Tarnished Beauty

Tarnished Beauty

a novel

cecilia samartin

ATRIA BOOKS
New York London Toronto Sydney

ATRIA BOOKS

A Division of Simon & Schuster, Inc.
1230 Avenue of the Americas
New York, NY 10020

First Atria Books hardcover edition March 2008

ATRIA BOOKS and colophon are trademarks of Simon & Schuster, Inc.

For information about special discounts for bulk purchases, please contact Simon & Schuster Special Sales at 1-800-456-6798 or business@simonandschuster.com.

Designed by Davina Mock-Maniscalco

Manufactured in the United States of America

10   9   8   7   6   5   4   3   2   1

Library of Congress Cataloging-in-Publication Data

Samartin, Cecilia.
Tarnished beauty : a novel / by Cecilia Samartin.—
1st Atria Books hardcover ed.
p.   cm
I. Title.
PS3619.A449T34   2008
813'.6—dc22   2007020049

ISBN-13: 978-1-4165-4950-5
ISBN-10:   1-4165-4950-1

For Vickie and
the Hope Street Family Center

Tarnished Beauty

1

I T WASN'T THE FIRST TIME a girl cried rape when her belly bloomed beyond the confines of her waistband. Yet in Lorena's case, no one doubted it was true. She'd always been a serene and modest girl, and when her passage through puberty transformed her into an alluring beauty with dark and mysterious eyes, her humility proved sincere, for she wasn't moved by the compliments lavished upon her by friends and strangers alike. She merely accepted their praise with no more than a gentle bow of her head.

Mothers in the village used her as an example for their daughters to follow, but most of the other girls preferred playing with their emerging sexuality, as if they'd happened upon the switch that turns on the sun, and couldn't be persuaded not to touch. They tried enlisting Lorena in their teasing games with the hope of convincing their mothers that the Blessed Virgin herself was not in their midst. But Lorena didn't need to unfasten the third button of her blouse or sneak her mother's lipstick to be noticed. She was simply beautiful the way the dawn is beautiful, without embellishment or pride.

It was rumored by some that she'd been born to royalty and had floated in a basket across the ocean to Mexico the way Moses floated down the Nile to Egypt. Of course, no one could conceive of a destiny appropriate for royalty in the dusty village of Salhuero, outside Guadalajara, where Lorena lived. And when imagination succumbed to jealousy, it was the same group of girls who reminded all interested parties, especially the young men, that she, along with her older sister, Carmen, had been born in a brothel the next village over and had been taken in by the devoutly religious widow Gabriela. Nobody was certain what had happened to their mother, whether she'd died in childbirth or had abandoned her children, as so many women in her situation did.

Such undesirable parentage would have discouraged better prospects, but countless suitors, intrigued by the modest beauty, overlooked her past and made their intentions known as honorably and fervently as they could. And when the time was right for Lorena to consider marriage, she tolerated endless suggestions and directions from her mother and sister about who was the best match, as this was an opportunity for the family to better its station by a prosperous arrangement.

Lorena herself was growing fond of a gentle boy with light eyes who visited on Sundays after church. He was the son of a wealthy merchant who exported tropical fruits north, across the border. Carmen, rough hewn and heavy, especially when compared to her sister, insisted he wasn't man enough and that she should consider the butcher's son, a dark and swarthy young man with eyes that wandered shamelessly down the blouse of whichever woman happened to be standing before him. Carmen insisted, with a bright cackle and a smack to her prodigious thigh, that a man like that would know how to handle a woman. Nevertheless, Lorena made her preference known and preparations for the wedding began shortly thereafter.

Rumor and careful calculation placed the rape at about the time of the Posada, in mid-December. And the villagers were fairly sure about the identity of the assailant. He'd been seen a few times before during major events such as weddings and funerals, when it was easy to partake of refreshments without drawing too much attention—a drifter looking for a drink and a place to sit so he could watch the young girls fluttering like pigeons in the square. He'd once been a handsome man. His sturdy frame and even features gave testament to the fact, but time and alcohol had degraded him so that only the most astute observer might suspect his former glory.

They say he lured Lorena into a derelict house as she was making her way to the celebrations, on the pretext that he'd hurt his leg and needed assistance. Lorena, having been raised on the milk of her mother's religion, didn't hesitate to respond. And once she was within his reach, the violation was as swift as it was efficient. She told no one about the incident, and as her custom was to dress modestly, she was able to effectively hide her growing middle even from herself. But two weeks before the wedding, Gabriela walked in on her while she was bathing and almost fainted at the sight of her daughter's belly and breasts, as heavy as bags of dried chilies ready for market.

The young man, desperately in love as he was, wanted to proceed with the marriage anyway, but his family forbade it and, for good measure, moved away, in case their son should prove more willful than they suspected. Four months later Lorena learned that he'd married another, but she didn't have the strength to weep or comment, or to even get up from her chair. The baby was due to be born any day.

Many prayers were said and candles were lighted after the atrocity was known. In this humble village where every child was considered a blessing, there was even secret hope that she might lose the baby and be spared the culmination of this hideous crime. The pregnancy, however, was a healthy one, and at nine months and two weeks, Lorena found herself unable to think of the shame she'd suffered because of the excruciating agony shooting through her body, worse than anything she'd ever known.

The labor was brief, and the baby slipped into the world so quickly that the midwife almost dropped it onto the dirt floor, laughing at her near blunder when she usually frowned, as her expertise required. She'd been delivering babies for more than fifty years, but she was particularly nervous about this birth, as all knew well of its origin.

"It's a girl," she announced, once composed. The baby whimpered instead of bellowing with the fullness of her lungs, but she was breathing well, and her eyes squinted at the dim lights as she responded to the voices around her with slight spasms of her chubby arms and legs. It was a beautiful child, perfectly formed, even angelic in the perfection of her features. Never had the midwife seen a newborn with such clear eyes so soon after delivery. Her coloring was warm like honey rather than the angry purplish red so common for newborns. The midwife's scrutiny softened to a glowing smile, as if her efforts had everything to do with the perfection of the child, and for an instant the unsavory origin of the birth was forgotten, and she could only gaze upon the splendor of new life that wriggled in her hands.

Nearly unconscious with exhaustion, Lorena fell asleep as the midwife and Lorena's mother took the baby to the basin. The midwife moistened a cloth with warm water and began to clean the little face, the arms and belly, the sweet little private area, small and demure as it should be, and the thighs and feet before turning her over to finish the bath. It was then that Gabriela smothered a gasp and for a second time the child almost slipped through the midwife's hands.

The mark, thick and red, like an open wound, covered her tiny shoulders and back, reaching down to her buttocks and all the way to the backs of her knees. With hands now trembling, the midwife dabbed at the mark briskly, hoping it was the harmless remnant of the afterbirth and nothing more, but it could not be wiped away any more than could the bright eyes and little mouth puckering for food. She hastily placed the infant back on the table and declared, "I've seen many birthmarks of all shapes and colors, but nothing like this. It's . . . it's as if the child sat on the hand of the devil himself."

She collected her modest fee and left without her usual instructions about how to give the breast while taking care of the mother's discomfort and other remedies she knew. Gabriela finished cleaning the infant and wrapped her snuggly in a blanket, intent that Lorena's first sight of her baby should be of her beautiful unblemished face, so much like her mother's. The next morning Gabriela would walk on her knees to the church, starting at the fountain in the middle of the plaza and not stopping until she'd reached the principal altar. All the way there and back, she'd pray for the Lord to take the mark away. Lorena had suffered enough for one so young, beginning life as an orphan and losing her one chance at marrying well. This disfigurement might prove too much for even the strongest of women to bear, and Lorena, disciplined as she was, had grown brittle, like dry kindling that could ignite in a warm wind. Gabriela had worried she wouldn't survive the pregnancy and every morning had asked Carmen to make sure that her sister was still alive and breathing on her bed.

"Sleep now, child," Gabriela said when she heard Lorena stir. "Your baby is fine and you can see her later."

"I didn't hear her cry."

"She's fine. You rest for now," Gabriela said, knowing she was going to need much more than rest to survive what lay ahead.

"I'll name her Jamilet," Lorena said with surprising certainty, for she'd refused to entertain any discussion about a name during her pregnancy. "It came to me the moment she was born, like a faraway chant, and I felt such peace when I heard it."

"Then Jamilet it is," Gabriela said, placing the sleeping baby in her box crib.

※

Despite Gabriela's best intentions, and careful avoidance of improper reference to the mark, Jamilet came to be known by everyone in the village as the angel with the devil's mark. She grew up familiar with the expression of troubled awe in the eyes that gazed upon her, sometimes directly, at other times peeking around corners or on fleeting faces that appeared like a parade of phantoms spooked by the living. Her own large eyes began to reflect a certain tenderness born of pity, so that by the age of three she was able to look back at the strangers who gawked at her with the serenity and wisdom of a priest who understood all the mysteries of life and death.

This only served to deepen the fear the villagers felt toward her. A child who was the perfection of human form in face, but hid a hideous swirl of blood and disfigurement that few had ever seen, but all had heard about. It was said by some to resemble a freshly gutted cow, by others to writhe like many snakes in a pit of blood. The few who had actually seen it, perhaps at the market when she pulled off the blanket her mother always kept around her despite the warm weather, said it was beyond description, and that they were unable to sleep for days after seeing it.

Lorena managed her fate like a chronic illness that throbbed steadily through the years, depleting her of what little energy she had left. Nevertheless, she wore her martyrdom like a crown and held her head high whenever she ventured out of the house, which wasn't often. If she was admired before, she was now revered as a woman of supreme courage who was able to endure the curse of her child with unfathomable dignity and grace.

"She's wise to keep her home as she does," they commented when she was seen walking alone down the very road where she'd been accosted.

"So young and beautiful. She might still find a husband if not for her obsession with the child. She would do better to abandon her, as she was abandoned."

Heads nodded like heavy fruit ready to drop from its branches. "She's devoted to her and spends what little money she has on trying to rid her of the devil's mark. Strange people come to the house at all hours. Sometimes very late at night, but they close the windows and I can't see what they do."

"Poor Lorena," they all said. "Poor, poor Lorena."

Lorena was able to muster a bit of hope when it came time for Jamilet to attend school, since she knew that her daughter possessed a unique mind. By the age of two, she was able to speak in full sentences and shortly thereafter began imagining and telling the most amazing stories about anything she happened upon. The insects she found in the chili patch behind their house were helping her to till the earth and preferred the darkness under the rocks because they were shy. The birds that landed on the windowpane gossiped about the neighbor who spent the entire night in the outhouse, relieving himself of the agony of too much tequila. And then there was the moon's frustration with her children, who were scattered about the heavens, refusing to do their chores.

"So you shouldn't be so mad at me, Mama," she'd say. "I am not as misbehaved as the stars."

Lorena's upset would ease, and she'd allow herself a rare smile. Surely her daughter's gifts, once they were discovered, would overshadow everything else, and the mark would be overlooked or perhaps forgotten altogether. And then, when the time was right, she'd find the courage to tell her daughter of its existence. As it was, when the *curanderos* applied their treatments, Lorena instructed them not to mention it, and to say instead that they were ensuring the child never became ill. If the treatments were painful, they were to explain that it was normal for badness to sting when leaving the body.

The first day Jamilet was to attend school it was well over eighty degrees, but Lorena insisted her daughter wear long sleeves and a sweater as well, making her promise not to remove it until she returned home at midday. Jamilet held her one and only schoolbook closely to her chest. This too she'd been instructed not to lose. Her grandmother complained that they'd spent more on that little book than they had on an entire week's worth of food.

Jamilet took a moment to admire the picture on the cover. A boy and a girl were walking to school with books of their own, and she smiled when thinking that she was now on the verge of becoming like them. Jamilet longed for the company of other children and watched daily from the window as they passed by like a colorful and noisy river of laughter and hijinks.

She would have preferred to walk with the children, and without her mother, but knew better than to argue with her. Lorena controlled her, not with anger or punishments, but with a sadness that loomed large and heavy, like black moons, in her eyes. Jamilet avoided looking at her mother too much or else found herself feeling that she had little energy to play or laugh, or tend to the peppers in the back field. Only when Lorena slept did her sadness lift, so that in the middle of the night, when other children were prone to waking with nightmares, Jamilet felt most at peace as she snuggled against her mother and found the comfort she craved.

On that first day, Lorena took her daughter's hand as they walked out to the road, and the children became silent all at once. As some crossed to the other side, Lorena's grip tightened, and Jamilet's fingers were aching by the time they reached the bend in the road, no more than a few hundred yards from the school yard.

"Go on, Jamilet," Lorena said. "I'll watch you from here."

Jamilet did as she was told and didn't turn around to look at her mother, although for once in her short life she truly wanted to, for she sensed the other children watching her, how she walked, and how she held her book in front of her like a shield. She looked neither left nor right, but down at her feet, mesmerized by the shiny buckles of her new shoes that winked at her with every step. She heard the children whispering, but it was not the carefree and happy whispering of a harmless joke or plans for play. Jamilet was only too familiar with the hushed sounds of fear.

Keeping her eyes downcast, she noticed tiny pebbles bouncing on the ground. They reminded her of the way the wind swept the dirt up in the back field when she was tending the chili patch. She thought it looked like backward rain making its way up to heaven. Her grandmother, not easily distracted from her work, had actually straightened up to gaze upon the dark cloud rising as Jamilet told the story of the backward rain and how the dirt in the field had come to life when touched by the breath of God. She knew her grandmother was more likely to listen if she gave the story a religious slant, but she'd tell the children a different version they'd like better. She was thinking of how to begin when she realized the pebbles had become larger, palm-size rocks the wind couldn't possibly have lifted. One smacked her soundly on the ankle, causing her to stumble.

It was then that she heard her mother's frantic call, and she saw the children lined up across the road, only a few hundred yards from the school grounds. Some held rocks in their hands, and others were hunched over, looking for more in the dirt. Lorena was running toward her with eyes that weren't sad, but were alive with fear. Jamilet had begun running as well, eager for the safety of her mother's embrace, when a deafening blow to her temple caused her arms to go limp. Before the darkness came, she felt the warm flow of blood in her ear, and heard a ringing so loud, she couldn't be sure if the children were jeering or laughing, as they did when she watched them through the window.

When Jamilet opened her bleary eyes, the first thing she saw was her mother's face, spongy with sadness once again, as she placed a cold compress on her daughter's head. Then she heard Gabriela fussing in the kitchen, banging pots and pans like she was prone to do when complaining about the scant help she got from her daughters and only granddaughter with the chores around the house. Although on this afternoon the noise she made was for another reason altogether.

Jamilet winced against the clatter, and reached a hand out for her mother. "Why did the children throw rocks at me, Mama?"

Lorena gently guided Jamilet's hand back down to the bed. "Quiet now. I only just stopped the bleeding."

Jamilet spoke up so her grandmother could hear her. "I was going to tell them the story of the backward rain, Abuela, but I never got a chance."

"It's a clever story, Jamilet," she responded tersely as she dropped a large pot in the sink and another on top of it.

Jamilet felt a piercing pain in her head, and held her breath until it had settled into a dull ache. She turned to her mother once more. "Why did they throw rocks at me, Mama?"

Lorena placed her daughter's hand on the compress and left the room without a word. She returned moments later carrying under one arm the mirror they kept in the front room, along with a smaller handheld mirror. She instructed her daughter to lie on her side, and pulled her nightdress up as high as it would go, positioning the larger mirror behind her.

"Be careful what you do, Lorena," Gabriela said, but Lorena didn't hesitate as she gave Jamilet the small mirror, guiding it so that her daughter could see the full expanse of the mark. Jamilet peered into the mirror and thought she'd caught sight of the wound on her head. "Am I still bleeding?" she asked, alarmed.

"It isn't blood," Lorena said, forcing her voice to sound strong, as one does when imparting news of a family death. "You were born with the mark on your back, and the children must know about it. They don't understand . . ." She hesitated, her voice trailing off, but she regained her composure. "The midwife who delivered you wasn't discreet."

Carmen had slipped into the room, and was slathering butter on a fresh tortilla. "Discreet?" she said while stuffing the tortilla in her mouth. "After the old bitch died she was devoured by rats, and they found her black tongue lying in a pile of bones and hair because even the rats refused to eat her filthy tongue."

"Carmen!" Gabriela gasped.

"It's true, Ma. Why shouldn't I say it when it's true?"

Normally Jamilet would have asked her aunt many more questions about the rats and how they happened upon the corpse and all matter of gruesome details, but she couldn't tear her eyes away from the formidable bloody landscape that spread across her shoulders. It seemed impossible that she was looking at something attached to her own body. She reached a cautious hand around to dab her finger at the red edges on one shoulder. Her skin felt thick and alien, and it bubbled and puckered in places, like an overcooked tortilla. But this thing was uglier than anything she'd ever seen before. Uglier even than rats and snakes and slimy creatures that lived under rocks, causing most women and children to scream, and men to demonstrate their bravery.

Finally, she found the strength to ask, "Will it go away, Mama?"

Lorena took the mirror from her daughter and smoothed her nightdress back down as she considered what to say. Then her eyes brightened, and she set her jaw firmly. "Of course it will. We just haven't found the way to do it yet, that's all."

"Be careful what you say, Lorena," Gabriela warned again, but she'd spoken with her daughter too many times on the subject to expect her to listen now.

Lorena stole a glance at her older sister, who was preparing her second tortilla for consumption. "It's true, Ma," she said with an uncharacteristically defiant nod. "Why shouldn't I say it when it's true?"

Once or twice a year, Jamilet retrieved her schoolbook from the high shelf in the kitchen, where the spices were stored, to look upon the picture of the boy and girl on the cover. The blood had dried and faded into a faint shadow across their world. And when she opened the pages to study the shapes, and the intricate markings that she knew to be the mysterious code for words and stories, she felt a sadness quivering in the very center of her heart that she didn't dare share with anyone. The people in her small world appeared perfectly content with their illiteracy. They managed by asking neighbors and even strangers coming to the door selling seed and wire fencing and such to help them decipher this or that. Once, Gabriela bought a soft, plastic, bristle broom, completely useless on her rough floors, so the salesman would do her the favor of reading a letter that had just arrived from Mexico City, only to discover that it had been delivered to the wrong address.

In the quiet hours, when the work of the day was done, the women often sat around the kitchen table mending clothes, or doing their needlework. At these times Jamilet asked quietly, almost chirping like a cricket so as not to disturb the moment, if she might be allowed to return to school, but her request was never considered with a serious mind before it was dismissed, and she was left with nothing to hang on to but that resigned sadness in her mother's eyes. Weary and detached as they sought a moment's rest, genuine interest could only be generated by a new recipe for red beans they'd heard about at the market, or the latest gossip that the milkman's son had fathered yet his third child out of wedlock. Sometimes their talk turned to more practical matters, like the need to hire a handyman.

Upon hearing this, Jamilet would say, "If my father was still alive, we wouldn't have to worry about paying a handyman."

The only sure way to get their attention was to bring up the subject of her father, and Jamilet took every opportunity to do so. She was intrigued by the furtive glances exchanged among the women, followed immediately by an increased concentration on their needlework. Eventually, one of the three would respond, sometimes by reminding Jamilet that her father had died many years ago, and how unfortunate that he was trampled to death by six horses at once so that there was nothing left of him. The year before it had been a drowning accident, and the year before that a tragic encounter with several bandits who had, for some reason, shot their pistols all at once while pointing at the same target between his legs.

2

CARMEN LEFT FOR THE NORTH soon after Jamilet's seventh birthday. It wasn't a surprise to anyone. She'd been complaining for years about the lack of jobs, and the backward stupidity of the villagers, and her desire to live in a modern world where people weren't so concerned with how many men she danced with on a Saturday night or if she really had a mole the shape of a sickle on her butt. This prompted Gabriela to scold her daughter about how much of her generous figure she'd made public knowledge, and she warned her that a bad reputation was like the foul smell of the unwashed, even worse in that it wouldn't go away, not even after a long, hot bath. This would inspire Carmen to launch into a fit of foul language that could be heard almost a half mile away.

After she left, things were definitely quieter, and there was plenty of extra work to keep everyone busy. There was the washing of the clothes, the feeding of the chickens, and the tending to the chili peppers that sprouted like Christmas ornaments all year long. There was the matter of sweeping out the dirt that blew in from the open fields, and helping Gabriela with the cooking. She was getting old and it was difficult for her to chop the onions and grind the garlic and chilies into the paste she used as the base for just about every meal.

Aside from looking after the peppers, Jamilet enjoyed her kitchen chores most, and became a fairly acceptable cook. When money ran short, it was on this premise that she accompanied her mother six days a week to work at the family house owned by Americans in the city. It was located in a fashionable neighborhood of Guadalajara where the streets were cleaned daily and the windows festooned with lace curtains and fresh flowers. Children attended school with nannies attached to their hands like pets, and returned home for lunch in order to enjoy the delicacies created by their family cooks. Although Lorena applied for the position with no credentials or recommendations whatsoever, the Millers decided to take a chance on her. They found the lovely sad-eyed woman and her daughter to be unusually refined, considering that they, like all the others, were peasants from nearby Salhuero looking for work. Her daughter was lovely as well and would make a fine companion for their only daughter, Mary. They were hired on the spot, and six days a week for five years, Jamilet and her mother boarded the bus from their village so they could report to work promptly at seven and have breakfast prepared before Mr. Miller left at eight.

Jamilet and Mary, who was only a few months younger, became good friends. Jamilet enjoyed the way Mary laughed for no obvious reason, as though happiness had just alighted on her like a butterfly in order to tickle her mercilessly until she relented with a good-natured prank or a game of some sort. After Mary came home from school in the afternoon, they spent countless hours together pretending to fish in the courtyard fountain, or playing hopscotch on the smooth ceramic tile that Lorena scrubbed on hands and knees every morning. They braided each other's hair and wove flowers throughout, as though they were fairies, or queens. But what Jamilet enjoyed most was learning the American songs Mary insisted she memorize so they could sing them together. Songs with strange names, like "Jailhouse Rock" and "Blue Suede Shoes." Mary told her they were very popular where she came from, and that every girl and boy had a record player.

She told Jamilet other things about her country, the way the roads were firm and paved even beyond the cities and in the places where the poor people lived. She described buildings, much taller than anything in Guadalajara, constructed of all glass and shiny as mirrors. "They're as tall as mountains that reach the sky," Mary said, blue eyes wide as she chewed and popped her gum. "That's why they're called skyscrapers."

After her first year with the Millers, Jamilet was speaking good English, and it was dismaying to the Millers that Mary hadn't picked up Spanish in the same manner. They suggested that maybe the girls should talk to each other in Spanish instead of English, but Mary refused, saying, "I like being the teacher, and besides, Jamilet can't read, and you can't be a teacher if you can't read."

Jamilet bowed her head to acknowledge the shameful truth, and the matter was dropped.

�֍

One morning, as Mary arranged daisies throughout Jamilet's hair, she caught sight of the upper edge of the mark peeking out beyond her collar. She passed her finger over it to see if it would change color with her touch. When she saw that it did, she dropped the daisies. "What's that?" she asked, pointing with her little finger, as though fearing it would leap out and bite her. Jamilet smoothed the hair back over her collar as the heat rose to her cheeks, but she was thinking harder and faster than she ever had in her life, intent upon not losing her only friend. "It's kind of a scary story," Jamilet said, turning around and opening her eyes wide for emphasis. "If I tell you, you might not sleep at night."

Mary bit her lip and thought awhile. "That's okay, I watch scary movies all the time and I can sleep really well as long as I keep the light on."

They settled themselves down in a quiet corner of the court-yard and Jamilet began to tell her a wondrous tale involving witch-

es and *cucuys* that lived under children's beds. When they were in
their deepest sleep, these evildoers would creep out and attempt to
steal unsuspecting children from their homes. They would snatch
them in their mouths the way dogs carry their young, and jump
out the window with them before they awoke. "I was lucky," Jamilet concluded, taking note of Mary's quivering bottom lip. "I woke
up before the old witch could get me to the window, but she left
her mark on me just the same."

Mary digested the story and recovered rapidly from her fright,
her pale face broadening to reveal two front teeth wrapped in
metal and wire. "Let me see it again," she said, reaching out for
Jamilet's collar.

But Jamilet blocked her hand. "It's private."

"That isn't private," Mary returned, pointing between her legs
as demurely as she could. "This is."

"Well, it's private for me," Jamilet said, stoic and unconvinced.
"It's the most private part of me."

Jamilet wondered what Mary would do if she knew that the
mark sprawled across her shoulders, down her back, and all the
way to the bottom of her knees. Would she be capable of smiling
then? She decided not to test Mary's good humor. It was best to
keep this a secret even from her only friend, just as she and her
mother had agreed before beginning work at the Miller house.

"People are afraid of what they don't understand, Jamilet," she
said. "And there's enough to fear in this life as it is."

But it was Lorena who broke the vow of secrecy when Mr.
and Mrs. Miller asked about the mark their daughter had seen.
Jamilet wondered if she'd understood her mother correctly when
she was called into the study and directed to turn around and lift
her blouse as far as it would go so the Millers could see the mark
for themselves. Jamilet studied her mother's eyes. They were not
sad, but were glittering with life, as they did on rare occasions.
When Lorena repeated her request, Jamilet did as she was told
and waited for the gasp of horror that would inevitably follow, but
there was only silence and the distant sound of water dancing in

the fountain where Mary waited for her friend to return. Jamilet wondered if American people expressed their shock differently from Mexican people, who were prone to make loud appeals to the saints and the Holy Mother when confronted with illness and deformity. For a moment, Jamilet thought the Millers had fainted standing up, but she dared not turn around to see for herself.

Then, Mr. Miller inhaled loudly, as if he'd suddenly remembered how to breathe. He cleared his throat to cover up. "We know a doctor," he said, calming his voice with palpable effort. "He was trained in the United States, but he has a practice here, in Guadalajara."

"I don't have money for that kind of doctor, sir," Lorena said, unashamed. She knew exactly what she was doing.

Mrs. Miller's reply was shrill and immediate. "We'll take care of it. You can put your shirt down now, dear," she said, and then whispered something to her husband that Jamilet couldn't hear.

Lorena had always told her daughter that somewhere in the world there was bound to be hope for a miracle, and that the north seemed as likely a place to find it as any. Surely, if they could build shiny metal buildings that touched the sky, there was a doctor there who'd know how to cure the mark. They'd long ago lost faith in the *curanderos* who waved leaves and lit candles while chanting and pouring acid medicines on Jamilet's skin, resulting in nothing but unbearable pain and blisters on top of the ugliness.

The sessions ended as always, with Jamilet exhausted on the bed, bandaged and bleeding and unable to sleep on her back for days. They were told that if the mark didn't disappear in three days, it never would. And as always, the three days came and went, and most times, the mark was redder and more inflamed than before.

The night before the appointment with the Millers' doctor, the expression in Lorena's eyes was not sad, but unusually hopeful. "I feel something wonderful in my heart that I've never felt before," she said, although she'd never looked so pale.

Jamilet traced a finger along the tiny beads of perspiration that had sprung up along her brow. "Will it hurt, Mama?" she asked, knowing it would make no difference.

But Lorena didn't answer. She'd already fallen asleep, her lips still moving in silent prayer.

Jamilet and Lorena waited in the lobby of a sleek office building with carpet instead of tile and pictures of perfect, unblemished fruit hanging on the walls. They sat on the edge of a small sofa feeling awkward and out of place as well-to-do, fashionably dressed clients announced their arrival to the secretary, who knew each of them by name. Several were young girls about the same age as Jamilet. They complained about the sprouting of acne on their cheeks, but try as she might, Jamilet couldn't see what they were talking about.

One young man did have a problem more severe, and Jamilet tried not to stare at the red welts, like tiny raised volcanoes, scattered over his face and neck. She understood his withdrawn and sunken expression, as he sought comfort in the internal universe that was his alone. There he could transform the sound of his beating heart into a symphony—anything to distract himself from the critical stares around him. Jamilet wondered how it would be if she spoke with him. Would he answer her? Would he even allow himself to hear? She wondered until she forgot where she was, until her imagination took over and she could no longer feel her mother's hand sweating on her knee.

"Is this your first time here?" Jamilet asks him, whispering so that her mother won't hear.

"No, I've been seeing Dr. Martinez for a long time, but it hasn't helped much, as you can see."

"This is my first time and I'm a little scared."

He studies her face from brow to chin. *"There's nothing wrong with you."*

"If you saw my back, you'd understand. I've been burned and scrubbed by curanderos *and village doctors ever since I can remember, but no one can get rid of the mark. They say it's the worst they've ever seen. It even scares the ones who claim to have powers over evil spirits."*

He shakes his head. *"If it's as bad as you say, then you might as well leave right now. I have a good mind to leave myself."*

Jamilet whispers so the secretary won't hear. *"I hear the best doctors are in the north."*

"That's what they say," he whispers back. *"And I have the money to get there, but I don't speak a word of English."*

Jamilet nearly falls off her chair. *"I happen to speak wonderful English. My best friend taught me. And I know a lot of American songs too."*

They stare at each other for a moment or two, knowing what they must do, but afraid to say it out loud.

"When do we leave?" Jamilet finally says.

"How about right now . . . before they call our names?"

The receptionist's voice boomed, jarring Jamilet out of her reverie. "Jamilet Juárez. The doctor will see you now."

Dr. Martinez was a small but imposing man with soft, thick hands. He began with the usual pleasantries, stating that his good friends the Millers had described the nature of Jamilet's problem when they'd asked him to see her.

"They're good people," he said to Lorena as he approached Jamilet. "And they're fond of you and your daughter."

"We're grateful to them," Lorena mumbled. "And to you for seeing us."

He instructed Jamilet to lie facedown on the examining table and assured her that he was only going to look at the mark and that he would let her know if he was going to touch her and that, when he did, it would be only with his fingers, no instruments or needles. Jamilet relaxed considerably, although she could see her mother's hands twisted into a knot on her lap.

Dr. Martinez pulled Jamilet's blouse up to her shoulders, and her skirt up to her hips to assess the full dimensions of the mark. She listened to his breathing, steady and low as it entered and exited his lungs, and felt the heat of his gaze on the mark. After a few minutes, she was surprised to hear, not derision, but fascination in his voice. "I've never seen anything quite like it," he muttered. "The medical term for the mark, as you call it, is a hemangioma. The condition is not uncommon. Approximately one in every one hundred children are born with some sort of birthmark, but this particular one . . ." He seemed at a loss for words as he pressed down on the protrusion at the base of her neck, thick with veins, like noodles in a little broth. "This one is quite extraordinary." After several more minutes, he asked Jamilet to sit up, indicating that his examination was finished.

"In many ways you're lucky," he said. "A fair number of hemangiomas like these appear on the face. And I've even read of cases, although much rarer, where the entire body is affected, and then other complications come into play, but I gather you've not had problems, say, with your heart or liver . . . seizures?"

"What are seizures?" Lorena asked, her hands white and stiff on her lap.

"It's a neurological problem," Dr. Martinez said, searching for words his humble patients might understand. "Something that happens in the brain. The electrical impulses are interrupted and—"

"Jamilet is as healthy as a horse, doctor," Lorena said. "She's never been sick, not even a sniffle." She dropped her head and stretched her fingers out, as if looking at them for the first time and marveling at their ability to move independently. "But . . . sometimes she stares into space and won't answer me when I talk to her. I believe she's daydreaming."

"Is that so?" Dr. Martinez turned to face Jamilet. He produced a tiny flashlight from his jacket pocket, and passed the light across her eyes several times. He placed his hands on his hips. "Do you hear your mother at these times when she says you're daydreaming?"

"I like to make up stories, and sometimes I don't hear anything but my own voice in my head."

Dr. Martinez furrowed his brow. "How long have you been making up these stories?"

"Since I was little, even before I learned how to talk."

"Is it only your voice you hear? Or do you hear other voices as well?"

Jamilet inched herself to the edge of the examining table. "I hear many voices. It's like a whole play in my head, like the ones they do in church during Easter, except I'm the one who makes up all the words, and if the play is really good, I can see it all in my mind too."

Dr. Martinez smiled at the curiosity of this simple child, speaking with such zealousness about her stories. "I don't think there's anything to worry about here." He gently thumped her forehead with his finger. "There's a very good brain inside that lovely head." He turned back to Lorena. "I should also add that there is some evidence to suggest that hereditary factors may be associated with this condition." He considered the baffled expression on her face and continued. "It can be hereditary and passed down from relatives, like eye color and height. I assume you don't have anything . . ."

Lorena shook her head, her lips pressed together, preparing for what she knew would come next.

"And the father? Do we know . . . ?"

"My husband died many years ago, Doctor, and he didn't have the mark, or whatever it is that you called it."

"He was killed by bandits," Jamilet added, as she'd recently decided that this was the version of his demise she found most worthy of retelling. "They shot him right between the legs."

Dr. Martinez's eyebrows flickered in surprise, and then he politely coughed and reached for a chart on the counter.

Lorena's voice was shrill. "And what about a cure, doctor?"

"A removal, you mean?"

Lorena nodded anxiously, her eyes teary as she opened her purse in search of a tissue.

Dr. Martinez's expression, which had been so confident before, grew doubtful. "I'm sorry to disappoint you, but I'm afraid there's little we can do at this stage in the way of removal. Perhaps when Jamilet was younger we could have treated it aggressively, but now it would be impossible to remove without risking severe injury."

"It's okay, Mama," Jamilet said when she saw the tears streaming down her mother's face.

"But, Doctor," Lorena implored, no longer caring if she appeared composed or appropriate. "How can she go through life with that horrible thing living on her back? Look at her face. She's a beautiful girl, my Jamilet. There must be something we can do, somewhere else we can go."

"I understand your concern," Dr. Martinez said, and his eyes crinkled with well-rehearsed compassion. "There are some new treatments I have little experience with, involving the use of lasers, a kind of very intense light. There have been some promising studies, but I sincerely doubt that in your daughter's case—"

"Where can we find these treatments?" Lorena snapped.

"In the north . . . in Los Angeles I believe a few clinics are beginning to use the laser on more superficial birthmarks."

Lorena wiped her brow for the third or fourth time. She was breathing heavily and her eyes appeared to float, as though loose in their sockets.

"Are you quite all right, Señora?"

"I'm fine," she said, her head dropping. "Just a little tired."

"Mama!" Jamilet jumped off the examining table as her mother slipped off the chair and collapsed in a heap on the floor.

Lorena was diagnosed with heart problems, and hospitalized for several days. When she was discharged, she was no longer able to work at the Miller house or anywhere else, for she was to rest her heart as much as she could and be spared any and all bad news. She was to sit on the porch during the day when the weather was agreeable, or stay in her bed and face the window overlooking the back field so she could watch Jamilet play and tend to the chili plants.

The Miller family visited a couple of times, and brought along boxes filled with cans of beans, vegetables, and meats that were already cooked, a rare luxury. Not possessing a can opener, Gabriela demonstrated her proficiency with a hammer and knife, and was so delighted with the gifts that she barely flinched when the knife slipped and she cut her finger.

Jamilet took the opportunity to show Mary the garden she'd tended for so many years. The peppers were bright and plump and considered to be the best in the market, she was proud to say. Mary considered them briefly, and agreed that they were indeed beautiful, although she did not care for peppers, as they burned her tongue and caused her to sweat profusely. Jamilet directed her attention next to the brook that ran several yards behind their modest house, which was even smaller than the shed where the Millers kept their car and gardening tools.

"On the other side of that river is the end of the world," Jamilet informed her friend, for she always thought it was so, and had never been any farther north than that.

Mary nodded, not particularly impressed. She seemed much more concerned with the condition of her new shoes. After she'd stepped in the loose earth that Jamilet had recently turned and watered, the satin finish became spotted with a fine smattering of mud. "That's no river," Mary said, swiping at her shoes with her bare hand. "If you want to see a real river, you should go to the Rio Grande. It's a hundred times bigger than this." She stood up, irritated with her lack of progress in removing the dirt. "Do you have a napkin or something for my shoes?"

Jamilet looked about for something that would do, but seemed at a loss.

Mary said, "That's okay, just show me where the bathroom is."

Jamilet pointed to the river and smiled.

That was the last time she ever saw Mary. Months later they learned that the Millers had moved back to Texas. Jamilet pictured her American friend with her blond ponytail swishing back and forth as she walked along the paved streets, smooth as plates, lying end to end. She was laughing and enjoying her reflection in the glass of the buildings, as tall as mountains. And she was happy, very happy, to have clean shoes.

Lorena's heart trouble, which had been well managed with repose and inane conversation, took a turn for the worse. Jamilet, now seventeen, evaluated her own practicality in the face of her mother's imminent death and it troubled her. She should have been devastated by the prospect of losing the person she loved most in the world, but her sadness was suspended somehow and hovering just out of her reach, and she was strengthened by a yearning she could not easily explain to herself or to anyone else.

She'd become aware of it when she saw the mark for the first time. At that moment, it felt like her intestines had tied themselves to the bedpost to keep her from lifting off the mattress and bursting out through the roof of the house. She'd also felt it gather fiercely within her when she'd finally accepted that she'd never go to school, and that the most she could hope to receive from the villagers was stiff regard, born of pity in the best of circumstances and restrained loathing in the worst. She'd learned, having had more than ample opportunity to study the phenomena, that people didn't merely enjoy their fear, they savored it as steady and reliable entertainment. When she went to the market, or ventured down the street on an errand, she reminded them that they were lucky no matter what their circumstances were, for at the end of the day, when they washed in the river or the well, whether they had the benefit of soap or just friction and water, they'd be clean from head to toe, front and back.

"Her mother is dying and she doesn't shed a tear," the villagers said. "Her face is perfect, like a statue. Not a tear."

"Does that surprise you?" they whispered. "She has the heart of the devil, and the devil is not saddened by death."

"There is rumor that she will leave for the north after her mother dies."

"I've been praying for years that she would. Ever since she was born, my fields have yielded much less, and hers seem to flourish. She's cursed us all."

"Yes, she has. My baby died three weeks after Jamilet was born, and I have no doubt that Jamilet should have died instead."

***

As her mother's illness progressed, Jamilet's stories evolved beyond the imaginings that had served her as a child and into deeper longings that had the power to soothe her soul. She passed the hours away with eyes semiclosed and fluttering as her mother slept. Gabriela instructed Jamilet to pray whenever she felt that her heart would wither with pain, but her fantasies, as impossible as she knew them to be, eased her pain better than anything else.

***

"Wake up, Mama. It's time for breakfast and you've been sleeping too long. Do you expect me to do all the work around here?"

Lorena's eyes open and she smiles. "How long have I been sleeping?"

"Too long," Jamilet says, pulling the covers off. "Come and see what I've made for you." Lorena gets out of bed and wraps a shawl around her shoulders as she's led into the kitchen. The table is set with a breakfast of tortillas, chorizo, and eggs, with fresh chili sauce and two steaming cups of hot chocolate.

They watch each other from across the table as they eat, incredulous with joy.

"You seem so happy, Jamilet. I've never seen my little girl so happy."

"I have a surprise for you, Mama."

Lorena claps her hands like a child. "Another surprise? What is it?"

"We're going north, Mama. We're leaving today. We're going to make a new life in the place where the shiny buildings touch the sky. I talked with Mr. and Mrs. Miller and they already have jobs for us there. And there's an extra room in their mansion that they don't use. They say we can have it until we find our own house, and we can take all the time we need to find just the right one."

"What about your grandmother? She's too old to live alone."

"She doesn't want to go, Mama. I've already asked her and she's very sure she would be miserable there and very happy here with the chili patch and chickens to look after. The doctor told me today that she's as strong as a horse, and that having a little extra room would do her good."

Lorena accepts this without question. "Well then, I suppose we have some packing to do."

"I packed while you were sleeping, Mama. All we have to do now is go."

"And what about the mark, Jamilet? I can't bear to think that we'll have to explain it to a whole new group of people . . . people who won't understand."

Jamilet places an envelope on the table.

"What is this?"

"I received it yesterday, Mama."

"Should we find someone to read it for us? Maybe if we call Rolando's son Pepe, down the road . . ."

Jamilet takes up the envelope, unfolds the letter, and begins to read in a loud, clear voice. She reads about an appointment next week with a well-known doctor in the north who is certain he can remove the mark in a matter of hours, or three days at the most. The procedure will be painless and the cost can be paid off over time.

Tears are streaming down Lorena's face. "Jamilet, I have never heard such wonderful news. And when did you learn to read? I had no idea."

"I just figured it out one day while I was waiting for you to wake up. I had that little book in my lap and I prayed like Abuela told me, and suddenly all the lines on the pages began to speak to me with their own voices. They came together like pictures and it all made sense to me, just like that."

"It's a miracle."

"The world is full of miracles, Mama. All we have to do is find the ones that belong to us."

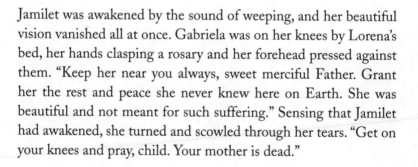

Jamilet was awakened by the sound of weeping, and her beautiful vision vanished all at once. Gabriela was on her knees by Lorena's bed, her hands clasping a rosary and her forehead pressed against them. "Keep her near you always, sweet merciful Father. Grant her the rest and peace she never knew here on Earth. She was beautiful and not meant for such suffering." Sensing that Jamilet had awakened, she turned and scowled through her tears. "Get on your knees and pray, child. Your mother is dead."

3

J AMILET DECIDED it would be best to cut her hair to just above the ears. She performed this task with little ceremony, as she did when trimming the stems from the tomatoes when they were ripe and ready for the table. Next, she flattened her breasts by wrapping her torso with the fine white fabric she found under her mother's bed. Gabriela told her it was sacrilegious to use fabric intended for her mother's wedding dress in such a manner. But Jamilet paid no attention, and noted that although it was uncomfortable, she could still breathe, and the layers under her shirt would provide her with additional warmth during the night. She appraised herself critically, using the only mirror in the house. Wearing a pair of loose slacks and a broad-rimmed hat low on her brow, she appeared to be an underfed adolescent boy with weak shoulders and smallish feet. And if she lowered the pitch of her voice a bit when she spoke, the transformation was complete.

Gabriela tried to discourage Jamilet from leaving as she swept up thick tendrils of black hair from the kitchen floor, but she chose a different argument from the one she'd employed with Carmen years earlier. "Who's going to look after my garden?" she wailed into her hands, careful to leave enough space between her fingers to peek through. "Relying on charity is a slow death in these parts."

Jamilet's expression remained smooth and unyielding. "Tía Carmen sends you money every month and I will too. Everybody knows that money is easy to earn in the north. And remember, I speak English."

Gabriela lowered her hands and stared at her granddaughter through eyes weakened by cataracts. Even with her hair chopped off above the ears, she was lovely. "Life isn't like one of your stories you can twist around in your head so the endings are always happy. There's no cure for your mark, not even in the north. I've known this is true since the day I walked on my knees to God's holy altar after you were born. I never told your mother about it because I knew she would only suffer more, but if I can prevent you from making this horrible mistake, I'll tell you now." She leaned on her broom, and her face softened with the memory. "I was praying for a miracle, looking up at our Lord as He hung on the cross, when a beam of light entered through the window above and illuminated His crown. At first I didn't know what it meant, but then He spoke to me." She closed her milky eyes, and swayed a bit on her feet. "He told me that you must bear your mark bravely and give your suffering to the Lord. It is your very own crown of thorns, and one day it will bring you glory." She opened her eyes, as clear as the desert night. "So you see, if you go north you'll be disappointed as always and this time you'll be alone . . ."

"I'll be with Tía Carmen,"

"That's even worse!" Gabriela began sweeping again with such a fury that dust clouds rose up all around them. "God alone knows what kind of life that girl's made for herself. She tells me she goes to church every Sunday, but I don't believe her, and I'm sure she's drinking more than ever. It's a miracle she's able to send any money at all."

Jamilet captured her grandmother's broom and set it aside. She took hold of her hands, pressing them into her own. "I never told you this before, *Abuela*, but God spoke to me too. When I was deep in prayer as Mama was dying, He told me I should go north and there I would find the cure." Jamilet waited for her revelation to take effect.

"How did He sound?" Gabriela asked, intrigued and moved that her granddaughter could have had a religious experience when she usually couldn't be bothered to say Grace before a meal.

Jamilet looked directly into her grandmother's eyes with some regret, for she wasn't comfortable telling tales about that which her grandmother held so dear. "It wasn't like the voice of a person. It was more like soft thunder, holding back its strength so you'll listen and know that it's God without feeling afraid."

"Soft thunder," Gabriela repeated twice. "That's how he sounded for me too."

The twelve-hour bus ride was the only rest Jamilet would get for several days. She tried her best to sleep, but was so exhilarated that she couldn't keep her eyes closed for more than a minute or two. She studied the words on the paper that she knew to be her aunt's address in Los Angeles, and tried to recall the woman she'd last seen, over ten years ago. Everyone always said that they'd never known two sisters to be more different. Jamilet pictured her mother sitting quietly in the corner, observing the world through large dark eyes and offering a hesitant smile if circumstances required. Carmen liked to laugh out loud at her own jokes, and she was always looking for a reason to fill her enormous lungs with air and bellow out her good humor or anger—whichever the case might be, as if breathing like everybody else wasn't interesting enough.

Jamilet watched the Mexican desert sweep past her window, smudges of tan and green layering over each other and blurring into the panorama of endless horizons as the rhythmic sounds of the engine and wheels became an anxious lullaby, more appropriate to bouncing than rocking, but soothing nonetheless. In this hypnotic repose she clearly remembered her aunt sitting at the

kitchen table, feet propped up like the man of the house, unconcerned that her broad thighs and buttocks were partially visible to
whoever was present.

"Lower your legs," Gabriela would say. "Do you have to show
all the world your business?"

"The world? Do you see the world in here, Jami?"

Jamilet looked around the room, eager to demonstrate how
well she was able to follow directions, and then shook her head
in agreement. But if the world should happen to appear in the
form of Pepe from down the road, offering a plate of his mother's
tamales in exchange for a bag of chilies, or the milkman with his
weekly delivery, Carmen didn't lower her legs, or adjust her skirt,
not even an inch. Instead, she'd smile wickedly and watch to see if
they stole a glance at her generous behind, which they always did.
Then she'd laugh, as if she'd just proven something very important
to herself, although Jamilet couldn't imagine what it was, but she
laughed along just the same, and returned her aunt's triumphant
wink when the show was over.

The truth was that Jamilet agreed to most things her aunt
proposed, and Carmen was prone to sharing her opinion on a wide
variety of topics: the need for a cold beer first thing in the morning to clear the mind; the energy wasted on too much courtesy;
the secret arrogance that lived in the hearts of the overly modest,
just to name a few. But for Jamilet, the important thing was to be
in Tía Carmen's good graces, and to bask in her laughter when it
filled the house like a party of twenty or more.

When Lorena turned up her nose at her sister's foul language
or when Gabriela gave up an irritable plea for the Lord to guide
her lost soul, Jamilet was quiet, and in the stillness of her thoughts,
at the very center of her cautious admiration, she cheered. How
could she harbor criticism in her heart for Tía Carmen, the only
person she knew who wasn't afraid of the mark? In fact, Carmen
didn't pay it much attention at all and wasn't spooked or bothered
by the idea of curses and punishments from God. Jamilet knew
that Carmen would teach her how to be strong and how to face

the world with her chin up and shoulders back. She'd undoubtedly approve of Jamilet's manly disguise and they'd laugh until they were rolling on the floor like drunken horse hands. She could imagine every detail of their exchange, and clearly heard her aunt's voice booming above the droning motor of the bus . . .

❋

"And you can forget about all those dainty rules your mother and grandmother fed you since you were a baby. They won't do you a damn bit of good here."

"I'll forget everything, Tía," Jamilet says, smiling. "I'll even forget my own name if you want me to."

Carmen stares at her quizzically. "Don't get ahead of yourself," she says.

Together, they walk out into the city. The ground beneath their feet is polished marble, like the floor leading to the altar at church. The buildings surrounding them are a multitude of angular shapes and colors that reach beyond the clouds. Tía looks around, and even she, who's never been too impressed by anything other than a good-looking man's backside, is momentarily reverent.

"There's no dirt on the ground here," she says. "And look up." She points to the uppermost edge of the city, where concrete and glass give way to open sky as blue as any ever seen. "These are the kinds of miracles you can believe in here."

❋

In less than two days, Jamilet was crossing the desert, her path illuminated only by the light of the stars because flashlights might attract unwanted attention. It was more dangerous to attempt crossing without an experienced coyote to guide them, since coyotes knew the passes through the canyons, and the bandits who roamed the border looking for Mexicans to rob. But Jamilet had joined six others near the border who, like her, had no way of securing the money for such a luxury. They'd decided to brave the crossing on their own. They'd be safer, and traverse many more miles walking through the desert during the cooler nights. In three days' time, if all went according to plan, they'd cross the Rio Grande at a calm, shallow stretch of river and emerge on the other side where all was prosperity and hope—the North.

Jamilet felt a nervous kind of elation at the prospect of being so close to her goal. The journey had been easier than expected. She had been prepared to devote days, and even weeks, to the crossing, well aware that many were caught and returned to the border only to attempt it again the very next day. This could go on for weeks, and often the more stubborn were detained and incarcerated for months. But here she was, taking part in a plan as simple for her to understand and execute as any of her household chores.

Juan, a soft-spoken man with an easy smile, was the only member of the group Jamilet trusted. When some complained that the scrawny boy was slowing them down, or not collecting his share of the firewood when it was time to set up camp, Juan reminded them that they'd be wise to conserve their energy for the Rio Grande, and that the bandits were always on the prowl, so bright, burning fires were a bad idea anyway. Jamilet made certain to walk no more than a few paces away from him, and when it came time to rest, she always lay as near him as she could.

Juan appraised his young traveling companion with increasing suspicion. He was familiar with the degradations of the north, of the open prostitution and of the men who dressed like women and danced nearly naked in the clubs located in the seedier parts of the big cities. Surely Jaime was headed for such a place. In Juan's village, his sort were hung from trees and flogged until the priest could be assured that the evil had been beaten out of them. Juan took note of Jaime's delicate wrists. This one had never been hung from a tree, and such tender skin wouldn't survive too many lashings of the whip. Feeling more pity than disgust, he prodded Jamilet on the shoulder, more roughly than necessary, aware that the others were watching, and told her that his brother was to meet him across the border and take him on to Los Angeles. With his fair share of money for gas, Jaime was welcome to join them, he said.

Incredulous and tearful when confronted with such good fortune, Jamilet reached for the money she kept stuffed in her sock, and gave it all to him before he could change his mind. She was now penniless, but she trusted her skill at discerning character, and she had no doubt that Juan was a good man who wouldn't harm or deceive her.

The night before they were due to cross the river, it was so close that they could hear the thundering chorus of water that passed swiftly between the land of the north and the land of the south. Jamilet imagined the sound to be the voice of God, not so different from the false description she'd given her grandmother days before, although it felt like a lifetime ago. She closed her eyes, and tried to decipher the meaning of it all. Was the message an ominous or a hopeful one? She couldn't be sure, but she had no doubt that there was a message for her there. Before sleep claimed her thoughts, she lifted her eyes to the night sky, and promised upon the light of every star in the heavens that if she wasn't rid of the mark in two years time, she would end her life. She wouldn't wait for God to take it from her as her mother had done. She'd simply climb to the top of the tallest building in the city and jump to her death. She found comfort in the thought that it would be impossible to distinguish the mark from the bloody mess that would be left of her. Anyone who jumped from such a high place would look exactly the same, and in this way at least, she would have succeeded.

The next morning, Jamilet awoke to see the dusty boots of her companions at eye level, as they stood over her. One or two were laughing nervously, and the others drifted off to begin packing their meager provisions. When she turned to do the same, she was unable to move her hands and feet, and realized they had been tied while she slept.

Juan, who had been watching and waiting for her to wake, sat near her on his haunches in order to address her privately. "I'm sorry, Jaime," he said, "If you'd known what else they were planning, you'd thank me. These boys don't understand your kind, and I guess I don't either, but that's no excuse for cruelty, I know . . ."

Jamilet struggled to release herself, but the more she pulled, the tighter the ropes dug into the flesh of her wrists and ankles. In minutes she was winded from the effort.

"You're wasting your time," Juan said, shaking his head at the pitiful sight. "I'm an expert when it comes to tying knots."

One man kicked dirt in Jamilet's face as he walked by, and mumbled a curse under his breath. He was clearly glad to be rid of the degenerate young man, and eager to get on with the next phase of the journey before it was too late. As he prepared to cross the river, he proceeded to unfasten his belt, and remove his boots and all of his clothing, until he stood fully naked in the sun. Jamilet had never before in her life seen a naked man, and despite her fear and confusion, she became momentarily transfixed by the sight and the curious patches of hair that grew all over his body, making him look as though he'd been dipped in egg and rolled in batter, some places sticking better than others. Most curious of all was the man's penis, which reminded her of the deformed and feeble arm of an infant.

"The *joto* wants you, Jose," one of the men shouted when he noticed Jamilet's gaping interest. "Maybe you should give him a taste."

"Leave him alone. It's bad enough we tied him up like this," Juan replied.

"You want him for yourself . . . ," the troublemaker jeered back, but he was too busy with his own preparations to take it any further.

"You took my money," Jamilet said, craning her head around and up to look Juan in the eye.

He glanced at the other men, and then quickly retrieved the bills she'd given him from his back pocket, and stuffed them into her boot, making it appear as though he was only tightening the ropes. And as he did so, he whispered, "The rope is lightweight. A few strokes across a sharp rock and you'll be free. Then you should go back home, and pray to God that He forgives you for your perversions. Besides," he said, glancing toward the river, and shivering at the prospect of what awaited him, "small as you are, you'll never make it across."

As Juan left to join the others at the bank of the river, Jamilet contemplated telling him that they were mistaken about her, but the sight of so many naked men, and the realization that she would have to do the same, led her to conclude that her situation would worsen rather than improve. She kept quiet and watched sullenly as Juan stripped down like the first man, rolled his clothes and provisions into a tight bundle, and then carefully tied it all on top of his head and under his chin with his belt. It was well-known that a group of Mexican men slinking through the fields with their clothes dripping wet was certain to arouse suspicion and a call to *la migra*. The ranchers who lived near the border could spot them like eagles, and it was rumored that even their wives made calls to the authorities while keeping watch from their kitchen windows as they did the dishes. The illegals were often caught and detained before the dishes had dried. But if they managed to keep their bundles out of the water as they crossed the river, in a matter of seconds they'd be dry and dressed, and dispersing into the adjacent fields, easily blending in with the other ranch hands in the area.

Soon the men could be heard screaming, blubbering, cursing the frigid water and slippery rocks like wounded cows. Their bellows endured for some time, and several required much coaxing before they felt brave enough to cross. Eventually their boisterous complaints faded into the roar of the river, and Jamilet couldn't be sure if they'd perished or made it to the other side.

It took little more than an hour for Jamilet to release her hands, using the strategy that Juan had suggested. She spent the rest of the day and most of the evening crouched at the bank of the river watching it flow past like an enormous glistening snake, carrying twigs and branches and the occasional plastic bag and tin can along its undulating back. She ate the last of the apple she'd been saving and drank frequently from the river. She listened to the wind whispering through the trees, and even more intently to the stillness that settled itself in between the sounds of nature all around her, hoping to hear the true voice of God somewhere in its midst telling her what to do next. But all she could be sure of was the beating of her own heart, and the breath entering and leaving her body reminding her that she should be grateful to be alive, and nothing more.

The moon was high in the sky when she removed her clothes and rolled all she carried into a neat bundle. Everything, that is, except her boots; certain, as she remembered the complaints of the men earlier, that she'd be more sure-footed with them on while stepping on the slippery rocks that carpeted the river bottom. With the bundle tied securely to the top of her head, she stepped into the river, and braced herself against the water that swirled about her ankles and up to her knees, her thighs, and filled the warm spaces in her groin with a turbulent cold that was excruciating and terrifying all at once. Although she was panting and trembling violently, she continued to go deeper into the river that surged up to her waist, lapping at her breasts like a hungry sharp-toothed child. She clamped her eyes shut against the pain, gathering as much strength as she could, and before long found herself gazing into the familiar and hideous face of the fear and rejection she'd lived with all her life. If truth be told, the river water was warm by comparison, the sticks and debris that pounded into her body no more threatening than a friendly poke to the ribs.

And then, when she felt herself on the verge of succumbing to the bitter cold, the river sang to her. "Life without despair is possible," it sang over and over again within the deepest heart of its roar. "If you can endure . . . If you can endure . . ." The voice, more powerful and captivating than the ugliness of her past, plowed a valley through her consciousness, deep to the core of her soul, and she followed its call through the darkness until she heard nothing and felt nothing except for a numb and deathlike peacefulness. She was certain that she'd been taken by the river and that she was floating like a leaf on the surface of the water, spinning and dipping along with the currents, moving with a power that surpassed her most paralyzing fears. And there was nothing she could do but let herself go wherever it led.

When Jamilet collapsed on the bank of the river, she was unable to move, and hardly even to breathe for a long while, but her mind soared with the joyous realization that she'd made it to the land of miracles. When she was once again able to feel the blood pumping through her arms and legs, and had determined that she hadn't suffered any serious injuries, she dressed in clothes that she had managed to keep mostly dry, and spent the remainder of the night huddled at the base of a thorny bush that smelled of orange blossoms and mint. And there she slept soundly.

The next morning, she was awakened by a strange prickly sensation all over her body. She opened her eyes to discover an army of plump black ants. She leaped to her feet, ripped off her clothing in a flash, and jumped into the river without a thought of the horrifying experience of the night before. Back on shore she began to whip every garment she'd been wearing against the trunk of a tree until she was certain that all of the ants were gone. But as she made her way toward what appeared to be a dirt road leading away from the river, she thought she felt one or two surviving ants crawling down her back. They remind me that I'm a survivor too, she thought with satisfaction.

She hiked for several hours through a forest of willow and cottonwood trees draped dreamily over one another. Although she found the dappled shade of the forest refreshing, she became concerned when she detected no sign of previous travelers. She'd been told that the best trails were littered with trash and human excrement. Because of this, it was said that if you lost your way at night, you need only follow your nose to find it again.

Her canteen was nearly empty when she spotted a farmhouse less than a mile in the distance. As she got closer, she could see that it was a simple one-story structure with a wide covered porch. A laundry line could be seen in the front yard, off of which hung several pairs of denim jeans and long-sleeved shirts. Judging by their impressive size, it was clear that they belonged to a very tall and stocky man. Jamilet approached cautiously, crouching low as she emerged from the shade and protection of the forest. She decided it was best to follow a thicket leading away from the house, toward the barn where she hoped to rest for no more than a couple of hours. If she was lucky, she might find something edible as well. Animal feed would do, anything to stop the nagging ache in her belly.

The barn door was ajar, and she slipped through with little difficulty. On the ground was a burlap sack that smelled of manure, but no matter, it was large enough to serve as a cover. Taking it with her to the darkest corner of the barn, she curled up like a cat, but before she had the opportunity to settle in beneath it, the barn door yawned open, and the silhouette of a small person, perhaps a child, was visible in the doorway. Also visible was a double-barreled rifle poised at the hip. After more careful inspection Jamilet saw that it was not a child, but a young woman, no more than twenty, and obviously in the last weeks of her pregnancy. She wore a dress several sizes too big for her frame, and workmen's boots that reached up to her knees. Her reddish hair was loose around her face, and looked as though it hadn't been brushed in days. But her most distinctive feature was an enormous bruise on her left cheek and eye, swollen enough to make her otherwise pretty face appear lopsided. Jamilet could clearly see it illuminated in the shaft of light that entered through the uneven slats of the barn wall.

But the young woman's injury didn't impair her vision. She quickly spotted Jamilet crouching in the corner. Jamilet scrambled to her feet, and as she did, the young woman pointed the barrel of the shotgun directly at Jamilet's head. "Get the hell off my property," the young woman commanded. "I already called the border patrol when I saw you skulking around, and they move fast, so you better do the same if you know what's good for you."

Jamilet reached for her bundle to do just that, and the woman said, "I'll shoot you in the nuts if you try anything stupid." She lowered the barrel until it pointed directly at Jamilet's crotch this time. *"Los huevos,"* she said in Spanish, suspecting the stranger didn't understand English. "Bang bang . . . *los huevos.*"

Jamilet responded in English, "I don't have *huevos.* I'm a girl just like you."

The young woman lowered the barrel slightly, and then raised it again with a start, peering into the darkest corners of the barn, as though expecting someone or something to jump out at her.

"I'm alone," Jamilet said softly. Even with a rifle pointed directly at her, she was unable to muster the strength to feel even a little bit afraid.

The redheaded girl lowered the rifle a bit. "I never heard of a girl crossing on her own before. And I sure as hell never met a wetback that speaks English so good." The woman appraised Jamilet with guarded fascination. "And why are you dressed like that?"

"I thought it would be safer to travel as a boy," Jamilet answered with a shrug, realizing that she couldn't have been more wrong.

"We don't need any more Mexicans here, boys or girls. I don't understand why you don't stay in your own country where you belong, why you keep sneaking over like thieves."

"I came to see a doctor," Jamilet said.

"They got doctors in Mexico."

"Not the kind of doctor I need."

A momentary glint of intrigue softened the woman's expression, and Jamilet wasted no time. She pulled her shirt up and turned around so the worst part of the mark, where the skin was thickest and shiny red, was visible.

"Holy shit!" the woman exclaimed. "It looks like you were skinned alive!" She was about to say something more, but was interrupted by the crunching sound of wheels rolling across the gravel driveway outside. Moments later, a car door could be heard to open and close, followed by steps up onto the wooden porch. A man's voice called out, "Nancy. Hey, Nancy!"

The woman became momentarily flustered, and seemed confused about what she should do next. She lowered her shotgun so that the barrel pointed at the floor, and stared blankly at Jamilet, watching her as she tucked her shirt back into her pants. "Wait here and don't make a sound," she said, and then she left, taking the extra time to close the barn door securely behind her.

Peeking through the slats of the barn wall, Jamilet watched the woman who she assumed to be Nancy make her way across the yard and over to the porch to join the men waiting for her. She leaned casually on her shotgun, and crossed one boot over the other while conversing in an offhand manner with the two officers in dark green uniforms. A long bus of the same color with windows covered in wire mesh was parked in the drive. Four Mexican men were sitting in back, three sleeping and one watching the scene on the porch. Jamilet immediately recognized Juan, and when he lifted his hands to scratch his nose, she saw that he was handcuffed as well. In spite of everything, she felt bad for him. He had protected her as well as he could under the circumstances and she hoped that his detainment would be a short one.

Nancy pointed out beyond the road, toward the woods that Jamilet had traversed, and then entered the house, returning moments later with a can of beer for each officer. They accepted her hospitality with a nod before stepping off the porch and climbing back into the bus. As it headed down the road in the direction that Nancy had indicated, a thick cloud of dirt rose up from beneath the tires, obscuring the vehicle from sight although it was possible to hear the rumble of the engine for some time afterward.

When all was silent again, Nancy returned to the barn, without her shotgun this time, and instructed Jamilet to follow her into the kitchen. There, she prepared a meal of leftover fried chicken and corn mash. Jamilet tried to eat politely, but after a few dainty bites, she couldn't help but shovel the food into her mouth like a wild animal. Nancy watched her from the sink as she filled the canteen with fresh water from the faucet. The last time Jamilet had seen water running from a faucet like that had been at the Miller house.

"How'd it happen—that thing on your back?" she asked after Jamilet had almost finished her meal. "Did someone beat you bad?"

Jamilet shook her head and swallowed the last of her corn mash. "I was born with it."

"Does it hurt?"

Jamilet shrugged, and took a closer look at the bruise on Nancy's face, noticing that her front tooth was chipped as well. "Does that hurt?" she asked, pointing to her cheek.

"Only when I smile," Nancy answered, wiping her hands on the skirt of her dress and glancing out the window toward the clothesline. "I . . . I got an old foul-tempered horse in the barn. I should probably get rid of him."

"You probably should," Jamilet agreed, certain she hadn't seen a horse when she was in the barn. "Or put him out to pasture, and pray that somebody steals him." Nancy laughed easily, ignoring the pain, and took Jamilet's plate to the sink.

Jamilet felt an immediate connection with Nancy and began to speak without thinking too much about what she was saying. As she began to tell Nancy her story, she realized she'd never felt so compelled. And her close encounter with death had given her newfound confidence. Instinctively she knew that it was rare to find such a kind and interested listener. She told Nancy of how she'd been born with the mark that the villagers believed to have come from the devil, and all that she had suffered because of it. She told her about her years at the Miller house, and her mother's long illness and death, and her decision to leave home. She told her about how she'd traveled across the desert at night, and how she'd been tied up while she slept. She trembled when she described how it was to cross the river alone, and how it reminded her of the fear and repulsion she'd lived with all of her life. Surviving it had made her feel more capable than she'd ever felt before, and gave her hope that she'd find the cure she sought in the north. All the while, Nancy listened, enraptured, as her hands made lazy circles over her belly. When it seemed there was nothing more to say, Jamilet felt suddenly ashamed that she'd imposed in such a manner, and awkwardly thanked Nancy for her time and hospitality. Then, standing up, she asked her which way it was to Los Angeles.

"Los Angeles is real far. You gotta take the bus, and it ain't cheap."

Jamilet retrieved all the money she had out of her boot, and placed it on the table for Nancy's inspection.

"That won't get you nothing here. It's Mexican money," Nancy said, and she disappeared wordlessly into the pantry, returning moments later with a small wad of bills folded in her palm. "There should be enough here for a one-way bus ticket to Los Angeles, and a little to spare. You'll find a bus station in the next town, five or so miles down the road. Just stay close to the trees in case the border patrol comes back this way."

Jamilet was overwhelmed with emotion in the face of such generosity. "I . . . I can't take your money."

"You're not taking it—I'm giving it to you." She grabbed Jamilet's hand and pressed the bills into it. "You know what they say, when you got money and no purpose for it, it . . . it starts to stink so bad that even an old horse can sniff it out. It's best I get rid of it."

※

That afternoon, Jamilet found herself seated on a Greyhound bus headed for Los Angeles, the place where her aunt Carmen lived, and where Lorena believed that miracles could be found. With the few dollars that remained, she bought a hamburger, potato chips, and a small Coke. It was the first hamburger she'd ever tasted, and she ate it reverently while gazing out the window and thinking about Nancy. It was getting dark, and in the window Jamilet was certain she saw the reflection of her mother's face wavering beyond her own. And if she partially closed her eyes, the vision became more distinct and impossible to dismiss. And when her mother spoke, her voice was like the melody of a lilting flute, and more real than the droning rumble of the engine.

❋

"I'm very proud of you," she said. "I didn't think you'd get this far. You have more courage and strength than I thought you had."

Jamilet replied, "When I stepped into the river, I realized that fear and courage push each other along, like best friends."

"That's true," Lorena said, and then she instructed her daughter to be quiet, and put her head down so she could sleep. Jamilet obeyed and felt the gentle strokes of her mother's fingers on her temple, and she heard the beautiful lullaby her mother used to sing to her when she was very young.

"Don't stop singing until we get there, Mama. Please don't stop."

❋

The next day, as Jamilet stepped off the bus, she glowed with the warmth that had remained with her since her encounter with Nancy. Still, she felt the force of the wind that swept through the skyscraper canyons of downtown Los Angeles. It was no different from the wind that blew through the desert canyons she knew back home, except that here the lonely howl was replete with the feverish pitch of automobiles honking, and sirens wailing, and a buzzing urgency she'd felt only in times of trouble at home—when the river flooded, or a fire broke out in the fields. It seemed that people were rushing with purpose instead of alarm, and this intrigued Jamilet more than a little.

It was truly a wondrous thing to walk among these people as if she were invisible. When she dared to stare straight into their faces, in most cases they never looked back or even noticed that she was there at all. Slinking around in her dirty disguise would have aroused alarm in her village, and certain confrontation. Within moments of her arrival, Jamilet decided that justice was alive in this place where everyone was dismissed with so much equanimity and that superstition couldn't possibly thrive in the crevices of polished glass and concrete the way it flourished like a fungus at home.

After showing her slip of paper with Carmen's address to those strangers who appeared to have softer, somewhat less preoccupied eyes, Jamilet eventually made her way to the east side of the city where the multitude of colors and races she'd never seen before gave way to people mostly of the brown race that she belonged to. In this place everybody was Mexican and spoke Spanish, or English with a Spanish accent. On every corner was a Mexican-style market or restaurant. There was even a small circular plaza identical to what could be found in every village and town south of the border.

The street where Carmen lived was so busy with traffic that Jamilet was certain she saw more cars drive down in five minutes than she'd ever seen pass through her village in her whole life. Overhead was a crisscrossing of wires strung between the houses like a canopy. In some places pigeons were perched in long lines along the wire, watching the frenetic world below with calm reserve. The house itself was a small Pepto-Bismol pink bungalow, but it was easy to see by the scabs of paint chipping off here and there that it had once been an even more disagreeable blue. It was surrounded by a chain-link fence that reached an inch or two above Jamilet's head. The gate was closed, but the padlock had been left open. After checking the address three times to be sure, she let herself into the yard, and walked up the broken concrete path leading to the front door. She knocked, and waited, expecting at any moment to hear her aunt holler out a welcome, but all was silent, and the shades that were drawn in the window hadn't moved. She concluded that her aunt was probably still at work, so she dropped her bundle and eased herself down on the front steps to wait, wincing at the stiffness in her legs. Even after working in the field for hours on end, she hadn't feared that her bones were going to dislodge from their sockets, but she did now. The journey had taken its toll, and she felt like rolling up into a ball and sleeping for several days.

But it wouldn't do for her aunt to find her niece asleep for their reunion, so Jamilet forced herself to stay awake and found her gaze wandering with interest over the front yard. It was mostly dirt, with a few patches of dry grass clinging to the soil here and there. The trash that blew about had become trapped along the base of the fence, and she preoccupied herself with trying to see if she could recognize any of the American brands. As best as she could tell, her aunt had a definite preference for Cheetos and Oreo cookies.

Straining forward, she looked up and down the length of the street, noting that most of the houses were more or less the same size and nondescript style. Some had blankets hanging in the windows, and thick overgrown gardens tangled in among a scattered collection of discarded furniture and mechanical parts rusting in the sun.

Jamilet leaned back and stretched out her legs, grateful that the hot afternoon sun had shifted so she could rest in partial shade. She removed her hat and finger-combed her short hair before replacing it. Would she still recognize Tía Carmen after so many years, and would Tía Carmen recognize her? As she contemplated this, she noticed a young man across the street waiting on the porch in much the same manner she was, with legs outstretched while resting back on his elbows. He wore a white tank top and his dark hair was cropped short above the ears. Even from such a distance, it was easy to make out the clean line of his jaw, and the curved flange of muscle flaring at his shoulder. He had an athletic build, much like the young men who traveled around looking for work on the ranches back home. Women liked hiring hands like these, especially if their husbands were prone to long stays in town.

She adjusted her hat so that she might continue to watch him without looking so obvious. Then he stood up and stepped off the porch, making his way to the edge of the property closest to her. He indicated with a flick of his head that she should do the same, and Jamilet jumped up on her feet, oblivious to the pain in her legs as she made her way to the fence.

"She won't be home for a while," he called out over the noise of the traffic in a friendly voice. It was odd to hear a Mexican boy speak English so perfectly, with no trace of an accent. Jamilet's English was good, but she knew her accent was as thick as fresh salsa. "That's okay, I'll wait," she called back, forgetting to lower the timber of her voice, as she had done before, but she was none-theless pleased with her selection of words and lack of grammatical errors. She'd heard Mary call out many such phrases over the years. No doubt she'd make use of the others she'd stored away in her memory bank.

The boy's eyes flew open in surprise when he heard her, and he braved the traffic, managing to get across the street in two or three long strides. Up close like this he was taller than he appeared from far away, and his brown eyes were bright with curiosity. A smile tugged at the corners of his mouth. "Say that again," he chal-lenged, and Jamilet was momentarily struck by how handsome he was, even handsomer than the ranch hands back home who could saunter into a dance and have their way with any girl of their choosing.

"Say what again?" Jamilet answered, nervously, as she read-justed her hat.

The boy placed his hands low on his hips and shook his head. "You're a chick. I can tell by your voice and . . ." He leaned in closer to get a better look. "Your face and stuff."

Jamilet felt her cheeks color.

"Why are you dressed like that?" he asked boldly, like someone who was not easily fooled and was accustomed to getting answers.

Jamilet shrugged, not sure if she should tell him the reason for her clever disguise. She'd heard many warnings about not letting on that she'd crossed the border illegally, and thought it wiser to stay quiet. The color in her cheeks intensified as he waited for an answer. She detected something in his eyes, more prominent than his curiosity—kindness, and it was this that prompted her to be honest. That and the fact that she didn't know how else to explain her appearance, and it felt very important for some reason that she explain it adequately. "I crossed the border a couple of days ago. I dressed like this so . . . so I wouldn't get caught."

"Ah . . . you're a wetback," the boy said, nodding wisely, but he'd stepped closer still, and took hold of the fence between them, looking at her through the wire as though she were an animal at the zoo.

Jamilet realized her status hadn't been elevated one bit, but she smoothed her collar with as much dignity as she could muster. "My name is Jamilet."

"I'm Eddie." He flicked his head, his eyes never leaving her face. "My girlfriend, Pearly, lives across the street."

Jamilet was intrigued with how he spoke, and with the way his lips spread smoothly over his teeth when he smiled in a wide unhurried way, as if the world and everything in it were there for his own personal amusement. When she didn't respond to his last comment, there was a brief silence between them, and it felt as though he'd crawled into her eyes, diving in deep to where it was dark and cool, and the passing of time didn't matter. She could not, in spite of her growing discomfort, look away.

He eased back from her gaze, perhaps a bit uncomfortable himself, and glanced toward her aunt's house. "She's pretty cool. She buys us beer sometimes when she's in a good mood."

"She's my aunt," Jamilet said, basking in the unexpected de-

light of their conversation, and realizing that she'd have to respond
in some way if she hoped to prolong it.

He shook his head and wrinkled his brow. "You look nothing like her," he said. "And that's a compliment 'cause, no offense . . . but your aunt's nothing to look at." At that moment
something prompted him to glance back over his shoulder and
his body stiffened, as though someone had poured a bucket of
cold water down his back. A striking young woman was walking across the street toward the house where he'd been waiting,
her thick platform shoes smacking the pavement with every step.
Jamilet was fascinated by her lips, which were painted a deep red,
so as to appear almost black, and her long, dark hair, which was
streaked with shades of red and gold. But it was the quality of her
skin that captivated Jamilet the most. Practically nude in a tank
top and miniskirt, it shimmered gold in the sunlight. Her legs,
front and back, from ankle to thigh, were powdery smooth. The
flesh of her shoulders running down the length of her arms, the
curve of her throat and chest beyond her cleavage, was as perfect
as if she'd been spun from the finest silk thread. Not a blemish could be seen anywhere, just clear uninterrupted skin going
on and on. Jamilet knew that this had to be Eddie's girlfriend,
Pearly.

Without another word to Jamilet, he sprinted back across the
street to her, but she shrugged him away with her creamy shoulders when his arm encircled her waist. Eddie wasn't easily discouraged. He followed her up the steps to the house and placed his
hand on the curve of her hip, resting it there as if she belonged to
him and no other. While she turned the key in the lock, he whispered something in her ear, and she pushed him away playfully
this time, forgetting her upset. Their smiles were dreamy as they
entered the house, and Jamilet was certain she heard laughter after
they closed the door. She wondered if they'd immediately rip off
their clothes and make love, or if they'd wait a respectable amount
of time, maybe have a snack first. Jamilet remembered that Tía
Carmen and her boyfriends always ate something before they left

to fondle each other in the bed of the old rusted truck that was abandoned in the back field. Tía insisted on it.

All at once, Jamilet felt the weariness return to her limbs. She sighed, and slowly walked back to the front steps of Carmen's house, and waited there until evening announced itself as a steely gray dusk that was nothing like the black nights of her village. In this place the lights of the city effectively fought off the encroaching darkness, and the constant traffic stirred up the dust to create a perpetual haze. Even so, Jamilet could no longer help herself. She curled up, well hidden from the street by the wide post on the porch, placed her bundle underneath her head, and fell soundly asleep.

A strong hand on her shoulder moved her to and fro. "Wake up, you're scaring the shit out of me." The voice was both firm and familiar.

Jamilet's eyes flew open, and she found herself face-to-face with a woman who looked somewhat like the Tía Carmen she remembered. This woman had the same squat nose and broad face, the same coarse black hair that curled away from her forehead in little cowlicks all around. But she was much bigger than the Tía Carmen she remembered. This woman was easily three Tía Carmens in one.

Jamilet sat up with a start and stared into dark eyes as sharp as razors.

The woman switched to Spanish. "Are you my sister Lorena's girl, Jamilet?" she asked, peering suspiciously at the short hair and boy's pants.

Jamilet felt her lips tremble with emotion. It was wonderful to be recognized in this strange place and to hear her mother's name spoken as if she were still alive. She was filled with a wave of hope and nostalgia that left her momentarily dumb. She could only nod.

"You showed up a lot sooner than I thought you would," she said as she jabbed her hand into her purse. She immediately produced keys that jangled like wind chimes. "Some get stuck for weeks trying to cross."

"I crossed the river alone," Jamilet replied, finding her voice, but it was wimpy and girlish sounding, when she wanted to sound so confident and strong. She scampered up and gathered her belongings together before Carmen could unlock the screen door, and the two locks on the main door after that. This gave Jamilet a moment or two to appraise her aunt's hairdo, as massive as it was intricate, like an elaborate fountain frozen around her face. At her other end were small fleshy feet tightly packed into leather shoes. And in between the two was an impressive girth, as big and round in front as it was in back.

The door was finally opened and Jamilet followed her aunt into the dark house. A foul bittersweet odor wafted around them, the stale odor of filth left to its own devices. When the light was switched on, her suspicions were confirmed. The furniture was obscured by layers of clutter and trash that appeared to have fused together over time, like wax melting in the sun. If one looked carefully, it was possible to discern the approximate location of a tattered couch, and the television on cinder blocks set right in front of it. The coffee table in the center of the room was a bit easier to distinguish, and on its surface sat the recent residue of Carmen's domestic life: empty beer cans, grease-stained paper plates, and a multitude of colorful wrappers, their contents long ago devoured.

Carmen appraised the scene as if for the first time, and shrugged. "Excuse the mess," she said, after which she tossed her purse on the couch and proceeded to the kitchen, which was in even worse condition than the living room. Jamilet couldn't help but gape wide-eyed at the sink overflowing with dishes, the counters cluttered with opened boxes of every kind of ready-made food imaginable. Some of the boxes were chewed through, and small pieces were scattered about the floor and counters. Jamilet was familiar with this; the handiwork of rats, and from what she could see, they'd been cohabiting comfortably with her aunt for some time.

Carmen plowed straight through the obstacles in her way, kicking whatever trash she encountered this way and that as she headed for the refrigerator. She swung open the door with a jerk and retrieved a can of beer. Then she stepped aside, raising her eyebrows as an invitation to Jamilet, who politely declined. Carmen didn't bother closing the door before she popped the tab, and swigged down half the beer in one swallow. She finished it with another large gulp, tossed the empty can on the counter, and popped open another before slamming the door shut.

"Now," she said as genteelly as she could, "I feel human again."

She pushed a pile of newspapers off the counter stools and onto the floor, inviting Jamilet to sit. She herself experienced some difficulty with this maneuver as she slid her ample bottom up and over the seat.

"So," she said, stifling a burp, which caused her eyes to water. "Now that you're here, what are your plans?"

Jamilet still held her little bundle close. She was shocked by her surroundings, but nonetheless exhilarated by the question. No one had ever asked her such a thing before. Her life's course seemed always to have been predetermined by the chili plants, the remoteness of the village, and the mark. "I want to get a job," she replied.

"The old lady expects you to send money home, too, does she?"

"Some, but I'm going to save most of it."

"Yeah? What for?" Her saucy brown eyes were reading into every second it took Jamilet to respond.

"I want to save money for . . . for the future."

Carmen narrowed her eyes, not quite convinced. "Don't think you're getting a free ride here or anything."

"I'll pay my way," Jamilet said, delighted that her aunt would let it go at that. She was one of the few who'd actually seen the mark, but it was easy to see how her new life in the north had reshuffled her memory. In this place it wasn't necessary to know about the best time to plant corn. One could survive without remembering that on the way to the market you should walk in the shade, not only because it was cooler, but because it was also the best way to avoid the snakes, who preferred the sunny spots. Jamilet was tantalized by the possibility that details about her mark were not among her aunt's scattered collection of memories. Could it be that she'd forgotten about it altogether? Jamilet felt a glimmer of hope. To be hundreds of miles away from anyone who knew about the mark was the closest thing to a cure she'd ever experienced.

"Let me show you around," Carmen said brightly, beer still in hand as she slid off the stool. She led the way out of the kitchen and through the living room with Jamilet following close behind. "I didn't have time to fix up your room, so don't get all excited."

Carmen stopped at the last door at the end of the hallway and flipped on the light. The room was the size of a large closet. It was crammed from floor to ceiling with boxes, shoes, and old clothes. So many layers of dust had settled on top of everything that it all appeared to be draped with a thin gray blanket. In the far corner, propped up against the wall, was a stained and mottled mattress.

"I use this room for storage," Carmen said as she shoved the box closest to her away with her foot. "Most of this stuff I probably don't need anymore."

Jamilet attempted to find a pleasant place to rest her gaze, aware that Carmen was watching her, but she was well-practiced at hiding her feelings. She'd learned long ago how to keep the muscles of her face relaxed, and her eyes steady and calm, even when a storm of emotion was raging inside her. At that moment she knew that if she allowed herself a moment of weakness, she'd collapse to the floor in a puddle of tears. "This will do just fine, Tía," she said brightly. "I'll clean it all up in the morning, but tonight, if it's okay with you, I'll sleep on the couch."

Carmen stared at her niece. "For an instant there, you re-minded me so much of your mother," she said, uncharacteristically wistful. Then she shrugged, kicked off her shoes, and waddled back down the hall on bare feet that were as thick and square as waffles. She flicked on the lights in the bathroom, in the center of which stood an enormous claw-foot tub, before waddling back toward the living room. Staring at her niece for some time, she folded her arms like a giant pretzel. "Okay, we need to get some things straight if this is going to work out," she said. "You were still little when I left, so you probably don't remember the only surefire way to piss me off."

Jamilet shifted on her sore feet, and shook her head.

Carmen considered her niece with a wary eye, looking her up and down. "You can call me a fat bitch and it won't piss me off. You can say I'm the biggest slob north of the South Pole and it won't piss me off either. You know why?" Her mouth twitched into a near smile, and then she was dead serious once again.

"Why, Tía?"

"Because it's the truth, that's why. But if you tell me I'm the cutest thing on two legs, I'll be pissed as hell."

Jamilet met her aunt's fierce gaze, and fought the temptation to return a smile. She remembered that sometimes her aunt was funny without trying to be, or wanting to be, and it could get you in trouble. "I won't lie to you, Tía," she said as sincerely as she could.

Carmen waved her arms about in a sudden gust of good humor. "I don't mean just you . . . anybody. I don't like liars, that's all."

Jamilet placed her bag on the arm of the couch, not quite sure of what to do next. Carmen left for a moment and returned with an old blanket that she tossed at Jamilet.

"Tía," Jamilet said, unfolding the blanket. "Don't you eat dinner before you go to sleep?"

"Naw . . . I ate at the bowling alley. A big cheeseburger, like I do every Wednesday on bowling nights."

Jamilet lowered her gaze. The mere thought of a cheeseburger made the saliva overflow in her mouth. The last time she'd had anything to eat was that morning—the remainder of her burger that she'd saved from the night before. Her stomach had been complaining since noon, although she'd been able to quench her thirst by drinking from the faucet in the yard.

Carmen propped her hands on her hips. "Are you actually hungry . . . now?" Jamilet could only answer with the unmistakable gaze of the famished. "Well, I . . . I didn't know you were coming tonight," Carmen said, flustered and perturbed. "There's nothing here, except maybe some crackers." She thought for a moment and added. "Maybe . . ."

Jamilet considered the hopelessness of the situation and brightened. "That's okay, Tía. Right now, I need to sleep more than I need to eat."

"You sure?"

"I'll be fine." And that was enough to send Carmen on her way to bed without another worry.

After ridding the couch of all the beer cans and food wrappers, Jamilet made her bed as best she could. She closed her eyes and tried to forget her hunger by remembering Eddie and how he'd peered at her through the fence earlier that day. She sensed a rare tenderness in his soul, and imagined that he was the sort who'd go to great lengths to catch a spider in the house and release it unharmed, no matter how loudly the women protested. "You're a chick," he'd said to her, and she liked how he'd smiled, as though he was pleased, very pleased to know that she was.

4

JAMILET APPRAISED the fruits of her labor. In the kitchen, she surveyed the gleaming counters, and the coffee cups stacked neatly next to the coffeepot, ready for tomorrow's breakfast. In the living room, there wasn't a beer can to be found. They had all been gathered up, along with load after load of food wrappers, and deposited in the trash cans outside until they bulged, their lids tilted off center like cockeyed hats. The couch had been thoroughly cleaned and the cushions propped up evenly from end to end, and it was no longer necessary to squint through layers of greasy dust to see the TV screen. In the bathroom, the tub was scrubbed, the mirror polished, and the floor mopped. In her own little room, Jamilet threw away what was obviously trash, organized and rearranged the myriad boxes into one corner, and swept out the rat filth along with everything else.

The only room she didn't touch was her aunt's bedroom. She did peek in, however, and was not surprised to find that the clutter had invaded this room as well, although to a somewhat lesser degree. There was clothing draped everywhere, and various books and magazines were strewn about on the bed. They were similar to books she'd seen thrown into a pile in one corner of the living room. Jamilet had organized them as best she could so that they all faced in the same direction. Now and then, she flipped through the pages with her thumb, first in one direction and then the next, enjoying the cool slip of air on her face, and the smell of ink on paper.

She studied the pictures on the covers next. They were different, and yet all the same. Beautiful ladies swooning in the arms of athletic men whose muscles bulged as they struggled to control their wanton passion, for there was almost always a breast or a thigh poised to reveal itself. Their expressions were also fascinating, with eyes half closed in breathless rapture, nostrils flaring, and lips parted as though preparing to bite into a succulent peach. Never had she been more curious about the kinds of stories that could provoke such a frenzied state.

As she cleaned, she returned to the books several times in order to stare at the faces and wonder. While polishing the mirror in the bathroom, she tilted her chin, and narrowed her eyes in an attempt to imitate one woman's expression: passion laced with anger; the tender surprise of a fawn covering her naked bosom; and the seductive eyes, ready to submit or be taken by force. All the while she played this game, she pondered the most intriguing question of all: When and how had her aunt managed to learn how to read?

※

When Carmen came home, she stood frozen in the doorway. The grocery bag she held in one hand slipped through her fingers and dropped to the floor with the unmistakable clunk of a six-pack. Her purse was the next to go.

"My God," she said, tugging on the loose flesh under her chin. "I didn't realize how big this place was . . ."

She drifted in as though in a trance, not sure of where to look next, and then turned suddenly toward the kitchen. There she stood in the center of the room, mouth half open and eyes blinking slowly. Swiftly, she ducked her head under the counter, as if she might catch someone there, and here too her eyes met with a wondrous sight. Where yesterday it had been impossible to accommodate her feet, it was cleared out and spotless. She straightened up slowly, her face slack with the shock of it all. It was rare that Carmen should ever find herself speechless, and it took a few moments before she could shake the feeling and find her bearings. "How did you do it all in one day?" she finally asked.

Jamilet felt herself pump up with pride, and she straightened her shoulders in spite of her fatigue. "I'm a hard worker."

"You sure are," Carmen said, heaving her massive chest as if she were out of breath just thinking about it. "You did the work of ten people here, Jami." Then she burst out laughing. "Oh man, Louis is going to shit his pants."

"Louis?"

Carmen propped her hands on her hips, feeling much more herself. "Oh, you'll meet him," she said all a flutter. "He's coming over tonight." She glanced at her watch, waddled quickly to her bedroom, and stood before her door, uncertain about whether or not to enter.

"I didn't clean up your room, Tía," Jamilet said. "I thought I should ask you first . . ."

"Next time, don't ask," she said brightly before disappearing into her room.

While Jamilet was putting away the beer Carmen had left in the living room, she heard a knock at the door. She opened it to find a middle-aged man with skin as dark as strong coffee, and a shabby gray mustache that curled over his lips. He dropped his own bag of beer on the same spot Carmen had used moments earlier, looking even more amazed than she had.

"Excuse me," he said, taking a tentative step forward. "Am I in the right house?" He repeated his question in a louder voice so that Carmen would hear him in her bedroom. "Am I in the right house, woman?" He was on the verge of laughter now and Carmen responded with, "Yes you are, old man," and a cackle of her own that busted him up with pure pleasure. "I guess I am," he said, turning to Jamilet with a jolly crinkled smile. Unlike Carmen, he took his own bag straight to the kitchen while Jamilet trailed after him.

"You do all this?" he asked, looking all around as he popped open his first beer.

Jamilet noticed that Louis was able to drink beer even faster than her aunt. "I did it all today," she replied.

She watched his Adam's apple bob up and down three times before he set the can down on the counter and swallowed a belch. "That's amazing . . . what's your name?"

"Jamilet."

He nodded, his eyes slightly glazed. "You're the cousin, right?"

"The niece."

He snapped his fingers and pointed at her face. "That's right, the niece. Carmen told me you were coming."

"I don't think she expected me so soon," Jamilet said, hoping he'd tell her she was all wrong about that, and that her aunt had been looking forward to her arrival ever since she'd learned of her sister's death, and that she'd been worried sick about her only niece.

Louis ran his finger along the rim of his empty beer can, seemingly preoccupied with whether or not to have another one so soon. "Let me tell you about your aunt," he said with the gleam of admiration in his eyes. "She never expects nothing and she never plans for it if she does. If she knew a year ahead of time you were coming, it would've been the same to her."

Jamilet took his empty can and tossed it in the trash, hoping he'd taken good care to notice where it was.

"You must be real tired," he said, leaning on the counter as he took note of the dark circles under her eyes and the pale lips.

"Tired" didn't begin to describe it. She was now drifting and managing to move and breathe by drawing on what strength she could garner from the filaments of anxiety that sparked her into action just when she was ready to collapse. "I didn't sleep too good last night," she said.

"You probably didn't eat too good either," he said with a knowing wink.

Jamilet shrugged. Her mouth was past watering. It was positively dry, and the aching in her stomach had started to throb in her ears since the afternoon, and hadn't been relieved except for a few minutes when she gobbled down the stale crackers she found in the kitchen drawer next to an unopened package of rat poison.

"She's a good woman, your aunt, but she's no hostess," he continued. "She's got no sense for it."

At that moment Carmen made her entrance wearing a red dress cut so low that her cleavage must have measured at least a foot in length, yet there was plenty that still wasn't showing. Her black hair was teased big and high and she wore hoop earrings that could've strangled a cow.

Carmen smiled from ear to ear, delighted to see Louis's eyes bugging out at her cleavage and the slit in her skirt, cut way up to reveal a mighty thigh. Standing next to her, Jamilet thought that he looked small and bent, like a stick somebody had snatched out of the fire before it turned to ash. She imagined that if her aunt were to embrace him, he'd disintegrate in her great arms and ruin her dress.

But Louis was gushing and smiling, and sucking on the scraggly ends of his mustache as if they'd been dipped in honey. "You're a whole lotta beautiful woman," he declared.

Carmen giggled and shoved his shoulder. He bounced away and sprung back at her. "A whole lotta sexy woman," he added while sweeping his hand along the voluptuous contour of her buttock before placing it on her shoulder, and assuming a more sensible expression. "Your niece is very hungry," he said, nodding at Jamilet. "She spent all day cleaning for you and I think we should get her some dinner before we go out."

Carmen's face went suddenly pale and loose about the jowls, apparently disappointed that the compliments had ended so soon.

"That's okay," Jamilet said. "I can eat something here."

"Eat what?" Louis said. "There's no food in this house, never has been. Isn't that true, Carmencita?"

Carmen was pouting and examining a loose thread on her sleeve. "I like to eat out mostly."

"Yes, well, your niece needs to eat too . . . my little flower . . . ," he said, cajoling her with the confidence of one who'd met with frequent success using such tactics. "How about if I stay over tonight?"

This cheered Carmen up enough to prompt her toward the refrigerator for her first beer of the evening. She offered another to Louis, who accepted by holding his hand up in the air like an outfielder. She turned to her niece, and Jamilet surprised herself by doing the same. In a few seconds beers were flying across the kitchen like frigid bombs. Jamilet caught hers like a pro, and flicked open the tab with an easy snap of her forefinger as it burped in a friendly sort of way. She'd never been curious about the taste of beer, but was certain that anything would be better than the stale soda crackers and tepid tap water she'd been consuming all day.

She took a cautious sip and felt the cool fizz dance over her tongue and throughout her mouth, bitter and toasty, like burnt bread. Her gums began to tingle with the next sip and she bit down on the bubbles escaping down her throat. After a few more swallows, her cheeks and ears were glowing and a pleasant numbing sensation had spread over her lips and part of her face. The hunger she'd felt earlier was almost gone, and she was swaying on her feet, listening to the talk between her aunt and Louis, and trying to discern its meaning. For a moment she thought they might be speaking another language—a language that wasn't Spanish or English, because she couldn't understand one word they said. She concentrated instead on the hairs of Louis's mustache, which fluttered like palm fronds in the wind when he talked. Moistened with beer, she imagined it was both windy and raining and that at any moment it would blow a gale. She swallowed her private giggles along with another swig of beer.

Next thing she knew, Carmen was guiding her by the shoulders to the door. "Okay, let's get something in your stomach, lightweight. You act like this is your first beer."

Jamilet felt as if her feet were loose at the ankles, and she was afraid they might fall off if she walked too fast. "It is my first beer," she said, taking another sip, most of which dribbled down her chin.

Carmen and Louis were laughing as they helped her into his old Pinto. She sat in the backseat sipping away and feeling happier than she had in months—light and free and not worried about how hungry she was, or about finding a job, or even about the mark. All worries had disappeared in this effervescent moment, and she felt wonderfully warm as the golden liquid flowed through her veins.

The engine started with a cough, and she looked out the window, across the street, and saw Eddie sitting on the porch with Pearly. She'd been looking out for him all day, and now there he was watching her drink a beer in the back of this old man's car while his hand rested on Pearly's perfect thigh. Pearly hadn't noticed that his attention was diverted, and was talking all the while, fluttering her long-nailed fingers in the air as though conducting an orchestra of admirers.

They drove to Tina's Tacos a few blocks away, leaving Jamilet in the car, and returned a few minutes later with a white paper bag stained with grease. It was piping hot, and its contents smelled so delicious Jamilet was certain that even her teeth were watering.

Back at the house, Carmen handed Jamilet the key. "Let yourself in and leave it under the mat."

It was difficult to find the handle and open the car door, and when she went to get out, she almost dropped her precious bag of food in the gutter.

"You need any help?" Louis asked.

Tía Carmen waved an impatient hand at him. "She only has to get to the door, for God's sake."

"Yeah, but she's drunk as a skunk."

"She's fine."

They waited until Jamilet made it to the front steps and then drove off as she was opening the door. She was preparing to slip the key under the mat as instructed when she looked up and saw them still on the porch. Eddie was kissing Pearly's neck like a vampire, and his hand was straight up her shirt, as though pumping the blood from her heart for his meal. Forgetting her hunger, Jamilet hid in the shadows and watched as they twisted and contorted themselves like snakes, slipping their hands between the spaces of their clothes, moving their lips as though eating from each other's mouths. She watched until her knees grew weak and she could no longer stand the growling in her stomach.

When she finally went inside to eat her dinner, it was barely warm.

5

JAMILET SLEPT UNTIL NOON the next day, and woke with a pounding in her head. She looked around and remembered where she was. She also recalled, with nauseating effect, the two additional beers she'd drunk after she finished her dinner, and vowed that this would be the first and last hangover of her life. In her village, she'd seen plenty of what happened to people who turned to liquor for comfort. They were men mostly, and they wandered the streets like ghosts searching out a new corner to haunt and from which to beg for change. They often met death on the side of the road or in somebody's field, their bodies bloated and forgotten for days or weeks until they were found, usually by horrified children playing beyond the watch of adults.

For women it was worse somehow, although the alcohol hit them more subtly in the early stages, flushing their cheeks a flattering crimson and giving them the courage to speak and move with that alluring lack of inhibition that made men notice them. These were the same women who burned candles until late at night. If you passed by their houses, you'd see shadows moving in the windows, and hear the low, sensuous laughter of betrayal and forbidden things enjoyed to an extreme. In the morning the men's wives would show up pounding at their doors and would leave weeping into their aprons. This might go on for years, until one day the woman would emerge with red-rimmed flabby eyes, wondering where everybody had gone, and why the nights were now so dark and the days even darker. No, there would be no more beer for Jamilet.

Over the next few weeks, she busied herself with housework. She began by throwing out, with her aunt's approval, all the junk that had been accumulating, untouched, for years. She dedicated one full week to the laundry alone, and most mornings when Carmen left for work, Jamilet could be found outside, hanging freshly washed clothes and sheets out on the line to dry. She also started cooking in the evenings, preparing recipes that the Millers had enjoyed. Carmen was pleased with the home-cooked meals she returned to every night, and began to arrive earlier so she could converse with her niece about the daily drama and frustrations of her life while the meal was in its final stages of preparation.

Jamilet also enjoyed these times, and found comfort and amusement in her aunt's forward opinions about everything, which confirmed that the north hadn't changed her that much after all. In fact, there were moments when Jamilet felt as though they were sitting around the kitchen table in Mexico, with Lorena quietly sewing, and Gabriela grumbling about Carmen's lack of concern for her modesty or her health. Jamilet had always laughed along and sided with her aunt, but now she felt more sympathy for her grandmother's view of things, and hoped that with a clean house to live in and good food to eat, Carmen would be motivated to live a healthier life.

One evening, after guzzling her third beer, Carmen caught her niece's critical eye. "Don't look at me like that," she snapped. "Who do you think you are, the Virgin Mary?"

Jamilet sighed and tossed the empty cans in the trash without bothering to answer. She knew that there wasn't an answer she could come up with that would get Carmen to listen. During the few weeks she'd been there, she'd exhausted them all. She reminded her aunt of the broken lonely women from back home, and of the early undignified deaths that befell almost all drinkers. When that didn't work, she turned to the fact that too much beer resulted in enormous bellies on men and women alike, and that their noses became big and red. At this Carmen laughed in midswallow, and nearly choked on her beer. "You must think I'm pretty goddamned stupid to believe that," she said. "Louis drinks three times what I drink, and he's skinny as a bird." She cackled once more, took another swallow, and then grew thoughtful. "There is a part of him that gets big and red though . . ." She leveled her eyes at Jamilet, almost bursting with laughter. "But it sure as hell ain't on his face."

Other times Carmen remained with a scowl on her face and drank her beer in exaggerated loud slurps, but Jamilet knew her aunt's foul mood would lighten as soon as Louis arrived. He came over almost every night, about an hour or so after Carmen got home. Before then she was certain to change into something that accentuated her cavernous cleavage even if in the process she had to reveal the appalling state of her midsection. But Louis thought everything about Carmen was endearing, and if he could make her laugh it was all the better, as he liked nothing more than to watch her breasts jiggle. He looked for any excuse to declare, "I like my women big and sassy," often with his mouth full of Jamilet's homemade dinner, and his hand slipping under the table to caress Carmen's generous thigh.

Late one evening, Jamilet was awakened by a strange wailing, quite different from the sloppy lovemaking sounds she'd grown accustomed to on the nights Louis stayed over. This was the eerie low-pitched moan of death making its claim and preparing for victory. Cold with fear, Jamilet got out of bed to check on her aunt. Her bedroom door was ajar, so Jamilet peeked in to find her sprawled naked on the bed, her breasts smeared across her body like too much whipped cream on an enormous sundae. She was whimpering and calling out for Louis, who was nowhere to be found, although the pillow on his side of the bed betrayed the fresh imprint of his head.

"Tía, what's the matter?" Jamilet asked, overcome by the sight of so much naked flesh.

Carmen made no attempt to cover herself as Jamilet entered the room. "He's a fucking bastard." She attempted to raise her head a few inches before dropping back down to the pillow. "The bitch threatens him with the police and he's gotta run off to them . . ." She suddenly turned and swiped the phone off the nightstand, sending it to the floor, where it landed with a series of discordant jingles.

"You mean Louis?"

"'You mean Louis?'" Carmen mimed with disgust. "Of course, who else?"

"Is he in trouble with the police?"

Carmen's thinking about this question seemed to prompt some modesty, and she reached for the sheet and pulled it over her midsection. "He's in trouble with his wife, that's who. Who does she think she is calling here at this time of night? And how the hell did she get my number? That's what I'd like to know."

Jamilet was speechless. In spite of his obsession with beer and his even greater obsession with Carmen's full figure, she thought Louis was a basically kind and decent person. She appreciated how he thanked her for dinner every night and how he made it a point to comment on how things had improved since she'd arrived. "It's starting to feel like a home around here," he'd say while planting a kiss on Carmen's cheek. "And we can thank your niece for that."

"Louis has a wife?" Jamilet finally asked.

"And three snot-nosed kids," Carmen replied, now turning on her side. "And I don't want to hear any lectures from you, got it?"

"I'm not going to lecture you."

"Yeah, right."

"It's just that . . ."

"Here it comes . . ." Carmen grabbed the pillow closest to her and wrapped it around her head and ears.

"I thought you said that you couldn't stand people who lie," Jamilet said, loudly enough to penetrate her aunt's pillow barrier.

Carmen turned so that only half her face was visible as she directed one squinty eye at her niece. "Yeah, so?"

"How can you stand Louis if he lies to his wife and kids? Every day he's here with you, he's lying to them, isn't he?"

Carmen turned on her back again, and managed to prop her head up a few inches so that her chin rested on her chest. She stared wide-eyed at the ceiling, contemplating this bizarre dilemma, this affront to her philosophy of life. Then her cheeks puffed up as her eyes fixed on Jamilet like a warrior. "He doesn't lie to me though, does he?"

Before Jamilet could answer, Carmen pointed a fast finger at her. "No he doesn't, so shut up about it." She collapsed on the bed and began moaning anew.

Jamilet pulled down the sheet to cover her aunt's feet, writhing in sync with her agony. "I'm sorry you feel bad, Tía. Do you want me to bring you anything?"

Carmen's feet became still, and she answered with a whimper, "Warm milk with vanilla and sugar, the way you made it for me the other night."

Jamilet was back in minutes with a steaming mug and placed it next to her aunt, where the phone had been. Carmen took several tentative sips, and appeared somehow fortified.

"I don't want to hear his name mentioned in this house again, do you understand me?"

"I understand, Tía."

Jamilet waited a few minutes longer, and when it seemed that her aunt was calmer and on the verge of sleep, she started to tiptoe out of the room. But then Carmen stopped her with an unexpected question. "Do you think he's making love to her, Jami? Do you think that while I'm here suffering, that skinny bastard is making love to his bitch wife?"

"No, I'm sure he's not," Jamilet replied.

"Why not? How can you be so sure?"

Not thinking, Jamilet replied, "Because it's late and he's probably tired."

Carmen brought her fist down to the bed in a fury. "Damnit,
you're supposed to say it's because he loves me, and not her. You're
supposed to say that he's with her only out of obligation, but that
his heart belongs to me. "

"He loves you, of course he does," Jamilet replied hurriedly.
"What I mean is that it's just too bad he's married."

"Yeah," Carmen sighed. "It's too bad."

Carmen didn't go to work for the remainder of the week. She
directed Jamilet to call the gas company and tell them that she'd
come down with the stomach flu and couldn't come to the phone
because she was on the toilet with constant diarrhea. "They won't
ask too many questions if you tell them that," she said.

During the day she stayed in her room, sleeping or reading
one of her many books with the pictures on the cover of half-
dressed men and women embracing. But these only seemed to fuel
her misery. Sometimes Jamilet would walk in to find her weeping,
and the book she'd been reading spread-eagled like a wounded
bird, on the opposite side of the room.

In the evenings, Carmen preferred to sit sprawled on the
couch watching TV and drinking beer after beer until she doubled
over on her side and fell asleep. Twice, Jamilet was unable to wake
her and had to leave her there for the entire night.

Toward the end of the week, there was a light knock on the
door and Jamilet opened it to find Louis, with a lopsided grin
and a nervous foot tap-tapping on the threshold. Jamilet hurriedly
stepped outside and closed the door so Carmen wouldn't notice he
was there. She'd almost finished her first six-pack and was beginning to fade.

"She's very upset," Jamilet whispered. "You better leave."

Louise glanced up from his feet. "She usually is," he said, looking like a penitent child. "But she gets over it."

"You mean this has happened before?"

Louis raised his eyebrows and placed a wise hand on Jamilet's shoulder. "And it'll probably happen again." With that he stepped past her, walked into the house, and plopped himself on the couch next to Carmen, a shy smile playing on his feathery lips. Carmen didn't blink as she helped herself to another beer, acting as if a fly had landed on the couch next to her and not the man she'd been pining over for three torturous days.

Undaunted, even amused, Louis began to beg for her forgiveness in a fit of poetic despondency, talking about the lack of meaning in his life without her, the emptiness in his heart, and so on.

Jamilet took a seat across from them, entranced by the scene. She'd been judging Louis very harshly during the past few days, and had convinced herself that he wasn't as kind and sensitive as she thought, but rather a liar and a trickster who couldn't be trusted to take out the trash. She was then surprised to find herself hoping that Carmen would give in to him, or at least respond in some way. But Carmen didn't even flinch, and proceeded to examine her fingernails one by one. Louis persisted, making more and more desperate declarations of his love for her, the joy he felt in her presence, his realization that no other woman could ever compare. His face reddened and his eyes watered, but still she refused to acknowledge him, or even to glance in his direction.

"You could at least answer him, Tía," Jamilet said, no longer able to contain herself.

"You shut up," Carmen answered, her eyes twisting in their sockets.

Louis jumped in. "She sees how cruel you're being."

Carmen took a giant breath, and writhed with the overwhelming desire not only to answer but to bellow at him with all of her might. Louis licked his lips and waited. But when it was clear that she'd somehow found the strength to resist him, he sighed as despondent a sigh as he could muster, and said with convincing resignation, "I can see that this time you really mean it. My heart will be breaking for the rest of my life, but a man knows when he's wasting his time."

He exhaled as though giving up his last breath and pushed himself up from the couch. He shuffled to the door and Carmen blinked once. He reached for the doorknob and her mouth twitched. He opened the door and her lips, which had been pressed tight, loosened and she began to speak words that were unexpectedly soft. "Why don't you leave her if I'm all that?"

"We've talked about this before, Carmencita. You know I can't leave until the children are grown and out of the house. That won't change."

He put his foot over the threshold and Carmen spoke again. "Where are you going?"

"Where can I go?"

"You can stay if you want, you bastard. That doesn't change either." And Louis promptly slammed the door and planted himself next to Carmen, where they stayed snuggled for the rest of the evening until they retired to the bedroom. That evening Jamilet fell asleep to the ardent, slap-happy sounds of their lovemaking, but it was the best night's sleep she'd had in three days.

6

◦─◦

T HE BATHROOM, with its enormous tub and bright white tile,
was the most pleasant room in the house. Here, Jamilet
found peace and solace from her worries, although here
too was the place where she examined the mark. It was possible
to see most of it if she adjusted the two mirrors over the sink
so they reflected onto each other, and she turned herself halfway
around and looked over one shoulder. The first time she did this,
the breath caught in her throat. Under the harsh light, the mark
was like red lava frozen in time, spilling over her shoulders, her
back, covering her buttocks and trailing in thick ribbons down her
thighs to the tops of her knees. It was worse than she remembered
and appeared all the more alien when observed against the stark
whiteness surrounding her.

It seemed that the weeks she'd spent not looking at the mark
had affected her memory somehow, fading the horror to a mere
shadow, an unpleasant annoyance. But now she had to once again
accept that the mark was not this kind of problem. It was not a pile
of rat-infested filth, or months of accumulated laundry that could
be dispatched with a heavy dose of discipline and resolve.

It was no wonder that she'd waited so long to get on with her
plans to find a job and begin saving the money she needed to be
rid of it. She'd taken respite in dusting and organizing, and stir-

ring pots on the stove, all the things she did in Mexico. She found comfort in the knowledge that at least for now, nobody knew of her disfigurement. Ashamed, but not discouraged, she lowered her body into the scalding bath and promised herself that from that day forward she would study the mark on a daily basis, from the base of her neck to the top of her knees, so she would never forget the reason she'd come north.

That very afternoon, when her aunt arrived home from work, Jamilet followed her into the bedroom and waited until she'd begun to remove her panty hose, a formidable undertaking. "Tía Carmen," she announced. "I think it's time I get a job."

Carmen kicked the hose to the corner of the room. "Haven't you got enough to do around here?"

"I want to earn some money I . . . I need to pay you rent."

Carmen thought about this for a moment and shrugged. "I don't need help covering the rent." She eased herself down on the bed and began to rub her sore feet. "Things have been going real good around here. Why don't you go to the community center? They can teach you how to read over there, like they taught me, and it won't take you all day, so you can still keep things up around here."

Jamilet hesitated. This was a tempting thought, but she was anxious to get on with her plans. She dreaded saying what she knew she had to say next, but she also knew she could go round and round like this with her aunt for days, and get nowhere. "I want to get a job so I can save money, and see a doctor."

Carmen froze in a rare moment of selfless concern. "Are you sick?"

"I'm not sick. It's . . . it's the mark, Tía. I want to see a doctor, and it's going to cost a lot of money to get rid of it."

It took a moment for the revelation to register on Carmen's face. There was no doubt now, as her memory clarified with every blink of her eyes, that she had indeed forgotten all about it. "Oh *that*," she finally said. "You still worried about *that*?"

Jamilet hardly knew how to respond. Her aunt referred to the mark as if it were a silly pimple or mole, easily hidden by a bit of makeup. Suddenly, Jamilet's anxiety was compounded by shame because the truth was that she wasn't worried—she was obsessed. The mark was like a thorn buried between her brows. "Yes," she mumbled, red faced. "I'm still worried."

Carmen stood up and grabbed her own belly with both hands, so that it resembled an enormous slab of meat. "Look at this," she demanded, giving it a shake with every syllable she uttered. "I carry this shit around with me everywhere I go, and you don't see me worried. And I still got myself a man," she concluded in a huff. She then proceeded to pull on a pair of sweatpants with a matching bright pink tube top that was two sizes too small.

Jamilet felt she might burst into tears. She'd trade her mark for a massive roll of belly like that any day of the week. In fact, she'd welcome it, and consider herself blessed. How she'd love to wake up at dawn every day and run through the streets, wearing a tank top to show off her smooth meaty shoulders to the world. She'd eat Jell-O, and broth for breakfast, lunch, and dinner. That would be great. She'd love to be enormous and immensely fat, like a circus act, if that meant being rid of the mark. But there would be no more discussion that night. In a matter of minutes, Carmen was relaxing with her feet up in front of the TV, and her first beer consumed. Jamilet knew better than to question her any further that evening.

⚜

A few days later, Carmen came home and tossed an envelope on the kitchen counter. "Go ahead," she said to Jamilet, who was busy dismembering a chicken for their dinner. "Open it."

Jamilet wiped her hands on a dish towel and opened the envelope, discovering a card with words and numbers on its front and back. She looked questioningly at her aunt.

"With that little card," Carmen said, quite pleased with herself, "you can get any job you want."

"I can?"

"You sure can, as long as you remember that your name is Monica, not Jamilet." She dropped her purse and proceeded to the refrigerator. "I paid good money for that. With your English, nobody will ever know it's a fake."

Jamilet was well aware of the false documents for sale in many parts of the city. With good-quality papers it was possible to find the better jobs that paid minimum wage, and sometimes more. Without them, most people had to settle for work in one of the many sweatshops downtown that were reputed to be raided by immigration officials on a regular basis. "What if I get caught?" she asked.

"Oh, I don't know. They'll probably throw you in jail for a while, feed you bread and water once a week, and then ship your ass back to the border. And that's if you're lucky." She turned to Jamilet, her face set hard. "So, keep the card safe, and don't show it around. Is that clear?"

Wearing a navy skirt that reached down below her knees, and a crisp white blouse, Jamilet felt secure that the mark wasn't visible. She then carefully placed her false identification card along with her birth certificate in a small cloth pouch, and pinned it to the inside of her bra to make sure it was safe. It would always be with her, over her heart. Her plans for finding employment were just as straightforward. The man at the supermarket had told her that with such a pretty face, and sweet smile, she'd be bound to get a good job at the department stores downtown that sold fancy clothes and shoes to the businesspeople, so that's where she was headed.

Carmen gave her the once-over when Jamilet emerged from the bathroom. "Hold on a second," she said and rushed to her room, returning moments later with a bright pink scarf fluttering from her fingers. She circled it around her niece's neck, tied it this way and that, and then stood back to appraise her work. "They'd be crazy not to hire you," she said.

Later that day, with one shoe dangling from each hand, Jamilet turned the corner to her aunt's house. Carmen's pink scarf hung limply around her neck as she walked with her head down, trying to avoid stepping on the dried chewing gum that was stuck to the sidewalk.

"What happened to you?"

Jamilet turned to see Eddie's brown eyes smiling down on her. This was perhaps the only moment since her arrival that she would have given anything not to see him. She swallowed hard. "I was out looking for a job," she answered in a small voice.

"No luck, huh?"

Jamilet shook her head and swallowed again, a giant lump, thick as a fist. She longed for the quiet sanctuary of her bath, where she could assess her wounds in private and find strength in her secret visions.

Eddie narrowed his eyes with practiced good humor. "You got papers?"

Jamilet nodded, even more ashamed. She might have found an excuse in not having any.

"Where'd you go looking?"

Jamilet told him and he rolled his eyes and whistled. "Are you crazy? They don't hire Mexicans in that place. You should try down by the garment district. You'd have better luck."

"But they don't pay as good."

He was still shaking his head, both amazed and amused by her lack of judgment. "Lemme see your papers," he said, extending his hand and rubbing his fingers together impatiently. Jamilet hesitated and glanced in the direction of the house. "C'mon, hand 'em over, I'm an expert," he said, ignoring her discomfort.

Jamilet dropped her shoes and reached into her shirt for the pouch. She produced the card and handed it over, praying to God that her aunt wouldn't catch her.

Eddie studied the card, front and back. "This is good. It

must've cost some bucks." He returned the card and his gaze shifted up toward the canopy of wires above them. "I think I know of a job for you. It pays decent, but it's not for everybody." His eyes dropped back down to Jamilet's face. "You ever heard of Braewood?"

"What is . . . ?" She attempted to pronounce it exactly as he had. "Braewood?"

"It's a nuthouse. You know, a place where they put the crazy people who talk to themselves and shit. It's not too far from here."

Jamilet listened to him talk about the place, noting that his easy demeanor had stiffened. She could have told him that she wasn't easily frightened, but she preferred listening to him go on about his cousin who'd just quit her job there, and how she came home every day with stories that made it difficult for her little brothers and sisters to sleep at night. He told her, while stuffing his hands into his pockets as though suddenly chilled, that his cousin thought the place was haunted, but then, she was also the type to freak out when the cat brought home a dead rat. He stopped abruptly, as though suddenly aware that he'd been talking for several uninterrupted minutes, something rarely experienced in the company of a girl. "So, you interested or what?"

Jamilet nodded. "How do I get there?"

He attempted to give her directions, but Jamilet didn't know the area well enough to understand them. "Okay, listen," he said in a hushed voice. "If you meet me down the street, by that tree"—he pointed to a large sycamore a few yards down from Carmen's house—"let's say . . . tonight at around nine, I'll walk you over. It's on my way home, but it's just between you and me, okay? I don't want Pearly to find out."

"Okay," Jamilet said, feeling the rush of something unfamiliar and wonderful. "I'll be waiting by the tree."

Standing underneath the branches so that the leaves brushed the top of her head, Jamilet felt like a creature well accustomed to the night, and an unsettling sensation born of hunger and anticipation filled her. She'd been thinking about Eddie while lying in her bed since they'd made plans to meet. Many stories came to her, leaving her almost breathless, although she lay very still on her bed. They were somewhat far-fetched, and in one version, she had to admit that she might have gone too far. Pearly had found them, their limbs desperately entwined like the thirsty roots beneath her feet, and she challenged Jamilet to fight for her man, but Eddie stepped in, concerned only with Jamilet's welfare. The drama grew more and more outlandish, with each turn serving only to confirm Eddie's remarkable love for Jamilet, and growing disgust for Pearly.

She tried to put these stories out of her mind and satisfy herself with the true knowledge that in a few moments, she'd be with him, but they conjured themselves up like a chorus of jealous ghosts, each fighting for their time to haunt her. Try as she might to resist them, she always gave in for fear that they wouldn't return when she needed them most.

Jamilet stepped out from her hiding place when Eddie approached, but he said nothing, motioning with a flick of his head that she should follow him. His stride was brisk, and for several blocks not a word passed between them. After they crossed the second streetlight, he relaxed a bit, and slowed his pace so that Jamilet could keep up without needing to break into a trot every now and then, but it was clear he wasn't interested in conversation. He grunted when Jamilet thanked him for showing her the way, and when she asked him how long his cousin had worked at Braewood, he answered, "Don't know."

They walked on in silence, as the fantasy inspired by what could be contained within her aunt's romance novels took over in her mind.

Eddie's watching her, looking for an opportunity to act on his manly desire. "It can be pretty scary here," he says. "If you're afraid, just stay close to me and I'll protect you."

"What's there to be afraid of?" she replies with a shrug, unaware of how alluring she is to him, how the curve of her hips is driving him wild.

He opens his eyes wide, pretending to be shocked. "You're not afraid of total nutcases? Don't you know that they'll skin you alive if you give them half a chance?" In spite of his desire to stay in control, Eddie takes her hand and attempts to embrace her, but Jamilet gently pushes him away, teasing and drawing him in with her forced bravado.

"Don't worry about me. I'm used to taking care of myself," she says with a sly little smile that effectively turns his knees to jelly.

Eddie has been staying close, strategizing his next move, when they arrive at a gate that appears to be chained and locked. But strong and capable as he is, he opens it wide enough for them to slip through. Jamilet can't help but notice his well-muscled forearms as she "accidentally" brushes them with her breasts. There's a tangle of trees rising on either side of the narrow path leading up to the hospital. It's dark, but Jamilet insists on taking the lead even though she's starting to feel afraid.

"Did you hear that?" Eddie whispers.

Jamilet stops to listen and stumbles back into his waiting arms. She's trembling and scared this time, and she doesn't push him away, but looks up into his face, her lips parted and moist. Eddie devours her with his eyes for a moment or two, then with passion burning in his heart, he slowly lowers his face to hers so that his mouth gently . . .

"What's wrong with you? Can't you hear me?" Eddie asked, clearly annoyed.

Jamilet turned to find him standing at least ten yards behind her on the path, and she shook her head, confused. "Is . . . is something wrong?"

"I don't like the sound of this." He headed out to the middle of the main road, Jamilet close behind. "There it is again," he said under his breath.

It started as a steady hum, reverberating as though underground, and then escaped into the cool night air, low and eerie, moaning like a ghost through the trees. It grew steadily all around them, swirling and surging between and through them, quickening the blood in their veins. They heard the call of a tortured soul crying out for release from the sheer agony of existence. And then it sweetened into the haunting song of a wandering heart, cool and then warm again, waning at the memory of life and love, hesitant in the face of another, remembering. It was no doubt a human voice, singing and wailing for whoever or whatever was brave enough to listen.

Jamilet stood still and closed her eyes, swaying to the sound of the singing as it grew louder. Then, without warning, Eddie grabbed her wrist and pulled her, stumbling behind him, as he ran at breakneck speed back toward the gate through which they'd entered moments earlier. He released her as they approached the gate, and pushed himself through the narrow opening first. He kept running down the street without looking back. But Jamilet felt no need for alarm. She calmly passed through the gate, and when she finally caught up to him at the corner, he was still panting, doubled over, with one hand on the lamppost to steady himself. When he glanced up at Jamilet, his eyes retained a glint of the wild fear that had possessed him, while Jamilet covered her mouth to stifle a giggle.

"I'm glad you think I'm so funny," Eddie said, straightening up.

"I'm sorry, it's just that . . ." She shrugged contritely. "I once saw a man run from an angry bull that had the biggest horns you ever saw, and he still didn't run as fast as you."

"Okay, you made your point." He wiped his sweaty hands on his pants legs and pointed a thumb behind him. "That's the way home," he said, and then he pointed back the way they'd come. "And now you know where Braewood is." He turned to leave.

"Are you mad?" Jamilet asked.

He answered without turning around, raising one hand and then letting it drop to his side in a beleaguered fashion. "Nope."

"Yes, you are. I can tell."

Eddie turned around. The light from the streetlamp over his head made him look like a lone actor on a stage. "I'm just freaked out, I guess."

"Freaked out?" Jamilet wasn't so familiar with this expression.

"You walk straight through the gate like you own the place, and when I tell you to slow down, you don't even answer me, you just keep going like some kind of zombie." He shook his head, still dazed. "It was pretty weird."

Jamilet was prepared to offer excuses, but he stopped her with a more decisive hand this time. "Save it. I . . . I hope you get the job."

Jamilet watched Eddie walk out from under the streetlight and slip into the darkness down the street. Moments later, her fantasy resumed.

"Don't you think the singing was beautiful, Eddie?"

He takes her face in his hands, and his fingers softly stroke her cheek. "Yeah, it was, but not as beautiful as you."

"You're crazy, Eddie."

"I know I am," he says, right before he kisses her for the first time. "I'm crazy about you."

7

THE WORDS CAME OUT however they could: "I'm applying for the housekeeping job." Jamilet was certain that her accent was worse than ever, but the pale woman behind the desk understood her perfectly, and responded without looking up from her work.

"You need to speak with Nurse B." The woman glanced up at Jamilet's startled face. "Who shall I say is applying?"

Jamilet took a deep breath, and her lungs quivered when she exhaled, making her voice sound like an out-of-tune violin. "My name is Monica Juarez."

The woman took the application Jamilet had completed the night before, and returned within less than a minute. She directed Jamilet to follow her through a narrow passageway behind the front office. They had proceeded down a labyrinth of halls painted chalky green before the woman opened one of several office doors and indicated that Jamilet should enter on her own.

Nurse B. was sitting behind her desk. She was an older woman with a fleshy face, graying yellow hair, and eyes so deep set that it was difficult to be certain of their color. In her white uniform, she resembled an overstuffed pillow. With a flick of her hand she directed Jamilet to sit in the chair across from her, and Jamilet promptly dropped into it, grateful that her trembling knees might be less apparent from a seated position. She folded her hands on her lap and waited for her application to be reviewed. Jamilet had asked Carmen to fill it out for her the night before and to make sure there were no mistakes.

Nurse B. studied Jamilet when she'd finished, her brow twitching sporadically. Then, quick as a flash, she produced a piece of paper and a pen and whisked it across the desk toward Jamilet. "Write down your name, your address, and . . . the reason you want to work at Braewood Asylum," she said.

Slowly Jamilet took up the pen. As she started to trace aimless patterns on the page, her face smoldered with shame. For an instant she considered confessing the truth about her illiteracy, but suspected that this was not a woman who would soften when encountering vulnerable disclosures or hard-luck stories, no matter how heartwrenching they might be. The brooding lines engraved on her face were clue enough.

Jamilet's pencil dragged across the page. With her nose only inches from the paper, she wished that she could somehow fold herself into it and disappear. From the corner of her eye, she saw Nurse B.'s thick fingers tapping on the desk, almost dancing with joy, like a troupe of jolly little men rejoicing at the prospect of witnessing this impending humiliation.

It was then that a firm and furious knock was heard at the door, and a red-faced young woman burst into the room, followed by the same pale receptionist who'd shown Jamilet to the office. She was muttering her objections with the effectiveness of one trying to speak underwater.

The young woman didn't notice Jamilet sitting in the chair, and when she spoke, her voice was shrill, and louder than necessary. "It's been more than a month and you said it would only be two weeks."

Nurse B. clenched her jaw. "I'm in the middle of an interview, as you can see."

But the woman seemed incapable of understanding, and continued to rant about the time that had passed, the agreement they'd made, and other complaints she was no longer able to contain. Jamilet wondered if she might be an escaped patient, but she didn't look like a mental patient, and her anger, although extreme, didn't sound like the ravings of a lunatic, but more like the frustrations of an overworked employee.

"I'm not going back up there, and if you try and make me, I'll call the union." She stood back from the desk, a bit wild-eyed, as if she was looking for something she might throw. "I think I'll call them anyway. There's gotta be a law against sticking someone up there for hours on end like that."

Nurse B. took two deep breaths, her eyelids fluttering slightly with each one. As she listened to the woman, a crimson glow gathered about her ears. "You may call the union, the president, or the pope if you wish, but if you're interested in discussing the matter with me, you'll have to wait until I'm finished. As you can see, I'm in the middle of an interview," she repeated, pointing to Jamilet, who sat slumped in her chair, the pencil still propped in her fingers.

When the woman took notice of Jamilet, she calmed down considerably. "Oh," she said, stepping back from the desk. "I didn't realize . . ."

Nurse B. addressed the receptionist, who was still in the doorway, wringing her hands. "Ms. Clark, please see Veronica to the waiting room. I'll let you know when I'm ready to see her." The two women left as abruptly as they'd entered, and the silence that followed was punctuated only by the large woman's breathing, deep and low in her throat.

Jamilet watched as Nurse B.'s eyes roved across the ceiling, and her lips twitched into a smile. "Why continue this ridiculous charade, Monica?" She leaned over her desk so that her ample bosom spread across it. "Why not admit the truth?"

The pencil slipped from Jamilet's fingers as she considered which of the shameful truths she should admit to first: the fact that she was an illegal alien presenting false documents for employment, or that, with the exception of her true and false names, she was unable to read or write a single word. Until that moment, she hadn't realized how difficult it was to lie. She'd thought it would be just like prompting her imagination to take over and guide her, as she did when she created her stories. But lying was nothing like that. It didn't make her feel free, like her stories made her feel, but constricted and locked up about the heart and throat, making it difficult to speak and breathe.

Nurse B. chewed slowly on her tongue as she considered the application more carefully. "My guess is that you've never had a job before in your life," she declared flatly.

"I'm a good cleaner and a hard worker," Jamilet said. "Even when I don't get paid for it."

Nurse B.'s great head nodded, her fingers still tapping on the surface of her desk. Jamilet felt a twinge of encouragement upon seeing this, and piped up again. "And I'm not afraid of ghosts," she added confidently. "I'm not afraid of anything."

Upon hearing this, the collection of creases radiating out from Nurse B.'s eyes and mouth deepened into a smile. "That's very nice, but I'm afraid the janitorial position was filled yesterday afternoon. Of course, I do have another job that's just become available. It's yours if you want it."

The next morning Jamilet arrived twenty minutes early, and waited in the lobby as she listened to the sounds of the asylum beginning to stir. Although many corridors separated her from the patients' area of the hospital, the acoustics created by tiled floors and metal doors made it possible to hear every loud bang and echo from beyond. Voices called out their terse commands, as shrill as trumpet blasts. They were met with lingering groans that blended and twisted like smoke curling around and through the walls and doors that held them in. Laughter soon followed, disquieting laughter, devoid of cheerfulness. A chill stole up Jamilet's spine, and she glanced up at the clock on the green wall. Ten more minutes to go.

The sounds beyond the door grew into a cacophony of noises, bells buzzing, screams and complaints from patients, orders barked by the nursing staff, and finally, the sound of showers and faucets flowing from a hundred different sources at once. It was at this moment that Nurse B. appeared. She was in a hurry, and her thick-soled shoes pressing on the tiled floors produced a muffled smack and squeak with every step she took. This, combined with the zipping sound of her stockinged thighs rubbing together, made her breathy words barely understandable. It didn't help that Jamilet's own hard-soled shoes created a deafening sound, so much so that Nurse B. suddenly halted her march to inspect Jamilet's shoes. She frowned, but said nothing.

Nurse B. proceeded through endless tunnels of green until she and Jamilet arrived at a metal door larger than the others. Next to it was a clock at chest level and a series of bracketed frames into which were inserted numerous cards. Nurse B. showed Jamilet where her time card would be kept, and how to punch it into the opening at the top of the clock upon her arrival and departure every day. "I'm too short staffed to provide you with a full day of training," she said as she grabbed the keys that hung on a peg nearby. "I'm putting you straight to work." Having found the proper key, she inserted it into the lock, then braced her foot against the door as if expecting a gale-force storm on the other side. "Follow me and stay close," she commanded. Jamilet had no intention of doing otherwise. She nodded and held her trembling hands together to steady them. It wouldn't do to show her fear, especially after she'd bragged about her courage the day before.

When they entered, Jamilet was assaulted by the pungent smell of cleaning solution masking the unmistakable odor of human urine. Green, gleaming corridors radiated in all directions, but there were no patients visible anywhere. She followed Nurse B. to the nearest nurse's station, and stood nearby as she inspected one of several charts there. At that moment a small group of male patients still in pajamas and hospital robes peeked out from inside one of the rooms, and waited until Nurse B. was fully engrossed in her reading. They then approached Jamilet, who'd been watching them as well. She was trying to guess their ages, but it was difficult, for although some were wrinkled and gray, they appeared motivated by a childlike enthusiasm rarely seen in adults.

They stood before her, their eyes wide with wonder, as the spokesman for the group, a small man with a head as smooth and shiny as a lightbulb, asked the question Jamilet would hear at least a hundred times that first day, and every day thereafter. "Do you have a cigarette?" he whispered, holding out his tar-stained fingers as though confident that his request would be instantly fulfilled, but it was Nurse B. who responded. "You know the rules, Charlie," she said, admonishing him with a thick hand. "You'll receive your cigarettes at the canteen after you've showered and changed, and from the look of you, it would seem that soap and water is long overdue."

Upon hearing this, he hung his head and the group disbanded, their unity disrupted by such sudden and absolute failure. Nurse B. said, "They think every new face belongs to a fool, and more often than not, they're correct."

Nurse B. and Jamilet began their long march through the wards, and Jamilet became increasingly aware of the hollow stares and shadowy figures lurking behind bed curtains, slumped in chairs, and peeking out of half-closed shower doors. Those who didn't stare seemed lost, as though waking from a dream, too confused to direct their energy toward anyone or anything outside themselves. Jamilet couldn't help but stare back and was suddenly afraid that she too might become lost if she stared too long, for some of the patients, with eyes deep and wide as lagoons, looked as though they could possess her. There was an inexplicable power in their countenance, as if the only thing that held them up on their feet or upright in their chairs was the strength that came from too much suffering and hopeless longing.

When Nurse B. approached, some of the patients ducked behind curtains and doors, trying not to be noticed, but there was little chance of that. She continued her march, looking neither left nor right, but straight ahead, her jowls jerking along with the rhythm of her step.

By the time the elevator had deposited them on the fourth floor, Jamilet felt her nervousness somewhat lessened. The brisk walk had produced a soothing warmth that radiated through her arms and into her hands. This was true despite her observation that with every floor they'd traveled up, the patients seemed to become more mentally disturbed, the lost and wandering look in their eyes more intense, their rambling conversations with unseen companions more animated.

Nurse B. had barely uttered one word. For a moment Jamilet wondered if she'd forgotten that there was a new employee following her like a loyal puppy dog, walking when she walked, and stopping when she stopped. Then, quite suddenly, as they stepped out of the elevator, Nurse B. turned around to face her. "I think I should inform you," she said as her pinlike eyes quivered in their sockets, "that you'll be looking after only one patient. He is unlike the others you've seen."

Jamilet felt the knot that had loosened in her stomach begin to tighten once again. She said nothing as she followed Nurse B. to another door and, rather than take the elevator, they started to climb up a narrow staircase. Nurse B. sputtered for breath as she awkwardly maneuvered her feet on the narrow steps. Jamilet didn't follow so closely this time, for fear that her hefty superior might squash her on the way down, should she stumble. But they reached the fifth floor without incident, although Nurse B. was flushed and gasping for air.

If the wards below were stark, then the fifth floor was absolutely barren. The lime green paint freshly applied throughout the rest of the hospital was absent here. Bare lightbulbs protruded from the walls, but only one was still working. It emitted a thin yellow light that cast a strange pallor over the place.

Once Nurse B. was feeling better, she led Jamilet down the corridor to the office at the far end. This room was a bit more cheerful, due to the large window overlooking the grounds below.

The only furniture was a desk, completely cleared except for a black phone placed in the center, and an oversize chair. Nurse B. promptly sat down and the chair groaned as it accommodated her bulk. "This," she said, leaning back, "is where you'll be spending the majority of your time. The charge nurse on the fourth floor has orders to call up and check on you, and you can call her if you have questions or if there should be a problem." Nurse B. leaned forward and pressed her hands together so hard her fingers turned pink. "Now let's talk about your patient. He is disturbed, but quite clever. I recommend that you avoid all unnecessary conversation with him. Experience has taught us that he can become quite disagreeable if given the opportunity, and that's when you'll want to leave, like all the others have." Nurse B. stood up and smoothed her uniform, and pulled at her girdle. "He has refused to leave his room, not because he's not allowed to do so, but because every time he's attempted to leave, his condition worsens. Unfortunately he's also refused treatment by a psychiatrist, but he won't be able to refuse for long," she said with a gleam in her eye. "If he doesn't demonstrate some measure of progress in a few months, he'll be transferred to a more secure facility for his own good, whether he wants to go or not. But that isn't anything you need to worry about now. In fact, I think you'll find that this could be the easiest job you ever had." She thought about this for a moment and addressed Jamilet with enough enthusiasm as to make her appear almost cheerful. "If you make it past one month, I'll give you a raise. How do you like that?"

"I like it very much," Jamilet answered. "I have only one question."

Nurse B. raised her eyebrows in response.

"What are my duties?"

Nurse B. was momentarily taken aback. "Your duties are simply to do as he asks," she said, fluttering her hands, and clearly annoyed with having to explain it yet again. "Bring him his meals and his mail, tidy up his room, and make sure he has everything he needs."

"You mean, like a maid?"

Nurse B. squared her shoulders. "Yes, it's not at all misleading to think of it that way. Follow me," she said, and left the office to stand before the only other door in the corridor. A small, thick window had been cut into the upper third, far too high for a person of ordinary height to see through. There was a sign with small lettering directly underneath. Nurse B. spoke low in her throat, as if she were afraid of waking the dead. "This is your patient's room," she said, her eyes widening. "It's best that you enter alone."

"By myself?" Jamilet could hardly believe that her employer wouldn't be marching into this patient's room as she had throughout the entire hospital. But in just a few seconds, Nurse B. had changed. The charge of authority that had colored her cheeks moments earlier had disappeared, leaving her pale and perspiring. Lips that were previously tight, and perched on the verge of a command, had loosened into a flabby scowl. She pressed her back against the door she would not enter, as though gathering the strength she'd need to return to the comfort of her asylum.

"I've learned," she said, regaining some degree of composure, "that it's best when only one person attends to him at a time. Too many people upset him."

Jamilet thought about the corridors through which she'd just passed, the inconsolable eyes peeking out from behind curtains and the laughter laced with a pain well past anyone's idea of upset. She felt a quivering fear in the pit of her stomach, and thought for the first time that she'd made a terrible mistake. Not just in accepting the job, but in leaving Mexico and everything she knew.

Nurse B. instructed Jamilet to wait until half past the hour, at which point she was to go to the cafeteria to pick up her patient's meal. After delivering it, she was to promptly leave the room. She would do this three times a day, and every day thereafter, all the while avoiding as much unnecessary conversation as possible. This had proved to be the undoing of all who had come before her.

Nurse B. was all too eager to leave once she'd imparted the last of her scant instructions, stating that Jamilet could review them on her own, as they were written on the door. When she was alone, Jamilet stared blankly at the sign on the door, realizing that she didn't even know her patient's name.

The breakfast tray was elegantly set, with a large domed plate and a steaming pot of coffee. Someone had also taken care to tuck in the day's correspondence. Jamilet considered this strange, noting that the other patients in the cafeteria received their meals on portioned plates, with cartons of milk or orange juice. Coffee was to be purchased in the canteen along with the cigarettes.

It was easy to spot Charlie's bald head, in the far corner of the room. He was eating alone, but in a matter of seconds the other patients had taken his lime Jell-O, coffeecake, and orange juice. He appeared quite accustomed to the situation and began eating his lonely eggs without complaint. Jamilet took an extra serving of coffeecake from the counter, and placed it before him saying, "Eat quickly. I'll wait here until you're done." Charlie appeared more confused than grateful, but wasted little time in gobbling down his coffeecake, knowing that he was safe so long as a staff person was present.

She left the cafeteria after he finished, took the elevator up, and ascended the narrow staircase with the breakfast tray in hand. She studied the sign on the door, blinking slowly. The tray was getting heavier, and the words on the sign once again failed to deliver themselves, so she could only hope that Nurse B. had been thorough.

With her heart pounding wildly, she entered the darkened room. Meager sunlight slanted in through a half-open window. She placed the tray on the first surface she saw, a desk near the window, strewn with papers. She hadn't yet looked at the patient, but sensed him watching her from the other side of the room.

Once relieved of the tray, every muscle in her body urged her to bolt out of the room as quickly as she could, but that would appear weak and cowardly. So she forced herself to go to the window instead, and opened it a bit farther, hoping that fresh air would neutralize her fear. The rusty hinges moaned and complained at being moved back, and a gust of sweet air rushed in.

She turned, her heart now pumping at a ferocious rate. She would not be able to maintain this charade of calm for much longer. Nevertheless, she straightened her shoulders and lifted her chin, as she'd learned to do back home when children and adults assaulted her with their jeering remarks.

She was almost to the door when a silken voice addressed her with words tempered by a Spanish accent refined enough to lend them the eloquence of a count. "Young lady, didn't you read the sign on the door instructing you to knock before entering?"

Jamilet turned to the sound of the voice, and beheld an imposing elderly man who was in bed and leaning on one elbow. He had a full head of snow white hair that curled about his head like smoke. His black eyes were devoid of emotion, absorbing her with unblinking intensity.

"No, sir," she muttered.

He watched her for a moment longer and then sat up straighter to get a better look. "What were your instructions?" he asked.

Jamilet wasn't sure whether or not to answer. Could this be considered unnecessary conversation? She decided that not answering might upset him, and that too was to be avoided. "I . . . I was given the same instructions as the others," she said.

"Yes of course, you're to bring my meals three times a day, call downstairs if a problem arises, and, this is most important, you're not to engage me in any unnecessary conversation. And if you are able to keep your position for a month, you'll have the benefit of a raise." His eyebrows, black as his eyes, rose to the top of his forehead. "Correct?"

Jamilet nodded and felt a cold finger tracing down her spine. She couldn't look away from him.

"What is your name?" he asked.

"Monica," she answered, surprised she'd kept enough of her wits about her to use her assumed name.

"Well then, Monica, please allow me to complete your instructions." For the first time since she'd entered, he shifted his gaze away from her face and she was able to breathe a bit easier. "You are to knock before entering, and you are not to enter unless I give you permission. You are to leave the windows, the furniture, and everything else you see in my room exactly as you find it and you are never," he said, both raising and deepening his voice to a seething pitch, "to place anything upon my desk. Is that quite clear?"

"Yes, sir."

"I expect my room to be cleaned thoroughly on a daily basis, including the bathroom and under the bed." Jamilet looked around the room as he spoke. It was elegantly furnished with a four-poster bed and rich-looking carpets and pillows similar to the kind she'd seen at the Miller house. There was also an elaborately carved desk upon which his breakfast tray steamed. The bathroom was at the far end of the room, and Jamilet could see the corner of the tub from where she stood.

The patient continued to list his expectations in excruciating detail. His outgoing mail was to be placed upon Miss Clark's desk no later than ten every morning. His breakfast eggs were to be cooked so that the yolks ran, and the whites stayed firm. His coffee was to be hot enough to scald the feathers off a chicken, and if he found even one hair in his bathroom, she would be fired on the spot, and denied her wages for that day.

As the list of duties grew, the patient's voice softened and he relaxed into his pillow, quite pleased with his ability to demand and command. He concluded the litany by adding, ". . . and don't tell me you weren't hired to be a maid, or I guarantee that you won't last a week."

Jamilet looked about the room briefly. "Where would you like your tray, sir?"

He patted his lap with both hands. "I prefer to take my morning meal in bed."

Without hesitation, Jamilet took the tray to her patient, lowering her eyes when at arm's length from him as she gently placed it on his lap. With a polite nod, she turned to leave, but he spoke once again. "And I expect you to address me by my proper name."

"Yes, sir," she said.

His massive white head was cocked to one side and his eyes sparkled. "Yes, what . . . ?"

"I'm afraid I don't know your name, sir."

"How can that be? Didn't your employer inform you?"

"No, sir, she didn't."

"Well, it's written on the door, for God's sake. Didn't you read the . . ." But he stopped, and muttered to himself as he buttered his toast, "This time she's managed to hire not only a fool, but an illiterate fool."

Overcome with shame, Jamilet was unable to deny this or defend herself as he swiped the domed lid off his breakfast and tossed it to the floor so that it landed just inches from her feet.

While poking at the yoke of his eggs with a fork, he said, "My name is Señor Peregrino. Repeat it so that I'm sure you're able to pronounce it properly."

"Señor Peregrino," Jamilet said in a quiet voice.

"Again," he repeated, holding up his fork like a conductor.

"Señor Peregrino," she said a bit more loudly.

He squinted at his eggs, obviously not pleased. "Your pronunciation is good, but your accent quite vulgar. Where are you from?"

"Mexico."

He glared at her as though momentarily stunned by the depth of her stupidity. "Obviously, but where in Mexico?"

"Guadalajara," Jamilet answered, preferring to avoid mentioning her village.

His eyes held her, as they had earlier. "You're lying. You're from a place with dirt roads where people wash in the stream and take care of their bodily functions in much the same manner as dogs." He applied blueberry jam to his toast and continued, "Your mother probably birthed you in the fields and you were as likely to have learned your first words from the hogs as you were to have learned them from her. She's still there, waiting for you to send money because the hogs were sold and there's been a drought . . ."

"My mother is dead."

He prepared his coffee next, adding a teaspoon of sugar and a touch of cream. "Good for her, it's probably the smartest thing she ever did." He continued with his litany of insults, and as before, the more hateful his words became, the more serene his demeanor. He might have been talking about the sweet succulence of the fruit on his plate, or the likelihood of showers in the evening. It was also clear that his tirade would continue so long as she stood before him and listened. She had to find a way to get out, even if it meant interrupting, and possibly upsetting him in the process.

"Excuse me, Señor Peregrino, may I be excused, please?" Jamilet asked. "I need to use the . . . the bathroom."

"I'm not finished," he said, scowling. "Nevertheless, you asked for permission to leave without specific instructions to do so." He waved her toward the door with his fork. "You may go."

Jamilet left the room calmly, and waited until the patient's door had closed completely before running down the corridor to the adjacent office. Once there, she flung open the window and leaned out as far she could, breathing deeply and allowing the fresh air to fill her lungs and quell the nausea brewing in her gut. Feeling somewhat better, she glanced back at the clock on the wall. She'd been in the patient's room for less than fifteen minutes, and couldn't imagine how she'd survive the rest of the day. A month was out of the question.

8

⁓

"J UST QUIT," Carmen said. "You shouldn't be working in a hellhole like that anyway."

"But it pays well, and they didn't have any problem with the papers."

"Nobody's gonna have a problem with those papers," Carmen said while stuffing a meatball sandwich into her mouth. "You can take them anywhere. You'll see." She took the remainder of her sandwich with her to the couch and propped up her feet. She was eating rapidly, dispensing with a napkin and cleaning up the sauce that escaped from the corners of her mouth with the bread. Louis would be over soon and she didn't like to overeat in front of him. She'd enjoy a regular meal with him later, and her appetite would appear a bit more ladylike. "I'll bet the old man's a child molester. That's why they got him locked up," she concluded as she swallowed the last of her sandwich.

Jamilet shrugged. "All I know is that he has so much hate in his eyes. It scares me just to look at him."

Upon hearing this, Carmen tossed the wrapper on the coffee table. "Is it something like this?" she asked, leaning forward and giving Jamilet a frighteningly cold stare that seemed to stiffen her body from head to toe. This was the kind of look that kept stray dogs out of her yard, and Jehovah's Witnesses from knocking on her door a second time.

Jamilet couldn't help but feel its effects, and shudder a little bit. "That's pretty good, Tía, but I think Señor Peregrino's look is even worse than that."

Carmen dropped her face. "What the hell kinda name is Peregrino?"

"I don't know."

"You say he's a Hispanic guy?"

Jamilet nodded. "He acts like he's the king of Spain or something."

"I'll tell you what he's the king of," Carmen declared. "He's the king of perverts. Now bring me a beer. I got cheese breath."

Jamilet brought Carmen her beer, and a napkin besides. "What does the word 'peregrino' mean, Tía?"

She popped the lid and took a swig as she thought about it. "It means pilgrim, I think." She took another swig. "Yep, I'm sure that's what it means. His name is Mr. Pilgrim, if you can believe that."

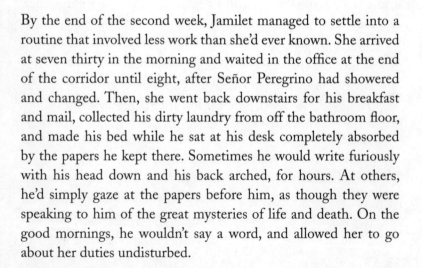

By the end of the second week, Jamilet managed to settle into a routine that involved less work than she'd ever known. She arrived at seven thirty in the morning and waited in the office at the end of the corridor until eight, after Señor Peregrino had showered and changed. Then, she went back downstairs for his breakfast and mail, collected his dirty laundry from off the bathroom floor, and made his bed while he sat at his desk completely absorbed by the papers he kept there. Sometimes he would write furiously with his head down and his back arched, for hours. At others, he'd simply gaze at the papers before him, as though they were speaking to him of the great mysteries of life and death. On the good mornings, he wouldn't say a word, and allowed her to go about her duties undisturbed.

The mornings Jamilet dreaded most were those in which he was not reading or writing, but was staring off into space as if lost in a horrible dream. At these times, he looked for every opportunity to distract himself from this inner unpleasantness however he could. He'd study Jamilet while chewing on his pen, and for his own amusement was quite adept at identifying her weaknesses. "I notice that you hunch your shoulders, rather like a troll. What is it you're so ashamed of, Monica?"

"I'm not ashamed of anything, Señor," Jamilet said.

"Oh, but you most certainly are ashamed of something."

Jamilet continued straightening his bed just as he'd instructed her to, without tucking the sheet in under the mattress, as it caused him unnecessary trouble when getting back into bed. She dared not look at him when he watched her like this for fear that she'd be lost in the black oblivion of his gaze. It was best to avert her eyes, and when she had no choice but to look at him, she did so with muted attention.

"I believe it isn't just your inability to read and write," he mused. "It's something else . . . something much uglier. It might have something to do with your family. I won't denigrate the memory of your dead mother, but you've said nothing of your father. I would imagine that he's probably a drunken fool, a misshapen soul who's forgotten he's a man and that he has a daughter."

Jamilet fluffed the pillow and dropped it into place. She was getting better at deflecting him, and could easily have found a way not to answer, but something prompted her to do otherwise. "I never knew my father, Señor. But I heard many silly stories about the way he died, and I know people make up stories when they don't want to admit the truth. So . . . he probably was even worse than you say."

This revelation, as honest and direct as it was, prompted Señor Peregrino to be silent. But she sensed him still watching her as she collected his dirty laundry from the floor, then left the room. A good while later she returned with his laundered shirts, and arranged them in the closet as he'd instructed her to do the first week, like colors together, short and long sleeves separated. His eyes followed her as she went to his bathroom with fresh towels. She took her time hanging them on the racks, one by the sink and two by the bath.

When she returned he had not moved. "You think yourself to be very clever, don't you?" he said.

"How could someone who doesn't read or write be clever?"

Señor Peregrino's lips flickered with a smile in spite of his desire to remain severe. "I'm curious," he said. "Don't you wonder why I'm up here, why it is that I don't have a file like every other patient in this hospital? Not that you could read it if I did, but I would think that you would have asked a few questions by now."

"I don't know why you're here, Señor." Jamilet shifted her weight onto her other leg. She wanted anything but to be engaged in a guessing game with him, one that he could twist and turn about her throat until he strangled her with his vile humor. But she knew that she must indulge him, or suffer his disagreeable moods later. "People are here because they're crazy. So, I guess you must be crazy too."

Señor Peregrino clapped his great hands together, and then bowed his head with exaggerated humility. "You certainly pushed your mind beyond its limits to arrive at that conclusion. Bravo!"

Jamilet allowed herself a rare moment to look fully into his eyes. "But you don't seem like the others downstairs." She shook him out of her eyes, and muttered, "I don't know . . ." Señor Peregrino's own eyes widened and in the corners there appeared a momentary softness, a veil of tears remembered and withheld. "Those poor souls you see writhing around in their own excrement below are the lucky ones. Nevertheless," he said, "I'll make it worth your while if you're able to find out something about me—why I'm here."

"I don't understand, Señor."

His face hardened. "Open your mouth for once and ask questions."

Jamilet lifted her chin and tightened her arms around the laundry. "That's not my job, Señor. Why should I do this?"

"Because . . . because if you manage to make any accurate discoveries before the end of the week, I promise I will not speak a word to you until you've completed your month's tenure. Then you'll most certainly have earned your raise, and as paltry as it must be, I'm sure you'd be delighted by the extra pennies in your wallet."

"The end of the week is tomorrow, Señor . . ."

"Then you haven't much time, have you?"

"And I'm assigned up here. I'm not supposed to leave."

"That does make things more difficult, but a clever girl like you would be resourceful."

Jamilet hated being manipulated in this way, but the possibility of making it to the end of the month without having to endure his constant barrage of insults was too tempting to pass up. Perhaps when the month was over, after she'd received her raise and proved her worth as an employee, she could request a transfer to another department. And even if she had to continue attending to Señor Peregrino, at least she'd be able to save the money she needed more quickly.

Jamilet decided to begin her inquiries with the kitchen worker who prepared Señor Peregrino's meals. He was a young blond-haired man with a red, ruddy face that made his eyes stand out like bright blue beads. "They don't tell us anything down here," he said, wiping his chapped hands on his apron. "All I know is, he gets whatever he wants. The only other time that happened was a while back when this rich lady came in. But she died after a couple of weeks. That old man's been here . . ." He looked up to the ceiling as he made his mental calculations. "It's been about three years."

She next approached the charge nurse on the fourth floor, a perpetually flustered woman with thick glasses that were constantly slipping down her nose as she scribbled in one of a pile of charts on her desk. She squinted at Jamilet as if seeing her for the first time. She had in fact spoken to her on two previous occasions, and each time appeared just as bewildered as she did at this moment. "You want to know about Señor who?" she asked, shoving her glasses up her nose.

Jamilet bit her lip. "Señor Peregrino . . ."

"Who's Señor Pere . . . whatever you said," she stated.

"The patient . . . on the fifth floor."

"That's not his name, for goodness sake," the charge nurse said, and then she reached for the clipboard underneath her desk, and began running her finger down the names on the list. She jabbed at the spot with her finger when she found it, and showed it to Jamilet for good measure. "See here? His name is Antonio Calderon."

Jamilet studied the place where she pointed, feigning the thoughtful gaze appropriate to reading. "Yes, of course, but he *thinks* his name is Señor Peregrino."

The charge nurse seized this opportunity to instruct and criticize with relish. "You should never encourage patients in their delusions." She pointed to a thin man scuffling by in his robe and slippers as he muttered unintelligibly to himself. "On some days, that patient you see there believes he's Gandhi. Do you think I go around saying, 'Come and get your medication, Gandhi' or 'Have you showered today, Gandhi?' She stared at Jamilet with her unblinking fish eyes. "Of course I don't. That would only confuse him all the more." She slapped her chart down, causing a minor avalanche on her desk.

Jamilet was heading back up the stairs to her post when a low, muffled voice prompted her to turn and peer into the darkened corner behind her. "You want to know about the old man on the fifth floor?" it asked.

Jamilet turned around with a start and found herself looking into the gray face of Richard the janitor, who was as thin and bedraggled as the mop that was his constant companion. She'd seen him around, slinking through the corridors, and leaving his watery trail where ever he went, although he never went up to the fifth floor. She alone was expected to perform any and all cleaning services that pertained to her patient.

"You know my patient?" Jamilet asked.

He lifted his ashen hand and circled it haphazardly before it flopped back down to his side. "I know 'em all." He glanced down the hall and lowered his voice, so that Jamilet had to lean toward him to hear. "I know 'em better than the nurses and the docs," he said, smiling secretively. "You know Charlie, the one you're always sneaking food to?"

Jamilet was shocked that he'd seen her do this. "Only once in a while," she muttered.

"Nope," he said. "I've been watching you, and I seen that you give him stuff every day. It was chocolate pudding yesterday, and today you gave him two extra rolls. I saw you pull 'em right out of your pocket. Anyway," he continued, once he believed Jamilet to be sufficiently impressed with his observational skills, "the reason Charlie's so bald is because every morning, and every night, he spends hours in front of the mirror pulling out his own hair. He keeps the nails on his right hand long so he can use 'em like tweezers. And sometimes he wears a towel like a diaper, and walks around sucking his thumb. It's a sight to see," he said, chuckling.

"But why is *my* patient here?" Jamilet asked, "The one on the fifth floor."

The janitor pursed his lips for a moment, as if savoring a delicious candy. "I heard the doctors say that he killed his wife. Just went berserk one day and chopped her up into a thousand pieces." Reacting to Jamilet's incredulous expression, he raised both hands, almost dropping his mop in the process. "I swear to God. They found him curled up like a baby in his mother's womb after he did it. Wouldn't leave his house, and didn't talk for months. You know he's never left his room since he came here?" He examined Jamilet with a certain concern. "You should be careful with him, young and pretty as you are. He has a taste for young blood too, I hear. Why do you think nobody ever lasts up there with him?"

❇

With the lunch tray balanced expertly on her forearm, Jamilet softly knocked on the door and waited until she heard his permission to enter. He was at his desk, as he almost always was, reading through the same papers over and over, as if he'd never seen them before. He did not acknowledge her as she set his lunch tray down, and she walked lightly to the door, hoping that he'd forgotten the challenge he'd posed to her earlier.

"Do you have anything to say for yourself?" he asked, not bothering to look up.

Jamilet stood to attention, her mind a blur.

"Should I take your silence to mean that you've failed at your task?"

Jamilet blurted out the first thing she could think of. "Your name is not Señor Peregrino."

He turned around in his chair, obviously intrigued. "Really?"

Jamilet tried not to look at him as she spoke. "It's Antonio Calderon." She glanced at him briefly. "Señor Calderon," she corrected.

He crossed his arms. "What else?"

Jamilet dropped her eyes to the floor, and became aware of a quivering sensation about her knees that was spreading very quickly.

"Look at me," he commanded, and her eyes shot up to his. "What else did you learn?"

"You've been here for three years, you haven't left your room, you're rich. And that . . . that . . ." Her tongue felt like jelly. "You killed your wife, and cut her up into a thousand pieces."

His eyes narrowed. "Who told you that?"

Jamilet hesitated to answer. "The janitor. He says he knows everything that goes on around here."

He looked away for a moment, a worried scowl cutting across his face. "You're quite young, and perhaps too young to understand the ways of . . ." He scratched his chin as he searched for the proper words. ". . . certain men."

Jamilet's back stiffened as she stepped toward the door. She'd never felt personally threatened by Señor Peregrino. He'd never so much as glanced at her in a suggestive way, but Richard had warned her, and Señor Peregrino hadn't denied what the janitor revealed about him. Perhaps he was correct about the old man on the fifth floor and his lecherous ways.

Jamilet's nervousness sharpened her tongue. "I may be young, but I'm not a fool, Señor."

He was not moved. "But of course you are, my dear. You are a fool in the same way all young and pretty girls are fools. Even more so in that you don't have your vanity to protect you."

"I don't understand what you're saying, Señor."

He sighed and turned to his papers. "I don't know why I waste my breath with you. Nevertheless, you've earned your reprieve. Aside from any essential communication, I won't direct a word to you for the remainder of the month."

It was late in the afternoon when Jamilet left the office to collect the lunch tray. Señor Peregrino was easiest to manage at this time of day, as he usually napped after his afternoon meal. Now she couldn't help but wonder and worry if he'd truly been sleeping. Perhaps he was pretending, only to catch her unaware at the moment he decided to strike.

She entered the hallway, and was at the door of his room when she heard someone coming up the stairs. Moments later, Richard appeared in the corridor, wearing a grim smile and carrying the ever present mop.

"Came to change the bulbs," he said, propping the mop against the wall. "Maybe a little more light will make things less spooky up here."

Jamilet felt a wave of relief spread over her, and hoped Richard would stay until she was safely back out with the tray. He was a small man compared to Señor Peregrino, but between the two of them they'd be able to subdue him if he decided to try anything.

Richard hadn't yet moved to change the bulbs. "You okay?" he asked.

"I'm fine," Jamilet said.

"Are you happy to see me then?" His sleepy eyes suddenly widened, as though he'd been prodded with a sharp stick.

At that moment, his mop slipped down the wall, landing at Jamilet's feet, and when she bent down to retrieve it for him, he leaped on top of her, pushing her to the floor with all of his weight, one hand groping and clutching between her thighs, under her skirt, as the other clamped tight over her mouth and nose so she couldn't scream or breathe. His own breath was thick in her ear when he said, "You sure are a pretty thing. Why'd they stick you up here where no one can see you?"

Gasping for breath, Jamilet inhaled the harsh smell of cleaning solution on his hand. His knee was pressing on her back, and he'd worked it down toward her buttocks, and almost had it wedged between her legs, when she bit down on the flesh of his palm with all her strength. He yelped and snatched his hand back.

Jamilet flipped over and began fighting him off, kicking and striking out with her fists in a furious volley, but every time she managed to make contact, he laughed wildly, as though he were engaged in a boisterous game, and she was overcome by his breath, foul with the stench of cigarettes and the decaying teeth that she clearly saw in his gaping mouth when he laughed. But in the end he was quicker than she, and when he'd had enough of the game, he grabbed her wrists and held them down on either side of her head. She writhed underneath him, but with amazing strength the skinny man was able to pry open her legs with his knees, while holding both of her hands in one of his own and deftly unbuckling his belt with the other.

Jamilet wretched with the realization of what was about to happen, and let go an unholy scream. It seemed to emanate from somewhere deep in her bowels, and now all she could do was close her eyes and disappear somewhere into the furthest and darkest corners of her mind.

Suddenly, she heard a door open and a dazed and perplexed Richard was lifted up from on top of her as though he were not a man, but a marionette, his arms and legs loose and flailing about. He went flying through the air, and his head made a sickening flat sound as it hit the wall opposite her, causing him to bite his tongue. When he lifted his head, drool and blood were dribbling from his lips.

Jamilet didn't move from where she lay, staring up at Señor Peregrino, who stood between her and the bleeding janitor with clenched fists. Richard began to laugh again, unaware, it seemed, of the red fluid that was now flowing freely out of his mouth and cascading over his chin.

"Are you hurt?" Señor Peregrino asked Jamilet, never taking his eyes away from Richard.

"I . . . I don't think so."

"Get up and go home then," he commanded.

Jamilet scrambled to her feet and ran as fast as she could, stumbling down the hall as she rearranged her blouse and skirt. Richard's horrible laughter followed her down the stairs, away from the hospital and into the streets. It rang so loudly in her ears that she couldn't hear the roar of the traffic or the pounding of her feet on the pavement, or the howling of her own breath. She didn't even return Eddie's greeting when she passed him, although she saw him sitting there on the porch waiting for Pearly. In her state, she couldn't conceive of how to return a greeting that would make any sense, and briefly it passed through her mind that Eddie would have no doubt now that she was thoroughly insane.

She burst into the house, breathless, and grateful that Carmen wasn't home. She froze as her brain struggled to discern what day it was—Wednesday. Carmen would be meeting Louis at the bowling alley after work. She went straight to the bathroom and prepared her bath, stripping off her clothes and stepping into it before it was ready. She sank in below her shoulders, concentrating on the liquid warmth that reached beyond all the places Richard had violated. She felt the thick skin of the mark on her buttocks and shivered again with the reassuring loneliness of her secret. Perhaps it would be better if people knew she was different. Then they'd understand the constant torment that set her apart and excused her from ordinary suffering. She already possessed the mark—that should be enough for anybody.

9

J AMILET COULDN'T BE SURE how long she'd been asleep in the
bath, only that the water was cold and judging by the darkness
in the room, that it was already night. She felt remarkably calm
and confident that she might even be able to forget the vicious
attack of a few hours ago. Perhaps it was nothing more than a
horrible dream. With this thought, she stepped out of the tub and
dried herself with a towel. She flicked on the lights and, as was
her habit, attended to her underclothes first in order to carefully
unfasten the pinned documents, and ready them for the next day.
But they weren't in their usual place. She quickly searched through
the rest of her clothing, and then searched again, more frantically
this time, tossing her things about the room in such a manner
that her bra ended up floating in the bathtub, but the papers were
nowhere to be found.

Wrapped in a towel, she rushed out of the bathroom and into
the living room, her horror refreshed by the thought that she'd
somehow lost her documents. The little card with the nine numbers, along with her birth certificate, could be somewhere on the
street or at the hospital. She didn't know which was worse, and
concluded that either circumstance could easily destroy her life.
She collapsed onto the sofa and tried to think. She'd run from the
hospital so quickly, and was so upset, that she couldn't remember if

she'd seen anything on the floor, or if she'd felt the documents slipping out. All she remembered was Señor Peregrino looming over
Richard, and commanding her to leave. For all she knew, Richard
was at this very moment squashed against the wall like a fly and her
documents were soaking in his blood. The more she thought about
it, the more certain she was that they had to be somewhere on the
fifth floor. As Richard groped at her they'd become unpinned, and
she'd been too terrified to notice. Señor Peregrino couldn't be bothered to retrieve his own napkin; how likely was he to concern himself with papers on the floor? The documents were there. They had
to be. Her first thought was to rush to the hospital immediately
to begin her search. But if she were to run into one of the charge
nurses, or Nurse B., God forbid, they would demand to know why
she was there at such a late hour. And should Tía Carmen get
home and find the house empty, she'd also demand an explanation,
and Jamilet was certain that her anxiety would give her away. She'd
have to wait until the next morning to look for her papers.

Too upset to eat, she attempted to calm herself with the habits
of normalcy, and proceeded with her bedtime ritual. She went to
the front window, and stood there until she felt as still and inani-
mate as the furniture in the room. Then, ever so slowly, she raised
her hand and shifted the curtain to one side. They were there as
always, gazing out at the traffic. With every passing car Eddie's
hand traveled farther up Pearly's thigh, but on this night Jamilet
couldn't watch them anymore, so she went to her room. Light-
headed and dizzy, she tried to sleep, but when she closed her eyes,
all she could see were her precious documents lying on the floor
outside Señor Peregrino's room, unfolding like a flower, and revealing her true identity to whomever passed by.

❋

Having slept uneasily if at all, Jamilet's eyes flew open at the
first light of dawn, and she wondered how early she could report
for work without arousing suspicion. She dressed quickly and

dispensed with breakfast. Her stomach was tight as a knot, and the only thing that provided any relief for her anxiety was the thought of getting to the hospital as quickly as she could.

She clocked in a half hour early, but attracted no attention from the nurses and other staff who were scurrying about in the midst of the morning shift change. With heart pounding she ascended the staircase to the fifth floor, and entered the corridor where she hoped to find her documents. Even if they were lying in a pool of blood, or torn up in a corner, she would've been overjoyed to see them. She slowly paced the corridor, but after the second pass knew she had no choice but to enter Señor Peregrino's room and attempt a search before he woke for his morning shower. Perhaps he'd found them and set them on his desk without realizing what they were. He must have been exhausted after his confrontation with Richard.

She stood outside his door, calming her breath. She removed her shoes, then opened the door, holding the handle so that it wouldn't click, and slipped in. He was still sleeping, just as she'd expected. She padded silently across the room, toward his desk, and peered down at his papers, fingers hovering over them while her eyes adjusted to the dim light.

"What are you searching for?" Señor Peregrino asked calmly, as though he'd been waiting for her.

She turned to see him, sitting up in bed. "I just thought I'd get started early today, Señor."

He appeared amused, and gave up a beleaguered sigh. "You're not a very good liar, are you . . . Jamilet?"

She gasped when she heard him speak her true name.

"I must say, 'Jamilet' is a definite improvement. Although your assumed name, bland as it is, suits you better." He studied her for a few seconds, his black eyes shiny as marbles. He appeared troubled, but not nearly so troubled as Jamilet.

"I need those papers," she said. "They were a gift from my aunt and I can't work without them . . . Señor. I mean, can I please have them back, please?"

At this Señor Peregrino yawned, and stretched his great arms. "Desperation can drive certain people to civility if they're not careful," he said.

"I've always been civil to you."

Señor Peregrino nodded and his eyebrows flickered to acknowledge as much. "Is it civility that you owe me? Or perhaps something more . . . ?"

"I don't know what you mean. I never know what you mean when you talk like that." She wavered on her feet. "I will not dishonor myself for my papers if that's what you mean."

Señor Peregrino's hand that lay idly on his lap constricted and then relaxed. "I don't esteem you enough to be offended by such a remark. If there's one thing I've learned," he said severely, "it's that, aside from the cheap entertainment they sometimes provide, fools are of little use to me. I certainly don't take their prattle seriously."

"Then what is it that I owe you, Señor?"

He appraised her like a disappointed teacher, and all of a sudden she knew exactly what he meant. "I didn't thank you for helping me yesterday, is that it?"

"Helping you? I believe it more accurate to say that I saved your miserable hide from becoming even more miserable."

Jamilet nodded, feeling not only foolish, but contrite. "Forgive me for not thanking you before."

"Very well. I accept your apology." He shooed her to the door with both hands. "Now you may leave. It's far too early for this sort of thing."

But Jamilet didn't move from her spot. "And my papers?"

Señor Peregrino became suddenly preoccupied with the arrangement of his blankets, and began smoothing out the layers one at a time. "Are you referring to the illegal documents you used to obtain employment here?"

"Yes I am," was Jamilet's soft reply.

Señor Peregrino was almost jovial. "Well, I do have them. And I'll return them if you're willing to entertain a certain proposition. Honorable, of course." He paused to consider his phrasing. "I realize that you've been directed to avoid all unnecessary conversation with me, but I ask that, from time to time, you . . . you listen as I tell you my story from beginning to end. When I have finished, I will return your illegal documents to you and say nothing to anyone of their existence."

Jamilet stared at him in disbelief. "You want me to listen to your story?"

"Yes, it will fully explain the reason I'm here," he said, settling back onto his pillows and closing his eyes.

"How long will it take, this story of yours?"

With eyes still closed, he answered, "It will take as long as it takes." And without another word, he yawned, turned on his side, and fell soundly asleep.

10

After enjoying a hearty lunch, and proclaiming that the roast chicken was especially delicious, Señor Peregrino took his usual nap. Every afternoon at this time, Jamilet quickly removed his lunch tray from the room without disturbing him, but on this day she stood for a long while watching the gentle rise and fall of his chest as he slept. He appeared so peaceful, so completely unaware of her presence.

Ever so quietly, she approached his bedside and reached out her hand until it floated directly over him. It trembled slightly as she inched closer, while bending at the waist. A few inches more and her fingertips were just touching the rim of his shirt pocket. He mumbled something in his sleep, and she froze, but she held her position, hardly breathing, eyes closed lest the heat of her gaze upon his face awaken him. Slowly she opened one eye to find that his were still closed, and, ever so carefully, she reached into his pocket. Suddenly, his eyes flew open, and she jumped back several feet.

When Señor Peregrino realized what Jamilet was up to, he frowned. "You said you wouldn't dishonor yourself for your papers and I believe that you're doing just that," he growled.

Flustered and shocked, Jamilet almost choked on her response. "I thought you were asleep, Señor."

"My state of consciousness does not excuse your behavior."

"I was only trying to get back what is mine. There's no dishonor in that," Jamilet said, upset now for having attempted such a foolish thing.

Señor Peregrino lifted himself up on one elbow with considerable effort. "What, then, do you consider the honorable thing for me to do under the circumstances?"

"Return my papers, of course."

He dropped his head to his chest for a moment, so that only the snowy crown of his head was visible. He raised it slowly, bitterness tracing the line of his smile. "And not to report the illegal nature of your employment to the authorities? You are, after all, committing a federal crime. The hospital could be fined severely, perhaps even shut down if you were discovered. What would happen to the patients if the hospital were forced to close its doors?"

Jamilet could say nothing. Instead, she turned to take his tray and then thought better of it. "You said you'd return my papers if I listened to your story, Señor."

He muttered something to himself and it seemed he might drop back to sleep, but Jamilet was surprised to hear him speak with a different voice, one that lacked its usual harshness.

"Where should I begin?" he asked. "It is always troublesome, this question."

Jamilet searched herself for an answer that would get the whole thing rolling. The sooner he got started, the sooner it would end, and the sooner she'd have her papers back. She plopped down in the chair nearest him, and leaned forward. "Perhaps you should begin at the place where the story gets interesting," she offered.

Señor Peregrino nodded wisely, as though acknowledging a great and undeniable truth. "Yes, that would be the best place to start, and also the best place to end this wicked business." He took a deep breath.

Jamilet nodded eagerly in order to demonstrate her cooperation, but she soon realized that he was paying her no attention whatsoever. He was reaching beyond the moment for something more, and it seemed to take all of his concentration, and all of his will, to find it. Weary, and without his anger to defend him, he appeared as flustered as an old stork that has lost its way while on a long migratory flight. Jamilet stayed quiet and soon his voice found its strength and filled the room.

There are spirits that sing, Jamilet. They sing beyond the spaces where the firmament of heaven conceals them, filling the chambers of our universe, and creating a most lovely echo that only some can hear. I was ten years old when I heard them, as well as the whisperings of the saints and angels around me. I saw spirits peeking out from behind the trees too as they watched us go about our lives. When I told this to my mother and father and to the other people in the village, they paid me little attention and thought I was a most imaginative boy. As time went on, however, it became unsettling for them to hear of my stories about spirits, and the mysteries of life and death that they shared with me. The amusing smiles I at first received turned into patronizing grins, to be followed by stony countenances and the occasional scowl.

My father was a patient man, and slow to anger. But one day, not knowing what else to do, he beat me with a switch after I told him another one of my fantastic stories. I knew it was fear and not anger that motivated him to behave in this way, for in those days, fear was a shadow one could never escape. It was most commonly challenged not with understanding, but with a greater fear, however inspired. In this case my father was hoping that fear of the switch would cure my foolishness.

Mind you, all I knew about the world was what life in a rural village in Spain could teach a young boy. But when I had my visions, I felt as though I were being carried along on a great river more splendid and more powerful than anything I'd ever known. Sometimes late in the afternoon, after I'd finished tending the sheep, I'd watch the sun settle right on the crest of the mountain, as liquid gold streamed down upon us in warm shafts, filling the bowl of the valley. At these times I was moved to singing alone, religious songs because that's all I knew. I was overheard by many, and because of my singing, combined with my unique sensibilities, my fate for the holy life was eventually sealed. In other words, it was decided by everyone who knew me, and most especially my parents, that I should become a priest.

I was not, as you might imagine a young boy to be, frightened by the prospect of such a life. My family was poor, and the priests in my village were highly regarded and enjoyed as much respect as the wealthiest of men. They lived in better homes, with polished wooden floors, near the quiet of the churchyard. They wore elaborate vestments during mass over their well-tailored clothes, and their shoes rarely showed traces of mud or wear.

My good friend Tomas was directed to a holy life as well, but for different reasons. Aside from being born to the wealthiest family in the region, he had a weak disposition and one leg slightly shorter than the other, so that he didn't exactly limp, but he swayed a bit, as though he couldn't decide whether to walk to the left or to the right. Every family of standing was expected to have a son or daughter dedicated to the church, and it made sense that for Tomas's family he be the chosen one.

After the decision was made for me, all was well again, and I felt quite fortunate. My older brother often complained that while my future was assured, he would have to continue proving his worth by the sweat of his brow and the number of healthy offspring he could produce to help him in his tasks, worries I would never have.

Mine became a life of rigorous study, for there was much to learn in preparation for the seminary and I was excused from the physically exhausting chores of a poor sheepherder. Tomas and I were quite happy with our books. What little free time we had was spent dreaming about the exceptional future that awaited us. While other boys our age fancied themselves great warriors, Tomas and I prayed in the shadow of the mountains and spoke of one day going to Rome, and exploring the marbled splendor of the Vatican. Already, we were bestowed a certain reverence by the villagers and even by our own families. I was the first child to be served at mealtime, even before my eldest brother. And the same villagers who had scoffed at me before, now asked for my advice about important matters regarding the marriages of their children or the decision to sell a piece of land or build a new house.

All progressed very well in this way until the age of sixteen, when my visions quite suddenly stopped. The emerging strength of my body seemed to overtake the fortitude of my spirit, so that a strange and unholy discomfort began to plague me, like a warm humming coursing through my veins. I became acutely aware of it on a particular summer night when attending a dance at the village square, as I had every year since my birth. Why anything so remarkable should happen to me in such an unremarkable place made it all the more astounding, but the sensation was undeniable and I can only describe it as this: As I watched the dancers in the square, children, parents, men and women of all ages, I found my eyes drifting toward a certain young lady I'd known all my life. Her name was Matilda, and when we were younger she sat next to me in class, and I remember thinking it very amusing that when she laughed her freckles lit up like tiny lanterns all over her face. I'd make up silly things to say just so she'd laugh, and I could watch the spots burn on her cheeks and over the bridge of her nose. But on this night, I was not the least interested in her freckles. Instead, I was mesmerized by the gentle rhythm of her hips as she danced. Through the many-layered skirt she wore I became aware of the womanly form of her body, and as I watched her, the warm humming intensified and grew hotter and hotter, until it became a monstrous cycle of pleasure and shame that fed itself without my consent. I could not turn away. My eyes were transfixed on her body. And then thoughts began to formulate in my mind, wicked thoughts I'd never entertained before about the truer form that moved beneath the layers of her clothing and the delicacy I might find there.

It was Tomas who interrupted my tormented reverie. "You look as though you've seen a ghost, my friend," he said, laughing.

"Perhaps it is just as well that I look upon my own death."

Tomas followed my uninterrupted gaze, for even as he spoke to me I continued to watch her. "She's grown lovely," he said. "I never would have thought it possible. She was so ugly as a child."

"She's not a child anymore," I observed, feeling some relief at being able to speak my mind.

Tomas remained near until the dance came to an end, and Matilda disappeared into the crowd to join her family. The heat that had accosted me earlier began to dissipate, until I felt only guilty exhaustion in its place. A familiar heaviness fell over us both and we didn't need to speak a word to know what the other was thinking. As children, the reality of a life without knowing women seemed not like a sacrifice, but a blessing meant to spare us the trouble of dealing with such a messy business. But with the dawning of manhood upon us, it grew into a sacrifice of new proportions. Now I understood the prayers the priests had prayed over us as children when our parents made their intentions for our lives publicly known. Prayers in which they supplicated the Lord to spare us the discomfort of our earthly passions so that the totality of our beings might be devoted to the spiritual. In this way, celibacy would not prove such a heavy cross to bear, but would become more of a perpetual splinter that might sting from time to time, serving to remind us of our weakness and to ensure our compassion for the ordinary man.

But as I grew older, it seemed that I bore the full weight of man's lascivious nature on my shoulders alone. The fact that women were forbidden to me made them all the more alluring, and it didn't help matters that I was attractive to them as well. My stature was remarked upon, as was the elegance of my profile, so that I was considered by many to appear not the son of a humble herding family but of a nobleman. With my destiny in the church well established, I was also a favorite dancing partner—safe, but handsome and clever all the same. I dare say the

young ladies danced all the closer to me because of my disquali-
fied status.

I was despairing in my deception, and only Tomas knew the
truth. He implored me to hold strong to my convictions, for it
seemed that I could think of nothing else but that which was denied me. And in the worst of my torment, they all looked beautiful
to me. Even the homelier girls with crossed eyes, I would have
accepted as a gift from heaven.

Tomas commiserated with me as a loyal friend would do, but
I could see that he was not as tormented as I with this matter. He
looked forward to his priestly duties without concern for what he
was sacrificing. I envied his composure, the way he accepted the
communion wafer so serenely on his tongue, when the host in my
mouth seemed to burn.

There is nothing worse than to live a lie. At eighteen years
of age, when we were shortly to enter the seminary, my stomach
turned sour. And there is nothing that will concern a mother more
than her son's sudden loss of appetite, so my mother insisted that
I see a doctor. After a thorough examination, it was determined
that for some mysterious reason I was unable to get enough oxy-
gen into my lungs, and that this had unbalanced my entire organ-
ism. The good doctor recommended that I take daily walks, and
he prescribed a glass of strong spirits to accompany my meals.
Nevertheless, the weight continued to drop off my body, until I
appeared much as I do today—a six-foot-three skeleton with eyes
as big as plates.

In this state I even lost interest in my obsession and no longer
fantasized about how it would be to hold a young woman in my
arms. I had energy only to stay alive, attend to my studies, eat
what little food I could keep down, and find my way into bed at
the end of the day. I drifted off to sleep many a night hoping never
to wake.

Up to that time, I had rarely spoken to my father, and only
when he spoke to me first. The few questions he directed my way
were meant not to inquire, but to strengthen my responsibilities,

and my direction in life. Thankfully, however, he listened carefully to my answers.

"Did you find the ewe we lost last week, Antonio?"

"Yes, Papa. I found her in the glen where she always likes to hide."

"How many books did you read last week, Antonio?"

"Three, Papa, including the one from the widow Robledo."

"Do you want to be a priest, Antonio?"

"I don't know, Papa. I doubt that I'll live long enough to find out."

The pilgrimage to Santiago de Compostela is an ancient journey for the faithful and the faithless alike. It winds through the north of Spain, following the milky way of stars above, and culminating at the venerated Cathedral of Santiago de Compostela, the very place where the apostle James is buried. Walking the path is meant to clear the mind and cleanse the soul. This is how it has been for almost a thousand years, since the saint's body mysteriously appeared on the Galician shores. And so it was decided by the priests and elders of the village that I should make this pilgrimage as soon as the worst of winter had passed. Tomas was to accompany me, and he was to remain vigilant and tend to my vulnerable disposition. Upon my return, it was hoped that all matters would be resolved.

I felt as if new life had been breathed into my body. My appetite returned stronger than before and I resumed my previous healthy state. With the possibility of a different life before me, my obsession moderated to a balanced interest that no longer gnawed mercilessly at my senses. I was feeling like myself again and I awaited the return of spring as never before.

One brilliant morning in early May, Tomas and I set off from our village for Puente la Reina, almost six hundred kilometers from our destination in Santiago. We were to undertake the entire journey on foot. We had enough cheese, bread, and wine to last only a few days, knowing that we'd find food and drink at the *refugios* along the way, but I tell you that I had enough hope in my heart to last for a thousand years.

11

THE MEAL WAS PREPARED with exceptional care. The chicken was stewed slowly, until the meat fell off the bone. Nothing but homemade tortillas would do, and the sauce was enriched with a double dose of tomatoes and peppers. Jamilet hid two of her freshly prepared enchiladas in the refrigerator, behind the milk and eggs, as Carmen didn't like to leave food uneaten, and chicken enchiladas were her favorite.

For almost a week, Señor Peregrino had refused to continue with his story, saying that he wasn't in the mood to go on with it, and when he was he'd let her know. She tried to disguise her impatience, and knew she'd be wiser to appear uninterested; then perhaps he wouldn't enjoy withholding as much as he did. Nevertheless, if her chicken enchiladas were able to sweeten Carmen's mood after the end of a hard day, Jamilet suspected they'd have a similar effect on Señor Peregrino.

The next morning, she placed the tray on his lap, as she always did, and cleared her throat, announcing that she'd cooked something special for him to try with his breakfast. "I think you must get bored eating the same thing all the time. And . . . I'm a good cook," she concluded.

He removed the dome over his plate and stared at the enchiladas for several seconds. For an instant, his face flashed a grateful expression, and then settled back into a scowl. "How do I know it's not poisoned?" He gave Jamilet such a leering look that it was almost comical.

She was flustered by such an unexpected accusation as this. "I . . . I wouldn't poison you, Señor."

"Oh, but I think you would," he said while pushing the plate away with the very tips of his fingers. Then he crossed his arms and glared at the new food, as if expecting it to speak, and betray its maker.

Jamilet stood idly by until she could no longer keep quiet. "Señor, if I poisoned you, I'd never get my papers back, as I have no idea where you've hidden them."

"You must be fairly certain they're somewhere in this room. Once I succumb to the toxin, you'll be free to look anywhere you please."

It was Jamilet's turn to cross her arms and shake her head. "You don't have to eat it, then. I'll take it back home to my aunt. My chicken enchiladas are her favorite."

It was as if Señor Peregrino hadn't heard her at all. Then he suddenly took up his fork, and held it out to her. "They do look delicious. Why not have one now?" He said, forcing a gracious smile.

"No thank you. I had plenty of breakfast."

His eyebrows flickered. "Isn't that convenient?"

Jamilet sighed, and arranged a far too generous portion on her fork. It was a challenge to keep it all in her mouth, and as she chewed dribbles of salsa escaped from the corners of her lips.

"For God's sake, have you no manners?" Señor Peregrino grabbed his napkin and waved it at her while turning his face away.

"I'm just trying—"

"Enough! I'll lose my appetite entirely if you force me to look upon that mastication you insist on displaying."

Jamilet swallowed hard and wiped her mouth with the napkin. "I'm sorry, Señor, I only wanted to prove to you that it's not poisoned." Immediately after uttering her apologies, she felt like stamping her foot. Why should she be apologizing to him? Once again, she felt every bit the fool he accused her of being.

Señor Peregrino assembled a more civilized portion of chicken enchilada on his fork. He chewed slowly, and his eyes grew soft, as they had on the day he'd begun telling his story. "You are indeed a very good cook . . ." He stopped himself and collected his unspoken emotions into a heavy sigh before taking another bite. "You're trying to bribe me for your papers, is that it?"

"Maybe I just wanted to do something nice for you, Señor. Because I like your story."

"Ah, but if I gave you back your papers today, I believe you'd be looking for a new position tomorrow. My story hasn't captivated you so much as to change that truth. And only the best stories are able to change the truth."

He finished every bit of the enchiladas, leaving the rest of his breakfast untouched. Then he poured himself a cup of coffee, and continued.

The first part of our journey from our little corner of Spain to Puente la Reina took us several days, although it felt that we were not walking, but floating, as we could hardly believe that we had embarked upon such an adventure. I hadn't in all my life traveled farther than ten miles from my place of birth. Sometimes, for no reason at all, I would break out in laughter, startling poor Tomas. I was only trying to expel the anxious joy I felt accumulating within my breast and keep myself from bursting altogether. Tomas, in spite of his desire to remain stoic, would find himself caught up in my energy and laughed along, so that, rather than serious pilgrims, we must've appeared more like two happy madmen making their way down the road.

In this way, we passed through countless villages that looked like charming clusters of mushrooms that had sprung up between the folds of the mountains. These mountains grew more and more imposing each day we traveled, and our narrow path eventually led us through a series of thick forests where the wind howled between the black shadows deep within, chilling us to the bone. Eventually, our weariness began to overcome our good humor, as we'd been sleeping only a few hours each night in barns near the roadside when we could, and under the stars when this wasn't possible.

It was almost dark when we saw the lights of Puente la Reina up ahead. Tomas had wanted to stop and rest earlier that afternoon, but I had persuaded him to continue the march until we reached our destination. And he was glad that I had, for after we crossed the bridge over the River Arga, we found ourselves in an impressive town with fine stone buildings several stories high, and many fountains. The main *via* was teaming with pilgrims from throughout Spain and Europe. There were even some from as far away as Greece. It was exhilarating to hear so many languages mixing about like a delicious stew, its aroma delighting our senses at every turn.

Feeling truly free for the first time in my life, I longed to sing out with the whole of my heart in the middle of the square. But I refrained from making a spectacle of myself and waited until we were safely tucked away for the night in our *refugio*, which was adjacent to a small chapel. Earlier we had followed the sound of the church bell that we were told rang to announce its presence to pilgrims in need. This, like many other lodgings we encountered on our journey, was a simple and clean establishment near the main pilgrim route, offering modest lodgings in exchange for a small donation or a prayer. Few things were considered more sacred than a pilgrim's prayer. So Tomas and I, along with twenty or so others, were offered a meal of bread and cheese, and were then permitted to lay our blankets on the wooden floor of the chapel for the night. All had succumbed to the exhaustion of a full day when I began to sing softly to myself, as was my custom. I suppose that I must have sung more loudly than I intended, for when I stopped almost everyone in the room was watching me with wide eyes reflecting the moonlight that shone through a small stained-glass window above our heads.

A large man with an overgrown beard and a thick Basque accent asked, "Why did you stop? When I hear you sing like that, I'm reminded of the reason I will torture myself with this journey. Please continue."

There were many murmurs of agreement, and I was grateful for the semidarkness that hid my embarrassment. Although, I was pleased to be admired by strangers from so many different countries and traditions. I believe that an old man such as I has earned the privilege to delight in his past accomplishments without being accused of indulging in excessive vanity, so let me say that I sang quite beautifully that night and continued to sing until every soul within the sound of my voice had fallen into a deep and restful sleep.

From that day forward, I was regarded by all as the singing pilgrim—one who possessed a voice capable of easing the hardships of the journey. Tomas and I were never without company because of it. This was distinction enough, as we had already agreed to keep secret the fact that we were seminarians. If the purpose of my journey was to discover the true life I was meant to lead, why should I predispose myself and those around me to a foregone conclusion?

We were a colorful and noisy group. Among others, our band of traveling companions included three merchant brothers from the north of France, two middle-aged Italian nuns, and three convicted thieves from the Basque country whose sentences would be commuted if they could prove to the courts that they'd completed the pilgrimage. Our day typically began before sunrise when, after a quick wash at the well, we'd begin walking after a small piece of cheese and bread for our breakfast. When the weather was agreeable, and the path not too steep, we were able to cover more than ten miles before noon, at which point we'd reward ourselves with a well-earned rest and a more substantial meal. This was the fa-

vorite time of day for most of the pilgrims, but I was most fond
of the mornings. The Spanish sunrise contained within its light
the ancient lore of the land. It was as though time began while
we witnessed this miracle with the sleep still in our eyes. At those
moments I was renewed in my faith and conviction to serve the
Church. God revealed Himself to me in the wavering gold of
dawn's light. I heard His voice in the tender silence of the morning, and felt His love in the mist that embraced the land.

Tomas awoke in the middle of the night, when we'd been almost a week on the road, and leaned on my arm, whispering softly,
"Any inspiration so far?" he asked.

"I've been walking in the clouds since we began," I responded,
hoping he would leave it at that.

"I gather that since you haven't been walking in the company
of a young lady, you're back on the right path."

No doubt Tomas had noticed my eyes drifting toward the
lovely ladies we encountered in the villages through which we
passed, as well as the attention I received in return. A few nights
before, the innkeeper's daughter had made it a point to place the
wine and food nearest me, and she smiled so sweetly that someone
in the group asked me if I knew her. But I managed to politely
discourage her attention without feeling those familiar spurs dig-
ging into my sides.

Still, I hesitated in answering Tomas too soon. We had weeks,
perhaps even months of the pilgrimage ahead of us if the weather
proved difficult, and with all of the kindhearted patience he dis-
played toward others, with his best friend he could be quite impatient.

I turned away from him so he wouldn't see the slight smile on
my face as I answered. "Whatever my path turns out to be, I'm not
running, but walking slowly to make sure I don't miss anything
along the way."

"But you must have some idea where you're headed, Antonio,
and I think it wise that you tell me so I can guide you."

Upon hearing this, my smile threatened to burst into laughter. Tomas fancied himself my moral and spiritual superior, and I indulged him in this. "You can guide me best, dear friend, by your gracious works. The kindness and sensitivity you showed Renato is the best inspiration that I or anyone else can hope for." I was referring to the young man Tomas had befriended a few days before. Renato had a sallow complexion and eyes the color of weak tea. He did not walk, but flapped and slithered and dragged himself across the Spanish landscape like a broken insect. We were told that he rarely spoke, and had made his way from the French border to Pamplona without uttering a single word. All believed that he wasn't long for this world, but I suspected that Tomas, blessed as he was with the patience of a saint, would draw him out. And sure enough, one fine afternoon, while sitting under the shade of a giant olive tree, we saw the first hint of a smile on Renato's pale face, followed by a tentative yet clearly discernible request for water. All had agreed that Tomas's kind attention had been the reason, and I knew that a reminder of this would keep Tomas quiet for the rest of the night. I was right.

I awoke the next morning eager to resume our journey. On that day, we were due to reach the larger town of Logroño, and in this place was the Church of Santiago el Real, a most beautiful sanctuary and a favorite for many pilgrims. I knew that if we began walking before sunrise, and made good time, we'd be there by midmorning. Luckily, the others were of similar mind, and after a quick breakfast, we donned our packs and were on the road just as the first hint of dawn touched the sky.

The landscape changed considerably as we made our way out of Navarra, and descended into the region of Rioja. The green, mountainous terrain we'd been traversing for days softened into lush rolling hills more suitable for farming, and this offered us a welcome respite. As we continued on our way, the dark, rich soil beneath our feet became red and sandy, and on either side of the path could be seen vast stretches of yellow wheat fields that seemed to go on and on, as far as the eye could see. When we neared the Ebro River, we were delighted to find that the water flowing there was clean and sweet, as some other rivers we'd encountered were bitter, and rumored to be poisonous to people and horses alike. We filled our canteens and drank without concern until we were quite satiated. Hovering above the fields we beheld the delicate spires of countless churches and monasteries. So many that we soon lost count. I would have liked to have seen them all, and to have offered a prayer to Santiago while kneeling upon every altar, but we tended to stop not when inspired by the beauty of the facades or the charm of the villages we encountered, but when directed by the condition of our feet, which urged us to go on while they still felt fresh.

Upon our arrival at Logroño several hours later, we were exhausted but delighted to have arrived only an hour or so behind schedule. Some members of our group went to inquire after lodgings, as it appeared that foul weather would impede further travel on that day, but Tomas and I went directly to the Church of Santiago el Real. When we entered we were immediately embraced by the comforting hush of prayer and the sweet fragrance of incense. We made our way down the central aisle toward the knave, and stood in awe before the altar, which appeared to us like an enormous and intricate network of fine vines twisting and looping over each other, reaching up and up until it culminated in a single shining star that shone throughout the interior of the church and upon all who worshipped there. We felt as though we were standing at the entrance to heaven, like archangels preparing to enlist in God's army, rather than humble pilgrims, darkened by the dust of the road. After our prayers, we crossed ourselves with holy water before emerging onto a sunlit square that was overflowing with pilgrims, most of whom we hadn't seen before. They must have arrived soon after we had, eager to find shelter before the storm hit. Already, billows of white clouds were blowing across the sky, leaving us in shadows one moment and bright sunlight the next.

"Sing for us," Rodolfo, my Basque companion implored me, his wine flask quite empty. "Sing so that we may better understand God's glory as we rest in His shadow."

I turned and allowed my gaze to wander up among the sculptures and intricate carvings that reached toward heaven. That the human mind could conceive of such beauty, and human hands create it, was incomprehensible to a simple shepherd boy such as myself, but there I was, preparing to sing to God's glory while humbled by the artistry born of it. My throat became suddenly tight at the prospect, and I yearned to escape into the quiet sanctuary I'd just visited. But how could I disappoint my companions, and God, who was watching from beyond this majesty of stone and glass?

Tomas gave me an encouraging shove and began to sing quietly, so that only I might hear him. It was a simple hymn he'd heard me sing many times before, and my voice joined his until I was transported beyond my petty self-consciousness and was singing with all my soul. I felt an inexplicable love surging within me, and my spirit soared as the pure melody of my song flowed through my lungs and throat like a mighty river.

When my song was finished, I felt a strange yet familiar sensation throughout my body, as one does after taking a long, hot bath, and changing into clean clothes. At that moment I glanced down at my hands, and was stunned to see that they were clean, and that the thin black line of dirt packed under my nails was completely gone. My clothes too were spotless, and as fresh as the day I had put them on at the start of our journey. Mystified, I looked out upon the silent crowd that mirrored my reverie, and then came a thundering applause and an explosion of cheers from all corners of the square. I managed a hasty bow, and the people cleared to let me pass, as I was eager to find my companions.

As many people congratulated me, and complimented my singing, I looked all around for them, but Tomas and the others seemed to have been swallowed up by the crowd. I headed toward the cafés, certain I'd find them there. All the while I was shaking hands with many as I went along, then suddenly I stopped. The throng of road-weary pilgrims around me became silent. It was as if they had all disappeared in a puff of smoke.

I stood alone in the middle of the square with a woman I mistook at first for an angelic statue. She wore a red shawl over her head that slipped to her shoulders, and revealed a dark-haired beauty with eyes the color of the sea. I do not know what captivated me more, the perfection of her face, or the mysterious aura that surrounded her.

In the moment that it took me to blink and confirm that she was in fact real and not a vision, I was lost.

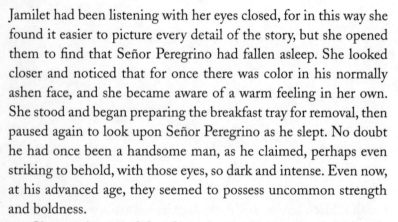

Jamilet had been listening with her eyes closed, for in this way she found it easier to picture every detail of the story, but she opened them to find that Señor Peregrino had fallen asleep. She looked closer and noticed that for once there was color in his normally ashen face, and she became aware of a warm feeling in her own. She stood and began preparing the breakfast tray for removal, then paused again to look upon Señor Peregrino as he slept. No doubt he had once been a handsome man, as he claimed, perhaps even striking to behold, with those eyes, so dark and intense. Even now, at his advanced age, they seemed to possess uncommon strength and boldness.

She tore her mind free from the imaginings that held her. It was time to get back to work.

12

THERE WAS LITTLE DOUBT in Jamilet's mind that the best time to ask her aunt for anything was in the evening, after she'd had her second beer. Before that, she was far too irritable and filled with complaints to listen to anyone. She'd complain about the idiotic places they put gas meters in some houses, making them impossible to find and read, and she'd complain about her boss, who expected all his employees to answer the phone with a smile, and about her fellow employees who got all the best assignments. And then there were the complaints about her constantly aching back, miserably sore feet, and incessant heartburn. If her workday had been tolerable, then she'd find something else to complain about—the fact that the grass was green, the sky blue, and the earth round instead of square. Of course, if Jamilet waited until after Carmen had consumed her third beer and more besides, she'd agree to almost anything. The problem was that the next day she wouldn't remember what it was she'd agreed to.

On the afternoon Jamilet decided to ask her for a favor, she waited until the second beer was downed, and posed her request directly, feeling a bit odd as she did so. When she asked her aunt a question, it was usually for the purpose of doing something for her, and not the other way around.

"Tía, would you like extra cheese on your tacos?"

"Tía, do you want me to change your sheets?"

"Tía, will you need your jeans washed for tomorrow or can you wait for the weekend?"

But now it was, "Tía, will you take me to the library?"

Carmen flipped through the TV guide without looking up. "Yeah, sure . . . where is it, anyway?"

"It's only a few blocks away. We could even walk."

Carmen tossed her empty can at Jamilet. "Why do you need to go there?"

"I just want to learn something about Spain."

Carmen looked up from her TV guide, and scrunched up her nose, as though she detected a foul odor. "Spain?" Then she narrowed her eyes. "Does this have something to do with that old pervert you're looking after?"

Jamilet hesitated to answer, not quite sure of her own motivation. "He's not a pervert, Tía. It's just that he's been telling me things about where he came from, and I . . . I just want to know if they're true and if he's really crazy."

"Of course he's crazy, and you are too for working with him," she said before starting on her third beer. She glanced up at her niece's hopeful eyes. "Okay. If I'm not too tired, we'll go tomorrow after I get home from work."

The next day Jamilet waited anxiously for her aunt to get home from work. When she heard the car in the drive, she watched through the window as her aunt walked to the door, her gait heavy and lumbering from side to side. The keys slipped from her hand to the ground, and she kicked them all the way to the steps, putting off bending down for them until the last minute. It had been another bad day at work, and Jamilet could well imagine the long list of complaints she'd be subjected to that night. Swallowing her disappointment, she opened the front door before her aunt got to the steps and reached down for the keys herself. On bad days like this, Carmen's back pain was absolutely excruciating.

"You're a lifesaver, Jami," Carmen said with a sigh.

Jamilet didn't bother to remind her aunt of their plans to go to the library, but later that evening, after the dishes had been washed, and Carmen and Louis were engrossed in an episode of *Starsky and Hutch,* Jamilet slipped outside the house through the side door, and made her way to the tree where she'd met Eddie before. She waited for him to pass by, as she knew he would, between nine and nine thirty, after kissing Pearly twice and giving her a firm pat on her bottom.

He approached right on schedule, hands stuffed into his pockets, shoulders hunched forward against the fresh night air. She waited until he was a few feet beyond her hiding place, and then stepped out. "Eddie," she called softly.

He whirled around, squinting with alarm into the darkness. When he recognized Jamilet, he relaxed, but only a bit. "What are you doing there? You scared the shit out of me."

"I'm sorry. I didn't mean to scare you again, I just need a favor."

Eddie's face went stiff. He didn't seem to appreciate any reminders of how badly he'd been spooked before. He said nothing.

"It's not a big favor," Jamilet added, taking a cautious step toward him.

"What is it?"

"I need you to go with me to the library. I already asked my tía Carmen, but she gets too tired after work."

Eddie stared at Jamilet as if she were speaking Russian or Chinese. When he was certain he'd understood her correctly, he flicked his head to the left without moving his eyes away from hers. "The library's just around the block. You don't need my help to find it."

"I need you to go with me so I can look up some stuff about Spain . . ."

"Look," Eddie said, his irritation mounting. "I got a girlfriend, in case you didn't notice." He lowered his voice, and stole a glance at her porch.

"I don't want to cause trouble for you, Eddie, I just need you . . ."

"Why can't you go alone?"

Jamilet felt her face get hot as she considered how best to answer him. Her eyes watered, and she was grateful for the darkness. "I can't read," she muttered.

"What?"

"I can't read," she repeated, raising her voice as though to banish the shame. "I don't know how—not in English or Spanish. I can't—"

Eddie held up both hands to shush her. "I heard you. Shit, they heard you in Canada."

Jamilet felt her heart beating furiously and waited for it to slow down before saying anything more. "So, now that you know, will you go with me?"

Eddie stuffed his hands in his pockets, but said nothing.

Jamilet stepped in closer to him. "Will you go with me, Eddie?" she asked again.

He shook his head slowly. "I'm really sorry, but I can't take the chance that Pearly will find out. You don't know how jealous she gets."

"You must love her a lot," Jamilet whispered, but her heart was pounding again worse than before because of what she was contemplating to say next. She hadn't realized until that moment how desperate she really was, and the feeling was at once completely alien, and yet strangely familiar to her. The words that came out of her mouth had been borrowed from another life it seemed, and when she spoke them she felt the thrill and power of breathing fire. "If you don't go with me," she said, "I'll tell Pearly you took me to the hospital that night."

If he'd half-expected something like this from Jamilet, Eddie might have smiled coolly and put her in her place without a second thought, but the shock gave him pause, as if Mickey Mouse had suddenly hauled off and socked him on the jaw. He shook his head in disbelief. "I was wrong about you," was all he said.

They met the following afternoon behind the first stack of bookshelves nearest the entrance. Eddie's face was set in stone and he didn't respond when Jamilet greeted him. She expected as much, and knew that she probably deserved it, but it was too late to take any of it back now.

"Let's get this over with," he said, barely glancing at her. Jamilet struggled to keep up as he walked briskly through the building, looking for someone who might offer some assistance. But the proverbial librarian, sitting at her desk, eager to guide thirsty young minds in their quest for knowledge, was nowhere to be found.

"Can't we look for what we need ourselves?" Jamilet asked him after they'd passed through the same corridors three times. She pointed to the shelf nearest them. "Maybe we can start looking here."

Eddie rolled his eyes. "You won't find anything that way," he said.

Jamilet shrugged, intrigued with the way his temper flared. He was still awkward with it, as though wearing shoes too big for his feet. But in spite of his sour mood, she enjoyed the fact that words were passing between them, and that his attention to her, however contrived it might be, made her feel alive and wonderful. Jamilet said, "Maybe if we just try."

Exasperated, Eddie replied much too loudly, forgetting where he was. "There's probably more than a million books here. Who knows? Maybe a hundred million and you're saying we should just start looking here . . ." He pulled his eyes back into his head, grabbed the book nearest him, and opened it like an angry professor who was sick to death of his ignorant students. His eyes focused and then refocused on the words he read. "This book here," he said, looking up at Jamilet, who was nothing less than fascinated, "is about postdepression economics and all the things that have to do with that. It has nothing to do with Spain," he said, pronouncing the "ain" in "Spain" in a long and exaggerated manner meant to emphasize his disgust with this whole business.

Jamilet was clearly impressed with Eddie's command of the written word, and his use of such sophisticated phrases. "What is . . . postdepression economics?" she asked.

Eddie rolled his eyes, irritated once more by the need to explain something so painfully obvious. "It has to do with how people lose their money when they get sad, like when somebody in their family dies or something."

Jamilet thought it very interesting that a whole book should be devoted to such a subject, for she'd known many who'd suffered in just that way. They were widows mostly, like her grandmother who worked the land for a meager living as best she could and accepted the charity of good-hearted neighbors, and the money that her daughter and now granddaughter sent her on a regular basis. "I think I've known a lot of people with postdepression economics," Jamilet said while nodding her head gravely and savoring the words on her tongue. They'd been in the library less than five minutes and already, she'd learned something very interesting.

Eddie narrowed his eyes at her and slammed the book shut, causing Jamilet to jump. "You're wasting my time. I got to be at Pearly's in an hour and if I'm not there she's gonna wonder why."

"Just tell her you were running late. Everyone has the right to be late sometimes, don't they?"

Eddie peered into Jamilet's face, his eyes slowly widening as he did so. "I got it. I just figured out what this is all about." He pointed his finger at her, and shook it. "You want to ruin my life. You woke up one day wherever it was you used to live, and decided to cross the border so you could ruin somebody's life, the first poor bastard you laid eyes on. And I'm the lucky one. That's the real reason you came north, isn't it?"

Jamilet smiled in spite of the small pain his suspicion produced. "That's not the reason I left Mexico," she returned softly.

At that moment the librarian appeared, and promptly instructed Eddie and Jamilet to quiet down or take their conversation outside. Eddie took the opportunity to enlist her help. He tried to explain but Jamilet quickly took over, and in a matter of seconds, the woman was leading them to the far corner of the building. When she located the desired shelf, she retrieved three heavy volumes and laid them on the nearest table, reminding them once more to keep their voices down.

Jamilet took her seat, and waited with chin in hand for Eddie to do the same. Reluctantly, he took the seat across from her and began flipping through the pages of the first book, turning on several occasions to glance at the clock on the far wall, and sometimes flipping through a fair number of pages while looking away entirely. He handled the pages with so much force that at times he nearly tore them out of the book as he muttered, "This is such bullshit . . ." and other things. He asked Jamilet to repeat what she was looking for several times, "The pilgrimage road to Santiago—in Spain."

He continued flipping the pages back and forth, and Jamilet wondered if anybody could possibly read so fast. She observed an older woman sitting near them. Her eyes serenely floated across the page. It took her a long time to turn the page (Eddie had flipped ten or more pages in the same time she took to turn just one), and when she finally did, her eyes landed on the next page like a falling leaf, grateful to have found its resting place.

Eddie was already charging through the last of the three books, shaking his head resolutely, his eyes blank as the pages came and went before them. She anticipated his words, certain that he'd thrust his hands in his pockets as he stood to say them. He pushed his chair back, and was true to her expectations. "There's nothing about that place here," he announced. He even attempted an expression meant to resemble disappointment. "It's probably not a real place."

Jamilet stacked the three books and placed them in front of Eddie, as they'd been before he began. "You didn't read them."

"I did too."

She stared him down with every ounce of character she could muster, just like Tía Carmen did when she was angry, and Señor Peregrino did when she disturbed his papers. The effect on Eddie was the same as it was on Jamilet. His face burned, beginning with his ears, and a watery guilt began to glaze his eyes. He pulled his hands out of his pockets and sat back down with an audible thud. "Damn," he said. "Damn, damn . . . ," he repeated, while looking through the table of contents more carefully this time, and eventually trading anger for concentration as his finger trailed down the column of topics and finally stopped midway down the second page. He opened the book and began to read, not moving or even bothering to glance at the clock for a full minute.

"You found it, didn't you?" Jamilet asked after almost five minutes had elapsed.

He nodded and turned the page like the older lady had done, as if time were hovering, and space had opened up to make the mind forget itself and flounder happily in a newfound dimension.

Jamilet stayed quiet, although she sensed the thrill of his discovery and yearned for it as well. Eddie was able to read about the place in Señor Peregrino's story. He was able to learn about this distant world because he knew how to transform those strange and beautiful little squiggled symbols into something meaningful. It was a wondrous thing, and he was all the more beautiful in her eyes because of it. She gazed openly at him, feasting upon this moment that she knew would pass too quickly. She noticed that his lips twitched slightly while he read and that there was a softness in his eyes that eased in along with the mysterious knowledge he was gaining. She wished to touch her fingers to his forehead and sweep aside a lock of the thick brown hair that seemed to impede his vision, but she kept her hands folded on her lap and waited. Finally, when she could no longer keep quiet, she asked, "Can you read it to me?"

Eddie raised his head and shook it slightly. "Nah, I don't read too good like that." But his earlier apprehension was gone. Jamilet waited a bit more and watched as the expression in his eyes shifted from wonderment to concern and then back to wonderment again. "It's a real place; all right," he said, looking for a strong foothold to begin. "It's old too, like nine hundred years or something . . ."

He reached for the book again, as though to check his figures, and then thought better of it. "People started walking to this big church . . . a cathedral, because they believed that Saint James was buried there. You know," he said, searching for confirmation in Jamilet's eyes, "he was one of those saintly guys that hung out with Jesus, at church and in the Bible, and stuff." He turned a bright shade of red. "I can't believe I'm talking about this."

"Where did people start walking from?" Jamilet asked, ignoring his discomfort.

He gave a resigned sigh. "From all over Europe mostly. Some walked more than a thousand miles to get there. And this was back in the days when they didn't have good shoes or sunglasses or nothing like that. And there were bandits, too." Eddie's eyes began to sparkle. This part seemed to have especially captivated him. "They hid behind trees, like you did the other day, and waited for pilgrims to walk by so they could"—he threw her a cold stare— "ruin their lives. The lucky ones were shot in the head."

Jamilet ignored this. "Why did they go if it was so dangerous?"

"Hell, I don't know," he said. "In those days people believed a lot in miracles and stuff. They believed in all kinds of crazy shit that people don't believe in anymore."

"Like what?"

Irritation started to nip at Eddie's heals. "How should I know? Crazy stuff. Like . . . believing you'll get rid of your warts if you splash holy water on them. Or, that you'll be able to walk even if you've been a cripple all your life, or that your mom won't die if you say a few lousy prayers even when the doctors say she will." Eddie stared hard at nothing for a long moment and then pushed the books away as he prepared to leave. Jamilet would have tried to say or do something to delay him, but she was transfixed by his last comment and was trying desperately to remember if she'd ever said anything to him about her mother's death. She was almost certain that she hadn't.

"Fair's fair," Eddie said, standing up. "I did what you wanted, and now you have to promise to keep your mouth shut."

Looking up at him, Jamilet put on a serious face, like she did when she haggled for chickens at the market near her village. "You didn't tell me a lot and I have more questions, but . . ." She smiled cleverly. "I guess you kept your end of the bargain."

"I don't think you can call it a bargain, exactly. And don't pull this on me again or I might be the one to tell Pearly some stuff. She won't mind calling you out."

"Calling me out?"

"Yeah, she'll jump you if she thinks you're trying to mess with her man," Eddie said with a gleam in his eye.

Jamilet was far too intrigued with the idea that a girl would fight another girl over a boy to react to the threat right away, and Eddie was eager to leave. He mumbled a word or two to announce his departure, not sure that the moment merited much more, and walked away as Jamilet remained still and reflective in her seat. Eddie was almost to the exit when she pushed herself away from the table and ran in the direction he'd gone. She caught up to him at the main entrance and pulled on his shirtsleeve as though she were a child.

He whirled around to face her. "What is it now?"

Jamilet was breathless. "I can't explain it, but I know something about you. I just know." She tried to compose herself. "Your mother's sick, and you're afraid she's going to die and leave you alone."

Upon hearing this, Eddie's face melted before her eyes, and his posture weakened, as though he'd lost his breath and forgotten who he was and where he was going, all at once. "You got to leave me alone, Jamilet," he finally said.

She felt the warmth gushing forth from her heart. She wanted nothing more than to connect with him, and ease his pain somehow. "When my mother died, everyone believed I didn't love her, because I didn't cry at her funeral, but that isn't my way. I just don't cry the same way other girls do." She blinked hard, afraid she might prove herself a liar at that moment, she was so overcome with emotion.

Eddie took several steps back. "Like I said, you got to leave me alone. If you know what's good for you," he added before turning and walking away.

Jamilet watched him for a while. The sun had begun to set, and it appeared as though he were wavering in an ocean of orange light as he made his way to the corner, then turned toward Pearly's house.

"You're good for me, Eddie," she whispered.

After a satisfying supper of chilies rellenos, Carmen relaxed on the couch, nursing her third beer. She was watching *The Price Is Right*, the program she endured until her favorite show came on, *Wheel of Fortune*. Jamilet thought this would be a good time, a perfect time, in fact.

She eased herself down on the couch next to her aunt. "Tía Carmen?"

"Yes, *mi hija*."

"Do you love Louis?"

It took a few moments for her aunt to digest the question. "That old bastard?" she said, her lips curling into a smile. On this night Louis hadn't come over because he wanted to watch his daughter's softball playoffs at Lucas Park. They'd had some words over it earlier and Carmen had slammed the phone down, as was her custom when they argued. But Jamilet had no doubt he'd be by later, after the game, and she'd be awakened in the middle of the night by their reconciliatory ardor.

"I guess I love him," Carmen said.

"How do you know it's love?"

"God, I don't know. How does anybody know?" Carmen swished a mouthful of beer like she was gargling, and swallowed. "I guess it's because when I'm with him I feel so good, I just want to die. And other times I feel so bad, I just want to die." She poked Jamilet's shoulder. "Or kill him. Whichever comes first."

She turned to face her niece. "Why you asking? You got something going on with somebody?"

"No, Tía."

"Because I don't need you coming home pregnant. If you're going to have babies, you'll have to find somewhere else to live. You can come back when the kid's about thirteen."

"I'm not having a baby, Tía."

Carmen eyed her suspiciously. "It's that boy across the street you keep looking at through the window, isn't it?"

Jamilet was shocked that her aunt had noticed when she thought she was being so sly. "I don't look out the window." But her voice was weak and unconvincing.

"Right. And I'm a size-six petite." She cackled and looked hard at Jamilet. "Besides, you could do worse. He looks pretty good to me. I think he looks good to his girlfriend too," she concluded with an all-knowing nod. Carmen turned back to the TV when she heard the music that announced her program. Jamilet stood and hovered about with two empty beer cans ready for the trash. They were just introducing the contestants, and in a few moments the games would begin and the opportunity would be lost.

"Do you think she's pretty?" Jamilet asked suddenly.

Carmen shook her head so her jowls jiggled against the collar of her shirt. "I don't understand all the fuss over Vanna. She's a bleached blonde with a big nose."

"I don't mean the girl on TV. I mean Eddie's girlfriend. The one across the street."

Carmen appeared to seriously consider this question. She cocked her head to one side and momentarily closed her eyes. Then she turned herself fully around to face her niece, looking as though she were about to burst with a secret so tantalizing that she required Jamilet to sit down on the couch to receive it. She tossed the empty beer cans that Jamilet held onto the table, and took Jamilet's hands into her own enormous fleshy palms. "Now listen good, because I'm gonna tell you something some girls learn early and some never learn at all."

Jamilet was speechless. Never had her aunt spoken to her with such compassion. She nodded, her eyes riveted on her aunt's expressive face.

"First I need to ask you something." Jamilet nodded. "Do you think I'm pretty? Be honest, 'cause you know I'll be pissed if you lie."

Jamilet didn't sense one of her aunt's jokes about to rescue her from responding, and pressure was building up in her chest. "I think . . ." She hesitated, feeling her aunt's grip tighten. "I think when you fix yourself up, you look really nice."

Carmen's gaze grew narrow and hot as she repeated, "But, do you think I'm pretty?"

Jamilet's fingers felt sweaty in Carmen's grip. "I . . . I guess not . . . not in the usual way people think of prettiness."

Carmen loosened her grip and her eyes relaxed with intelligent regret, as though she'd been reminded yet again that not only had she not won the lottery, but that her ticket had none of the winning numbers. But she wasn't finished. "Do you think Louis thinks I'm pretty?"

Jamilet thought of the way Louis fawned over Carmen every time he saw her. His eyes ate up every inch of her when she wore one of her revealing dancing dresses, and Jamilet often thought he'd die a happy man if he could just dive in and drown in her cleavage. "He thinks you're beautiful. I know he does. He looks at you the way Eddie looks at Pearly, like he can't remember what day it is or even his own name."

Tía Carmen dropped Jamilet's hands and nodded knowingly, as if she wouldn't have expected anything less. Then she pointed to her own head, still nodding. "It's all in the brains, Jamilet. Don't matter one bit what you look like."

"I don't understand, Tía."

Carmen turned back to her TV show. "Look. You asked me if

I thought Eddie's girlfriend was pretty. The fact is, she *thinks* she's the most goddamn beautiful girl on earth, and that makes her boyfriend believe it too." She waved a pudgy finger toward Jamilet. "And that's all that matters."

Jamilet applied a heavy slathering of her aunt's beauty cream all over her face that night before bed, and dabbed a small amount on the back of her neck where the mark could be seen, like the tip of Africa floating hot and red beneath her shirt. She had to sleep on her back so the pillow wouldn't get sticky with the stuff, but it smelled so good, she closed her eyes and inhaled the sweet fragrance that lingered like hope strung along the darkness on a thin wire.

13

THE RECEPTIONIST, Ms. Clark, was waiting and called out as Jamilet whisked through the front office on her way to the fifth floor. Ms. Clark had to repeat herself, as Jamilet had become unaccustomed to being called "Monica" ever since Señor Peregrino had discovered her true name.

"Nurse B. would like a word with you," Ms. Clark said, her lips flattening as though she tasted something sour. "Go on."

Jamilet hadn't spoken to her employer since her first day on the job, and the few times she had seen her it was only to receive one of the many stiff nods she distributed among the workers she happened to pass during her inspections of the lower floors. She hadn't ventured back up to the fifth floor since the day Jamilet began.

Nurse B. sat at her desk, with hands resting on the surface and fingers taut. She indicated that Jamilet should take a seat in the same chair she'd occupied during her initial interview. "Today," Nurse B. said, looking not pleased, but poised on the verge of irritation, "marks exactly one month since you began your employment. And as promised, I'm prepared to offer you a raise." She shuffled through the papers on her desk, hardly looking at them. When she found the form she wanted, she tossed it across the desk at Jamilet. "I need you to sign here for me if you could and . . ." She looked up, her expression sharpened. "Are you aware that Richard Mentz quit his job?"

"Richard Mentz?"

"The janitor. He's been here for over ten years, and his resignation was quite unexpected." Her hands continued to shuffle aimlessly through the papers on her desk while she studied Jamilet's reaction to the news. "He says he was attacked by the fifth-floor patient while changing a lightbulb. We're not equipped to manage combative patients in this hospital, and I may need to transfer him unless you have any additional information—"

"No, it . . . it wasn't his fault," she blurted out. "The janitor attacked me first."

Nurse B.'s hands became still. "Where exactly did this happen?"

"Up on the fifth floor. Señor Peregrino came out of his room when he heard me screaming. I didn't think a man as old as he could be so strong, but he lifted Richard off me and threw him against the wall. He saved me," Jamilet said, and then dropped her eyes to the unsigned document on the desk.

The color had drained from Nurse B.'s face, and she seemed at a loss for words. "Are you telling me that your patient actually left his room without trembling in fear?"

Jamilet nodded. "I think he was too angry to be afraid."

"How far did he get?"

"I . . . I'm not sure. Just a few steps out of his room, I guess."

"Well, that hardly counts," she muttered to herself, then turned back to her employee. "And why didn't you tell me about this incident, when you were instructed to report any and all problems to me immediately?"

"I . . . I don't know. Señor Peregrino told me to run away and go home, and I was scared."

Nurse B. took the document back from her and paused to think. "You are to refer to the patient by his real name. If you continue to indulge him in his fantasy, you'll only further confuse and upset him. If it weren't for the fact that he seems to tolerate you,

I'd dismiss you immediately for your poor judgment on both these matters; is that clear?"

Jamilet lowered her head. "Yes, Nurse B. It's just that he doesn't respond to any other name."

"That is not the point," she said, rolling her eyes in exasperation. "Do you remember any of your other instructions?"

"I'm to look after his needs, and I'm . . . I'm not supposed to talk with him."

Nurse B. pushed the document over toward Jamilet once again, and leaned across the desk. "The fewer the words that pass between you the better, but he'll try to engage you, believe me he'll try. Perhaps he already has?"

Jamilet reached for a pen and signed the document. She sensed Nurse B.'s growing agitation as the false words slipped over her tongue far too easily this time. "Not yet, but if he does, I'll let you know."

Nurse B. relaxed considerably and leaned back in her chair, her eyes still darting this way and that as she considered other matters. "And if anything else out of the ordinary should happen, you're to tell me immediately. Is that clear?"

Jamilet glanced at the clock. She was several minutes late in delivering Señor Peregrino's breakfast. She could picture him at his desk, wearing a scowl that could frighten a vampire, as he'd made it well known that he didn't appreciate tardiness.

"Excuse me," Jamilet ventured. "But I'm late, and his breakfast will be cold . . ."

Nurse B. understood Jamilet's concern, and waved her out of the room. "Don't forget your instructions, Monica. I guarantee you that I won't be so understanding if this should happen a second time."

Señor Peregrino was sitting at his desk, and he didn't look up from his papers when Jamilet entered the room. She placed the breakfast tray on his bedside table, and waited a moment to see if he would take it in bed, but still, he did not acknowledge her presence.

Jamilet cleared her throat. "I'm sorry I'm late, Señor. Nurse B. wanted to speak with me. I tried to leave as soon as I could."

He swirled around in a flash, his eyes glaring. "What did she want?"

She opened her mouth to answer, but Señor Peregrino cut her off with an agitated wave of his hand. "Don't bother, I already know. She wanted to inform you of Richard's sudden departure, and remind you of the rules regarding my care. Furthermore, she's considered having me transferred to another hospital. Am I right?"

Jamilet nodded, impressed and intrigued by his accuracy.

Señor Peregrino grew weary as he continued to recount the remaining details as surely as if he'd been there. "What's more, she doesn't want you to entertain me in any of my *delusional* talk." He crossed his arms and appraised Jamilet plainly. "And you," he said with a flick of his head, "how did you respond?"

"You don't know?" Jamilet asked, not sarcastic, but genuinely surprised.

"Although I believe that I've almost completely figured you out, there may still be room for error and I'm not in the mood for a guessing game, so won't you please tell me?"

Jamilet proceeded to recount every detail of her response, denying that there'd been any unnecessary conversation, and her commitment to inform Nurse B. of anything else that happened.

"Well done," he said, clearly pleased. "Should I take this to mean that you're learning how to lie?"

Jamilet's eyes felt scratchy and dry, as if she hadn't blinked in several minutes. "I don't know, Señor. But I think she believed me."

"Good." Señor Peregrino went to his bed and sat up against the pillows, as he did when he was ready to receive his tray. Jamilet brought it to him and placed it on his extended legs. "I'm not advocating dishonesty, and I know you're very high-minded about honor." He lifted the cover of his breakfast, and frowned. The eggs were cold and overcooked, but on this morning he didn't complain. "There are times, however, when it is not only advisable, but absolutely necessary, to lie." That said, he stabbed a sausage with his fork and popped it into his mouth, chewing pensively. "I've learned this over the years, and they've been painful lessons."

Basking in their new complicity, Jamilet indulged herself with a question she'd been wanting to ask for some time. "Why do you want me to call you 'Señor Peregrino' if it isn't your real name, Señor?"

He dabbed his mouth with a napkin and pushed his tray away. "You assumed another name in order to deceive, whereas I have chosen my name in order to reveal the truth about who I am and my purpose here." He stroked his chin, while his eyes wandered up toward the ceiling. "I'm not quite sure where I left off with my story. It's been several days . . ."

"You were singing on the steps of the church, and you saw the woman with the red shawl," Jamilet said. "And then you were lost."

Señor Peregrino held up his hand to silence her, his eyes widening as the recollection entranced him once again. "Oh yes," he whispered. "How could I forget? Although often, more than anything else, I have wanted to forget that moment."

※

Who can deny the beauty of the first days of spring, when tender buds begin to yield their secrets, and the sun spreads its glory across the land with unparalleled brilliance? I suppose there are some who when confronted with such beauty are not affected by it. The very same who happen upon the most spectacular of sunsets and continue their daily routines with little more than a glance. I am the sort who stops in my tracks to consider each subtle phase, every errant beam of light that dances across the sky. I am spellbound until the end, and so I was with Rosa.

I didn't speak to her the first day I saw her. I only managed to nod, and smile nervously before looking away. Even so, I remember precisely the way in which her hair reflected the sun like a dark glossy river and I followed its soft light until she disappeared into the crowd. By this time Tomas had found me and his voice implored me, much as a mother's does when waking her child from a dream. "There's a storm approaching," he said. "And if we don't take our lunch quickly and find lodging, it will surely catch us, and we'll have no choice but to sleep in the rain like dogs." Not getting a response, Tomas stood up on the step above mine so we were at eye level. "Do you hear me, Antonio? Or am I speaking to a deaf-mute as well as a fool?"

"Don't be cross with me, Tomas. I prefer your tender assurances to your admonitions."

He lowered his eyes briefly before fixing them back on to my face. "Look around you, Antonio. Look at this work of men inspired by God. Don't you want to be part of this glory?"

Again, I gazed up at the stones of the church that reached to the heavens, twisting as though from the human agony that yearns for divine understanding. And then all at once, I detected a mild breeze that had found its way into the square, as it meandered about the cafés and open windows above the marketplaces along the periphery of the square, carrying with it the aroma of roasting meat and onions.

My stomach grumbled as I clasped Tomas's shoulder, grateful for his friendship and perseverance. "Thank you, my brother. I will not fail, I promise you that. And I will discipline my mind and my body to strengthen itself against life's temptations. Even the greatest of the saints were tempted, weren't they? Even Santiago himself, I would think."

"They all were," Tomas said, exhaling his relief. "And their temptations only served to humble them."

"We're in good company then."

I decided that I would have nothing to do with the beautiful girl in the square, and hoped that she was perhaps an angel who'd alighted from a cloud, only to return to the paradise that had spawned her. At the very least, I suspected that with the throngs of pilgrims everywhere, and the great multitude of walking groups that had already formed their alliances, she wouldn't turn up again. Perhaps she wasn't even a pilgrim, but a local village girl taking a break from her daily routines in order to enjoy the diversion of a song.

But as providence would have it, I soon learned that she was indeed a pilgrim. And it took little investigative work to learn that her name was Rosa and that she was traveling from the south of Spain with her mother, who, like everyone else, was praying for a miracle in Santiago. When I turned away from one group talking about the beauty traveling with her mother, I'd collide with yet another.

It was rumored that they were gypsies and that the girl's green eyes were a gift from a Nordic soldier who'd visited her mother years earlier. Others said she was a spirit, and not at all human, for they'd never seen a mere mortal with skin of such porcelain perfection. Several of the men surmised that if she were a gypsy, then perhaps they could pay her to dance for them, and that if they weren't walking for a holy purpose they might consider paying her for something else.

To my dismay, Rosa's mother befriended Rodolfo when she lanced a nasty blister on his heel, and she and her daughter were invited by the ever grateful Basque giant to join our little group. It was then that Tomas took to watching me out of the corner of his eye, even as we followed the Najerilla River, passing through prime farmland that rivaled that of his family's holdings. While vast stretches of vineyards flanked us on the right and left, he watched me with obvious concern, ignoring what would normally have prompted his animated commentary. The vineyards gave way to fields lined with countless rows of golden haystacks drying in the sun. We knelt and prayed at almost every cross that we encountered, and afterward placed a stone at its base. In some places there could be seen small hills, more like mounds, alongside the road. When we got closer, we could see that these hills were actu-

ally piles of stones that pilgrims over the ages had left as a testament to their journey.

Days passed in this way, and I hardly spoke, and ate even less.
Occasionally it rained, turning the dirt beneath our feet into a
sticky quagmire, but still I walked the path more vigorously than
anyone and was frequently leading our little band of pilgrims along
its route. It wasn't that I enjoyed leading so much, but at the front
of the group I wasn't tormented by the sight of Rosa. Even when
gazing upon the back of her head under the mantle she wore, it
was difficult for me to bear. While the rest of us walked, it seemed
to me that she floated. When she gestured with a delicate arm out
toward the fields to the left or right, pointing out to her mother
something that caught her eye, it became the most sensuous of
dances. She was taunting me with her grace, so it was better for
me to walk ahead, leaving Tomas and Rosa and everyone else in
the dust of my shoes.

We were almost at Santo Domingo de la Calzada, where there
was to be music and other festivities celebrating the miracle of the
hanged innocent. The ancient legend told of a young man who'd
been unjustly accused of stealing by a young lady he'd rebuffed.
He was forthwith hanged, but came back to life when Santiago
intervened. This intrigued me, as I felt a certain kinship with the
hanged man's misery. We were to begin walking at dawn so as
to arrive by noon. Tomas chastised me as he arranged his sleeping blankets next to mine, and spoke to me in a brusque whisper.
"You'll make yourself ill if you continue in this fashion, Antonio."

"I'm as strong as a horse and I'm walking faster than anyone."

"Even a horse needs to eat and rest and pace himself. Don't
think that I don't know what has possessed you, because I do."

I smiled. Tomas never failed to amuse me when he acted the
seer, as he always appeared more worried than wise. I said nothing,
but braced myself for his words, which I knew had been seething
in his breast for almost a week.

"It's the girl with the green eyes and shy smile. I believe she's
been planted in our midst by the evil one in order to turn men's

thoughts away from their holy obligations and toward this un-healthy lust that plagues the foolish."

I spoke softly. "She did not ask to be blessed with such beauty. There's no need to make her out to be the devil."

"And what is physical beauty but a mask that wears with time, only to reveal the humanity of us all? Some of us show our humanity earlier than others, that is all. Have you any idea what she thinks or if her temperament approaches the sweetness of her appearance? While her face is like that of an angel, her heart may be as foul as a demon's."

I was silent as I considered Tomas's argument, and had to admit that I didn't even know the sound of her voice. She was, after all, human like the rest of us, with her faults and foibles. What's more, she required rest and food, and the opportunity to exercise the crudest of bodily functions in order to live. My obsession had conjured up a creature who was not made from the organic substances I knew, but from the mysterious elements that gave light to the stars. Perhaps she was truly a hateful soul, as Tomas had said. It would stand to reason if she was, for if there were a balanced equation of justice in this life, it would demand that one so externally beautiful should be ugly by equal measure on the inside.

Suddenly, I became ravenously hungry and proceeded to eat a healthy slice of cheese with bread and butter, and washed it all down with plenty of wine. That night I slept. I slept like a babe in his mother's arms.

14

IT SEEMED TO JAMILET that all things conjured up in her mind had, like a Popsicle left on a warm sidewalk, melted away. Her stories had become nothing more than a sticky residue that offered her little nourishment or distraction. She missed them most during her walks home from work, when she anticipated seeing Eddie sitting out on Pearly's porch. When they were still with her, they'd begin forming before she actually laid eyes on him, and they'd set the stage for anything that happened or didn't happen between them. A flick of his head became a secret code for their unspoken love, a flutter of his hands, a sign of their surreptitious surrender to passion. But after a few days, and then weeks, without her stories, Jamilet had to accept that they'd left her completely. Once or twice she tried to force the voices back to life, but the result was a strained and feeble sort of internal banter devoid of true emotion, and completely unsatisfying.

She blamed the loss on Señor Peregrino. His story had the power to sustain itself in her mind over time, while her own stories had always vanished within seconds of their conclusion, only to be replenished by fresh, equally disposable tales. Now she thought about Antonio and Tomas and how it must be to walk twenty miles in one day, and how it must feel to be as beautiful as Rosa. It occurred to her that maybe Rosa was not so beautiful after all, but merely thought she was, the way Tía Carmen and Pearly did, and had made Antonio think so as well.

Pondering this as intently as she was, she didn't hear the hollow pounding of Pearly's shoes as she crossed the street, nor did she notice Eddie waiting on the sidewalk for the traffic to clear so he could follow her. Moments later, Pearly's fist slammed into Jamilet's shoulder, forcing her to teeter on one foot before stumbling onto the neighbor's property. She managed to recover her balance while staring into Pearly's eyes—furious brown orbs glaring at her behind layers of mascara. Her face was contorting in many directions at once, while words sputtered out through her glossy purple lips. Her diatribe was interrupted only by the nuisance of having to flick away the strands of hair that kept sticking to her lips.

Slowly, Jamilet started to make sense of the words swarming around her head like so many angry bees. It had something to do with Eddie. Pearly moved in and shoved Jamilet on the shoulder again, and Jamilet crossed her arms over her chest like a penitent about to be baptized. But she was finally able to make out one full sentence: "Stay the fuck away from him!" Then came the blow to her jaw. Jamilet's head twisted around with uncanny speed, and the rest of her body followed. She staggered for a few seconds, arms out as though waking from a drunken dream, then crumpled to her knees onto the dirt. Heat flashed through her eyes, momentarily blinding her. She would have lost consciousness if not for the pain in her jaw, and the white light that hummed and swirled, filling all the spaces in her head. When her vision cleared, she saw Pearly's thick shoes marching up and down the sidewalk, and her toes neatly painted and curled up like ten tiny little fists.

Jamilet inhaled and was strangely comforted. The last time she was this near the earth, she was weeding the chili plants behind her house and creating stories for her own amusement. Any minute now, her mother would call for her to bring a pail of fresh water from the river before it got dark. She was remembering all of this while contemplating the fact that Pearly had not yet finished with her, and by the look of those shoes, which seemed to have been carved out with a crude ax, she realized exactly how the assault would end. Instinctively, she turned away to protect her face, but the blow never came.

Another pair of shoes appeared—Carmen's black Dr. Martens—and they were stepping all over Pearly's clunkers. Carmen was twice as big as Pearly, and with her black hair all frizzed out, she looked like an angry bear protecting her young. She grabbed Pearly by the shoulder, then swung back her arm, as thick as a tree trunk, and swept it across Pearly's face with ferocious strength. Pearly's ankles twisted in their shoes and she screamed, but the blow muffled her voice, making her sound as though she'd swallowed her tongue.

At that moment, Eddie appeared and threw his arms around Pearly so that she was unable to strike back. She struggled in his hold as purple lipstick mixed with saliva dribbled out of the corners of her mouth.

Carmen stood back, breathing hard. "You keep that bitch away from my family!" she said to Eddie.

Pearly screamed, "You keep that bitch away from my man!" She began to sob, and Eddie tightened his hold when it appeared she might struggle free. As they made their way back across the street, Carmen pulled Jamilet up by one arm and spoke low under her breath, but there was no mistaking the shame in her voice. "Don't you know how to throw a punch, girl? What would you have done if I hadn't come home early today?"

Jamilet's jaw ached, and her words slurred, as if she were drunk. "I don't know. I never threw a punch before."

Carmen sighed, but said nothing else until they were in the house. Then she turned on Jamilet, looking as though she was going to finish what Pearly had started. "What you doing with that boy across the street?"

"Nothing, Tía."

"You spend half your life looking for him out the window and his girlfriend wants to rip your head off, and you say nothing."

Carmen was perspiring heavily, and the moisture on her hairline created a tight little row of curls that reached from ear to ear. "Let me tell you something. There's some people you don't fuck with, and she's one of them. I can't keep saving your ass the way I did today, you understand me?"

Jamilet dropped her head. "I'm sorry, Tía," she mumbled.

Carmen went to the refrigerator and was back in seconds with a beer in one hand and a dish towel filled with ice cubes in the other. She inspected Jamilet's jaw and concluded that it wasn't broken, then instructed her to keep ice on it for the next few hours.

It was decided that due to the unusual events of the afternoon, Jamilet would be relieved from her cooking duties. Carmen went alone to Tina's Tacos down the street and returned with their evening meal. The tacos were delicious, as always, but Jamilet was unable to swallow more than a couple of bites. Tears came to her eyes whenever she chewed.

Señor Peregrino was at his desk when Jamilet entered his room. She welcomed the cool darkness of the place, and set the breakfast tray where she did when he was not in bed. She was careful to avoid making the slightest sound because she could see that he was quite absorbed by his papers.

"I'd like you to inform the laundry that my shirts were not properly starched," he said, not looking at her.

Jamilet nodded her understanding and turned quickly to leave. She didn't want to speak more than necessary, as the pain in her jaw was still intense and slightly affected her speech.

"Do you know the difference between light and heavy starch?" Señor Peregrino asked, turning fully around in his chair to face her this time.

"I'm sure I can find out, Señor," Jamilet returned.

"Yes, you do that." He leaned back in his chair. "Wait," he said, and he stood up to open the window wide. The light of day flooded in like a harsh and sudden tide, causing the room to glow. With the light filtering in from behind, and his white hair standing on end, Señor Peregrino looked as if he'd been transformed into an angel. Jamilet's eyes opened wide at the sight of him. She'd never seen him so clearly, the long, chiseled nose and eyes as black as a raven's.

"Someone has struck you, hard," he said.

Jamilet touched the right side of her jaw. The swelling had not reduced as much as she'd hoped, but at least she was able to chew. "Yes," she said.

"Are you in some kind of trouble?" he asked, still glowing like an apparition.

"No, I don't think so . . ." Jamilet hesitated. There was no doubt that Señor Peregrino would insist on an explanation, and the thought of putting her recent agony into words caused her to waver a bit. She had hoped that if she didn't speak about the incident, the memory of it would disappear with the swelling. "The girl across the street thinks I'm trying to steal her boyfriend," Jamilet said. "She hit me when I wasn't looking."

"She must be a big girl . . . strong," he said, somewhat intrigued.

"She's bigger than me, but not bigger than my aunt. Tía Carmen set her straight." Jamilet felt a sensational thrill at being able to recount this part of the story. "She was watching to see how things went and when she saw what was going to happen, she . . . well . . . she set her straight." Jamilet touched her cheek again and allowed the shame of her defeat to silence her. It wasn't right to borrow from her aunt's glory. She looked back to Señor Peregrino expecting to see the shame she'd seen on Carmen's and Eddie's faces, but found instead a strange smile floating there, as incandescent as the light that surrounded them.

Then he did something very strange—he laughed. She'd never heard him laugh before. It sounded like a rusty motor firing up for the first time in years, coughing out the dust of the ages before it could generate a spark. But eventually the thin wheezing in his chest grew into the loud and boisterous roar of laughter that caused the light around them to shimmer.

"You are, aren't you?" he asked, sitting down to catch his breath. His eyes danced, and his skin warmed with this breath of life, causing the tip of his nose and the curve of his forehead to glow a peachy rose.

"I am what?" Jamilet asked. She too felt like laughing, but hesitated, knowing that the pain in her jaw would be excruciating.

"You're trying to steal the girl's boyfriend. You want him for yourself." Señor Peregrino reached for a handkerchief in his pocket and wiped his eyes, moist with glee. "I suggest you admit it to somebody. If you keep it to yourself it'll only drive you mad, and bumps and bruises to the flesh are much more tolerable than the agony of the heart, I assure you."

Jamilet left the doorway and walked into the center of the room, standing in the circle of light as though she were on a stage, auditioning for this strange man who knew her without knowing her. The revelation felt like a deep, hot wound opening in her throat and filling with the disappointment and hope she'd labored so hard to ignore. She swallowed once, but was not able to keep silent. "I dream of being with him."

"Yes . . . ," he said.

"I don't have to look to know he's across the street. I feel it under my skin, tingling and making me cold, like I'm afraid, but I'm not afraid."

"Of course you're not . . ."

"Tía Carmen says I'm not allowed to look out for him through the window anymore, so I haven't gone near—"

"But he's calling to you isn't he?"

"It's worse than before."

"Denying it only makes it worse, my dear. It always does."

Jamilet felt tears dampening the corners of her eyes. She blinked once and they raced down her cheeks in a flash. "I don't know what to do, Señor."

"There's nothing you can do."

Jamilet blinked again and her eyes were cleared by the stark reality of her circumstances. "Tía says I can never talk to him again or even wave. She's afraid Pearly will come after us both, or send her friends."

Señor Peregrino crossed his arms and rocked a bit in his chair, so that it creaked and groaned as he thought about how to answer. "How does this young man feel about you?"

Jamilet chose her words carefully. "I think . . . he . . . feels sorry for me."

Señor Peregrino laughed again, but this time it came smoothly to him and purred through his torso full of steam and vigor. Jamilet smiled meekly, appreciating the result of her words on him.

Still entranced by his own merriment, he indicated that she should sit on the chair next to him. "I am feeling suddenly inspired to continue with my story," he announced. "Breakfast can wait."

Jamilet promptly sat down, and reminded him of where he'd left off. "You were finally able to sleep when Tomas told you that Rosa was just like everybody else even though she was so beautiful. You said that you slept that night like a babe in your mother's arms."

"Peace was mine," he said, leaning back in his chair. "However briefly it lasted, it was mine."

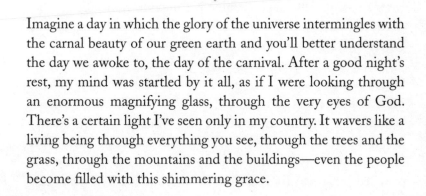

Imagine a day in which the glory of the universe intermingles with the carnal beauty of our green earth and you'll better understand the day we awoke to, the day of the carnival. After a good night's rest, my mind was startled by it all, as if I were looking through an enormous magnifying glass, through the very eyes of God. There's a certain light I've seen only in my country. It wavers like a living being through everything you see, through the trees and the grass, through the mountains and the buildings—even the people become filled with this shimmering grace.

And it is through this light that I saw her. She managed to walk ahead of me that morning, her skirt swishing about her ankles like an undulating sea. I tried to convince myself that I was less captivated than before, and that she did not compare with the delicate wildflowers of the fields, and that her hair was dull when compared to the raven's wing as it caught the sun. We walked at a brisk pace, while Tomas pointed out the beauty along the way, the patchwork of gold and green that spread far beyond the horizon, the medieval churches and stone villages nestled in the valleys of the Rioja looking as if time had been a none-too-frequent visitor, but when my eyes returned to her, my soul was fed.

A number of us arrived at Santo Domingo de la Calzada before noon. We washed our hands and feet at the well outside the village, forgoing a more thorough cleansing as we were eager to be nearer to the music in the square. The sound of the pipes urged us on and put us all in the mood for a celebration. Although I'd attended many such festivals before, my insides were tight with anticipation. I might have convinced myself that it was my love for dance and music that provoked such a state, but I was not so easily deceived. It had everything to do with her. In such a setting, I'd have plenty of opportunities to look upon her and not be concerned with what Tomas or anybody else thought of me. And what's more, I'd concluded that my previous strategy had been all wrong. In denying myself the pleasure of looking at her, I was actually enflaming my senses with greater desire. Perhaps it was wiser to get up close and examine her imperfections, the dirt beneath her nails, and the stench of her body after a long march. Surely then I'd be cured of my obsession.

Once in the square, we ate and drank wine until we were no longer aware of our aching feet. Tomas was careful never to leave my side, but he needn't have worried. I was absorbed by the dancers who spun together in the center of the square, their feet stomping to the infectious rhythm of the *jota*. It had been weeks since I'd danced and my feet began to tap along. All the while my eyes searched constantly for Rosa, but never found her. The next thing

I knew, I was pulled into the circle of dancers, spinning and leaping to the sound of the pipe and drum, until I closed my eyes and became lost in the music. But the *jota* is not to be danced alone, and before long I felt a small, soft hand slip into mine. Delicate as it was, I imagined it to be Rosa's hand. I dared not open my eyes, as we danced splendidly, our bodies flowing together as if we'd been born of the same musical spirit. When the music stopped, we stood, still facing each other, catching our breath, and that is when I opened my eyes. Rosa's face, only inches from mine, began to melt away, until it was not into her eyes that I gazed, but into the twinkling eyes of one of the sisters from France. She giggled and whispered that she'd once been a wonderful dancer. I smiled back and assured her that she still was.

I was unable to sleep that night. Even the moonlight that slipped through the window tormented me. That, and the knowledge that perhaps only a few feet away, on the same slat of wood upon which I rested, she rested as well, for this *refugio* was large enough to accommodate separate sleeping quarters for men and women.

Tomas fell asleep almost instantly. I tried to follow the rhythm of his slumber to find my own rest, but tossed and turned for a long while. It didn't help that the chamber was alive with snorts and snores and whistles in every key, a grumbling symphony of exhaustion for a frustrated audience of one. I slipped out of the room with my blanket wrapped around my shoulders, and made my way to the outer courtyard where it was bright with the blue light of the moon. I was drawn toward the small church across the square. The moon shadows created by the rough-carved statues of saints and the pilgrim saint himself seemed to beckon me. He looked down upon me from his concave perch with his staff held high, as though he might knock me over the head with it. I welcomed the beating if it would earn me a moment's peace.

The night was cold, but rather than entering the church, I chose to go around back to the graveyard. I sat on a large flat stone and prayed. I prayed for God to give me the courage to pluck the very eyes out of my head if it would help me regain my strength and purpose in life. As I prayed, the night grew strangely warm and comforting, as though I were being gathered into a mysterious embrace. I shrugged off my blanket, and was preparing to remove my shirt as well when I saw a lone figure at the edge of the grave-yard. Instantly, I recognized her, and as she approached, the hem of her skirt whispered with the dry leaves it swept over the tombs. Her eyes glowed a soft and misty color, and they held me so pow-erfully that when she stopped before me, only inches away, I didn't have the presence of mind to stand, as I knew I should.

"You're perspiring," she said. "Are you ill as well?"

The whole of my being shuddered. Had I been honest, I would have told her that I was sick with love for her and was very likely near the point of death, but somehow I managed a coherent if banal reply. "The night is warm. That is all."

She said nothing more, but turned away to walk among the tombs. She headed down the darkened path that led to an open field that earlier that day in the bright sunlight I'd seen alive with wildflowers and bees. She held her arms out to keep her balance on the stones, but made no sound, as though she were not a girl, but a spirit rising from the earth. I felt compelled to follow her, and stopped at the edge of the field to watch as she picked wildflowers and collected them in her shawl. She motioned that I should come nearer, as her shawl was beginning to overflow. I couldn't breathe for the pounding of my heart, which propelled the blood through my veins with the force of a cannon. I didn't see an innocent young girl picking flowers. She was a seductress, naked and expectant beneath her clothes, kneeling on the bed of the earth, teasing me with her physical perfection like a cruel baker tempts the hungry with fresh-baked bread. Quivering and sullen, I swallowed the de-sire that surged like bile in my throat. This girl, with her green eyes and pink lips, had the power to make me into a monster. She could skin the life off my bones by slipping her hand down the length of her hip and thigh as if searching for nothing more than a coin between the folds of her skirts.

Suddenly Tomas's warnings came roaring back into my head. It took every ounce of strength I possessed to turn away and return to the church. The night became cold again, and when I arrived at the *refugio*, I was shivering although sweat poured down my back. I don't believe I was ever more afraid in all my life.

15

LOUIS HAD BEEN STAYING over almost every night, and Carmen was giddy with happiness because of it. She was in such a good mood that occasionally she was moved to helping Jamilet with the evening meal. It was while peeling potatoes at the sink that she told her about Louis's wife, who had gone back to Mexico to look after her sick mother, taking her three daughters with her. She doubled over the sink and lowered her voice so Louis, who'd been dozing on the couch, wouldn't hear. "I hope she catches whatever disease the old lady has and dies herself," she said, and a slow grin stretched across her face as she fully appreciated the possibility.

Jamilet took the potato from her aunt's clenched fist. She'd been fingering it while chatting, and had made little progress. "What about Louis's daughters? If their mother died, Louis would have to be both father and mother to them."

Carmen's grin twisted and fell. She quickly grabbed a nearby dish towel and began to dry her hands, pulling on each finger as though she were trying to remove a number of rings that were too small. "Oh God, I don't know." She tossed the dish towel back on the counter. "You always make things so goddamned serious, Jamilet. Is it so bad to dream a little?"

Jamilet shrugged. "I guess not."

"I guess not," Carmen mimicked in a high-pitched voice. "You got a way about you, girl," she said, no longer bothering to moderate her voice for Louis's sake. "You take the fun out of everything, you know that?"

"I'm sorry, Tía. I don't mean to."

The scowl eased off Carmen's face. "I know you don't," she said with a sigh. "Your mother was just the same." She retreated to her bedroom without another word. She and Louis were planning to go out dancing for the night, and Carmen would need an hour or more to get ready. Her hair took her the most time. She liked to wear it high for special occasions, and pull curls down around her face. This way, she said, she looked taller and thinner. Jamilet thought it looked as if she had a hairy volcano on her head, but Louis loved it and told her she looked like a movie star, and every time a different one.

As Jamilet proceeded to peel and chop the onion, she didn't notice Louis get up from the couch and come into the kitchen. "I love it when your aunt's happy like this," he said leaning on the counter. "I feel like a young man again when she's so happy. I don't know what it is, but there's no one who can make me feel like she does."

Jamilet nodded and smiled. There was no arguing about Carmen's ability to change the weather with her moods. For the last couple of weeks they'd been graced with sunny skies and light breezes, without a cloud in sight. And Louis's presence made things all the better. With his easygoing manner and way of smiling past all upset, he diluted Tía's intensity to a lingering sweetness with just enough zing to make it interesting. When Louis was in the house, Jamilet could relax, and trust that things would always work out somehow. She wondered if that was the reason women liked having a man around, although she was certain that not all men were like Louis.

"Your aunt told me what happened the other day," he said, flicking his head toward the window. "With that girl." His eyes were pained, and he tugged at his mustache in an effort to get more of it in his mouth.

Jamilet colored visibly and continued chopping the onions with a steady hand. She inhaled and her eyes stung. "It was nothing," she said.

Louis sucked on his mustache for a while and carefully traced one nail under his other nine fingernails, flicking the residue onto the counter with every swipe. When he spoke there was such tenderness in his words that Jamilet felt compelled to set down her knife and face him. "I have three girls," he said. "And I watch out for them pretty good most of the time. They don't get in too much trouble with me around." He crossed his arms and glanced away nervously when he realized he had Jamilet's undivided attention. "I tell them to watch what they wear. I don't like my girls to go out looking like streetwalkers." He appraised Jamilet kindly, her long white blouse and the baggy sweats she exchanged for a navy skirt when she went to work. "I'm gonna tell you something different from what I tell my girls. I'm gonna tell you that you should fix yourself up a bit, okay? You're pretty and all, but if you want that boy across the street or any boy to notice you . . ." He shut his mouth tight, rethinking what he'd just said, and frowned. "You know what I mean?" he asked weakly.

Jamilet nodded as she knew she should, but hopelessness welled up inside. She felt suddenly sick, as if Pearly had taken an open kick at her belly and knocked the wind out of her all over again.

"Don't take it wrong," Louis said. "There's nothing wrong with you . . ."

"It's okay," Jamilet said, and she even attempted a smile.

"Carmen can take you shopping downtown."

"I'll ask her," she quickly responded.

Louis hung his head, then brightly snapped his fingers, pointing at Jamilet's face. "I know what," he said. "My girls have clothes they don't wear anymore. They're about your size. I'll bring some by for you." His eyes were watering with pity for her, and Jamilet felt the upset in her stomach ease a bit. How could he know that she was different from his daughters? That she couldn't waste time and energy on the normal concerns girls her age had about clothes and makeup and other things?

"Next time I come I'll bring the clothes," he said, and he placed a warm hand on her shoulder, right on the edge of the mark where the deep purple turned to red and then faded into a crisscross of tiny veins.

A couple of days later a paper bag appeared next to Jamilet's bedroom door. She emptied it on her bed and found several sleek little shirts in all colors, with stripes and gold piping. There was a short hot pink skirt she liked best, and a pair of high-heeled shoes similar to the ones Pearly wore except that these were white and had a black buckle when there was no need for a buckle. It was just for show.

Jamilet kicked off her loafers and tried the shoes on first. They were slightly too big, but she was able to adjust the straps and walk in them just fine. She looked down on herself and liked the way her ankle appeared, so slim and feminine. Next she stepped out of her navy skirt and slipped into the hot pink number. Again a little big, but a decent fit. Filled with excitement, she unbuttoned her blouse, almost popping a few buttons in the process, and selected a top with capped sleeves that slipped off the shoulders in an alluring slump. She'd seen Pearly wear shirts like this before. She was always pulling up at the sleeves just to let them fall again, mesmerizing Eddie with the smooth flesh of her shoulders that was covered and uncovered all the time. The shirt fit perfectly, snug and secure over her torso, the way it should. She could feel her hair just brush her bare shoulders, and imagined this was how it would feel if Eddie were kissing her there.

Even though she knew Carmen and Louis wouldn't be home for another hour or two, she peeked out of her bedroom door just to make sure, and ran as fast as her three-inch heels would allow her, down the hall and into the bathroom, where she closed and locked the door behind her.

She admired her reflection in the semidarkened room. In the gray light, the contour of her form, although somewhat thin, appeared well proportioned, the shape and length of her limbs graceful and pleasing to the eye. She struck a variety of poses, then imagined herself walking down the street as she collected admiring glances and catcalls from all the men who saw her, young and old alike. She continued to stare at her reflection from every angle until the encroaching darkness made it impossible for her to see anything but a sinewy outline against the white tile of the wall behind her.

When she was barely able to see even her hand in front of her face, she flipped on the switch and the bathroom was flooded with the cruel fluorescent light, forcing her eyes closed, until slowly she was able to open them again. Licks of red flesh reached over her shoulders like evil fingers. She need only turn a quarter of the way around and the burning stamp on the back of her legs was clearly visible. Down her arms and down her back it glowed and pulsated like a separate living thing, with its own will and its own mind. Sometimes Jamilet wondered what the mark would say if it could talk. She imagined it weeping and groaning most of the time. When it did manage to speak, it would say that it was as strong as it was ugly and for that reason alone it deserved to live. When that didn't convince her, it would say that it had rescued her from vanity, and the meaninglessness of an ordinary life. Without it, she'd undoubtedly be living in the village where she was born, married to a drunkard who'd saddled her with five children to feed, maybe more.

Back in her room, she examined the rest of the clothes carefully, concluding that with the exception of a purple shirt with long sleeves and a scoop neck, every piece would reveal significant portions of the mark. She would wear the purple one when she had an opportunity, and never forget to serve Louis his dinner with the chopped cilantro on the side, as he preferred to eat the green herb before it had wilted. Not that he complained. Louis never complained.

The heavily starched shirts had been hung neatly in the closet, long sleeves on the left and short sleeves on the right. The fine leather shoes were organized from dark to light, and Jamilet liked to arrange socks that matched, tucking them inside the shoes the way she saw them do in the windows of the fancy department stores. She often wondered why he bothered with shoes when he never ventured outside.

"You're proving to be quite a reliable worker," he said, glancing up from his papers.

"Thank you, Señor."

Jamilet proceeded to go about her duties, tidying up the bed-sheets, wiping the counters in the bathroom, and emptying the trash. She knew that when Señor Peregrino was at his desk, she wasn't likely to hear any more of his story until later that same afternoon, if she was lucky. Sometimes several days might pass before he was prompted back into that unique reverie from which his story emerged.

Jamilet came in from the bathroom with an armload of clothes she planned to take to the laundry after returning his lunch tray later that afternoon. She dropped the bundle of clothes on the floor and knelt to separate the darks from the lights.

"Yes, indeed," Señor Peregrino said. "You are an excellent worker, and one day I will reward you for your good work."

Jamilet's thoughts instantly went to her documents, which were undoubtedly hidden somewhere in the room, perhaps in the same drawer where he kept his papers. She was tempted to tell him that returning her documents was the only payment she'd ever want, but bit her tongue. "I'm paid fairly for my work here, Señor," she said, and then brightened. "But, perhaps if you con-tinue with your story . . ."

He smiled with the satisfaction of an elder statesman recon-
firmed to office. "Ah yes. I believe you've grown fond of my little
tale."

Jamilet stood up and brushed off her knees. Concern shadowed her small face. "It's a very good story, Señor, but is it all
true?"

He appeared affronted, and puffed up a bit. "Of course it's
true, every word or may God strike me dead at this very moment."
To punctuate his challenge, he held out his arms as though ready
to receive the deadly thunderbolt. Then, his arms dropped down
to his sides, and a drowsy smile emerged on his face. He was anticipating the delicate feast that his memory offered him. He enjoyed traveling nimbly through corners already turned, skipping
over rocks that had once caused him to stumble.

Jamilet needed no invitation to sit, and started him off, as it
was becoming her habit to do. "You thought Rosa was the devil,"
she said with the confidence of one who'd been there herself. "You
said you were never more afraid in your life."

When I closed my eyes to sleep that night, I couldn't rid my mind
of the image of this woman at once so beautiful and so terrifying,
the perfect trap to ensnare me. I thought of her still out in the
field with her nightshirt open at the throat. What was she doing
picking flowers in the night? Who ever heard of such foolishness?
I laughed out loud at the absurdity of it. My close brush with evil
seemed to have caused a momentary insanity.

I woke Tomas with my laughter, and told him of my encounter
in the graveyard. Together we prayed into the night, beseeching
our fatigue to leave us, lest she come into our very beds and take
us both, for Tomas readily confessed that he had dreamed of her
as well. In his dream her dress fell from her shoulders to reveal her
breasts, like two white doves fluttering their wings and blinding
him with their beauty. He longed to touch their feathery softness,

but just at the moment he reached out his hand, the wind blew so violently about them, that the clothing was torn from both of their bodies, and they stood naked before each other. Tomas said he felt the wickedness inside him like a wild beast he was unable to tame. "The devil has visited us both," he said.

We vowed not to look her way during the remainder of our journey. Our plan was to wake very early, before the rest of the group, in order to assure ourselves that she would be nowhere near us. We barely spoke to each other as we marched on the next morning. We passed through green fields glistening with dew, each drop capturing the sunrise like a tiny prism, but we hardly noticed, so solemn were we in our resolve, so shaken by the events of the previous night. We stopped only once for a hasty meal of bread and cheese, but I sensed her behind us on the trail, and as much as I tried to control my thoughts, I pictured her among the other pilgrims, that creamy oval face embedded with emeralds. She would be walking as she always did, with her mother on her arm, for the older woman appeared to be weakening from the journey.

Our destination being San Juan de Ortega, we passed through several small woods on the way and found little comfort in the cool shade of the trees, although the day was quite warm. When I laid eyes upon the cliffs that were known to have once been inhabited by hermits, I longed to climb the precipice and crawl into one of their dark holes so that I too might feed my loneliness. Not far from that place, we came upon several pairs of storks nesting high upon the rooftops of the village houses, and I wondered jealously at their lifelong commitment to each other, and at their tender dedication to their young. When we arrived at the *refugio*, our only contentment was to find that we were the first pilgrims of the day. We'd have our choice of spots to lay our bedding and a thorough wash at the well without concern that it should run dry, as it often did toward the end of the day. Nevertheless, we headed directly for the chapel in the central square and knelt down to pray with the dust of the road covering us from head to foot. Tomas's face was streaked with tears, his lips moving with half-formed words. He appeared so fragile and spent, I was afraid he might not be able to endure the journey, let alone the temptation of this woman.

We washed and ate our meal under the spell of the solemn mood with which we'd walked that day, and continued with our plan to sleep, wake early the next morning, and every morning thereafter. With any luck, we'd put days and miles between us and Rosa's group. This we confirmed with half phrases and knowing nods, too exhausted to formulate complete sentences. Our fear spoke for us.

But we were not so lucky. As we made our way across town to our beds, we saw the first of our group entering the square. It was the Basque man, Rodolfo, red faced and exhausted from his trek. He spotted us before we could duck into the *refugio*.

He said gruffly while taking my arm, "We could have benefited from the gift of your song today, Antonio." He turned to Tomas. "The reassuring calm of your presence. The young man died in the night," he said in a hoarse whisper.

"Renato?" Tomas asked, taking hold of Rodolfo's arm this time.

Rodolfo nodded, his eyes awash with sobering sadness.

"But he was doing so well," I said.

"He was going to Santiago to pray for his father's redemption," Tomas said to himself, remembering their early conversations.

"The others should be arriving in an hour or two. I ran ahead to get things ready for the burial. You see," he said, relieved to be sharing the burden, "we've been carrying the body with us for a proper burial. Will you help me talk to the innkeeper, Antonio? We were told he could help in matters like these if the priest were not available." This giant man with arms as big as tree trunks implored me with a child's eyes, wide and pleading. Feeling more than my fair share of guilt for having abandoned him and the others at such a time, I instantly agreed to help and informed him, having just come from the church, that the priest wasn't due back for another few days. The innkeeper would have to do.

Several hours later the rest of the pilgrim group arrived carrying the corpse on a makeshift litter between them. After my eyes had taken in the view of the dead, they immediately searched for the living beauty among them. I found her trailing at the end, radiant with the flush of exercise, her mother leaning heavily on her arm.

The next day we stood around the grave, freshly dug by Rodolfo and me, as the grave digger was nowhere to be found. The afternoon sun had succumbed to a fragrant light drizzle as delicate as a child's tears, which wet the old tombs around us, turning them a dark gray. The space of light we shared was shrinking and the shadows were closing in upon us as the day gave way to the night. I stood next to Tomas, head bowed, as was his. I heard the garbled words of the innkeeper and forced myself into prayer. But I knew she was to the right of me, her red shawl wrapped close against the chill. In half a glance I detected an unusual darkness in her eyes, which smoldered. Immediately, I recalled Renato's conversation one day soon after Rosa had joined the party. He was sure he'd never laid eyes on a girl more alluring. He'd laughed about it, wanting to appear robust and ready like the rest, although his lips remained pale and thin. Perhaps his last thoughts before death had also been of her, the curve of her slender throat and that small smile that could light up a ridge of mountains like a hundred suns.

At that moment she glanced up and caught me staring at her, and all at once she was surrounded by a golden light. I looked around to see if perhaps the sun had broken through the clouds, but they had only thickened. She nodded sadly to me, as though to acknowledge our mutual grief, but I could not respond. I was mesmerized by this mysterious light and realized that it emanated not from above or behind, but from inside her. Overwhelmed by the sight, I looked away, and didn't dare turn to look in her direction for the remainder of the service. Tomas had not lifted his gaze from his shoes. He'd stayed truer to his convictions than I.

We returned to the *refugio* after the burial with plans to retire. Tomas was cold as ice, and my concerns for his health were renewed. I covered him with my blanket as well as his own.

I was certain he'd drop off to sleep instantly and that I'd have a moment to collect my thoughts, yet his voice was overcome with emotion when he said, "She was up all night. That's why her eyes look so black with fatigue."

"What are you talking about, Tomas?"

He appeared even more tormented than the day before. "Rodolfo told me all about it while you were making arrangements for the burial. He told me that Rosa was up all night looking for herbs that might cure Renato's fever. She was by his side the entire night and didn't sleep to make sure that when he asked for water he had it, when he complained of cold she could stoke the fire. It was in her arms that he breathed his last."

My head began to spin with the realization. "So it wasn't flowers she was picking in the moonlight."

Tomas sat up, spellbound. "While we were up all night praying for God to protect us from the evil of this woman—"

"She was up all night doing God's work," I said.

"What are we to do, Antonio? When I close my eyes I see her face, I see those eyes and that hair and—"

"I don't know, but we can't allow our fears to control us. No matter the cost, we must not lose our composure."

That night we prayed as never before, and neither of us slept.

Señor Peregrino turned to Jamilet as he spoke these last words. The quiet of the room seemed to pulsate in the wake of his story. Then, his black eyes opened to appraise her sitting there with one hand covering her mouth, looking as though she might burst. "What is this?" he asked, disbelief creasing his brow. "Are you laughing at me?"

Jamilet squirmed in her seat and pressed her hand more tightly over her mouth, afraid that if she attempted to speak, she'd howl with laughter instead.

His eyes narrowed and his lips tightened with disdain. "Answer me, young lady. What is it that you find so amusing?"

Somehow, she managed to regain her composure and lower her hand, but it was impossible to erase the guilty smile on her face. "I'm sorry, Señor. Please don't think I'm being disrespectful. It's just a . . . a little funny to think of how scared you and Tomas are of a young girl, even if she is so beautiful."

He almost spat out his words. "I'm an old man now, but when I was young, men and women were different with each other. There was respect and . . . and reverence."

"I understand, Señor."

"Do you?" He smirked as his eyes swept over her from head to toe. "You live in a world where it's not unusual for a young woman to give herself to any man who offers her a . . . a six-pack of beer, and a . . . a ride in his car."

"Señor," Jamilet gasped. "I'd never do that."

He folded his arms across his chest and nodded as though burdened by the weight of too much wisdom. "You'd save yourself quite a bit of heartache if you stayed away from beer *and* boys until you're old enough to know that one should never persuade you in the other."

"I may be young, and there are many things I don't know, but I'm not like other girls," she returned with equal disdain. "And, I don't even like beer."

He met her firm gaze and held it, but eventually his arms unfolded and his palms spread out over his knees. For a moment Jamilet thought she saw regret shadow his expression, but he remained silent.

She stood to collect the laundry and paused. "I've been wondering, Señor, why are you telling me this story?"

He reached for a page on his desk and allowed his eyes to linger there, as if caressing every word. "I, like you, do not know many things. Although I don't have my youth to blame." His eyes grew misty and he turned to his papers again. The spare light of morning he liked best wouldn't last long.

16

WITH SPRING JUST AROUND THE CORNER, the window in Señor Peregrino's room stayed open most of the time, and a pleasant breeze, fragrant with flowers and fresh-cut grass, reached the fifth-story window. Jamilet often stood near it looking out and commenting on the pleasant weather, and how nice it would be to stroll the grounds and take a meal under the shade of the biggest tree, where there happened to be a welcoming bench. She couldn't imagine how a person could live in one room for so long and she knew that it would do him a world of good to venture out, but Señor Peregrino rarely responded to this talk. Once he replied that he would leave his room at the appointed hour and no sooner, no matter how much she suggested he do otherwise. When Jamilet asked him what he meant by "the appointed hour," he said nothing, and turned his attention back to his papers.

"You'll know soon enough," he muttered when she thought he'd forgotten the question.

It was while clearing the lunch tray one afternoon that Jamilet noticed Señor Peregrino watching her from his desk as he rolled a pencil between his palms. He'd been unusually pensive that day, and had eaten very little of his breakfast or lunch. Jamilet assumed he wasn't feeling well. "Leave that, and come here, Jamilet," he said.

"The kitchen will close, Señor."

"Please," he said with a nod. "The kitchen can wait."

Jamilet took the seat next to his desk, and Señor Peregrino pushed the papers he usually studied aside, and proceeded to retrieve several blank sheets from his desk drawer. Then, addressing Jamilet in a solemn tone, he said, "I understand the reason for your sadness."

"I . . . I'm not sad, Señor. I'm just serious most—"

He raised his finger. "Don't waste your nonsense on me, young lady. Any fool can see how you drag your grief around like a fifty-pound weight."

Jamilet was stunned by his words, and by the realization that her eyes were swelling with tears. She swiped at them quickly, hoping that Señor Peregrino wouldn't notice. She held her breath and concentrated on holding back the pressure building up behind her eyes, but she couldn't swallow to save her life.

"There's no shame in releasing your sadness, my dear," he said tenderly. "No shame at all in that."

Jamilet covered her face with both hands as wave after wave of emotion rolled through her, flooding her soul and pounding against her rib cage, until she could hardly breathe. It seemed that the tears she'd been saving all her life came forth at that moment. She was back again, as a child walking to school, hearing the doctor proclaim that there was no cure for the mark, at her mother's deathbed, and finally, crossing the river alone, with the cold rushing through her as everything she knew of the world, every shred of hope she'd managed to gather up, threatened to wash away.

Jamilet sniffled behind her hands, and Señor Peregrino shuffled to the bathroom and returned with a large wad of toilet paper that he placed on her knee. Without looking up, she wiped her face, feeling as though most of the life had been squeezed out of her. But there was a shimmering sensation coursing throughout her body as well. She felt wonderfully light and free, and when she took a breath it felt deeper and fuller than it ever had before.

"Do you feel better?" he asked.

Jamilet nodded, and looked around for a place to throw out the tissue.

Señor Peregrino took it from her and tossed it in the waste-basket under his desk while saying, "There's no need for anymore tears, because I'm going to help you." He turned to the blank paper on his desk and arranged it in neat rows, and Jamilet saw that the pages were not entirely blank, but that on each one was written a single letter in the corner. "Starting today, we'll take an hour, maybe two, out of each day for the purpose of my teaching, and most important, your learning how to read and write."

She stared at him for several seconds, unable to speak.

"Are you agreeable to this plan?"

Jamilet nodded, obviously shaken and moved by all that had just taken place. "You would do this for me?"

"I told you that I'd reward you for your good work, and I am a man of my word."

They began the first lesson immediately. Señor Peregrino instructed her to repeat the letters of the alphabet after him. Jamilet felt so awkward and eager, and overwhelmed with gratitude, that occasionally she stumbled, but by the end of the first week of lessons she'd memorized the entire alphabet in both English and Spanish, and was beginning to copy the letters next to his examples quite nicely. Although at times impatient, Señor Peregrino took obvious pleasure in his student's progress. Her best work he posted on the wall by his desk, and her worst he crumpled up and threw in the wastebasket in a huff. There were days when the trash was brimming with discards, but most of the time, the silence of their studies was interrupted only by the gentle sounds of paper ruffling on the wall when the breeze found its way through the open window.

Following the lesson, Señor Peregrino often found himself in the mood to continue with his story, just as he did after the first lesson, and Jamilet was grateful for the opportunity to rest her mind, and relax for a while.

His eyes grew soft as they focused on the far corner of the ceiling. "Let's see now, where was I?" he said. "Oh yes, the place where you found the agony of two young men so amusing."

"I did apologize, Señor."

"Yes, yes, of course," he said, waving the whole issue away. He was trying his best to remember where he'd left off.

Jamilet moved her chair closer. "Tomas couldn't sleep," she said. "You told him that whatever the cost, you had to stay in control, and not lose your composure."

"Ah," he said, clearly impressed. "The infallible memory of youth."

With each day that passed, Rosa grew lovelier in our eyes. I'd awaken every morning thanking God that he'd given me another day to gaze upon her, perhaps to exchange a glance or a word or two in greeting. When she was near, I felt a pleasant and peaceful sensation within me, but no longer did I believe that there was an invisible quivering string connecting her soul to mine.

Tomas, however, was as tormented as ever. If Rosa should pass by to fill her canteen at the well, he'd almost stop breathing in an effort to resist her. I couldn't help but laugh at those moments. "You have cured me, my friend," I said as we walked side by side. "You have become the mirror I sorely needed, and I see now that there is no reason for such lovesickness."

I started singing again, and many walked with us during the long miles in order to hear my musical veneration for all pilgrims, each with a singular purpose for walking the same path worn and hardened by pilgrims for nearly a thousand years. As we approached the midpoint of our journey, we were astounded by the immense flatness of the Castilian Meseta before us, and could see the land dotted by red-tile roofs that grew more numerous as we journeyed closer to the large and prosperous city of Burgos.

"The miles go by quickly when you sing," Rodolfo said. He was no longer as big as he'd been when he started. The walk had

taken at least thirty pounds from him, but his arms were still thick
and able and his neck the size of most people's thighs. Rosa lingered nearby as well. I know she liked my singing, but if I noticed
her stepping in accord with the cadence of my song, my heart did
not beat any stronger because of it. I thanked God for the freedom
I felt. I could gaze upon her and, unlike Tomas, still remember my
name and the place to which we were headed.

Everywhere we stopped to rest the pilgrim group changed.
Some pilgrims lagged behind due to injury or simple exhaustion.
Others shortened their rest to join our group, wishing to be part of
the joyful atmosphere we exuded. Sometimes young men studied
the female pilgrims who passed, for reasons that had little to do
with religious piety, and everything to do with their youthful lust,
enflamed by the loneliness of the road. Fortunately for us, Rosa
dressed modestly. With her red shawl over her head, these oppor-
tunists hadn't a clue to the rare jewel in our midst.

But one afternoon the sun beat down so vigorously upon us
that she was forced to carry her shawl slung low on her hips. I
daresay that even the birds flew more slowly over us as though
to appreciate the uncommon perfection of our species. At midday, when the heat of the sun was at its strongest, we arrived at
Burgos. Despite our thirst and fatigue, we made our way through
the labyrinth of the city toward its famous cathedral, larger and
grander than anything we had ever seen. We refreshed ourselves at
a nearby fountain intended for pilgrims, as indicated by the relief
of scallop shells at its base.

At first, we didn't notice the soldiers idling in the shadows
on the cathedral steps, but when we saw them our little band instinctively closed in around Rosa, like a herd protecting its young.
but we weren't quick enough. Almost instantly they started to stir,
nudging each other, and glancing our way. They were hungry li-
ons, conspiring and evaluating the herd before the attack. It didn't
take long for them to strike.

Moments later the sound of heavy boots could be heard
pounding across the square. Their gray uniforms were soiled from

the road, but the pistols and swords that hung from their belts shone brilliantly. Three of them made their way toward the fountain, their eyes riveted upon the prize, while dismissing the rest of us much like fodder to be kicked aside. Tomas was nearly trembling when the apparent leader, a tall blond man with shoulders as wide as a bull's horns, approached her first. Some of the soldiers stood behind, chuckling, while others retreated to a nearby café, poised and ready to watch the spectacle from their tables.

Rosa was helping her mother wash up at the fountain, and as usual, she was unaware of the commotion she caused. Yet we were all concerned to see that the soldier was obviously planning to speak directly to her, for it was not customary for a man to address a woman unless they'd been properly introduced, especially in a public place. The only women who were addressed so casually were women in the business of being . . . well, in the business.

His words startled her, and she dropped her red shawl to the ground. The soldier wasted no time in retrieving it. With a click of his heels, he presented it to her, and she accepted it with a nod as her cheeks flushed in a lovely way. Encouraged, he leaned toward her, not knowing which part of her to devour first. He reached out and touched her hair and Tomas groaned. My own stomach bolted, and I was aware of a smoldering deep and quiet within me, untended but ready.

Rosa stepped back, and her hair slipped out of his hand. He seemed amused by her discomfort and took the opportunity to admire her from this new vantage point. At that moment, Rosa's mother took hold of her daughter's arm and pulled her away. But they nearly collided with another soldier who'd been watching and waiting in case his services were needed. Although we were unable to hear their exchange, he had obviously addressed the older woman in a cordial manner, as he bowed his head, and he was successful in engaging Rosa's mother in conversation, a task not difficult to accomplish. With the mother's attention diverted, the blond man stepped forward again. He said that his name was Andrés and then pointed to the table his companions had already secured. He wanted her to join him for a glass of wine, perhaps a little lunch. Rosa declined his invitation with a furtive shake of her head. Her back was turned to us, but I could well imagine her face, luminous and polished as the moon, her eyes a flickering green. She could enchant a hermit monk with a half-smile, or a shrug of her dainty shoulders.

And so it was that the soldier began to melt before our very eyes. His mouth dropped, as though he'd suffered a sudden stroke, and his brow became shiny with perspiration. He trembled in his boots as he listened to her sweet, melodic voice making excuses perhaps, or explaining nervously about needing to remain with her sick mother. Feeling more confident, she maneuvered the red shawl over her shoulders so that her hair became caught in its embrace. Then she lowered her head and walked away. I'd seen her end many a conversation in this manner, and every time the conversant was left pondering his or her recent exchange with an angel. But this young man was not accustomed to having a peasant girl, however beautiful she might be, leave him with his words in his mouth. As she turned he took hold of her shawl and playfully pulled it away. Her eyes flashed as she whirled about.

Tomas, who'd been quivering and muttering his disapproval over the whole scene, stood up. "We must do something, Antonio," he said.

I looked about the square. Every other soldier and pilgrim in sight was watching the dance that ensued between Rosa and the soldier. She reached for her shawl and he reached for her hand. She tried to retrieve it, he stepped closer. She stepped away, he placed his free hand on her elbow. She protested, he laughed.

Tomas launched himself out into the square, nearly tripping on feet depleted from a twenty-mile hike while he cried out, "That is enough of that!"

The soldier took a moment to appraise Tomas, and a wry smirk cut across his chiseled face as he calculated that he probably outweighed him by fifty pounds. I had no doubt he'd kill Tomas if sufficiently provoked. With one blow of his sword, he'd split his skull in two. Nevertheless, I was overwhelmed with admiration for Tomas's bravery, and moved in to join him.

The soldiers who were sitting at the tables stood up and the pilgrims who were watching from the periphery closed in. A shadow seemed to fall over the square and suddenly, more swiftly than any eye could capture, the soldier struck a blow with his pistol and Tomas fell to the ground. He stood over Tomas, waiting to see if he would cause him any more trouble. And if need be, he seemed quite prepared to use his weapon properly next time, for he didn't return it to its holster. I took my position between Tomas and the soldier as Rosa fell to her knees behind me to tend to him. His appraisal of me was not quite so cursory. I stood taller than he, and although my shoulders were not as broad, I'm certain the intention he read in my eyes made them appear to fill the square.

"We don't want trouble," I said quietly.

"It's not trouble I'm after." He flicked his eyes down at Rosa, who'd managed to help Tomas sit up from his fallen position. "She tells me that she's not married, so I'm offending no one. It is this man who's challenged me," he said, thrusting his chin out. I understood what he meant, as it was well understood that a woman traveling without a husband, or a male relative to look out for her, was practically advertising her availability. It was amazing that this was the first problem she'd encountered while on her journey.

Where my next words came from, I do not know. It was as though they were spawned on my tongue by an unseen force, and I could only spit them out or swallow them. "She is not married, that's true," I conceded. "But she is not without family. I trust you'd understand a brother's desire to defend his sister's honor. Even if it involves confronting an obviously superior opponent."

The soldier's face went blank. "Her brother?"

I spoke loudly to be sure that Tomas and Rosa had heard me. "Yes, they are brother and sister, and as you can see, they are very close."

Upon hearing our discourse, Rosa's mother fell to the ground to join in on this spontaneous pietà. "Oh, my son, my son. What have you done to my son?" She grabbed Tomas by the shoulders with both hands, and pulled him to her bosom as though he were a suckling infant.

Disgusted by the scene at his feet, the soldier returned the gun to its holster and spun away to join his companions. We sat on opposite ends of the square during lunch, but his eyes never left Rosa's face.

17

⁓

JAMILET HAD JUST FINISHED her work and was making her way down the hill when she saw Eddie leaning against the hospital fence, with his hands stuffed into his pockets, and his head hanging. Even with his back turned to her, Jamilet knew it was him. There was no mistaking the dark hair just slightly wavy at the neckline, the length of his arms, and the breadth of his back. Her heart raced, and instinctively she scanned the street to see if Pearly was anywhere in sight. But Pearly would still be at work. She didn't get home until well past six and it was barely five.

Jamilet had obeyed her aunt's directive. It had been a month since the attack and, aside from his wavering image in her peripheral vision when she walked into her house, that was the last time she'd seen him. She was kneeling on the grass looking up at him as though she'd been caught defecating in public. She remembered the way he'd kept telling Pearly to calm down and relax, his voice like a velvet whisper. Jamilet had heard men talk like this when breaking wild horses, and it seemed to work pretty well on Pearly too, even as her nostrils flared while he pulled her away.

Jamilet's insides grew hot and tight as she remembered. To see Eddie here was almost a miracle, but she didn't want to feel the shame again. She stopped in her tracks and considered ducking into the trees. In forty minutes or so, he'd have to leave if he was going to be at Pearly's in time. Suddenly, as though sensing her presence, he turned around and saw her. He took hold of the fence, and indicated, with a flick of his head, that she should come closer. She had no choice—her legs kicked back into gear and began moving toward him without her consent.

When they stood close enough to speak, Jamilet could think of nothing to say. It occurred to her that maybe he wasn't waiting for her at all, but had decided to stand in that spot only to admire the trees and the fading light between their branches. Perhaps she should just pass through the gate and keep walking, but she stood where she was and tried hard not to drown in his nearness. But she had to breathe, and when she did, she inhaled the scent of soap and mint toothpaste, and died just a little.

He cleared his throat. "How are the nutcases doing?"

Jamilet tried to match his easy smile. "Fine," she said.

"You're still not scared working in that freaky place?"

Jamilet crossed her arms and uncrossed them, while shaking her head and smiling sheepishly.

Eddie nodded and stuffed his hands back in his pockets. The smile had left him. "About the other day. I wanted you to know that it was Pearly's sister who told her, not me," he said. "I guess she saw us at the library or something. And, I'm sorry if she hurt you 'cause I know she throws a mean punch."

Jamilet gazed at him through the fence with wide and vulnerable eyes. In his awkward attempt to apologize and explain what had happened, she considered him to be beyond beautiful. It filled her completely, and the warmth that surrounded them felt safe and separate from the rest of the world. And in this perfect space of time she hoped she might clear something up. "Why is Pearly so jealous?" she asked. "I didn't think girls like her were ever jealous."

"All girls are jealous."

"How do you know?"

"Because I know lots of girls and they're all jealous, especially if the girl they think is after their man is good looking, then they're crazy jealous, and they do crazy things like punch people they don't know in the middle of the street."

Eddie glanced left and then right. He shuffled his feet as though distracted, or searching for a way to end the conversation. Then he became still and his eyes burned bright with the fear that lurked behind them. "How'd you know?" he asked. "How'd you know my mom is sick?"

Jamilet couldn't find a way to explain how the knowing had come upon her that afternoon in the library, or how it was that over the years she'd learned how to read the expressions on people's faces in the way most people read books. It was simply a feeling that filled her in the same way she was filled with his torment at that very moment. "I just knew," she said after several moments of silence.

He nodded, his need to speak more profound than his need to understand. "She has cancer. It's in a place where they can't take it out . . . in her liver."

"That's too bad," Jamilet said, feeling stupid and inept. Nothing she could think of to say seemed right for the moment.

"Yeah, that's what I think," he said, cocking his head to one side. "That's just too fucking bad." He shrugged, mumbled a hasty good-bye, and walked away, his shoulders hunched forward as though braving a chilling storm. Jamilet waited until he was half-way down the street to begin her own walk home. She watched his shirttail floating behind him with every step, the way he pushed the traffic-light button with his elbow so he didn't have to bother removing his hands from his pockets.

When she lost sight of him, she replayed the scene over and over again in her mind, mostly to convince herself that it was real and not one of her own creations. When she thought of sweet beautiful Eddie suffering as he was, the sadness she felt gouged deep wells into a heart already weakened by its recent encounter, and the agony was so sublime, it was almost intolerable. Several times she stumbled, and imagined herself on the edge of a cliff ready to jump into the depths of something she couldn't under-stand. And then the glorious and unbelievable truth struck her—

Eddie thought she was "good looking." Good looking enough to make someone "crazy jealous." She was almost sure of it. She rubbed her jaw with her thumb in search of the dull ache that had only recently subsided in order to convince herself that it was true. And as she confirmed it, she was absolutely certain that she'd never been happier and more miserable in all her life.

Included with Señor Peregrino's breakfast one morning was an envelope that Ms. Clark herself gave Jamilet to deliver. And when he saw it, he opened it immediately and read it three or four times before taking another breath. Then his head dropped back on the pillow and he quickly mumbled what seemed like a prayer, his eyes glassy with tears.

"I hope it's good news, Señor," Jamilet said, mostly to remind him that she was still in the room.

Slowly he turned to her, joy beaming from his eyes, his entire being awash in wonder. He straightened up in his bed and refolded the letter carefully. "Do you believe in miracles, Jamilet?"

"Do you mean like magic?"

"What I mean," he said, the muscles of his face twitching, "are happenings, unexplained and wonderful, beyond your dreams, challenging your meaning of life, and your purpose within it."

She answered meekly, "I never really thought about it that way, Señor."

"Well, think about it," he said, as though ready to succumb to a mad gale of laughter. "What else have you to think about? What else has anybody to think about?"

Jamilet tried to appear pensive while keeping a wary eye on Señor Peregrino, who was acting strangely enough to cause her concern. The only thing that came to mind when she thought about miracles was the mark, and her hope beyond all others to someday be rid of it. "I think," she said cautiously, "that I would like to believe in miracles, Señor."

"You'd like to believe in miracles, would you? Well, let me tell you that in order for my eyes to open every morning, and look upon the world, I *must* believe."

Jamilet nodded as if these words made perfect sense to her.

He blinked happily. "What if I were to say to you that I'd found you a miracle?"

Jamilet was dumbfounded. "I . . . I don't know, Señor. I suppose that I'd thank you."

He chuckled and waved a hand at her. "Oh, you just think I'm just a crazy old man, but soon, when the appointed hour arrives, you will see that I am not so crazy after all." He sighed and refolded the letter, carefully placing it back into the envelope, his eyes glittering mysteriously. "I believe that I'll continue with my story now," he said. "Your lesson can wait until later. Sit. Sit," he commanded, and she obeyed, feeling somewhat relieved that this strange discussion had ended.

"Well," he said. "Where were we?"

"The soldier," Jamilet blurted out, happy to offer something useful. "The blond soldier was in love with Rosa."

"In love?" Señor Peregrino asked, raising his eyebrows.

Jamilet persisted. "He couldn't stop looking at her from across the square. He couldn't take his eyes off her."

"Is that love, Jamilet?"

She thought about this earnestly. "Maybe it's more like a seed. If it gets water and light, it can grow into love," she offered shyly.

"Interesting, I've never heard it explained quite that way before," he said, his black eyes flashing with every word. And then the Spanish day grew around them.

※

It seemed that the plains of wheat, waving their golden limbs up to the sky as they whispered their secrets to the weary pilgrims who passed, had grown eternal. The miles passed one after the other with little variation, save the occasional church perched upon an almost imperceptible knoll, or the appearance of dovecotes in the fields and dense flocks of doves as we neared the villages. While the monotony of our surroundings lulled most of us into a trance, Tomas embraced the role of protective brother with increasing enthusiasm, and Rosa's mother was ever so grateful to have acquired a son. She prattled on incessantly about it, and I do believe that even Tomas's boundless patience was tested.

Spending time with them as we did, it wasn't hard to understand why Rosa was such a quiet girl. No doubt she'd had to wait for days, even weeks, for an opportunity to interject a word or two of her own. Yet, she tolerated her mother graciously. One would never guess she felt the slightest irritation when commanded to cover her face against the dust of the road, to steady her walk over loose stones, to drink slowly lest her belly ache. Her mother fired these warnings and many others at her daughter, and Rosa wordlessly obeyed, her face always placid, betraying almost no emotion. It was impossible to know what she was thinking at any moment, and absurd to consider that she might have any feelings at all for me other than the same gentle friendliness she showed to everyone.

Once or twice, she caught me watching her and I became momentarily flustered, but soon regained my composure by asking her if she would like me to sing. The only time Rosa's mother ceased talking was when she slept or I sang. And so it was that the four of us were seldom seen walking the path one without the other. Tomas, with his new family, and I, the able friend who watched over them.

Before long, Tomas's obsession with Rosa grew into adoration. No more did he mention his dedication to the church, and I could swear that he was beginning to gain a bit of weight. And the timbre in his voice had deepened somewhat, so that once or twice I didn't recognize him when he spoke. He liked telling Rosa about his life in our village back home, and the vast stretches of land his family owned, the fine embroidered tablecloth they used even for plainer meals that never failed to include meat.

Rosa listened, while nodding politely, but she didn't appear to be impressed.

Her mother, however, was practically salivating and more than willing to give Tomas control of the conversation whenever it pertained to the subject of his family's holdings. She'd tuck his arm inside hers and laugh at something he said that was not necessarily intended to be funny. "You're such a clever young man," she'd say merrily. "I've always said that a man with muscle in the head is much more interesting, don't you agree, Rosa?"

As always, Rosa responded to her mother with reasoned caution. "I do appreciate thoughtfulness, Mother, in men and women both."

Doña Gloria cackled, and she quickened her step. "It's almost as though you were meant to be my son, Tomas."

More than once Doña Gloria spoke to me during those rare occasions when Rosa and Tomas couldn't possibly hear us. One time I remember clearly; I was waiting to fill my canteen at the well when she came up from behind and startled me. "Is it true what Tomas says about his family and their position?" she asked, her mouth twisted, as though we were partners in crime.

I couldn't suppress my indignation. "I assure you, Doña Gloria, that rich or poor, Tomas is an honest man."

"Yes, of course," she said, attempting to soothe me with her motherly tone. "But I'm sure you understand that a mother must watch out for her daughter, especially if her daughter is as beautiful as Rosa. You have no idea the fantastic stories I've heard. It's as if men take one look at her and suddenly become liars of the worst kind." She laughed, and covered her mouth with enough force to knock out a few teeth; and she hadn't many to spare. Feeling more composed, she whispered, "For many years I've been planning her destiny."

I was tempted to inform her that destiny could be determined only by God, but I had no desire to enter into a philosophical argument. I filled my canteen, and remained silent.

"I tried talking Rosa out of this foolish journey by telling her that God listens to her prayers no matter where she offers them, but she would have come with or without my approval. Oh yes, she's headstrong," she said, responding to my raised eyebrows, for I was surprised to hear that Rosa was anything but obedient. "She may appear meek and agreeable most of the time, but believe me, when she decides on something, nobody can stop her."

"And why is it so important for your daughter to complete the pilgrimage?" I asked.

Doña Gloria puffed up her cheeks and fumbled with her canteen, nearly dropping it. It was the only time I'd seen her at a loss for words. "Why is it important for anybody?" she asked, and left me to finish my chore.

That evening as we arranged our bedding for the night, Tomas was quite literally glowing. Earlier, Rosa had entered the dining hall with her hair still moist from a recent wash. There were several places at the table she could have chosen, including the chair next to mine, but she chose the seat next to Tomas. He recounted the way it happened several times. "Do you think she's fond of me?" he asked.

"I have no doubt."

Tomas smiled, unable to contain his delight. "It's a wonder to me when I remember how we began this journey. You were the one who was lost, and now I'm walking in the very shoes you shod, except . . . I don't believe I've lost my way at all, Antonio, but found it."

"I'm not sure I understand, my friend."

Tomas gazed up at the ceiling with glassy eyes. "It is I who wasn't meant to be a priest. I was meant to fall in love with Rosa, and she with me."

Every night he'd gather his blankets up around his chin and speak like a child full of promise, eager for the next day and what it might bring. Then he surprised me with a new theme. "I fear that as much as I love and honor Rosa, I cannot trust myself to be alone with her. I thank God that as we walk together arm in arm, playing the part of brother and sister, we are surrounded by our companions."

"What do you fear would happen if you were not?" I asked, feeling guilty, for I knew the answer to my question better than he did. I understood the inner fire that burns brighter than rational thought, provoking the will, and the flesh, toward the most intimate of desires.

His voice was shaky. "I fear that I will force my touch upon her."

"And then . . . ," I said, feeling like the very devil.

"She will relent, and allow me to touch her cheek and hair, caressing her as a true lover. Then she will press her lips against mine and embrace me."

I stayed quiet, simmering in shame after having heard such fantasies that, to my ears, sounded as pure as any sermon from the pulpit. By comparison, my thoughts were beyond perverse, and as wild as the Galician mountains that awaited us at the culmination of our journey, for in my dreams I'd taken Rosa to my bed countless times. I imagined how the turn of her ankle must lead to the bend of her knee, the exquisite length of her thigh, and the sublime softness beyond. Many an afternoon I placed my weary head upon her welcoming breast and slept as a cherub floating among the clouds, or we became as uninhibited as two snakes writhing in the tall grass. I came to accept my lusty thoughts as I did the sores on my feet and the aching in my legs, as something completely normal for a man of my age and circumstance. I would have to learn to live with it if I were to remain on the *camino*.

With our journey more than half complete, I no longer dreamed of standing in the shadow of the great cathedral and kneeling before the golden splendor of the apostle's crypt. It's true that I didn't indulge in the same romantic fantasies involving marriage and children that haunted Tomas, but I had no more conviction for the church because of it. What's more, I didn't long for the comforts of home, or the thrill of great adventures abroad. I was more than content to be a pilgrim on the path, taking each day, and each step upon it, as it came to me.

18

THE AROMA OF GARLIC AND ONION cooking in oil had permeated the kitchen when Carmen arrived home a bit earlier than usual. Jamilet was busy pounding away at a slab of meat on the counter with the butt end of an empty beer bottle, and the sound of Carmen's shoes landing in the corner of the room caused her to stop abruptly, with the bottle in midair.

"I didn't hear you come in, Tía," she said.

Carmen was already at the refrigerator. "It's no wonder with all that racket you're making." She gulped down a beer while waving a finger. "Don't bother with dinner tonight. Louis and I are taking you out for your birthday."

Jamilet set the bottle down and wiped her hands on a towel. "My birthday was last week."

"Yeah, so? Haven't you ever heard of the saying, 'Better late than never'?"

Jamilet put the meat and vegetables away for tomorrow's dinner and hovered about the kitchen, somewhat confused, and shaken. She'd never really celebrated her birthday before. Gabriela had always believed that birthday celebrations were an unholy exercise in self-indulgence, not to mention financially impractical. The most anyone received on a birthday in that household was a large piece of sugary-sweet bread they were expected to share four ways.

Not knowing what else to do, Jamilet took the dish towel and started to wipe down the counters as Carmen looked on. "For God's sake, stop cleaning," she said. "I told you, we're taking you out, so find something to wear. We might run into someone I know, and I don't want them to think my niece is a wetback with no taste."

With a hesitant smile, Jamilet retreated to her room and changed into the only other thing she had—the purple long-sleeved shirt Louis had given her, and a pair of jeans she wore only on weekends. She washed her face, and brushed her hair, which was now long enough to wear behind her ears, before shuffling back out to the living room, feeling self-conscious and red faced. Louis had just arrived, and raised a beer in greeting when she entered the kitchen.

"She cleans up okay, huh?" Carmen said proudly to Louis, who could only agree with a nod and a wink. He said nothing about the shirt. Carmen began searching through her purse while she mumbled and finally produced a tube of lipstick. Without asking, she took hold of Jamilet's face. "Do this," she commanded while puckering her own lips. Jamilet obeyed and closed her eyes, inhaling the waxy perfume of the lipstick as Carmen worked. Then Jamilet pressed her lips together and felt the creamy softness slipping between them. The makeup tasted somewhat bitter, although not unpleasant.

She opened her eyes to find Carmen and Louis studying her, as though they'd never seen her before. "It's amazing, isn't it?" Carmen said to Louis.

He nodded and popped open another beer. "The lipstick looks real nice," he said.

Carmen took hold of Jamilet's shoulders and turned her around. "Come on, girl. I'm gonna show you something." She walked her over to the bathroom mirror, and stood behind her while they both examined her reflection. They looked upon an oval face with smooth honey-colored skin and huge eyes—dark, and enormously sad. Jamilet thought the pink lipstick made her mouth look too big and out of place on a face where all the colors varied somewhere between black and tawny.

"What do you see?" Carmen asked.

"My mother's sadness," Jamilet immediately replied.

Carmen shook Jamilet's shoulders. "You know something? If I had your face and figure, I'd dress myself up every day and go dancing every night. I'd show off what God gave me, until I was too tired to move. Then maybe I'd die young, but I'd die happy."

"But the mark, Tía—"

"I'm not talking about the mark," Carmen barked. "I'm talking about you."

Having gone to bed later than usual after a lovely birthday meal, Jamilet reported to work a few minutes late, and went directly to the kitchen for Señor Peregrino's breakfast. When she entered his room, she greeted him twice, but he didn't respond, as he was intently working on something at his desk. She noticed that he'd taken all her work off the wall, an indication that he was preparing to embark on a new challenge. Jamilet sighed. As much as she appreciated his commitment to her education, she wished at times that he wasn't such an exacting instructor. The previous week, he'd become cross when she couldn't pronounce the *th* sound to his liking, and threw his pencil across the room.

Jamilet quietly placed his tray on the bedside table, and went about her duties in the bathroom. She was preparing to leave when he spun around to address her. "What's this? No 'good morning' or 'how did you sleep'?"

Jamilet nodded and mumbled a hasty, "Good morning, Señor," before resuming her retreat to the door. On the way, she snagged her skirt on the bed frame and snatched it back with a yank.

"My but you're irritable this morning," he said.

Jamilet pushed errant strands of hair away from her eyes and attempted to focus her gaze on him as sincerely as she could. "I'm not irritable, Señor."

Señor Peregrino widened his eyes and leaned forward in his chair. "Perhaps you prefer not to admit it, but you are and, if I may add . . . moody."

"You think *I'm* moody, Señor?"

"I do indeed." He waggled a finger at the tray, which meant that he wanted her to prepare his coffee and bring it to him. "The truth is that with you, I never know what to expect from day to day, whether you'll be cheerful, or positively sour. I daresay there are times when you frighten me with that venomous look in your eyes, and I wonder, as I do at this very moment, whether you might find a way to drench me with hot coffee, accidentally of course."

Jamilet stopped stirring the sugar abruptly. "You know I'd never . . . what a silly thing to say!"

"And now you're calling me a silly old man."

"I didn't say—"

"You'd do well to remember your place," he snapped.

"Of course, Señor."

"Yes, well . . ." he said, eyeing her with exaggerated suspicion. "I was going to ask you to join me in a cup of coffee while I continue my story."

"Thank you, Señor, but I don't like coffee. It's far too bitter."

"It's seems to me that your mood is even more so."

Jamilet at first ignored this last comment and brought him his coffee, noting the various exercises he'd prepared for the day's lesson. He'd been up late, no doubt, in order to have them ready by morning. "Of course, nothing would sweeten my mood better than to listen to your story," she said.

Sipping his coffee, his eyes glittered beyond the steam. "It is fascinating, isn't it?"

"Yes, and it helps me forget my problems."

He waved his hand as though to clear the nonsense between them. "When you have your health and your youth, there are no problems. Now where was I?"

Jamilet took a moment to gather her thoughts. "Tomas told you he was in love with Rosa and that he was afraid to be alone with her because of what he might do. You listened and felt guilty because the thoughts you had about her were much . . . worse, but you weren't lost like before. You were a pilgrim on the path, taking each day as it came, and you had no interest in—"

"Yes, yes, I remember now," Señor Peregrino said while raising a hand to silence her, but his eyes were dancing with good-humored mischief. "And you'd do well to remember that it's *my* story, Jamilet."

"Of course, Señor."

If the journey into Sahagún had seemed tedious, then the walk beyond that, heading toward León, was utterly desolate. The land was flat and interminable, with nothing to arrest our attention but the wind in the thistles, and the distant tinkling of sheep bells. It seemed that my only companions were the black hawks that circled overhead looking for a meal among the grain. Tomas had stopped sharing his thoughts about Rosa, and I noticed that he often walked more slowly when I sang, and that he and Rosa and Doña Gloria would lag behind, too far away to hear or sing along with me.

One evening while we sat alone near the fire waiting for our supper, I watched him as he sipped his wine and turned the glass in his hands. "I've always been satisfied to live in your shadow, Antonio," he said. "Since we were boys I was content to follow your ways, to wait for you at the base of the tree while you climbed to the highest branch, to clap my hands and stomp my feet while you danced, because I was unable to dance. Perhaps I didn't bother to learn because I knew I'd never compare with you." He sighed deeply. "We will return to our village at the end of this journey as changed men, but the difference between you and me will never change."

"Stop talking in riddles, Tomas," I said, trying to lace my voice with good humor.

He took a long swallow of wine, emptying the glass, his eyes gleaming with emotion. "You don't love Rosa, and I do. My heart and soul are devoted to her. Give her the opportunity to love me." He pushed the glass aside. "Promise me that you'll leave her to me."

I'd never seen him so desperate. "My promises cannot move a woman's heart," I finally said.

"I realize that, but I also know that if Rosa is not distracted by you, I'll have a chance with her."

"We're both wasting our breath, Tomas. You know as well as I that she has shown a preference for no man. I do believe her heart and mind must be otherwise engaged."

Tomas raked anxious fingers through his hair. "Perhaps, but I see how you look at her. She is only another beautiful woman to you, whereas for me there is only one . . . only Rosa."

Tomas was watching me intently, and I knew there was no use in arguing with him anymore. "Very well. I promise to leave her to you," I said with a weary sigh. It seemed to me that the pilgrimage had finally managed to drain Tomas of every ounce of patience he'd once possessed, filling him with a stubbornness that threatened to overflow from his ears.

I awoke early the next day, fortified myself with three cups of strong coffee, and left with a day's ration of food in my rucksack, knowing that Tomas would wait for Rosa no matter how long it took, or how much of her mother he'd have to endure. I traveled some miles along a stretch of Roman road, knee high in the mist that clung to the earth at such an early hour. As the sun rose over the windswept steppes, I caught up with a smaller group of pilgrims. There were several young ladies among them who I surmised were not from Spain. At least three of them spoke English, although it was evident that they had a more than cursory understanding of Spanish.

The most handsome of the three was blond and as spritely as

a new chick. Her Spanish was near perfect, and her chatter appealing enough. She walked with such a bounce to her step that I wondered how her feet didn't swell painfully after half a mile. She kept glancing back at me, and her smile left no doubt in my mind that she found me pleasing. But I didn't smile in return. I'd learned to acknowledge such attention with unblinking eyes that were more persuasive than any smile.

At midday we took our rest near a healthy stream that fed the River Esla. The three ladies took turns balancing on smooth stones in order to cross the stream and reach the wildflowers that bloomed on the other side of the bank. I pretended to take little notice of them as I ate my lunch, but out of the corner of my eye I watched the wavering form of the blond girl, which appeared to be not that of a girl, but of a mountain goat, stocky and sure footed as any I'd seen in the highlands. But then quite suddenly, her foot slipped and she screamed, toppling into the stream. Seconds later, I too had plunged into the stream, and was attempting to lead her out by the hand, but she was continually slipping from my grip and appeared near fainting, leaving me no choice but to carry her out onto the muddy bank, where we were met with more guffaws and giggles than concern.

We were both heavy with water, and cold, and somebody set about making a fire. The girl's name was Jenny, and when she removed her thick wool skirt, her two companions placed it near the fire. I stood near as well, as my trousers were all that needed drying but I couldn't very well remove them. So I took off my boots and socks and set them on a rock near the fire to dry. Jenny discarded the blanket she was given, and hovered about quite comfortably in her white cotton slip, asking many questions about my reason for making the pilgrimage, where I came from and with whom I traveled. I answered her questions, providing little detail, which seemed to frustrate her considerably.

All the while, her friends were busy tending to the fire and checking her skirt and adjusting it every few minutes, without concern for our conversation. When I commented on their attentive dispositions, Jenny explained that they were servants who'd been assigned to look after her en route and report any problems to her parents in America, who permitted her to do the pilgrimage because it was considered more of a religious exercise than a holiday. Her proficiency in Spanish was due to her family's successful businesses in Mexico, and the fact that she had lived there for much of her childhood.

"My parents believe that it's time I get married," she said, eyeing me boldly. "But I prefer to see the world without a husband in tow. And when I do marry, it will be to someone of my own choosing." She drew a line with her toe in the dirt between us, and I was struck by how different she was from Rosa. One woman had been blessed with incomparable beauty, and an unassuming spirit, while the other, who from this vantage point appeared as plain as any rainy Monday, behaved as though it were she who'd been blessed with the beauty. Fascinated, I allowed her to draw me in for a moment or two.

"A young woman who doesn't want to marry," I mused, impressing my own design in the dirt at my feet. "There is certain danger in that."

She laughed and immediately canceled my series of circles with her toe. "And that is the other reason for my pilgrimage," she said, leaning in closer. "I'm looking for a bit of danger. I imagine you are as well."

I stooped down to check on my boots. "No, Miss Jenny," I said, "I'm hoping to evade danger, if I can." I proceeded to pull on my socks while she chattered on about her trip, and her refusal to be tamed by it as her parents hoped she would be.

I collected my pack and strapped it to my back, hoping to make my intention of continuing on alone apparent to her and the rest. "It's been a pleasure meeting you, Miss Jenny," I said, bowing again. "I wish you a safe journey and . . . many dangerous blessings."

She smiled fiercely. "We will see you again, I hope," she called out as I made my way to the road. "I hear there's a turbulent river up ahead. I may need you."

I laughed and waved to her and the others before resuming my travels alone. At the end of the day, I found the *refugio* at the far side of town. I couldn't be sure that the others would join me. It had been a long day's walk and they might have decided to camp along the road rather than risk the night catching up. Even if alone, I looked forward to a glass of wine, and a hearty lamb stew for my dinner. I chose a small table near the window, where I could keep an eye on the road.

I heard them before I saw them, Jenny's laugh above all the clatter as the pilgrims entered the narrow cobblestone road like a flood, filling the spaces with laughter and song and the anticipation of a soft bed and a warm meal. Jenny led the group, like the figurehead of a mighty ship. Her fine clothes were covered in mud, as was her hair, which reminded me of a haystack blown about by a storm and then rained upon relentlessly. But her eyes were alive as she scanned the empty streets in search of the *refugio*.

I stood up to get a better look. The group had doubled in size, and I surmised that Tomas and Rosa were likely to be among them. Moments later, the dining hall was filled with pilgrims unloading their packs, inquiring about refreshments, and collapsing into chairs or on the floor when all the seats were taken. I was surrounded by a collective and exuberant fatigue, but still I kept my eyes on the road, not realizing that Jenny had taken the seat next to me and joined me in my vigil, mocking me, it seemed. Rosa and Tomas came into view toward the end of the throng, as I expected, with Doña Gloria limping more than usual. Tomas appeared sullen, and Rosa as stoic as always, her face shimmering and warm about the cheeks, while her eyes remained cool as the darkening sky. I couldn't help appearing a bit spellbound as I gazed upon her.

"She's lovely," Jenny observed.

Recovering from the startle of unexpected company, I settled down in my chair and came up with a response. "My friends. I . . . I was concerned they might not make it this far tonight."

"As concerned as you were," Jenny said, helping herself to a glass of my wine, "I'm surprised you chose to walk up ahead of them."

"I prefer to walk alone," I said, somewhat taken aback by her boldness. At this, Jenny's servants approached and informed her that they'd made arrangements at the best inn in the village.

"I thought I might sleep in the *refugio* with the others tonight," she replied, and they fell silent, quite obviously surprised.

Tomas and Rosa found their way to us, literally dragging Doña Gloria between them. She groaned on and on about the horrors of the day's walk and the deplorable condition of her blistered feet. I gave her my chair and she collapsed into it, barely interrupting her diatribe of complaints as she did so. Rosa knelt and pulled off her mother's boots and socks to reveal feet as swollen and red as boiled beets. The soles were covered with blisters, some reaching across the entire span of her heel.

Jenny placed a comforting hand on Rosa's shoulder. "I'm afraid she'll have to rest for a couple of days."

"Do you think so?" Rosa said, but she did not appear disappointed.

"I'm sure of it. Some ointment would do her good as well." Jenny directed her servant to fetch the ointment, and when she returned, Rosa massaged the foul-smelling grease into her mother's feet while Doña Gloria prayed for the Lord to release her from her misery. She went on and on about the poor sleep she'd been getting and how impossible it was to sleep in the *refugios*, so dank and crowded and full of vermin.

"Then I insist you take my room at the inn, madam," Jenny said while pouring Doña Gloria a generous glass of wine that she gladly accepted without her usual speech about drinking only on Christmas Day. As far as I could tell, she'd been liberally celebrating the holiday every day since we'd met her.

"That would be lovely—"

"We couldn't take your room, miss," Rosa responded, interrupting her mother for perhaps the first time in her life. "I'm afraid we can't pay for it and—"

"Nonsense. I've already paid for it, and this poor woman needs a proper night's rest without having to worry about vermin."

"That's very kind of you," Rosa said, visibly coloring. "But I assure you we've been very comfortable and"—Rosa looked about the bustling room to make sure no one had heard Jenny's disparaging remark—"my mother is afraid of the rats that sometimes scurry across the floor at night, that is all."

Jenny rolled her eyes knowingly. "Well, I was referring to the two-legged kind. They can be so much more dangerous," she added with a wink.

Once Jenny had convinced Rosa to accept her offer, she proceeded to order for the table and insisted that we join her. There were meat pies, fresh vegetables, and the best house wine. For dessert we enjoyed an almond tart, still warm from the oven. All the while Jenny told us of her adventures on the road and topped it all off with the story of how I'd saved her life. She embellished it beyond believable proportions, and had me swimming against the turbulent rush of the river to reach her. I reminded her that the water had barely reached up to my knees.

Upon hearing this, she cocked her head to one side and said to Tomas, "Has your friend always been so humble?"

"Not always," Tomas answered, "but I must say that modesty suits him."

By the end of the evening, even Doña Gloria's mood had improved. Rosa was obviously fascinated with Jenny and asked her many questions about her life in America. Jenny answered them, and when faced with the beauty before her, not the slightest trace of the jealousy such as I'd seen in other women was evident in her expression.

At the conclusion of the meal, our stomachs full and our hearts light, Jenny took my arm as we stood in the doorway watching Rosa and her mother walk across the square to the inn. Doña Gloria's limp had improved considerably and she was leaning less heavily on Rosa, while Tomas carried their packs, his head low as if in prayer.

Jenny said, "Your friend has hopelessly lost himself to love. But lucky for him, Rosa is as poor as she is beautiful. I'm sure Doña Gloria is already planning the wedding."

I stared at her for some time, waiting for the smile to vanish from her face. How could this woman who'd observed the three of us for no more than a few hours dare to be so bold with her theories?

I bowed politely. "I wish you a good night's rest, Miss Jenny. And if I don't see you in the morning, pleasant travels as well."

"And to you," she said. "But I'm certain you'll see me."

19

T HE SENSATION OF CASH in her hands—soft as fine leather, and the fragrance, slightly acrid and earthy—filled her with satisfaction, and made her feel that she was on the verge of transforming her dreams into reality. She imagined how she'd give the money to the doctor who would cure her. After accepting her payment, he'd produce a shiny instrument much like a gun, but with an intricate array of buttons and attachments that hummed pleasantly while emitting a continuous stream of light as though it were harnessing the power of an unseen force as mysterious as the stars. She would undress, and lie facedown on the examining table to wait. Despite her willingness to endure whatever pain necessary, the laser light treatment would prove no more painful than a near scalding bath. The results, however, would be immediate, and she would be given a mirror to see for herself—clear, unblemished skin from the nape of her neck to the bottom of her knees, only slightly red. The kind doctor would inform her that in a matter of days the redness would subside, and then it would be perfect.

Jamilet sighed as she placed the nearly two thousand dollars she'd saved back into the shoe box. Then she reached around to trace her fingers along the thick ridge of skin on her shoulders, easily discernible beneath the thin cotton of her blouse. She un-tucked her blouse at the waist and traced her fingers along her lower back, simulating the caress of a lover. Once she was free of the mark, this would be the most sensuous place for Eddie to begin his appeal, at the base of her spine, or the back of her neck. If he were as tender and romantic as she suspected, this was where their lovemaking would begin.

The front door opened then slammed shut. This was followed by the hollow sound of shoes kicked off and hitting the floor one after the other. Carmen wasn't due home for another couple of hours, and immediately Jamilet sensed that something was wrong. She hastily tucked in her blouse and ventured out into the living room. There she found Carmen collapsed on the couch, arms and legs spread out as though waiting to be executed. She hadn't even bothered to go to the refrigerator for her first beer of the afternoon. Never had she forgone this part of her routine. Often, she forgot to pull the plug after a bath, or put out the garbage on garbage day, but she never forgot her first beer of the afternoon.

Jamilet went to the refrigerator herself and placed a cold beer in the center of the coffee table. She waited a moment, but when her aunt didn't move, she popped open the tab as well, and placed it back on the table, an inch or two closer than she had before. But Carmen's eyes were glazed over as she relentlessly bit at her bottom lip. She didn't even seem to know that her niece was there.

"Your beer's there, Tía," Jamilet said.

Carmen responded with a weak grunt, but she didn't move a muscle.

"What's wrong, Tía?"

Her eyes cleared slightly, and it seemed as though she might speak when suddenly she thrust out her hand and grabbed the beer like a lioness striking at prey. She downed it in record time, and allowed the empty can to fall out of her hand and roll off the couch and onto the floor.

"Why did you come home early?" Jamilet asked, fighting the impulse to attend to the can right away.

Carmen's bottom lip started to quiver. "Why should I work all day when my life is over?"

"Did something happen with Louis?"

She nodded and plunged her head deep into the pillow next to her. Her body began to heave with violent sobs. Jamilet rushed to the bathroom, and returned with several yards of toilet paper that she placed near her aunt's closed fist. Carmen's fingers slowly opened and then closed around the enormous wad. She proceeded to wipe at her nose and eyes with the desperation of one trying to rid the carpet of a stubborn stain. Feeling more composed, she sat up, her face red and bloated. "It doesn't matter what happened. It's over," she said flatly.

"Things always work themselves out between you two, Tía, you know that."

"This time it's different."

"Why?"

Carmen's eyes twisted in their sockets. "Because the old lady didn't have the sense to die in Mexico like she should have. She tried to use her friend's papers to get back across the border. Any idiot knows you have to memorize birth dates and shit if you're gonna fool them, but the senile bitch got so nervous, she forgot everything. She couldn't even remember her friend's name when they asked her."

"That's too bad," Jamilet said, knowing that such an event would have resulted in detainment at the border, but she wasn't sure how this affected Carmen and Louis.

Carmen stuffed the pillow under her chin and hugged it tight, like a child hugging her teddy bear. "He came by work, when I was finishing my route, and told me he couldn't see me this weekend and maybe never again 'cause he feels so upset and guilty about his wife and daughters being in jail. He started to slobber and say all this stupid shit to me, so I told him, 'Hey, do I look like a fucking priest to you?' You should've seen the look on his face, it was sickening."

"Did you really say that?"

Carmen's eyes widened for an instant. "Do you think it was mean?"

Jamilet nodded, and Carmen threw the pillow she clutched across the room with all her strength. "Well, what the hell am I supposed to do? You tell me, if you're so fucking smart." Her eyes accosted Jamilet, with fear on the verge of something unfamiliar, but expectant—some semblance of hope.

Jamilet bent down for the empty beer can. "I don't know, Tía," she said. "Maybe we should wait and see what happens."

Carmen exhaled, and her chin dropped to her chest. "We can wait until my hair turns white, but it won't change a thing. It's over."

⁂

The call from the police came while Jamilet was getting dinner in the oven—chicken enchiladas that she hoped would brighten her aunt's mood. She still held the oven mitt as the officer explained that, while Carmen was being released under her own recognizance, she was in no condition to drive home and someone should come for her. Jamilet ran the entire four blocks to the station without stopping, and found her aunt sprawled on a wooden bench, her purse and its contents spilled out on the floor, near her feet. The officer behind the window handed Jamilet Carmen's car keys and driver's license while Carmen glared at her niece as if she were somehow responsible for her predicament.

They walked the first couple of blocks in silence. Jamilet was anxious to hear her aunt's version of the story, although the officer who called had already told her some of what had happened. The police were called to break up a fight at Chabelito's Bar. When they arrived they found Carmen with another woman's head in the crook of her arm. All the witnesses reported that Carmen threw the first punch, although she'd had to endure plenty of verbal abuse before she did. "If she'd backed off when we got there," the officer explained on the phone, "we might've let her go right then and there. But it took two of us to restrain her."

With black hair exploding from her skull, and one broken heel causing her to limp, they attracted quite a few stares as they made their way down the street, but Carmen didn't notice. She kept her gaze focused on the sidewalk, leaning on Jamilet once or twice when she felt unsteady on her bilevel heels. She mumbled something.

"What did you say, Tía?"

"I said," she repeated in a grizzly voice, "she should've known better than to bring up Louis."

"Is that what made you mad?"

Carmen turned to glare at her niece for a second time, and stumbled in the process. "Wouldn't you be mad if someone told you that your man had another girlfriend?"

Jamilet was silent.

"The bitch," Carmen muttered. "I know it's not true. I have my spies, and they say he hasn't left the house to do anything but go to work. She just said that to make me mad."

"Well, I guess it worked," Jamilet said, and she even managed to chuckle, but the tension didn't lighten and she felt ridiculous for trying.

"I never been to jail before, Jami," Carmen said, her voice soft with revelation. "You probably don't believe me, but it's true."

"I believe you, Tía."

"I just kept drinking and trying to swallow all this shit I feel inside, but it got worse. This time my anger swallowed me up instead of the other way around."

"I worry about you, Tía."

"Well, here's something else for you to worry about. I'm going to have to go to court in a few weeks and the judge might decide to send me to jail for a long time, maybe a couple of years."

They walked another half block in silence. "I don't know what I'm going to do, Jami," Carmen said. "Now it feels like my life is really over. Even if Louis came back to me, I don't think it would help."

Jamilet took hold of her aunt's arm to steady her, and Carmen began to weep softly. "I feel like a piece of shit," she said, tears running into her mouth. "No, shit is too good for me, too real . . . you can still see it and touch it. I'm more like a fart, a big silent killer of a fart, a smelly ghost."

"Let's get home," Jamilet said, straining under the weight of her aunt's misery. "You'll feel better after you get some rest."

"Yeah, let's go home," she said. "I want to sleep and never wake up."

Although Jamilet had never cared for the taste of coffee, by the time she finished her first cup, she had definitely changed her mind. Perhaps it had to do with the fact that Señor Peregrino had prepared it for her himself, while muttering that he was certain she'd prefer hers with plenty of cream and sugar, as most children do, and that it didn't do for a person from the Hispanias to dislike coffee, when it could easily be considered one of their greatest contributions to the whole of civilization. "It clears the mind and strengthens the constitution," he declared. "People who don't drink coffee are weak and feeble-minded; they usually don't have opinions about anything, but if they do, they're afraid to formulate them into words and speak out."

Jamilet accepted a second cup, shaken somewhat by the fact that he was doing the serving, but she continued to relate the events of the previous evening just the same. Until three in the morning she'd been attending to her aunt, who was so despondent after her arrest that she threatened to go to the First Street Bridge in her pajamas and jump into the L.A. River. When she wasn't contemplating the various ways she might end her life, she wept over the misery of her loneliness, and the humiliation of having been raised with the beautiful and perfect Lorena. "I know Mama wished I had died instead of her," she'd wailed. Jamilet had attempted to sooth her aunt's agony with herbal teas and sensible talk, but she was overwhelmed beyond her capacity to understand and do anything but acknowledge the enormity of her pain.

Although moved by Carmen's piteous condition, Señor Peregrino was far more concerned with Jamilet's obvious fatigue. "It's a love affair that's doomed to fail," he said. "And I don't think you should lose another night's sleep over it; there's only so much coffee a person can drink." Nevertheless, he proceeded to talk more about the wonders of caffeine. That civilization undoubtedly owed many of its achievements to the stir it created in the veins, and that the Old World was indebted to the New World for its discovery and transmission. He suggested that perhaps the coffee her aunt was drinking wasn't strong enough.

"She seems to like it," Jamilet said. "She drinks three cups, one right after the other, and doesn't bother with cream and sugar." She took a small sip while peeking up at him. "Besides, Tía Carmen has no problem speaking her mind, Señor."

When she was finished, she proceeded to organize his breakfast tray, and thanked him for the coffee.

"You may leave that for later," he said. "I wish to continue my story." And his eyes grew misty with the strain of remembering.

Jamilet sat on the edge of her chair. "Señor, you were—"

His hand shot up. "Hush for a moment. I can't hear myself think." He closed his eyes, as though to shut out everything that might interfere with his remembering, but still there was no indication that the story was about to resume. He opened his eyes. "Okay," he said. "Where did I leave off?"

Jamilet was so eager to answer that her chair scraped across the floor. "Jenny told you that Rosa was as beautiful as she was poor, and that Doña Gloria was planning the wedding." She hesitated for a moment. "You were upset with Jenny, even though she let Rosa and her mother have her room at the inn."

"That's true. I've never known anyone with so much talent for upsetting me." He set his coffee cup aside and began.

Doña Gloria awoke with her feet so enflamed that she was unable to get out of bed for breakfast. Rosa was distraught and asked us to join her at her mother's bedside so that we could help her decide what to do. Jenny came along, saying that she had experience with home remedies because her childhood nanny had a gift for healing and had taught her everything she knew. She chattered on with fantastic self-glorifying tales as we made our way to the inn.

We found Doña Gloria in bed propped up against her pillows, her mouth stuffed with biscuits and honey. She seemed quite comfortable, but when she pulled back the blanket to show us her feet, every one of us stifled a gasp. In the course of one night, her feet had swollen to twice their normal size. It seemed they would burst at any moment, and no one ventured to get any closer for a better look. No one, that is, except Jenny. She appeared more curious than aghast, and mumbled to herself while pressing down on the soles of Doña Gloria's feet, which were as shiny as pig tripe stretched and overstuffed with sausage meat.

"I'm afraid this doesn't look good," she said to Rosa. "There's no ointment that can help because the problem has to do with the way blood is flowing through her feet."

Rosa's voice wavered slightly as she asked for Jenny's advice on what to do. It seemed that my and Tomas's opinions were not so important anymore, but Tomas took the opportunity to make his thoughts known before Jenny could answer. "Surely if the problem is lack of rest, we should stay together and wait until Doña Gloria is well enough to continue," he said with inflated authority.

Jenny shook her head, not the least bit impressed with his apparent conviction on the matter. "I'm afraid she won't be able to resume walking in a few days. Maybe not even in a few weeks."

Tomas puffed up a bit, but he could think of nothing else, short of carrying Doña Gloria all the way to Santiago on his back.

Rosa covered her mother's feet, for which we were all grateful. "What do you propose then?" she asked, looking once again to Jenny.

"Your mother will have to abandon the pilgrimage if she ever hopes to walk again."

Doña Gloria ceased chewing on her biscuit and began to

whimper. Rosa patted her mother's shoulder. "And she should see a doctor . . . ?"

"Oh yes, definitely," Jenny agreed enthusiastically. "As soon as possible, but he'll only tell you the same thing."

"I'll inquire at the desk," Tomas said, and he rushed out of the room, hopeful, no doubt, that the doctor would disagree with Jenny's assessment. He was back in less than a minute, beaming triumphantly. "We're in luck," he said. "There happens to be a doctor of medicine staying right here. The innkeeper is talking with him now to see if he'll oblige us with a consultation."

Jenny turned to Rosa. "You mustn't worry about your mother; she'll be fine as long as she rests. Staying away from sweets and alcohol wouldn't hurt either."

The doctor arrived with traces of marmalade glistening on the tip of his gray mustache. He took a bit more time with his examination than Jenny had, although he seemed eager to distance himself from his patient, who insisted on expressing her distress like a baying mule. "I'm afraid she'll have to stay off those feet," he said, looking around, not at all clear about whom he should address. "It's a circulatory problem, and a pretty bad case from what I can tell. If it doesn't abate, it can become gangrenous and then well . . . she could lose her feet."

Doña Gloria began to wail with renewed vigor and Rosa tried to comfort her, to no avail.

"She should get home as soon as possible for proper treatment," the doctor continued, wincing at the screeches coming from the bed. "And, madam," he said, speaking with enough authority to prompt her total silence, "may I suggest that you refrain from indulging in sweets and that extra glass of Jerez after your meal." With that, he clicked his heels and left.

Arrangements began immediately for Doña Gloria and Rosa's return home. The innkeeper, eager to be rid of the infirm guest, was very solicitous and informed us of the various trains leaving for Barcelona. Rosa and Jenny went to make the arrangements and were gone most of the morning. Later, when Tomas asked where Rosa was, I felt only slightly guilty when telling him I didn't know, although I'd seen her enter the chapel with Jenny not ten minutes earlier.

The other pilgrims had left hours ago for León, and all was quiet. Tomas and I sat together watching as pigeons gathered at the fountain for a brisk bath. And then they started to flutter and hover about with a synchronized purpose, much like a swarm of bees. Before my eyes, they shaped themselves into a white, undulating form that evolved, stretching and condensing until I clearly saw the image of Santiago himself floating over the fountain while pointing his staff toward the road, urging us to leave the square immediately.

"Do you see what I see, Tomas—over the fountain?"

"I see a strange haze. It's hard to make out . . ."

"It's Santiago. He wants us to go, leave this place right now."

"And leave Rosa? I won't do it, Antonio, not even to appease Santiago."

At that moment, Rosa and Jenny emerged from the chapel, arm in arm and smiling broadly. Rosa was no less than jubilant when she dclared, "My mother has allowed me to go on without her." She turned to Jenny. "As long as I remain with Miss Jenny and her servants are able to attend to my mother on her trip home."

"What a blessing to us all!" Tomas cried, so loudly that the birds exploded with a splash from the fountain and flew back to their roosts under the eaves of the chapel.

"Yes, it is a blessing," Rosa agreed, taking hold of Tomas's outstretched hand, and for a moment I thought the two of them might take to dancing a jig in the center of the square. Never had I seen Rosa so expressive, but it was Jenny I watched with curiosity while she gazed at Rosa and Tomas as though she were admiring her own personal puppets on a string. Rosa excused herself, explaining that she needed to attend to her mother's final wishes before she left, and Tomas insisted on helping her, leaving Jenny and me to ponder this sudden change of circumstances on our own.

"You don't seem at all pleased that Rosa will be continuing

with us," Jenny said as the smile eased away from her face. "I'm surprised."

"That you're surprised by anything is quite a wonder to me, Miss Jenny. Things always seem to go exactly as you plan them." I was preparing to say more, when soldiers on horseback entered the square. The tall blond soldier from the earlier encounter was among them, leading his lathered and exhausted horse to the watering trough. It was obvious they wouldn't be riding through.

"You know them?" Jenny asked. At that moment, the soldier saw me and left his horse to his subordinates. He looked Jenny over thoroughly, impressed with the fine weave of her garments and female form, but the arrested gaze that overcame him when he looked upon Rosa was absent.

"I trust you are well, sir," he said with a slight bow of his head. "And that your companion and his sister Rosa are not too fatigued from the journey."

"Sister?" Jenny echoed, turning to me, with questioning eyes.

He extended his gloved hand to Jenny. "Allow me to introduce myself. My name is Captain Andres Segovia. I'm traveling the pilgrimage route on government business."

Jenny took his hand and introduced herself, as the well-bred lady she was. "So I can assume that your inquiry after Miss Rosa is related to government business?"

Andres blushed, appearing for an instant as though he were all of ten years old, but he quickly recovered. "I'm inquiring after the lovely Miss Rosa because I had occasion to speak with her earlier and found her charming." He turned swiftly back to me, perturbed by Jenny's probing stare. "You will give her my regards," he said. "And to her family, of course."

"Of course," I said with a slight bow of my head.

At this Jenny spoke up. "Her mother isn't well, Captain. She'll be returning to Barcelona by train this very afternoon."

"I'm sorry to hear it," Andres said, appearing intrigued. He would have asked more about it, but he was called away by his men. With a stiff bow to both of us, he turned on his heel and walked away, leaving Jenny dumbfounded. I took advantage of this momentary lapse and made hasty excuses about needing to pack, but she had the nerve to take hold of my elbow, forcing me to stop and face her or risk appearing a mannerless brute.

She was still and serious, as though trying to read my mind, like a gypsy. "Is she really . . . ? No, it can't be." Her expression warmed and her eyes crinkled at the corners from a smile. "It's all a trick of some sort, but why?"

I took exquisite pleasure in annoying her by replying, "All things are not meant for you to know, Miss Jenny. And," I continued, "some questions are better left unasked."

20

A FEW DAYS FOLLOWING HER ARREST, Carmen appeared to be feeling better. She stopped talking about Louis altogether, was up early for work, and came home at the usual hour. She appeared uneasy only when sifting through the day's mail, and every time she didn't find the court summons, she heaved a heavy sigh of relief.

"You know, Jami," she said after a full two weeks had passed, "I think I'm off the hook." Carmen settled back on the couch, put her feet up, and managed a healthy cackle besides. "I hear this kind of thing happens all the time. Clerical errors, they call it. Something goes wrong with the computer, and just like that," she said snapping her fingers, "my case is history."

Reassured by the thought that things were getting back to normal, Jamilet stopped at the market on her way home from work one afternoon in order to buy nopales for a special stew she'd been wanting to make. If she hurried, she'd be able to beat Carmen home and get the meal started. With a bag in each hand, Jamilet was hurrying down the street to get home when she saw Eddie, waiting across the street as usual. He nodded a greeting and Jamilet nodded back. This had been the extent of their interaction since the conversation outside the hospital fence, and on this day Jamilet was not quite as content with it. If she hadn't been late for dinner, she might have lingered outside to see if another conversation might bloom between them.

As it was, she hurried up the front steps noting that Carmen was already home. Jamilet confirmed it was her aunt's car parked out front by the soft pink dice that hung from the rearview mirror. Carmen said they reminded her that life was a gamble, and that up to now she'd been lucky. With her appetite back to normal, Jamilet expected to find her impatiently flipping through one of her magazines or channel-surfing with a vengeance. Carmen didn't like waiting for meals. She didn't like waiting for anything.

Jamilet opened the front door and called out, "Tía, I'm home. I'll get dinner started right away." There was no answer. She knocked softly on the bathroom door, and it swung open to reveal an empty tub.

A rush of cold fear shot through Jamilet, all at once, as she rushed to Carmen's room, and flung open the door, not bothering to knock. Carmen was lying on her bed with eyes half open and a letter resting on her chest. Jamilet didn't need to look to know it was the court summons. She took firm hold of her aunt's shoulders and shook her soundly. "Tía," she shouted. "Tía, wake up, Tía!" Carmen didn't move or blink, and her eyes remained perpetually drowsy, looking at nothing and no one. Only a thin line of spittle dribbled out of the corner of her mouth as an empty pill container dropped off the bed to the floor.

Jamilet slapped her aunt's face while shouting at her, almost choking on her own screams and trying to calm the wicked fear raging through her like a storm. She slapped her aunt's face until it was red, and until her hands were wet with her aunt's saliva. Frantic with the knowledge that she was dead or dying, Jamilet ran out of the front door and into the street in a bewildered state. "Eddie, you have to come!" she shouted. She called out in Spanish too and in English again, her voice nearly shrieking. And she was trembling so violently that she couldn't be sure if he'd heard her, so she continued screaming for him in English and Spanish. It seemed to her that she was screaming for close to an hour before he came, although later he'd tell her it was only seconds.

Somehow she managed to explain what had happened and Eddie ran into the house before she could finish. He shook Carmen's shoulders as Jamilet had, but even more roughly, so that her neck and shoulders bounced off the bed. There was no response. He instructed Jamilet to call the fire department, and as she did so he crouched over Carmen and began breathing into her mouth, deep breaths that caused her chest to rise and fall. Over and over again he did this, and every now and then he put his ear to her mouth, and then resumed breathing into her as if the earth would stop spinning if he didn't. He stopped only once to tell Jamilet to go outside and wait for the ambulance.

When the paramedics arrived, they pushed Eddie aside. Jamilet watched, dazed, from the doorway as several uniformed men cut off Carmen's clothes with large shears. Underneath she wore a matching set of bright red panties and bra—Louis's favorites. Carmen always complained about how uncomfortable they were, but joked that a woman needed to make sacrifices for her man if she hoped to keep him around.

"Is she dead?" Jamilet asked Eddie, who was panting softly.

"I don't know," he said.

One of the men inserted a long tube down Carmen's throat, while another tried to put a needle into her arm, but he couldn't find a vein through the fat. Eventually he had to stick the needle in her hand. Together, the men lifted her from the bed and onto the gurney. It occurred to Jamilet that Tía would hate to be sleeping while so many young men hovered over her practically naked body, but still her eyes remained vacant, neither open nor closed.

A quivering sensation grew strong in Jamilet's legs and she swayed a bit and leaned against the wall. One of the paramedics asked her if she planned to ride along in the ambulance, but she didn't answer until he asked her a third time, and then she turned to Eddie.

"I think you should," he said.

"Will you come with me?"

He hesitated and shoved his hands in his pockets. "I can't," he said. But he waited on the street and watched as Carmen was wheeled outside and put into the back of the ambulance, and once Jamilet had climbed in after her, the ambulance drove off to County General.

Three mornings in a row had been gray. The fog clung to the sidewalks, the houses, and the trees in a chilling embrace. It was difficult for Jamilet to be alone in the house. The quiet was the worst part. Even with the traffic buzzing outside, people calling to one another, planes rumbling up in the sky, the space in the house muffled the life outside with its thick, smothering silence. Sometimes it was difficult for Jamilet to breathe; it was as if she were inhaling the silence into her lungs and even the beating of her heart slowed to a lethargic pace.

In only a few days, the sink had piled up with dishes and the beds were unmade. Carmen's last beer can was still on her bedside table. It was nothing close to the calamity Jamilet had walked into when she first arrived, but the stench in the sink was a reminder that it was headed in the same direction. Before long the malodorous invisible thread would be pungent enough to follow her into the bedroom and haunt her through the night, but for now it was enough to close the door, close her eyes, and forget. Tomorrow after work she'd clean it up. She'd missed three days already and had no doubt that certain difficulties would be waiting for her. Each day she'd called to say that a family emergency prevented her from going in, Ms. Clark received her excuse with silence followed by measured questions about the expected length of her absence. It was apparent that Ms. Clark had heard such excuses before, and was not moved to pity or curiosity, but kept an eye on the practicality of replacement. On the third day, she was put on hold and Nurse B. came to the phone.

"This is highly irregular," she said. "What kind of family emergency are you dealing with, Monica?"

"My aunt is sick and in the hospital," Jamilet answered. "If I'm not there, she gets upset."

Nurse B. breathed hard, surges of air blowing in and out of the receiver as though she were jumping rope, but she was winded only by her upset. "If you don't report to work by tomorrow morning, I'll be forced to hire another replacement. When there is a change in his routine your patient becomes . . . ." She paused and made a gurgling sound deep in her throat. "He becomes detestable," she said.

Jamilet promised that she'd be there, and tried to settle her mind to sleep by reminding herself that she was no longer dealing with Carmen on her own. Louis was back, and in some ways it was better than before. He'd rushed to the hospital after hearing rumors circulating at Chabelita's Bar about Carmen's suicide attempt. He was at the bedside when after almost twelve hours of a deep, deathlike sleep, Carmen finally woke up. His were the first eyes she looked into, and they held each other as they wept for some time after that. Louis proclaimed to Carmen and everyone who came into the room—nurses, doctors, the janitorial staff—that this was the woman he loved, and that he was prepared to stop living a lie. He promised Carmen and Jamilet that when his wife returned, he'd inform her as well, and marry Carmen, as he should have years ago.

"Don't wait, tell her now," Carmen said when she was feeling stronger.

"I don't want to tell her when she's so worried about getting home, but don't worry, my little flower," Louis said. "I'm saving money to bring them over, but it's going to take me a while. It's four of them, you know."

"How much you need?" Carmen asked.

Louis's eyes glanced up to the ceiling as he did the calculations in his head. "Oh, I figure about . . . ," he closed one eye. ". . . two or three thousand."

"Shit!" Carmen said, bringing her hand down and splatter-ing a good deal of orange juice on the sheets. "You'll be dead and buried before you save that kind of money. Hell," she went on, *"I'll* be dead and buried."

Louis said nothing and took her hand to his cheek. Carmen shrugged happily when she normally would have found reason to argue and complain. She had her man back and for the moment that was all that mattered.

Even so, Jamilet wasn't able to let go of her worries for Car-men quite so easily. She couldn't be sure how long her aunt would be satisfied with the present arrangement Louis had proposed. Carmen's brand of satisfaction wasn't the lingering kind that ran deep, strengthened by faith and long-suffering patience. It lasted about as long as a good joke stayed amusing, and Carmen wasn't one to keep laughing for long.

Señor Peregrino's room was in disarray—laundry scattered all over the floor, and trays from the previous day's meals stacked in one corner, dripping from one level to the next like a gritty fountain left to years of decay. Señor Peregrino didn't turn from his desk when Jamilet stepped in and over the obstacles on the floor in order to place the breakfast tray on his bedside table.

By now an expert at walking silently in her hard-soled shoes, Jamilet drifted between the various piles on the floor, organizing the laundry as best she could.

She was making relative progress when he spoke gruffly without turning around. "Leave it," he said. Jamilet jumped and dropped the bundle of clothes she held.

"I told you yesterday," he continued sternly. "You are not to touch anything in my room, do you understand?"

"Excuse me, Señor," Jamilet said. "You never told me that."

Upon hearing Jamilet's voice, Señor Peregrino spun around, the legs of his chair screeching across the cement floor. He looked at her as if she were a dead relative come to life: overjoyed at first, but then his eyes narrowed and the line of his mouth stiffened into a neat little scowl. "So, you decided to return, did you?"

"My aunt was ill, Señor."

"Look at this place," he said, flinging both arms out at once. "Look at the filth I've had to endure."

"I'm sorry, Señor. I thought they'd send someone else until I came back."

"They're all idiots!" he declared. "I can't take time to train each and every fool who comes through here. It was difficult enough training you, and you're less foolish than the average idiot."

Still in his pajamas, Señor Peregrino stood and stretched, as though waking from a long and restful sleep. A fine growth of beard mottled his chin and jaw with a silver haze. "I'll be showering presently," he announced. "And when I'm finished, I expect to find the bed made, the floor cleared, and every one of those foul trays out of my sight. Then," he continued with an elegant half bow, "I'll take my breakfast in bed, after which we'll resume your lessons. And, if you're lucky, I may have a mind to continue with my story after lunch."

"Very well, Señor," Jamilet said. "And you'll be wanting your linens changed as well?"

He was heading for the bathroom. "Yes, and call down for another pot of coffee. This one will be cold by the time I'm ready for it. And . . . and be sure they make enough for both of us."

"Of course, Señor." Jamilet smiled to herself as she proceeded to separate the laundry on the floor.

But Señor Peregrino lingered in the doorway of the bathroom, and then addressed her in a softer voice. "I . . . I didn't think you were coming back," he said. "You should know that an old man like me is prone to worry."

Jamilet looked up from her work into eyes that were filled with tenderness, and felt a small ball of joy well up in her throat, warm and brooding, like a dormant seed that had refused to sprout and was now beginning to rattle with life. She swallowed hard on it for fear it might choke her. She could have told him that she'd been worried about him too, and that she'd wondered who was looking after him. But she thought better of it, and tightened the muscles around her eyes, brimming with tears, as she continued separating the laundry with impatient jerks this way and that. She even managed a weary sigh. "You know I'd never leave without my papers, Señor. And there's so much work to be done, I really don't see how I'll have time to listen to your story today."

He exploded with a resounding, "Ha!" and tried to sound bitter, but his good humor overcame him. "You'd get three or four times the work done if it meant a chance to hear more of my story, and you know it."

Jamilet smiled. There was no need to further validate what both of them knew.

Two steaming cups of coffee, one with plenty of cream and sugar, were waiting at the bedside once the morning chores had been completed. The trays and clothes had been moved into the corridor and still needed to be taken downstairs, but the room was spotless and the linens on the bed crisp. Jamilet opened the window and the midmorning sun stretched across the room like a soft golden arm, beckoning them to sit and meditate upon the warmth of its embrace.

Freshly shaven, and smelling of powder and soap, Señor Peregrino took both the coffee cups to his desk. Together they sat sipping, and watching the fine dust Jamilet had disturbed in her cleaning frenzy drift about like miniature stars between the light and shadow of the room.

"This time I remember where I left off," Señor Peregrino announced with certain pride.

Jamilet peered at him through the steam rising from her cup. She too remembered, but said nothing.

"I had managed to annoy Jenny as much as she had annoyed me by refusing to tell her the reason Tomas and Rosa were masquerading as brother and sister. Yes," he said. "I was quite pleased with myself until I realized that Jenny was capable of much more than annoyance." Señor Peregrino lifted the steaming pot toward her. "More coffee?" he asked, as though they were sitting in a fine parlor or sidewalk café.

"Yes, please," Jamilet said, and she held out her cup so that Señor Peregrino could refill it. Then she closed her eyes, listened to the trance-inducing melody of his voice, and felt that she was floating, much like the dust particles surrounding them. Perhaps it was the result of the two heaping teaspoons of sugar in her coffee and nothing else, but she doubted it.

Evening descended like a soft, dark shroud over León. In the small square where we stayed, candlelight wavered in every window and the space appeared as though haunted by shadows that moved with their own life. I'd spent most of the afternoon sitting at the same table and worrying about anything and everything imaginable. How was I to manage Jenny for the remainder of the journey? Was Tomas capable of losing his mind over Rosa? Every day that passed rendered him less and less like the man I'd known when we left our home a lifetime ago. And then there was my greatest worry—when would Andres make his move? For I had no doubt that he'd make it. He appeared to be a man of cunning who was not so foolish as to allow his passions to rule him indiscriminately. Instead they simmered in his soul, motivating and scheming a treacherous plan.

I had forewarned Tomas of Andres's presence and he was delighted that this would afford him the opportunity to play the role of endearing brother more convincingly than ever. As they crossed the square together arm in arm, the breath caught in my throat. She wore a simple dress and her dark hair was in a thick braid down her back, with no other adornment except the emerald of her eyes. Even the crickets were silenced, in awe.

Tomas interrupted his pompous entrance with a few nervous glances about the square as he looked for Andres. No doubt he'd told Rosa that Andres was near. There was a halted smile on her lips, but unlike Tomas, she dared not look about and invite a greeting that might lead to something else.

"Won't Jenny be joining us?" she asked when she saw me sitting alone at the table.

"I'm sure she'll be along shortly."

"Good," she said, smiling genuinely this time. "When Jenny is in our company, my heart feels lighter somehow."

"She does have a unique way about her," I said, pouring wine all the way around. Jenny joined us shortly thereafter. She looked decidedly pretty, her hair as shiny as bright copper and her eyes gleaming with perpetual delight. She prattled on about her desire for a warm bath and a soft bed, but was silenced by the expression of panic and horror that had suddenly registered on Rosa's face.

We heard his boots pounding on the wooden floor before we saw him. Tomas took firm and possessive control of Rosa's hand while Jenny's eyes glittered over the rim of her glass, like a child anticipating a fine game.

Andres bowed to us all, but his eyes were fixed on Rosa's face, which betrayed only the discomfort of being adored so brazenly.

"It is a lovely evening," Andres said, forcing his gaze to sweep over the rest of us.

"I agree," Jenny replied, then she turned to me. "Don't you think it a fine night for a dance, Antonio? Tomas tells me that you're a very good dancer."

"Perhaps," I returned.

"So you're a dancer, are you?" Andres asked, momentarily distracted from his adoration of Rosa.

"I've been known to enjoy a dance from time to time."

"I'm sure you've seen your brother's friend dance many times," Andres said, directing his conversation to Rosa. "Can you suspend your sisterly bias long enough to tell me if he's any good?"

"He is spectacular," Rosa said, meeting Andres's questioning gaze with unusual conviction of her own.

He was apparently delighted to hear as much, and brought

his hand down to the table with a resounding thud. "Then we will dance," he declared loudly, and then stood. "There are musicians about who'll oblige us, I'm sure."

Jenny clapped her hands excitedly, but what came out of her mouth next almost stopped my heart. "Oh, this is wonderful, Rosa," she said loudly, leaning forward and squeezing her arm. "But why does the gentleman refer to Tomas as your brother when he is no more your brother than mine? Is he referring to the fraternity implied by our pilgrimage? For if he is, then we're all one big happy family, are we not?"

The color drained from Rosa's face, so much so that it paled even next to Andres's white-gloved hand that he lifted to point at her and Tomas. "You are not brother and sister?" he asked.

"Of course not," Jenny answered, bouncing in her chair with every word. "They're playing a silly game, although no one will tell me why." Her face crinkled up in a smile that grew stiff and awkward as she waited for a response from someone, but there was only silence.

Finally Rosa spoke up. "We didn't intend to cause you offense, sir."

"I have no doubt, my dear lady," he said, "that you could convince a bird to stop flying and a fish not to swim if only for the knowledge that it would please you. I am not immune to your charms, but neither am I a bird or a fish." That said, he stood and left the table without another word.

I had never before felt capable of striking a woman, but in that instant it took every ounce of self-control I possessed to keep from slapping Jenny soundly. Tomas sat impassively in his chair, as though stripped of his identity and worth as a human being. And Rosa, as always, was impossible to read. She watched Andres walk off as though she could read the future across the breadth of his shoulders, but what that future might be was not revealed in her expression.

Moments later, musicians began assembling in the square. Tables were cleared and the weary clamor of the pilgrims was transformed into the boisterous and cheerful noise of a celebration. Feet that had been pounding the path for miles, swollen with blisters and aching with pain, began tapping to the sounds of instruments warming up. Music such as this, from the highlands of Spain, had the power to cause the dust of the road to fall away from those of us who were called by it, and to fill us with a surge of fresh energy as brisk as the mountain air. Although I was angry with Jenny, I couldn't help but feel it too and my heart began to skip along with the spirit of the moment.

Tomas tapped my shoulder and pointed toward Andres, who stood in the very center of the square shuffling his feet to the strains of the music. He was an imposing figure of a man, and standing alone as he was he looked rather like a military statue that had come to life. A sudden sweep of melodious wind filled the square and Andres began to dance in earnest. I knew this jig. It was a difficult one and best performed by men who possessed both athleticism and grace. He was doing a fine job, although his execution was a bit stiff. Nevertheless, it was rare to encounter anyone who could dance in such a fashion and the crowd was clearly impressed. Men gathered round to watch and applaud and before long one or two other young men were also dancing, but not with Andres's strength, and control. Next to him they looked like shadowy figures created by the dust of his boots.

More wine flowed and many pilgrims indulged beyond what their budgets would normally allow. To my surprise, Tomas raised his arm and called for the girl to bring us another pitcher as well, and our glasses were filled in an instant. Tomas was quivering with elation and relief as he brought his glass to his lips. He was convinced that Andres had made light of our little game, and that we needn't worry about further trouble. After all, could an angry man dance with such abandon? Could his mind be twisting with murderous designs while his body relented to participate in such frivolity? I should have told Tomas to stop drinking and keep his wits about him, that the danger had not yet passed, but I only kept quiet and watched.

When Andres had finished, many glasses were raised to him, but he bowed to our table alone, his eyes fixed upon Rosa, who nodded politely. He looked bereft as he stood there oblivious of the adulation bombarding him from all the wrong places. Then he turned his attention to me and held out his arm.

"He wants you to join him," Jenny said.

"I am in no mood to dance tonight," I returned blandly. "I'm rather tired."

"Tired from what? We didn't walk today. Some of those young men who were dancing just arrived and had barely a chance to sit down and—" But Jenny became silent when she heard Andres addressing the crowd and pointing in my direction, and gasped with delight when she caught the content of his speech.

"I have it on good authority," he said, "that in our midst is a wonderful dancer. Perhaps we can persuade him to share his talents with us." The crowd murmured its approval and looked about to see who this mysterious dancer might be.

"I'm sorry, Antonio," Rosa said, her face a portrait of regret. "I shouldn't have told him what a wonderful dancer you are. Perhaps I was wrong, and you are not so wonderful after all."

I hesitated to acknowledge Andres's request, but the crowd too was calling me out and challenging me. I stood and removed my coat, smoothing out my shirt as best I could, hoping the other pilgrims gathered would forgive the dirt on my shoes, and my wrinkled clothing. Standing in the center of the square, I painted a very different picture from Andres in his immaculate uniform and polished boots. Nevertheless, I closed my eyes and waited. The sounds of the square were silenced, and I heard only echoes from the mountains and a chorus of wind singing with a pure and lovely voice. The infectious rhythm of the tambourine prompted me to move the tip of my toe and find the ghostly pattern beneath the melody, the heart of my dance. The music soared and the musicians joined me as we searched for the union of body and spirit that is music and dance. We moved together, and I felt the music coursing through my legs, my arms, yet my control served as my abandon, and it was the precision and timing that inspired every move. I cried out with joy, and heard others calling out with me and clapping to the beat of my dance. When I chanced to open my eyes, I saw the wonder on their faces that they saw in mine, and we were all at once in love with the moment and the life that we knew. So long as the dance was alive, and the music played, and our voices rose above the stillness of the night, it felt as though we had conquered even death.

The roar of applause and cheering broke the trance, and I stood breathless in the center of the square before walking back through the crowd amid great praise. When I arrived at my table, the mood was not so jubilant. Although Jenny was nearly faint with wonder and took every opportunity to show her appreciation by taking my arm and even pressing my leg when I sat down, Rosa was clearly upset, and after a hasty compliment excused herself from the table with tears in her eyes.

Jenny explained to us as we watched Rosa weave her way through the crowd toward the women's dormitory, "She wasn't feeling well and wanted to get a good night's sleep before setting off tomorrow." Then she proceeded to pour herself another glass of wine. "But I'm enjoying myself immensely. I could stay up for hours. Perhaps I won't sleep at all," she concluded with a devilish smile. Then her face softened, and she addressed someone standing behind me. "Ah, Señor Andres," she said, "allow me to congratulate you on your dancing skill. For a moment I thought the very ground would shatter beneath you."

Andres was not alone. Standing next to him was a junior officer who held a small leather case. After Andres accepted Jenny's compliment with a dismissive nod, he focused his attention on me. "The lovely Rosa was correct. I must admit that your skill surpasses even mine." He nodded to his companion, who placed the leather case he held on the table between Tomas and me. "Whichever of you is more man than dog will open this case and understand what is implied by its contents," he said.

Tomas's shoulders jerked as though he'd been speared in the

heart, and his eyes accosted me with a furious fear that appeared to have left him paralyzed. I had reached for the case with every intention of opening it when Tomas slapped my hand away and opened it himself with such bluster and force that it nearly fell to the floor. Andres and the younger man sniggered when they saw Tomas's eyes water, and his mouth drop open at the sight of a long-barreled pistol nestled in black velvet.

"What is the meaning of this?" I asked.

"I am not accustomed to speaking with dogs, but in this case I will make an exception," Andres responded with a bow. "Your friend has accepted my challenge and I expect him to meet me tomorrow at dawn in the field beyond town."

"He has accepted nothing, and you know as well as I that dueling is illegal."

The young soldier laughed, but Andres silenced him with a scowl and spoke in a low and simmering growl. "My honor does not submit to trivial legalities. If he is not prepared and present tomorrow, as I request, I will hunt him down and shoot him in broad daylight if necessary. And I know this country like the back of my hand. There is no place he can hide."

I stood up. "Then I ask to take his place. He's never shot a pistol in his life; it would hardly be a fair match."

Andres appraised me with a serious eye, as he no doubt wondered whether I might be as good with a pistol as I was on the dance floor. But he needn't have worried. I'd held a gun only once or twice in my life, as it was never thought I'd have need of such a skill in the priesthood.

"I will have my satisfaction either way. Do as you wish," he said.

Andres left and we sat in silence for some time. Even Jenny appeared somber and reflective, but she couldn't resist running her fingertips along the sharp edges of the leather case on the table between us.

I could no longer contain myself. "It is your foolish and willful nature that has caused this," I said, fully hating her.

She didn't recoil, but remained pensive. "If the only way you can protect a woman's honor is by lying, then I feel very sorry for you both. And I'm sure Rosa feels the same."

The dagger in her words met its mark and I felt my pride warp and retire in the face of her judgment. Tomas was sputtering next to me, but in the end, we could say nothing, and she left us to our despair.

For the first time in our lives, Tomas and I argued heatedly about what to do and about who should face Andres the next morning. At the outset, Tomas insisted that this was his opportunity to demonstrate his courage, and that God had presented him with it for the purpose of winning Rosa's love, and he accused me of selfish cruelty for trying to rob him of it. Just at the point when I was prepared to concede, he succumbed to a violent fit of trembling that extended to his arms and legs, and it did not subside until I convinced him that it was preposterous for him to face Andres. Clearly, I had the better chance of survival, if for no other reason than I was not prone to such trembling fits.

As the night wore on, our thoughts took off in many desperate directions. We briefly considered the possibility of escape and concluded that Andres would eventually find us, as he'd promised, and that the life of a hunted fugitive would be intolerable. We reasoned that there might be a slight chance that Andres would miss his mark, or that his shot would result in wounding rather than killing me, and we discussed what action to take with each and every eventuality. Finally, once we had exhausted discussing all the practical matters that we could think of, we inspected the pistol carefully until we were satisfied that it was in good working order. Then, with only a couple of hours until daybreak, we rested our heads on the table and closed our eyes.

When the faint glow of dawn appeared in the window, I'd been awake for some time, listening to Tomas's hollow breathing. I shook him gently, and he woke with a start. The innocence of sleep was immediately supplanted by an anxious grimace when he remembered our dreadful circumstances.

"It's time to go," I said, taking up the pistol case. I felt unexpected relief in knowing that, if nothing else, the worst night of my life had finally ended. We washed our faces with the frigid water from the kitchen bucket before making our way out to the square. The stone buildings were black against the pale sky, and it was just possible to make out the path leading to the field beyond. There, I pictured the circle of trees that would obscure us from any observers who might happen by. The sound of gunfire wouldn't alarm or arouse anyone. This could be easily explained by the knowledge that hunters often ventured out in the early morning hours.

I was leaning on Tomas while retying my boots when I heard a door open and close across the square. The outline of two figures could be seen lingering in the doorway of the inn, but it was impossible to see them clearly through the mist and the darkness. One of them, a woman, began walking toward us and Tomas gasped faintly. It was Rosa. She wore the red shawl over her head, like a mantle, and her shoulders were hunched forward against the cold. She approached us, and held out her hand to me. "There will be no duel," she said. "Please, Antonio, give me the pistol." By this time, the other figure had also walked across the square. Andres stood next to her with his coat unbuttoned, and his bare chest visible underneath.

A seething anger burned in my throat. "What have you done, Rosa?"

"It is not what it seems," she said. "But I had to do something." Her hand remained extended, but I couldn't find it within me to give her the case.

Andres stepped forward. His voice had lost its bravado, and he sounded only tired and anxious to return to his bed. "Do as she says, I recant my earlier challenge . . . to you both," he said. "I will not trouble the lady again, and this will be the last day you see me. But I ask that you return the pistol, as it is one of a set and quite valuable to me."

Not knowing what else to do, I handed Rosa the case, and watched as she gave it to Andres. He glanced at her briefly. Gone was his adoring contemplation, although her face shone like a blessing in the gray light of morning.

We pressed her for an explanation as we made our way back to the *refugio,* but she shook her head, and smiled sadly, assuring us that she hadn't violated her honor and that that was all that mattered. I for one was convinced of the truth of this, for I couldn't conceive of any man releasing her so easily after he'd known the sublime pleasure of her company. But something extraordinary had happened between them, there was no doubt of that, and I suspected that this woman possessed a secret power even greater than her beauty. Later that morning, we heard the welcome sound of horse hooves on the cobblestones as Andres left the village with his men. And as he had promised, from that day forward we never saw him again.

21

SOMETHING ABOUT LOUIS had changed. He visited almost every night and was just as doting as ever, gushing about how sexy Carmen was, how delightful her voice and provocative her girth, but there was a difference, and it made Jamilet shiver just a little despite the warmth in the kitchen. She didn't like to think about it, but when she did she imagined that there was a little clock ticking away in his head, counting out the seconds and minutes and reminding him that every moment he was with Carmen, he wasn't where he should be. It made him jumpy and strange. Sometimes he didn't listen as Carmen told him funny stories that would normally have launched them both into a ruin of laughter, especially if they'd already had a few beers. And that was another thing—Louis hardly drank anymore. He'd force down a beer or two to play the part whenever Carmen scowled or asked him if he was planning on becoming the next pope. At these times, he'd smile sheepishly and explain that he didn't want to drink too much and get too tired because he was working extra hours to save the money he needed to bring his family back, and make things right.

Most of the time, Carmen was calmed by the thought that Louis was staying true to his promise to her, but at other times she leveled eyes at him that were boiling with suspicion. With every word he spoke, he seemed to shrink a little bit, and tenderize under the heat of her glare until his bones fell out of their sockets and he became a slithering mess, a pot of human flesh stewing in his own guilt. "It'll be different when the old lady gets back, Carmencita," he'd say, his palms outstretched to her.

"Yeah, right," she'd respond, flipping her head, and crossing her arms and legs so that all of her was twisted away from him, like a giant pretzel. She wouldn't even glance at him for the rest of the evening, and occupied herself with painting her toenails and laughing at things on television that she normally wouldn't consider funny. But laughter had always made Carmen feel strong, as if she could flip her upset on its head and make it dance for her awhile.

Nevertheless, he'd stay next to her on the couch, and even force himself to drink another beer. When Jamilet collected the empty cans, she noticed that the creases of his face had deepened, and he'd lost weight that he couldn't afford to lose, so that even his shoes were loose on his feet. But when he turned to look at Carmen, even if she was behaving badly, he was radiant with the glow of good health, and incapable, it seemed, of feeling anything but bliss.

One evening while she was doing the dishes, Jamilet managed to ask him when he thought his wife would be returning. Carmen was too proud to ask directly. She'd resort to making snide comments about never thinking she'd look forward to the old bitch coming back and the like, but nothing else.

Louis ran jittery fingers over his mustache and glanced at Carmen, who was sitting on the couch and happily munching her way through a giant bag of cheese puffs. "It's going to take a while longer than I thought," he said. "I got to send them money while they're there too. It makes saving real slow."

Jamilet wanted to be encouraging, but she feared that her aunt's nerves were fraying, and the next time she snapped it would be worse. "If you want, I can show them the way I came through the river. It wasn't so hard," she said, surprised by the desperation in her own voice.

"That's real nice of you, Jamilet, but my old lady's really old . . . like me. She can't be crossing rivers like a young girl."

Carmen shouted from the living room, "Louis, get your ass over here. You know I hate explaining the beginning of a movie to you."

"I'll be right there, Carmencita." He turned to Jamilet and whispered, "I think the real problem is . . . I got more woman than I can handle."

She wasn't sure if over the noise of the TV and the running water in the sink she'd heard him say "women" or "woman," but in either case, she could only agree.

For the second time in one week, Carmen couldn't find her car keys just as she was leaving for work in the morning. Jamilet helped to search for them while there was a barrage of accusations from Carmen, about being an obsessive "neat freak," as her aunt liked to call it, although on this morning her tone was devoid of its usual affection. After they turned the house upside down, the keys turned up in the laundry basket, tucked in the pocket of the trousers that Carmen had left on the bathroom floor the night before. Two days earlier they'd turned up in the refrigerator, and wouldn't have been found if Jamilet hadn't thought to defrost some chicken for dinner that evening.

"You see?" Carmen said, pointing the keys at Jamilet's face. "Just leave stuff where you find it." She rushed out to her car, leaving Jamilet to lock the front door.

Jamilet hated being late. Señor Peregrino would be disappointed and this would delay her reading lessons. He wouldn't sacrifice any time for that, and would be much more likely to postpone another installment of his story until the next day. Jamilet ran the first few blocks, but the stitch in her side forced her to slow down to a half run, and then to a brisk walk. When she saw Eddie leaning against the fence outside the hospital, she stopped completely. This time she had no doubt he was waiting for her.

Although it had been only a few days since she'd last seen him sitting on Pearly's front porch, they hadn't spoken since Carmen swallowed the pills, and it felt like an eternity of time, lengthened by worries and fears she could barely grasp, let alone manage. This was the first opportunity she'd had to thank him for helping her with Carmen.

As she approached, she realized she hadn't combed her hair very well that morning. She'd been so preoccupied with looking for her aunt's keys that she couldn't remember if she'd even washed the sleep from her eyes. She quickly passed a hand across her face, as though to make sure that her nose and mouth were more or less where they should be. Eddie pushed himself off the fence when he saw her.

They didn't greet each other, but Jamilet stood near enough to feel the warmth of his presence, and it moved her to the point of breathlessness. She waited for him to speak, hoping that if he didn't, she'd find words to justify the moment and lengthen it into something more than a chance encounter.

"How's your aunt?" he asked, as though the obvious way to start had just knocked him over the head.

Jamilet responded breathlessly, "Fine, she's doing really well. I . . . I didn't get a chance to thank you for helping her . . ."

"That's okay."

"I saw you on the porch, but I didn't want—"

"I understand," he said weakly. The conversation could have ended right there. Both Jamilet and Eddie waited for its natural conclusion to summon them, but they stayed where they were, watching the steam of their breath mingle and disappear. She looked more closely at him and noticed that his eyes were swollen, and dull. Men often looked like this when they'd been out drinking the night before, but in Eddie's case, she wondered.

He reached out and took hold of the fence to steady himself. His face was strained with something he didn't seem to know how to say. He opened his mouth and closed it, then opened it again. "I . . . uh . . . I know you have to get to work. I don't want to make you late."

"I don't mind," Jamilet said, almost before he could finish his sentence.

"I just started walking this morning. I didn't know where I was going or what I was doing, and I ended up here, I don't know why." His face softened momentarily and was then seized with an expression of grief, raw and achingly tender.

Instinctively Jamilet reached out and placed her hand on his arm. Her touch prompted him to speak and the words dropped from his mouth one after the other. "I guess it's because you knew she was sick, you know?" Tears glistened in the corners of his eyes. Jamilet kept her hand on his forearm, and said nothing. "I was pissed though." He chuckled while shaking his head, as though trying to make sense of a bad joke. "I didn't want to talk about it." He looked at her accusingly, and grew still. He lowered his head and his tears became streams of warmth between her fingers, still resting on his arm.

After several seconds of silence, Jamilet asked, "When did she die?"

Eddie lifted his free arm, wiped his sleeve across his nose, and sniffed. "Last night," he said.

❋

It was nearly impossible for Jamilet to keep her mind on the lesson. She listened with half an ear as Señor Peregrino reviewed the errors she'd made on her last assignment. She managed to respond somewhat coherently, but her mind wandered, like a kite that was constantly being teased off the ground. It was ready to lift off and soar into the sky, but there was Señor Peregrino, pulling on the string and forcing her back down to earth again and again with his insistence that she learn the difference between "knight" and "night," "hair" and "hare."

How could she concentrate on what Señor Peregrino was saying when she knew that that very evening she'd be meeting Eddie outside, by their tree, as they had the first night? It was his idea, and he offered it without hesitation, saying, "Meet me tonight, and we'll go for a walk or something . . . okay?" A smile found its way to his lips and Jamilet could only nod and agree to be there at whatever hour he asked, under whatever circumstances he wanted. It seemed that all at once, her life had a new purpose beyond itself, and she felt the irrational desire to laugh and cry and stare into space just to contemplate this miraculous turn of events.

Somehow she made it to lunch without appearing too distracted, although Señor Peregrino had been watching her with a certain curiosity. And when he pushed the chair by the desk out with his foot and asked her to sit while he continued his story, she promptly sat and waited for him to begin.

"Well," he said. "Where did I leave off?"

Jamilet flicked her attention to him, as she'd been studying the pastel blue of his sheets, wondering what she should wear that evening, for she'd already decided that her hair was long enough to wear loose. "I'm sorry, Señor . . . ?"

"My story," he repeated. "Where did I leave off?" He watched her squirm for an answer, and then leaned forward in his chair. "So, your memory isn't as good as you thought."

"I'm afraid not, Señor."

He sat back, somewhat self-satisfied. "Well, luckily for us both, I remember very well."

The higher we climbed into the mountains that guarded the entrance to El Bierzo and Galicia itself, the deeper we walked into her forests, and the more we encountered the rain. But unlike the others, I welcomed the rain because it encouraged long hours of introspection that I sorely needed. And it was while I stood on the riverbank one morning, watching Rosa find her footing on a slippery bridge, that many thoughts came to me at once: the humble manner in which she carried herself, and her patience with Jenny's constant prattle and airs. I thought of Tomas, whose pathetic countenance she met at every turn with kindness, always sensitive to his agony over her, of which she was undoubtedly aware. And then I thought of the mysterious way she'd saved our lives. This was truly an extraordinary woman.

A peaceful joy surged within me when I realized that what I felt for Rosa was not sinister or wrong. It had evolved into something quite wonderful, for I saw beyond her physical beauty and delighted in the total splendor of her being. I could no longer deny that I loved her more than life. Even so, I realized that telling her how I felt would only cause her to suffer. As always, she seemed concerned with matters beyond that of ordinary men, and I feared that my declarations of love would only add to her burdens. The most loving thing I could do would be to stay silent, and suffer alone with my love for her.

Late one evening after the others had retired, I was sipping my wine alone by the fire when suddenly I felt a warmth more ardent than the flames. I looked up to find Rosa standing before me.

"I'm sorry to disturb you, Antonio," she said with a slight bow of her head. "I'm finding it difficult to sleep. May I sit with you awhile?"

I straightened in my chair and reached for another to bring it closer to the flames. "You're not disturbing me at all. Please sit down. The fire is very pleasant." I poured her a glass of wine that she accepted with a nod, and I shivered pleasantly when the hem of her cloak brushed my knee as she took her seat.

Her face was taut with anxiety. "Nothing seems to upset you, Antonio," she said softly. "You are always so calm and sure of yourself."

There was a slight tone of accusation in her voice and I wasn't quite sure how to respond. "To use your words," I said, "things are not always what they seem."

She smiled and turned away, gracing me with her profile, more delicate than the glass she held to her lips. "I would like to tell you a secret, if you care to listen." The color rose to her cheeks.

"I would be honored."

"I've been thinking for a long while about how to say this, and now that we're so close to reaching our destination, I realize that I must do so now or lose my chance forever." She put down her glass, and turned to face me. "You must understand that I expect nothing from you. Only that you listen."

"I understand," I said, not understanding at all.

Her voice was slightly shrill, like that of a young girl confessing a minor sin. "I have told no other pilgrim until now that the reason I wanted to go to Santiago was to confirm my conviction for the church. My mother was never happy with my plans to become a nun. My family is poor and her desire has always been that I marry the richest man she can find—and I had many suitors," she said, not bragging, but lamenting the fact. "They came at all hours of the day and night, laden with presents and bursting with proposals, but I turned them all down. My hope and prayer was that the pilgrimage would convince her of my true dedication."

I'd been listening to her with my heart in my throat, as I couldn't believe that her quest was so similar to mine. I wanted to tell her that we harbored the same secret, but I remained silent and listened, as she had asked.

She gazed at me fully, her eyes pleading for sympathy. "I know that to speak as I am speaking to you now violates all rules of propriety. If my mother were here she would surely cut out my tongue, but I'm praying for a miracle, and I have great faith." She folded her trembling hands in her lap as tears welled in her eyes. "For you see, rather than strengthen my original intention, my journey has led me to a new one. I am in love with you, Antonio. Since the first day I heard you singing in the square, I have loved you."

Try to picture a young man after hearing such a confession from the most beautiful and perfect creature he's ever been blessed to know. Had I been standing, I would have fallen to my knees. As it was, it took effort for me to breathe and blink and make sure that this wasn't some kind of bizarre and fantastic hallucination.

We didn't speak for some time and she shifted her gaze to admire the fire while I stared at her, fearing that she might vanish into thin air if I dared to move.

Finally she broke the silence. "You've been doing a fine job of listening, Antonio. If you wish to speak now, I . . . suppose . . . what I mean is, don't worry about hurting me. I've been preparing myself, as it doesn't take a brilliant mind to discern your feelings for Jenny."

"My feelings for Jenny?" Her insinuation was like a bucket of ice water poured over my head.

Rosa became uncomfortable, as she was now betraying not her own secret, but another's. "I didn't mean to say it, it's just that I've seen how the two of you get on together, and under the circumstances I can't help but be interested." She managed a small guilty smile.

"I assure you, dear lady, that I have no special feelings for Jenny, none of the sort you intimate." Slowly, as though approaching a rare butterfly that might flutter off into the fields, I took her hands into mine and allowed the soft warmth of her touch to fill me. It was almost too much to look at her and touch her at the same time, but I remained composed while inhaling the sweet breath escaping her lungs. To think that she had no idea of my feelings for her caused me to falter for words, but I found them eventually, as any man would who must find his bearings to survive. "Imagine what you feel for me multiplied by a thousand, and you may come close to understanding my feelings for you. Not even I comprehend this love, but I am willing to submit to it completely, as I should have from the beginning."

"Don't tease me, Antonio." And she held her gaze upon me as though to discern my true heart, which I would gladly have ripped out of my chest to appease her. But she saw what she needed in my eyes, and graced me with a miraculous smile.

I brought her hands to my lips and from that moment our love was forever sealed.

Jamilet opened her eyes to find Señor Peregrino with his eyes closed, and a distant smile hovering about his lips. Behind his eyelids she saw the rolling movement, and she had the distinct impression that he was continuing with his story without bothering to tell it out loud.

"Excuse me, Señor," she said. "You stopped talking."

His eyelids fluttered. "I'm aware of that," he replied abruptly, but his smile still lingered. Then his eyes flew open, and blinked through the mist of his recollection. "I'm simply reflecting on the most precious moment of my life." He sharpened his gaze. "It's a curious thing—you weren't particularly interested in listening when we began, and now you don't want me to stop. That shouldn't surprise me considering your state of mind this morning."

"I'm always interested in listening to your story, Señor."

"Oh, Jamilet," he said, folding his arms and cocking his head to one side. "I'm not so easy to fool as you think." He nodded slowly while watching her, as though he could know everything about her by following the contour of her brow line, the curve of her cheek. Jamilet was prepared to complain, but he held up a hand to silence her and continued, "Your complete preoccupation today leaves no doubt in my mind that you're either in love or obsessed."

Jamilet blushed and fumbled with her hands, but said nothing. Then she began to gather the coffee cups and spoons together, but stopped. "How do you know if it's love or obsession?" she asked.

"At first you can't tell the difference," he answered. "It takes time to know what you're dealing with. But everything of true value will stand the test of time. It's no different with love."

"How can I love someone I hardly know?"

"It happens all the time," he said, leaning forward in his chair. "But be careful, Jamilet. When you're in this state of mind, things are not always as they appear."

22

⌣

A S LUCK WOULD HAVE IT, Carmen and Louis had made plans to go out to dinner and a movie, ensuring that they'd be gone for several hours. After they left, Jamilet slipped into her aunt's bedroom and studied the collection of perfumes she kept on her dresser. She selected the one in the twisted bottle that looked as if passion itself had made the glass writhe with the heat and deliberation of love. She dabbed a dot behind her ears and on each wrist as she'd seen her aunt do, but decided to forgo the extra pat on her cleavage. She was confident that the purple long-sleeved shirt Louis had given her would cover her sufficiently, and with a sweatshirt over that, there was no chance that Eddie would see anything she didn't want him to see.

She waited beneath the branches of the tree, beyond the light that shone from the streetlamp, breathing in her own scent and feeling a bit light-headed because of it. The perfume was stronger than she had expected. She plucked a moist leaf from overhead and started to rub at her wrists and behind her ears with it. What a fool she was to be dreaming of seduction at a time like this. Eddie wanted to talk about his mother's death, everything else he could get from Pearly. At this very moment they were probably grop-ing each other on the porch, as they always were, and this image helped Jamilet relax a little. She sniffed at the leaf to determine if she'd succeeded in rubbing off any of her foolishness, but her senses didn't seem to be working properly. She was surrounded on all sides by an alien buzz that blurred her vision and confounded her hearing. She took a deep breath to calm herself. Eddie would be there any minute. Or maybe he'd forgotten because Pearly was helping him manage his sadness in the best way girls can.

She heard a soft rustling, and Eddie appeared. "Let's go," he whispered, turning around and leading the way down the street, but he wasn't rushed as he'd been on the night they'd walked to Braewood Asylum. Jamilet had no difficulty keeping up with him, and a few well-timed glances revealed that he was more composed and rested than he'd been that morning. He was lost in his own thoughts, yet seemed to know exactly where he was going. There was purpose in his stride as he turned the corner after they'd walked a few blocks in silence.

Finally, he asked, "Do you like ducks?"

"Do you mean . . . the birds?"

He chuckled. "Yeah, you know. They have flat beaks, and they say 'quack, quack.'"

"I guess," Jamilet said, and she noticed that he carried a plastic bag that swung at his side.

Jamilet hadn't known the park existed, although she'd walked through that part of the city on several occasions when going to the market. It was set back from the street, behind a sickly looking grove of trees choked by the fumes of the constant traffic they were forced to inhale. Once behind the trees, the traffic noise softened into a mild whir, and Jamilet focused on the steady sound of Eddie's breathing as he made his way along the path that bordered a good-size pond. He was heading toward a bench perched on a slight knoll on the farthest side of the pond. He hopped up and sat on the table, with his feet on the bench seat, leaving plenty of room for Jamilet to do the same. She left two feet or so of space between them, so that when he opened the bag for her, she had to lean in a bit for a handful of bread crumbs.

He tossed out the first fistful, and they heard the splash of water and the muttering, throaty call of the ducks as they began to stir. In an instant it seemed the entire flock was waddling at their feet. Jamilet threw out another fistful, and the calls grew into little trumpet blasts, for they were not accustomed to such human generosity at this hour. Jamilet threw out another fistful of bread, and felt the urge to tell the ducks to quiet down. The last thing she wanted was for them to be found, because sitting on the park bench and feeding the ducks with Eddie was the closest thing to paradise she'd ever known.

In less than five minutes the bread crumbs were consumed, and the ducks, complaining and exasperated with such a swift conclusion to their good fortune, waddled back to their watery homes in the tall grasses near the pond's edge. The silence grew into the darkness again, and Eddie asked, "When did your mother die?"

Jamilet's lips trembled as she answered. "About a year ago."

"How long was she sick?"

Jamilet sighed. Although the night was warm, she was shivering from head to toe. "She had to stay in bed and rest her heart for a long time." Jamilet tucked her hands in under her armpits and told him about her mother's illness, leaving out that she was certain it had been caused by misery over her mark. Eddie listened closely, and Jamilet feared that he'd sense the gap in her story, the omission as obvious as a giant hole. But after she'd finished he merely said, "My mother wasn't sick for too long. Everyone says that's good 'cause she didn't suffer."

Jamilet wasn't sure how to respond. Eddie yearned to experience the comfort of their shared grief, but when her mother died she felt a freedom that wasn't seemly for a daughter to feel, as if for the first time in her life she could breathe full and deep. No longer did she have to look into those beautiful dark eyes that held her prisoner to unknown fears. When Lorena scrubbed the floors at the Miller house while Jamilet played with Mary, she'd look up from her work, a thick lock of her hair partially covering her eyes, but the pain in them was not obscured. As she sat in her rocker by the window watching Jamilet tend the chili patch, her mouth would turn in a lost smile, as though she were not looking at her daughter, but at the unspeakable future she could never change.

Eddie's foot moved an inch closer to Jamilet's, and she realized she hadn't been listening to him, as he had to her. "Has anyone told you that . . ." He stopped himself, and stuffed his hands back in his pockets. ". . . that you're different . . . kind of."

Jamilet felt her insides melt and turn a little. "Yes," she said.

"I don't mean that it's bad," Eddie said.

"That's okay." Jamilet turned away slightly and watched the headlights of passing cars beyond the trees seek them out, trying to penetrate the soft cushion of peace that surrounded them. The light didn't reach far enough to touch them, and found instead patches of green and dirt and trees, snapshots of normalcy within which their quiet adventure unraveled. She heard the scrape of his jeans across the splintered wood as he moved nearer, and felt his gaze trace the line of her profile. But she couldn't move, she couldn't even blink. She was paralyzed by her yearning to be found, and it wrestled fitfully with her fear of being truly discovered.

She felt the fabric covering her arm shift over her skin. Eddie was touching her sleeve, and still she couldn't move. "Aren't you hot with those long sleeves?" he asked.

"No, not really," Jamilet said and squeezed her armpits, which were moist with perspiration.

Eddie breathed deep and turned to look through the trees, as Jamilet was. He said, "I'm not gonna jump you or anything, so you can relax. I just wanted some company. I used to come here with my mom . . . that's all."

"When you were little?"

"Yeah. She used to walk me home from school every afternoon. She brought bread from the house 'cause she knew I liked to feed the ducks."

"She must've been a nice lady," Jamilet said.

Eddie leaned back on his elbows, so he was almost lying down, as she'd seen him do on Pearly's porch countless times. "Yeah, but she had a temper." He whistled softly. "She was nice most of the time, I guess."

Jamilet loosened her fists. She found the courage to turn and look down on him, and became momentarily lost in the broad line between his shoulders. A beam of headlights swept over them to reveal that he was studying Jamilet too, as though trying to understand his loss in the delicate bridge of her nose, and her soft wide eyes. He looked away again. "Do you think," he said, his voice almost a whisper, "that maybe she's here right now. I mean . . . you know, how some people believe that after you die, the ghost kind of hangs around to make sure things are going okay. You know, not like they're haunting or anything, just watching."

Jamilet pondered this question for some time. If ever she wanted to be spiritual and more like her grandmother, it was now, but being so near Eddie, it was nearly impossible to transcend the physical realm. Overwhelming sensations were coursing through her body. There was a pleasant tingling running up her thighs, and through her hips, and a delicious warmth was emanating from her abdomen and coloring her cheeks. She looked down at him again, his glistening eyes, his smooth mouth set tight against the relentless tide of grief surging within him, as it had that morning. All at once, she felt the tenderness a mother feels for her sleeping child. The next moment, she sensed his strength, as solid and real as his grief, and the allure of his complexity. All of this, and the wonder that they were sharing this moment alone together on a park bench in the semidarkness of a spring night. The whole of her trembled with a feeling she'd never known before, and it moved her to speak to his desires, and to find the words he needed to hear, even as she looked directly into his eyes.

"She's here right now, Eddie," she said. "She still loves you. That never changes."

The muscles of his face softened and relaxed into a smile. He lay back on the bench completely and put his hands under his head as he contemplated the night sky through the trees. "A lot of stars out tonight," he said. "Lie down and take a look." He scooted over to make sure she had plenty of room to lie down next to him.

Jamilet stretched out and beheld a smattering of dimly lit stars through a haze of city lights and smog. Still, there were enough stars to lose count if one were of a mind to do it.

"Hey, did you see that?" he asked with boyish enthusiasm. "It was a shooting star."

Jamilet strained her eyes hard, and shook her head. "I missed it."

They lay quietly for a while longer and then he said, "You know what they say about shooting stars, don't you?"

Jamilet said, "It's a soul going up to heaven."

"Do you believe that stuff?"

Jamilet had never thought about it before, but she answered, "Yeah. Don't you?"

Eddie's breathing quickened and then the silence around them grew heavy with grief. Although he didn't want to, he wept, his pain sputtering out between the tight fist in his heart. He brought one hand down to his side, and Jamilet thought he was searching for a handkerchief when she felt his fingers on her wrist. They lingered there for a moment, then slipped down to her palm, where they found the spaces between her fingers and folded into them, soft and warm.

They remained this way for a very long time, but neither of them spoke until Jamilet said, "My aunt will worry if I'm not there when she gets home."

They sat up and were preparing to leave, but Jamilet felt momentarily disoriented, and unsure of herself. It was as though she'd glimpsed the wonders of heaven, and the mysteries of the universe had been hers for a few precious moments. Now she was expected to resume a normal life back on earth as if nothing had happened.

They walked back the way they'd come, a proper and friendly

distance between them. They were almost to Jamilet's house when Eddie stopped a couple of yards from the tree, and announced blandly, "Pearly and me . . . we aren't together anymore. But it's still better for you if she doesn't see us."

Jamilet's eyes flew open. "You broke up?"

Eddie shrugged. "I'll tell you about it later," he said and his eyes flickered over her shoulder. "Isn't that the old man's car?"

Jamilet turned to see Louis's Pinto parked out front, with Louis and Carmen still sitting inside, enjoying a long and amorous good-bye. With barely another word, she quietly ran back to the house and managed to appear as if she'd just walked out of the front door when she heard the car drive up. She turned to look back, but Eddie was gone.

Señor Peregrino was glowing with pride as he taped Jamilet's latest writing exercise on the wall. "This," he said, with a ceremonious flair, "is your best work so far. Do you realize that you didn't make even one mistake?"

Jamilet blushed. "Are you sure, Señor? I usually make at least two or three."

"Not a one," he said. "And I can no longer teach you with blank paper and pen as I've been doing. We'll have to get you some real books from the library."

Jamilet clasped her hands together at the thought. "We can go together, Señor. I'm sure that if I speak to Nurse B. . . ."

"The truth is that with your current literacy skills, you really don't need me anymore." He sighed. "At any rate, you've earned yourself a nice rest—a little vacation. How about if you take a week or so away from your studies?"

"That sounds fine, Señor. And then you can spend more time telling me the rest of your story."

He said nothing, but eased himself back in his chair and began to tidy up his desk. "Well, I think you'll be glad to know that

I've decided not to continue with my story, Jamilet. I can't help but notice how preoccupied you've been lately, and well . . . it only stands to reason that what interests an old man wouldn't necessarily be of interest to a young woman. I'll be returning your documents forthwith and you can choose your course."

A few months ago, Jamilet would have been overjoyed by such news. But hearing it now, she felt that she was being cheated somehow and for the first time she could remember, it seemed very important that she speak out for justice. "This is unfair, Señor," she said with surprising forcefulness. "We had an agreement. I was to listen to your story, all of it, until it was finished, and then you'd return my papers, not before."

Señor Peregrino cocked his head to one side, a quizzical expression playing on his face. "I stole them from you. Don't you remember?" He shrugged. "Perhaps 'found them' is more accurate, but I forced you into this arrangement. There's no denying that."

"But . . . but that doesn't matter now." Jamilet talked very quickly, as though to keep herself from thinking too much.

"And why not, child?" He peered at her steadily, trying to see beyond the youthful sheen of her face.

"I just . . . I want to hear the rest of your story. I *need* to hear it because . . . because I don't have my own stories anymore."

"Your own stories?"

She nodded emphatically. "I used to make up stories all the time, but since I started hearing yours, I can't pretend anymore."

"I see," he said, slightly dismayed. "Once again you accuse me of pretending."

"Aren't you pretending at least some of the time?" Jamilet asked cautiously.

Señor Peregrino's gaze turned inward as he thought about how to answer her. Then he straightened in his chair and his eyes brightened. "What I have learned is that we're always pretending, Jamilet. From the moment we wake up in the morning to the moment we close our eyes at night. From the day we're born to the day we die—everything around us is an illusion. Reality emerges over time from those experiences in our lives that we choose to believe in."

Jamilet fastened her mind on his glittering eyes and tried to grasp his meaning. As usual, it eluded her, but she felt inspired nonetheless. She stood up, straightened her shoulders, and proclaimed, "Then I choose to believe in your story, Señor. It's my reality and it's wrong for you to take it from me."

He chuckled and then sobered, his cheeks quivering with emotion. "You're an amazing child, Jamilet. And it is my constant entertainment to be witness to that fact."

"Then it's only fair that you provide me with some entertainment in return."

"Well, I don't know about that . . ."

"And you can't possibly stop when you're at the most exciting part of the story, even though there have been many exciting parts."

"Yes, that's true," he said, getting caught up in her enthusiasm in spite of himself.

"There was the time when you first saw Rosa, and when you stood up to Andres, and the time Rosa saved you and Tomas from the duel, but this last part was the best of them all."

"Do you really think so?"

"Oh yes. But I have to tell you that I knew right from the beginning that Rosa was going to fall in love with you."

"How could you be so sure?" he asked, clearly delighted by her prediction.

"Because if she hadn't, there'd be no reason for you to tell me your story."

Señor Peregrino smiled while crossing his arms across his chest and appraising his student with newfound admiration. Later that afternoon, his story resumed.

In an instant, my world forever changed. What did it matter if night followed day, if it was necessary to eat when hungry, and sleep when fatigued? I was overcome by a whirling ecstasy that all at once rearranged everything I understood to be important in life. Rosa loved me, and there was nothing else that mattered next to that. I felt as unworthy as a worm plucked out of the dirt, and placed upon a golden throne. And, while I considered everything about my angel to be perfect, I wondered if she might not be a bit foolish to love me when she could have chosen from any number of wealthy and accomplished men. But this thought I pushed away from my mind whenever it arose. The love I felt in my heart overcame all of my doubts.

I wanted to declare my love for Rosa to the world, but she convinced me that it would be disastrous if Jenny and Tomas knew at this stage of the journey. Upon our arrival in Santiago, we would tell them both the truth. We had no doubt that the miraculous power of Santiago's love and healing would ease their pain, and our anxieties as well. Until then, we vowed to keep our love and our plan to marry a secret.

We marched on through villages with thatched-roof houses surrounded by green fields dotted by sheep and cattle. As we ascended higher along the lonely ridges, my love and imagination flourished with the heather, and broom, and wild thyme surrounding us. I pictured my homecoming, with Rosa on my arm. The road to my village was rough, and not unlike the one upon which we traveled. The first thing one sees is the old church with its weathered stone gate and tower. The bells would be ringing, of course, and my neighbors would be seen peeking out of their windows, toothless old ladies gaping at the sight, and children looking up from their chores to admire the dark angel, too stunning for words. My parents, already aware of my decision to leave the clergy, know it is because of a woman and are ashamed that their son should be as vulnerable to human need as their neighbor boys. They've already decided that no woman could possibly justify such a decision. But when they see her, their criticisms are silenced.

When they hear her voice and come to learn the workings of her sweet mind, they are convinced of her worthiness, and the infallibility of my decision, as surely as if Santiago himself had appeared before them to bless the union. The cold reception they planned is instantly transformed into a celebration for the new couple.

The hours on the road passed quickly when I occupied my mind with such thoughts, and the pain in my feet was easy to endure when I stole glances at my exquisite prize. But it was impossible to envisage a homecoming without thinking of Tomas. He would be there too, and when I tried to imagine him happy by our side, sharing in the joy of our love, my vision grew hazy and when the clouds parted, I saw his limp body hanging from a tree, eye sockets empty and bleeding from the incessant picking of birds. These thoughts too I pushed out of my mind by reminding myself that in Santiago, miracles awaited.

We arrived at Foncebadon as weary as we'd ever been, yet we agreed to walk a few more kilometers to the next town. We'd heard that there we'd find a hostel that, for a nominal fee, provided pilgrims with a tub of hot water in which they could submerge their entire bodies. The cost of this experience depended upon the number of people willing to make use of the same tub of water.

We walked the last few kilometers with renewed vigor as we anticipated this uncommon luxury. I had no doubt that Tomas was thinking, as I was, how to ensure that he was next in the bath after Rosa, for there was no doubt that this heavenly soup would satisfy any man for an eternity. I glanced at Tomas. He was watching Rosa with eyes blazing. He'd spoken little to me in the past several days, but there were precious few days left and I had no doubt that he'd attempt to speak with Rosa about his feelings for her soon, something best avoided if we were to keep our own love a secret.

When we arrived at the hostel, the bath was prepared in a small room off the kitchen. In this way it was easier for the attendant to carry buckets of hot water, one after the other, until the deep metal tub was filled. Once this was done, there was no need to question who would be first to bathe. Jenny sprang to her feet instantly, and disappeared without a word into the closet. Meanwhile, the three of us took in a bit of the rare Galician sun. The mist that hung low and thick for most of the day suddenly parted to reveal a world that seemed to have been magically colorized. Rosa sat at the edge of the field dozing before a vivid backdrop of green, her cheeks warm with the heat of the sun. I found a sharp stick to poke at the hardened mud encrusted on the bottom of my boots, and it fell to the ground in large chunks.

Tomas cleared his throat. "Rosa, I was hoping to speak with you after the meal tonight . . ."

"Tonight?"

"Yes, if you don't mind."

Rosa shrugged. "Why don't we talk here, right now?"

Tomas looked at me as though to implore me to leave, but I pretended to be far too absorbed with the matter of removing the mud from my shoes to notice.

"I believe there's a heavy brush in the kitchen that would do very well for that, my friend," he said, trying to sound jovial and offhanded in his attempt to get rid of me.

"This is working quite well, actually," I responded as I managed to wedge off another giant clump that disintegrated the moment it hit the ground.

Tomas stood and sighed, looking out toward the meadow, glistening with sunlight. A pleasant path wound its way through the field as it headed toward the foothills. He would ask Rosa to join him on a walk along this path, I was sure of it; and he was gathering the courage to do so when Jenny emerged from the kitchen amid a cloud of steam, wearing a rosy smile. Never before had I been so happy to see her.

"I feel human again," she announced. "I must weigh ten pounds less than I did before the bath."

Rosa giggled nervously, as relieved as I that, for the moment, the conversation with Tomas had been stalled. She left quickly, with excuses that she didn't want the water to get cold. Jenny also left, saying that she was ready for a long nap.

Once we were alone, Tomas sat down next to me, obviously annoyed. "I've never seen you take such an interest in the condition of your shoes, Antonio."

I held my stick out to him. "I can do yours next. I'm almost finished with mine."

He ignored my offer, and watched me closely, as though trying to read my mind. When he spoke, I heard that all too familiar tone of resignation in his voice. "You needn't worry about me, Antonio. If she doesn't return my love, I'll know what to do."

I threw my stick to the ground. "You're behaving like a fool! No woman is worth your sanity, let alone your life."

"And why not?" he retorted. "Doesn't the Bible instruct men to leave their parents and cling to their wives and to love them more than their own lives? I'd gladly go to my death if, in dying, Rosa understood how much I loved her."

I didn't know how to respond to this strangely transformed Tomas. I wanted to grab his shoulders and shake him to his senses. A few months earlier, he would have responded with laughter and a playful shove in return. Now I had no doubt that he'd consider such an action to be an attack and would retaliate like an injured animal.

And so, I was careful with what I said. "Perhaps it would be wiser to wait until you arrive at Santiago. There I believe we'll all find the strength to accept what we must. And we can continue our lives with renewed hope."

Tomas turned to me, his expression as resolved as I'd ever seen it. "That may work very well for you, Antonio. But for me, there is no longer hope or faithlessness, misery or joy. There is only Rosa."

23

For several weeks, Jamilet avoided looking at the mark. And when she bathed, she didn't run her hands along her shoulders and down the back of her thighs as she usually did. At these times she preferred to imagine Eddie touching the smooth, normal skin on her throat and breasts, as she wondered if true love was powerful enough to make miracles happen. Every evening that she prepared to go meet Eddie, she convinced herself that the world was full of miracles—that they were as plentiful as the stars.

They'd been meeting at the park every Wednesday evening, after Carmen and Louis went out. One time Eddie even took her to his mother's graveside, and told her that he hadn't been there with anyone else. Frequently, they held hands, as they had on that first night, but these occurrences were as fleeting as they were tender. Jamilet knew that the inevitable would follow.

During their last visit it had been a particularly warm night, and as they were walking back to the tree, Eddie asked, "Why do you always wear long sleeves and keep yourself so covered up?"

Jamilet should have been well prepared with an answer. But with all the potential scenes she'd been playing over and over again in her mind, with all the strategies she'd devised in order to gently fend him off without discouraging him, the possibility that he should begin with such a simple question had never occurred to her. The various ways she might answer rattled about in her brain—there were so many ill-formed lies to choose from, and each one seemed just as foolish as the next. She took a deep breath and came out with the first idea she could articulate. "My aunt doesn't want me to have a baby right now," she blurted out, quite shocked by her own pronouncement, and not at all certain about where it would lead. Nevertheless, she stumbled on. "She *makes* me wear this kind of clothing to keep the guys away." Jamilet left it at that, certain that her lie was preposterous enough to be funny.

But Eddie wasn't laughing. Instead, he appeared confused, and even slightly annoyed. "With the crazy stuff she wears?" he asked. "Why should she care if you show a little skin?"

Jamilet shrugged, and even managed a bit of annoyance of her own. "I know, that's what I say, but as long as I live in her house I have to do what she says."

"All the girls I know wouldn't care what anyone else thought, they'd just wear what they wanted, but I guess you're different . . . not like a normal girl."

And those words tormented Jamilet more than anything—*not like a normal girl*—because they were truer than Eddie could ever imagine.

Spring's mild temperatures gave way to the relentless heat of summer, and at times Señor Peregrino's fifth-floor room became unbearably hot. On some days it seemed that steam was rising from the floorboards, and the water from the cold-water faucet ran warm no matter how long Jamilet let it run. She wondered how Señor Peregrino was able to concentrate so intently on his letters when she was barely able to think. She took a break from her reading, and opened the window as far as she could, staring out at the still haze of the afternoon. Even the birds were resting and quiet, and the only sound was the drone of distant traffic, so constant as to be just another layer of silence. The occasional tinkling of the ice-cream truck could be heard, but it never ventured up the drive leading to the hospital. If it had, Jamilet would have run down the stairs and purchased ice cream for the two of them.

"You're daydreaming," Señor Peregrino observed. "Or perhaps you're indulging in one of your make-believe stories."

"I'm only thinking about how nice it would be to have an ice cream right now, it's so hot."

He nodded and wiped his brow with his handkerchief. "I believe it is the hottest day of the year, but it'll get hotter still, I'm afraid."

"How can you stand it, Señor? Why don't we go down to the garden and enjoy the breeze? We can read down there."

He turned back to his papers. "You go. I'll wait here for you."

Jamilet's physical discomfort prompted her to speak bluntly. "You're allowed to go outside, Señor. Nurse B. told me so herself, and she's in charge of this whole hospital. Why don't you ever leave your room, or walk in the grounds like the other patients?"

Señor Peregrino looked away, his eyes shadowed with a strange and bitter reverie. "Because I'm not like the other patients, make no mistake about that! And what's more, your Nurse B., as you call her, is not in charge of me! I'll leave my room at the appointed hour, and not when you or Nurse B. or anyone else thinks I should."

Jamilet hadn't the faintest idea how to respond whenever he spoke from that secret hate-filled space in his heart. So she said nothing, but when she dared look back at him she saw that his mouth was set in that familiar stubborn frown. She imagined that if he were to smile at that moment, his nose, eyes, and ears would very likely drop off his face. But to her surprise, his sour mood passed quickly, and an hour or so later he invited her to sit and listen to his story until the worst of the heat had passed. The hard lines on his face so secure in their downcast orientation a moment ago were lifted by their roots like dying branches summoned by a new day.

"I'm afraid," Rosa whispered to me early one morning in the dining room just before we set off. "But I don't know exactly what it is that I fear."

I tried to understand her meaning and the source of this fear. But my thinking was confused by my longing, and my overwhelming desire to protect her and spare her any pain.

"Put your mind at ease, my love," I said while softly stroking her hand. "I won't let anything happen to you."

We heard the latch on the door, and my hand quickly left hers. Tomas entered with an expression glazed by sleep and worry. He took in the sight of Rosa for his breakfast, as he did every morning, and found the strength to strap on his pack along with the burden of his love for her. For several days he'd eaten very little, and every night I heard the sounds of his tormented dreams. I tried to wake him once or twice, but it was no longer possible for me to comfort him.

Jenny joined us a moment or so later with her usual exuberance and talk about her plans for the day, how far she wanted to walk, what she'd determined to be the best destination, and the best places to rest along the way. One day Rosa said to me, "Jenny has the heart of a lion and the cunning of a fox. I wish I could be more like her, Antonio."

"Please, no," I said, exaggerating my distress in the hope of winning her precious laughter. "That's like saying you want to paint a mustache on the *Mona Lisa* or attach falcon wings on a pig to make it fly." But Rosa's eyes still glistened at the thought of becoming more like Jenny and I'm afraid that this overwhelmed her appreciation of my humor.

To the west we caught our first glimpse of the wild mountains of Galicia. The flutter of the pilgrims' excitement increased as we approached our destination, now only a week or two away. The words on every pilgrim's lips had something to do with the glory of the Santiago cathedral and the many miracles attributed to its saint. With my miracle secured, my only prayer now was for Tomas. He walked up ahead of the rest, turning every now and then to be assured of Rosa's presence. She was usually with Jenny, as we made it a point to never walk together.

As much as I anticipated my union with Rosa and taking her home as my bride, a strange sadness possessed me when I realized that our adventure was almost at an end. On the *camino,* my heart and mind had, along with the plodding of my feet, found a peaceful rhythm. Life's irrelevant distractions were gone. We had all that we needed, and every moment was complete in the present knowing of ourselves and our companions. Back in the world, I knew this would change. Even with Rosa at my side, it would change.

I doubled my step and caught up to Tomas in a couple of strides. He was mumbling to himself and his eyes were half closed. I wondered that he didn't trip, but his feet were sure and steady on the path. Aware that I was next to him, he raised his head and removed his hood, but he didn't smile kindly, the way he had before we began the *camino.* He simply stared at me with vacant eyes.

"You look tired today, my friend," I said, feeling guilty for my casual overture when my heart was weighed with the knowledge of what awaited him.

"And you look full of life, as though you were at the beginning of your journey and not at the end."

Afraid that the flush of my face would betray me, I stumbled on a loose stone. "I suppose it's my anticipation of seeing the cathedral that gives me renewed strength, and helps me think about something other than my aching feet."

The breeze that came down from the mountains suddenly whipped up, prompting us to pull our hoods over our heads. Rosa and Jenny were still walking arm in arm behind us, their scarves wrapped snugly against the cold. The wind began to stir the trees into a frenzy, and we heard the whining of cattle searching for shelter. Overhead a thick blanket of black clouds was drifting toward us at an uncanny speed. I spotted a shelter for cattle, thankfully unoccupied, and motioned in that direction. I was sure the storm would be upon us in a matter of seconds.

We huddled close under the crude thatched awning, watching the spectacle unfold. The sky darkened to a fearsome gray, frothing as the wind howled. Thunder reverberated across the sky in a shuddering roar, causing every creature, and even the stones, to tremble in its wake. We became one with the frogs and birds and beetles that scrambled for cover under our feet. The air was infused with a chilling cold as solid as the mountains in the distance, and we felt the pressure of it upon our chests. Soon the rain assaulted the land in thick sheets of ice and frost. It pounded the thatched roof above our heads and mutilated the foliage around us.

I moved nearer Rosa, who was staring out at the storm with green eyes like heavenly embers. The cold left me instantly at the sight of her, and my head swam with the ecstasy provoked by all that is beautiful and good in life. Careful that Jenny and Tomas couldn't see me, I searched for her hand beneath the confusion of all our capes and packs, and our fingers embraced as the storm raged on. My heart pounded louder than the thunder overhead as she caressed my palm, stroking each finger with exquisite tenderness. I returned the gesture and took my time exploring each soft finger from base to tip, my caresses interrupted only by a ring on her third finger. As Tomas shivered next to me, reciting the rosary, imploring God to spare us from certain doom, I perspired with ardor. I might have gone screaming out into the storm to cool off, but shuddered instead, and withdrew my hand for fear that I might lose my composure altogether and give our secret away.

When the worst of the storm had passed, Jenny was the first to speak. "I'm frozen from the inside out," she muttered, slightly breathless. "I need something warm in my stomach before I go on."

"There's a village just at the base of this hill," I offered.

Tomas returned his rosary to its leather pouch and was the first to leave the shelter to assess the strength of the wind. It had quieted to a soft purr and the rain was misting in fine gusts around us. Standing in the middle of the road, he held out his arms like a toreador taunting a bull. He glanced at Rosa and seemed quite pleased to see her watching him with certain interest.

"It's safe to go on," he proclaimed, as though he and the storm were on intimate terms. "But I caution you to watch your step, as the ground is slippery with mud and puddles. Follow me, Rosa, and I'll show you the best path to take."

The rest of us ventured out from under the shelter as if we'd been hibernating all winter. My muscles were stiff, but I felt reborn. Rosa's cheeks were emblazoned and her lips curled in a small smile as she watched Tomas meander along the path, skipping over puddles. I have to admit that I felt a slight pang of jealousy from seeing how amused she was, but I quickly comforted myself with reminders that her feelings for me went far beyond amusement.

Jenny shook herself from head to toe with the exuberance of one engaging in spring cleaning. "I for one can find my own way," she said, with a nod that let us know she was miffed by Tomas's oversight.

"Of course I'll help you as well," he said, somewhat embarrassed. He held his hand out to her for good measure, but she waved it away and proceeded to adjust her shawl with exaggerated care.

"We ladies can fend for ourselves. Isn't that true, Rosa?" she said, extending her arm so that they could continue walking as they had been before the storm. "Perhaps you boys should walk up ahead and find a proper café where we might redeem our humanity."

"I believe it would be wiser," Rosa said as she patted Jenny's arm in a warm and friendly manner, "if we stayed together."

Behind Jenny's yellow-gray eyes, sparks flew. "Nonsense," she returned, enunciating each word hard against her teeth, as if she might spit were she not such a lady. "We'll be perfectly safe. I can protect you better than either of these two," she said, coloring at her own remark.

She fumed in the mist, appearing to turn orange against the somber green of the darkened field. At that moment a glittery flash of light prompted me to look at her hands. My knees weakened as though I'd been kicked from behind by a horse, for on her third finger Jenny wore a ring—two golden snakes twisting into each other and crowned by a pair of wings. It was undoubtedly the ring I'd encountered moments earlier. Rosa was wearing no ring at all.

I felt Jenny's glare on my back like a spear prodding and poking me all the way down the hill toward the village. When we arrived, I sat by the fire apart from the others, and Tomas approached me with a mug of warm cider in hand. "Has the cold gotten to you?" he asked, genuinely concerned. He almost sounded like the Tomas of old, and I was unexpectedly comforted. For a moment I wished that we were back in our previous life, anything in order to avoid feeling like a foolish boy who'd been seduced by his own shadow in broad daylight.

"I'm okay," I responded, taking the cider and forcing myself to drink. With that, I glanced back with every intention of finding Rosa, but my eyes found Jenny instead. She had spread herself out over a chair with her shawl slung back across her shoulders, revealing the tight damp bodice that clung to her torso. She caught me looking at her and read my expression like a scholar of the most lurid intentions known to man. Her face, which had been slack and tired a moment ago, tightened with pleasure and she smiled at me.

I turned away and breathed in the cider, hoping that it would revive my sanity, but still, even after several cups of cider, and a meal besides, I could smell only her.

24

EXCEPT FOR THE SMALL LAMP that emitted a dim cone of light across the corner of her desk, Nurse B.'s office was dark. She attempted to stand when Jamilet stepped in, but thought better of it and dropped down the couple of inches she'd managed to lift herself. It had been several weeks since Jamilet had seen her, and even in the semidarkness surrounding them her deterioration was striking. The white uniform, once taut across her belly, now bulged, straining each button as it desperately clung to its position. The flesh encasing her face had grown denser in some places and looser in others, giving the impression that parts were melting away.

She indicated that Jamilet should take the chair across from her. She leveled her eyes at her and even attempted a weak smile, but it did little to improve her appearance. "It's been some time since we've had the opportunity to speak," she said. "The time has passed quickly, and I'm impressed with how long you've lasted—much longer than the others—and I'm trying to figure out why that is."

Jamilet lowered her eyes. "I do my job," she muttered.

"The others did their jobs too," Nurse B. said, lifting her nose as though sniffing the air for a clue. "And they had better credentials as well."

They stared at each other for an uncomfortable length of time and Jamilet was the worse for it. She felt the sweat on her palms begin to penetrate the coarse fabric of her skirt and dampen her thighs. "He doesn't seem so angry anymore, I guess," Jamilet said, eager to break the silence.

"He's been angry since he came here," Nurse B. shot back, but then her tone softened. "But perhaps," she said with a gentle, almost humble nod, "you have discovered something the others did not, something that has helped him to calm down. I would be most grateful if you told me what it was."

"Maybe . . . ," Jamilet said, "it's because I listen to his story. I know I'm not supposed to engage in needless conversation, but . . ."

Nurse B. leaned over her desk, eyes round and mouth loose and gaping with expectation. "Tell me about this story."

Jamilet tried to remember if Señor Peregrino had ever directed her to keep his story a secret, but she was almost certain that he hadn't. "In his story, he's a young man and he's on a journey to a legendary place called Santiago. On the way there he meets a beautiful woman called Rosa. But I don't think any woman can be as beautiful as he describes her to be. I think he must be pretending sometimes, and I told him so, and he got so mad at me for saying it that he almost stopped—"

"I'm not interested in your opinion about the story, Monica, just about the story itself." The flesh around her mouth forced a quick smile. "Please continue."

"He also had a friend, Tomas, who was in love with Rosa too . . ."

"So the young man, whose name is . . . ?"

"Antonio," Jamilet quickly answered.

"This Antonio. He was in love with Rosa as well, was he?"

Jamilet nodded enthusiastically. "Yes, but at first he didn't know if it was love or obsession. And then there's Jenny. He found her irritating most of the time."

Nurse B. continued to stare at her employee as a strange glaze spread over her eyes. "Go on," she muttered.

"As they walked on their way to Santiago, neither Tomas nor Antonio told Rosa how they felt about her until one day, Rosa told Antonio that she loved him, and they planned to get married when they arrived at the cathedral." Jamilet decided to stop there, startled by the strange effect her disclosure was having on her employer.

Nurse B. had closed her eyes while Jamilet spoke, as though trying to shut out what she was hearing, and her hands were balled up into tightly clenched fists. When Jamilet had finished, Nurse B. cleared her throat and shuddered in an attempt to compose herself, but she seemed altered and weaker than before. When she spoke again, she was breathless. "You mustn't indulge your patient by listening to these delusional stories about imaginary charac-ters—they'll only make him worse."

"But he's calmer after he tells me his story. That's why he's doing so well." Once again, Jamilet stopped talking when she saw the hideous expression contorting Nurse B.'s face, after which the nurse erupted with a cynical chortle.

"A young girl barely eighteen years of age understands the pain of an old man who hasn't set foot out of his room in years, and can't even tolerate the sound of his own name? Since the day he came here, he's refused the help of well-trained psychiatrists. Maybe if he wasn't wasting so much time talking with you, he'd talk with someone who could really help him."

Jamilet waited for a moment or two to find her voice. "I should probably go upstairs now," she said, standing up and taking several steps back toward the door. "He gets upset if I'm late."

"Yes, you do that. And you can inform your patient that be-cause you've violated your instructions, I'll be changing your as-signment immediately. I have no doubt that your presence is dis-turbing him deeply."

Jamilet didn't waste any time waiting for the elevator. Instead, she rushed up the five flights of stairs without stopping. She was out of breath when she knocked on Señor Peregrino's door and entered to find him still in bed, reading one of his letters. Approaching the bedside, she stood with her hands clasped in front of her as though in anxious prayer. "Señor, a terrible thing has happened," she said.

He looked up from his reading, and noted her flushed face, and the absence of the breakfast tray. "Don't tell me that once again they've overcooked my eggs? Well, I congratulate you for not wasting your time delivering them."

"Señor. This has nothing to do with your eggs. This is much more serious. Nurse B. is going to change my assignment—today, maybe even in the next few minutes."

His brow furrowed momentarily, and then he waved the thought away. "Nonsense."

"She said so herself, Señor. Just now."

He began to gather the folded letters that were spread out all over his bed. "Now why would she do such a ridiculous thing when you've been the only employee I've tolerated in years?"

Jamilet's face grew hot. "She's angry, Señor, and acting very strangely."

Señor Peregrino was unconcerned. "Yes. She gets that way sometimes."

At this, Jamilet lowered her head and began to wring her hands. "I'm sorry," she said. "I told her about your story, Señor. She wanted to know why you were doing better, and I told her about Rosa, and Tomas, and Jenny and about your walk to Santiago." Jamilet glanced up to see that his somber expression hadn't worsened, as she'd expected. "She became upset, and she told me not to encourage your . . . your . . ."

"Delusions?"

"Yes. And she told me I had violated my instructions, and that she was going to change my assignment immediately."

Señor Peregrino leaned back, and Jamilet took note of the cheery glint in his eye. "You're not angry with me?" she asked.

He shrugged. "Not in the least, but I think you should avoid telling her any more about my story if you can help it."

"I don't understand, Señor. Why did she get so upset?"

He shrugged, and continued organizing his letters. "Soon you will know the reason for her upset, and many more things besides. And you needn't worry, Jamilet. Nurse B. wouldn't dare change your assignment without consulting me first." He said this with such authority that, for the moment, Jamilet didn't doubt it was true, and she felt settled enough to go down to the kitchen to resume her duties.

By the time she returned with his breakfast tray, Señor Peregrino had already showered and changed. He immediately set about the preparation of two coffees and invited Jamilet to sit with him. He cleared his throat and began speaking with renewed urgency, although Jamilet suspected that the strain with which he spoke had little to do with their earlier conversation, and everything to do with what she was about to hear.

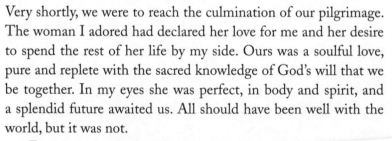

Very shortly, we were to reach the culmination of our pilgrimage. The woman I adored had declared her love for me and her desire to spend the rest of her life by my side. Ours was a soulful love, pure and replete with the sacred knowledge of God's will that we be together. In my eyes she was perfect, in body and spirit, and a splendid future awaited us. All should have been well with the world, but it was not.

Ever since our accidental encounter while waiting out the storm, Jenny was always nearby and took every opportunity to flatter me. Every time I looked up, she was there, and it was clear that whatever attraction she'd felt for me before had grown into an obsession. I could read it well in her eyes, and was afraid of what this feeling might provoke in her. In some ways, I was more concerned about Jenny than I had ever been about Andres. I thought about telling Rosa what had happened, and how I'd mistaken Jenny's hand for hers, but I didn't want to risk the possibility that she would misunderstand, and consider me some kind of scoundrel. Although I was young and inexperienced in these matters, I understood that once the fire of jealousy had been lit within a woman's heart, there was no extinguishing it. And, while Jenny could never compare to Rosa in beauty and spirit, there was no denying that she had certain agreeable qualities. My hope was that as the days passed, the event would fade into obscurity where it belonged.

But, Rosa took notice of Jenny's behavior toward me and of my resulting anxiety. She spoke to me about it while we rested near a small river, her eyes a darker green than the cool shadows surrounding us. "Do you doubt now that Jenny is fond of you?" she asked.

I wrenched myself out of my agonized reverie in order to ascertain the location of our companions. Tomas was filling his water gourd at the river, while Jenny was busy gathering berries in a nearby thicket. It was safe to speak openly. "I'm sure that it's nothing more than a silly obsession, but it's all the more reason to tell her and Tomas the truth about us. I think we should tell them now."

"Oh no, my love," she said, her eyes desperate with fear. "We mustn't tell them, not yet."

"But I want everyone to know how much I love you," I said. "I don't want to hide anymore."

Upon hearing this, Rosa's anxiety eased and she smiled sweetly. "There isn't much longer to wait, my love. We'll be in Santiago in a matter of days if the weather allows. Please, I beg you to be patient."

At sundown, we arrived at Ponferrada, a bustling market town that flourished at the intersection of two large rivers. The local priest, annoyed with having been disturbed during his supper, directed us to our lodging. It was a large room with a generous hearth, adjacent to the church, that was kept ready for pilgrims. We were grateful to have it to ourselves, as well as for the abundance of firewood stacked by the door. We purchased ham from the butcher and finished the day with a meal of bread and ham and more than a few glasses of the local wine. Tomas was unusually jovial that evening and made it a point to fill our wineglasses when they were only half empty, although I noticed that he barely finished his first glass. No matter, I welcomed the temporary escape from my anxiety and looked forward to a restful night's sleep.

After dinner we laid our blankets out on the floor. Tomas kept his rosary beads laced through his fingers as he prayed. Rosa and Jenny spread their blankets out on the far side of the room, nearest the fire, and Tomas faced Rosa, as always, like a flower turned to the sun for nourishment and warmth. I closed my eyes and waited for sleep to release me from my turmoil, if only for a few hours. Perhaps the next day I'd have the opportunity to speak with Rosa, and I prayed for the courage to tell her about what had happened between Jenny and me during the storm. I convinced myself that there was a good chance she'd understand it was all a mistake. Perhaps we'd have a good laugh about it. And it was with this comforting thought that I fell soundly asleep.

How she found her way to me in the middle of the night without waking the others, I do not know, for I was still dreaming when I felt her arms encircle me under the blankets.

"It's me, Antonio," she whispered, "it's your Jenny." And it was then that I awoke and focused my eyes upon her face. There was no mistaking her seductive smile, and the eager sparkle in her yellow-gray eyes.

Once I had recovered from my shock, I somehow found the strength to free my hand from her grasp. "Go back to your bed," I whispered, feeling like an animal caught in a trap.

"The way you caressed my hand during the storm," she whispered, every word hissing through me. "Now I know that you love me too." She took my hand again, but I wrenched it away from her.

"I don't love you," I responded, desperately worried that we'd wake the others.

Her face contorted with disappointment, and I almost felt sorry for her. And it was in that instant that I became painfully aware of her nearness and her feminine allure wrapping itself around me, taking my breath away. I shuddered in an effort to control myself.

This was exactly how she wanted me to respond—to give in to my lustful yearnings once and for all so she could claim me as her own, but I would not allow it. "Go back to your bed, Jenny," I said, gritting my teeth.

"Don't be a fool, Antonio. Don't you see that everything you've been dreaming of can be yours?"

"You know nothing of my dreams," I answered.

"I know that you long for certain . . . comforts, and that you were meant to be more than a shepherd," she said much too loudly.

"Quiet woman, you'll wake the others."

She calmed down and lowered her voice to a whisper. "You know as well as I do that Tomas is desperately in love with Rosa, and that he is able to give her a life that you never could. They are meant to be together, Antonio, just as we are," she said, on the verge of both laughter and tears. She attempted to encircle me in her arms again, but I stopped her. "Promise me that after we arrive in Santiago you'll come away with me," she said breathlessly.

"I can't promise you any such thing. Now get back to your—"

She placed her finger over my lips. "Promise me or I'll scream out and tell the others how you fondled me during the storm, and how you persuaded me to come to your bed."

Not knowing what else to do, and desperate to get her out of my bed, I promised her that, if nothing else, I'd think about her proposition and give her my answer at the end of our journey. Satisfied with that, she slithered away to her bed.

I was unable to sleep for the rest of the night, as I realized that confessing to Rosa was now out of the question. I couldn't risk the chance that Rosa would believe Jenny's story over mine, as I had no doubt that Jenny would prove to be a very convincing liar. The next morning I somehow managed to force down a bit of breakfast, and was relieved to see that Rosa appeared rested and that she ate heartily as she listened intently to Tomas's discourse on the accomplishments of the Templar Knights who had, since the Middle Ages, protected pilgrims on their journey to Santiago. He spoke with such authority that one would think he'd been a knight himself. But rather than getting annoyed, I was only grateful that Rosa and Tomas appeared to have no knowledge of what had taken place the night before.

At that moment, Jenny appeared looking rested and triumphant as she took her seat next to Rosa. I felt suddenly sick and pushed away what little was left of my breakfast.

"I'm beyond famished," she announced, after which she stuffed her mouth with bread.

"Did you sleep well?" Rosa asked.

"Oh, very well, and I had the most amazing dream," she said with a wink in my direction. "Have you ever experienced a dream so realistic that you can't be sure if it was only a dream?"

Rosa nodded with a smile, and Tomas set his coffee cup down, apparently intrigued.

"Well, let me tell you," she continued, "that last night I had a dream that was surely planted by the devil himself."

Before she could finish her sentence, I nudged the ceramic pot next to my elbow off the table and sent it to the tile floor below, where it shattered into a thousand pieces all about our feet. We sprang up, and together had the floor clean in an instant. Even Jenny helped and when we were finished stood by twirling the rag she'd used and smiling in a seductive manner.

"It's late," I said. "I suggest we set off or we'll be forced to take our lunch here as well."

All agreed and began their preparations to leave, but Jenny kept watching me, and spoke to me alone as I adjusted my pack. "What's the matter? Wouldn't you like to hear about my dream, Antonio?"

I ignored her and stayed close to Rosa for the remainder of our journey, unconcerned that our nearness should arouse suspicion.

Señor Peregrino refilled his coffee cup and offered to do the same for Jamilet, who shook her head, a solemn expression on her face.

"You usually take a second cup. Isn't it to your liking?" he asked.

"The coffee is fine, Señor." Jamilet placed her empty cup on the desk. "It's just that I don't like the way your story's turning out, not at all." She shot him a challenging look. "Does life always have to be so complicated?"

Señor Peregrino thought about this for a moment. "Perhaps not," he said, nodding slowly. "But it wouldn't make for a very interesting story if it wasn't." He leaned forward and filled her cup. "And it would make for an even less interesting life."

25

SECRECY WAS BECOMING as reassuring for Jamilet as a warm blanket on a chilly night, and she bundled herself up within its folds. Eddie didn't seem to mind. He understood that because of Carmen's strict nature, their meetings were limited to only those days when she and Louis went out, and luckily they'd been going out more than usual. And there was no doubt that secrecy added a touch of mystery to their already enigmatic relationship, although Jamilet suspected that Eddie thought of her as nothing more than a special friend who was helping him during a difficult time. They were occasional companions who spent time together in the park while Eddie talked and Jamilet listened, faithfully replying in accordance with what she knew would comfort him.

"Lots of boys cry, Eddie," she'd say. "Boys are hard on the outside and soft on the inside, and girls are the other way around." Or, "It's okay to be afraid. How else are you going to know when you're being courageous?" She didn't know where this wisdom came from or how she was able to conjure it up, but her longing to be what Eddie needed called forth thoughts from the pit of her unconscious, like a desperate miner.

But everything changed one afternoon when Eddie appeared at the park with a present. Jamilet reached into the plastic bag he gave her and pulled out a tank top. The light cotton fabric felt as soft as the finest silk in her hands. It had thin straps and was a hazy yellow color, like the sun drifting behind the clouds. Pearly had one in every color of the rainbow.

"Do you like it?" Eddie asked. "I bought it for you downtown."

"You didn't have to give me a present."

Eddie feigned upset. "I can if I want." He traced a stray lock of hair away from her eyes. "Wear it for me next week, okay?"

Jamilet lifted the softness next to her cheek, and inhaled the smell of new. For the moment, she could enjoy this beautiful gesture, this gift from the heart. She'd play the delighted girlfriend, anticipating how lovely she'd look for him when she wore it. On this day, she'd smile and tempt him with her seductive femininity by draping the top over her torso, and arching her back slightly to emphasize the curve of her breasts. All of this she was able to accomplish before asking, "Why next week?"

"Because I want you to meet some of my friends," he said.

Jamilet felt flush with emotion at the thought of being with Eddie in the real world, almost as though she were actually his girlfriend. But he wanted her to look the part. Long-sleeved Catholic schoolgirl shirts and navy skirts below her knees wouldn't do.

Jamilet asked, "What if Pearly finds out?"

"She's over me by now," he said.

Jamilet contemplated Eddie's face, the even brown skin and bright eyes swimming with confidence and humor, the full lips forming a smile so charming it could knock you off your feet if you weren't ready for it. Every time he flashed one of his amazing smiles she had difficulty finding words and correctly stringing them together. She could adore him endlessly.

"You're a sweet little girl, aren't you?" he said, leaning in to kiss her.

"I don't think so," Jamilet said.

He stopped, his lips close enough to brush hers when he asked, "You don't think what?"

"I don't think she's over you."

Jamilet hovered outside herself. Her body felt foreign, as if her arms and legs were moving like tentacles, all in different directions. Every cell was a hologram reflecting the endless possibilities born of her imagination, and a strange courage possessed her, obliterating familiar fears from which she'd never been weaned, and circumventing all that she knew was real. Was it love that caused this? She'd always heard that love was the greatest power in the world. That it could move mountains, and when it was pure, overcome even death. In its lesser forms it was the magic that misted the eyes and changed the physical shape of things, blurring the hard edges of disfigurement, fading it to nearly nothing. When there was love, the mind would see only what the heart allowed it to see.

And love required honesty no matter the cost, or it would wither and die. A hopeful seed might poke its tender shoots aboveground, and exalt in having reached the surface, but once the sun found it, death would come quickly. If true love were to grow between them, Jamilet knew that she had to show Eddie the mark.

She slipped the T-shirt he gave her over her head and pulled it down over her torso. The evening was balmy. Only old ladies wore sweaters on nights like these, and even then they didn't actually wear them, but kept them neatly folded over one arm in case they got chilly. Jamilet's freshly washed navy blue sweater was laid out on her bed. While she had every intention of revealing the mark to Eddie on this day, she saw no reason why the revelation should be a vulgar and unnecessarily shocking one. Situations like these needed to be handled delicately, and explained with care so the mind could slowly digest what the eyes struggled to understand.

Jamilet hadn't seen the mark herself for several weeks. She'd suspended the nightly ritual once her meetings with Eddie became more frequent, simply forgetting—so light was her mood and complete her preoccupation with the steady progress of their relationship. She convinced herself that dreams could partner with other dreams and encourage each other like good friends. If the dream of capturing Eddie's love was coming true, then wasn't it just as possible that the mark would lose its power? Perhaps it was nothing important, like Tía Carmen said. Perhaps it was her mother's infectious worry that had deepened her misery over it all these years, when it was nothing more than a blemish, a shadow—an illusion.

Carmen and Louis had gone out for dinner again to a place where Carmen said they served water and beer in fancy glasses, so that you always looked elegant. After dinner, they planned to catch a movie, which meant that Jamilet and Eddie would have plenty of time. Their plan was to meet at the park, as they had been, and then proceed to Eddie's house where a gathering of friends would be waiting for them. Jamilet planned to show him the mark when they were alone in the park, and no matter what he said, she'd insist on wearing the sweater around his friends, as they weren't subject to the intoxicating effects of their love, and would see only the mark.

As Jamilet made her way through the trees she spotted Eddie sitting on their bench, tugging at a loose thread on the inner seam of his jeans. She stopped for a moment to admire him, the broad line of his shoulders, the gleam of his dark hair. When he saw her emerging from the shadows, he stood up slowly to get a good look at her as well. The faint light of dusk made everything look silver and grainy, like a black-and-white photograph taken in the rain. Jamilet felt the mark pulsating beneath her sweater, as if it knew that freedom was near, and that with freedom came the healing sensation of fresh air alive with witnesses, the birds, the squirrels, the trees, everything in the world, including Eddie, of course.

As Jamilet approached, she tripped on the root of a tree and Eddie cracked a joke about whether she'd started partying early with her aunt. Normally she would have chuckled along with him, but she couldn't even smile, so intent was her focus on sticking to her plan. She'd rehearsed the words at least fifty times in the mirror, tilting her head this way and that, deciding how to hold her hands, and at what point to remove the sweater. It was as carefully choreographed as it was scripted, and she couldn't allow him to distract her as he always did.

"You wore it," he said, obviously pleased. "But what's the deal with the sweater? It's eighty degrees out." Eddie himself was wearing the male version of Jamilet's tank top, clean and white against his muscled chest.

Jamilet took in the sight of him and instantly forgot her lines. She should have been speaking by now, and describing the foolish fears of the backward villagers who thought her to be of the devil. She'd have to start at the beginning because, while she knew everything about Eddie's childhood, he knew almost nothing about hers. She estimated that it would take, without questions or sidetracking, almost half an hour before the unveiling. By then the twilight would have darkened to a shadowy gray, which was exactly what she wanted, the most forgiving light possible. Gradually, he would be allowed to see more and more of it, his love for her flowing into the stark holes of despair a little at a time, until the full revelation was complete.

He stepped up to her and placed a hand on her shoulder, but it soon became apparent that his intent was not a greeting or a kiss, but to remove her sweater. Jamilet slapped his hand away without thinking, but it wasn't a playful gesture, and its sting wasn't lost on Eddie. He looked surprised, but not as surprised as Jamilet, for she was sure that she'd never moved so fast in her life. She took a step back, and tried to remember, but she couldn't conjure up the words with him looking at her with those wounded eyes. Oh yes, she was to begin by telling him about the day the children threw stones at her. He would be moved and saddened to hear about this. His protective tendencies would become activated and ready to defend her from the evil that could provoke such horrible behavior toward his love. She'd ask him if he'd ever seen a birthmark before and that would lead her to tell him of her appointment with Dr. Martinez, and the true reason she'd come to the north.

"What's wrong with you?" Eddie asked. "I just want to see how you look without the sweater."

"Not yet," Jamilet stammered. "I want to explain something first."

"You look really cute," he said, his smile widening. "Even better than I thought you would." He stepped in closer. "I bet you have nice legs too, but we'll take it one step at a time."

"It's kind of hard to explain," Jamilet stammered, and then felt her thoughts evaporate in the heat.

"Explain what?" He stroked her cheek, and hunched down to peer into her face. "Why are your eyes watering?"

Jamilet averted her gaze, and felt her knees grow weak and wobbly. She clutched the sweater close around her with both hands, as the reality of what she was about to do hit her all at once. Was she crazy? What kind of insanity could make her believe that Eddie would respond to the mark differently than anyone else had? It was hideous beyond belief, and there was no love in the world that could overcome it. Her own mother hadn't been able to face it. Trying to do battle with it had surely killed her.

She glanced at Eddie. He didn't seem to know whether to smile or frown, and a nervous twitch tugged at his left eyebrow as he vacillated between the two. "I think I should go home," Jamilet muttered.

"Why?"

"I just think I should . . ."

"Is it your aunt?"

Jamilet shook her head. "I don't know . . . I . . . I should go." She turned and began walking back toward the trees at a brisk pace. She was within a few feet of them when she heard him running to catch up with her. He stopped her with a firm hand on her shoulder, and they stood together on a sunny patch of grass while she clutched her sweater closer.

Eddie took hold of her shoulders and shook her gently. "Talk to me, dammit. Don't just walk away."

"You won't understand," Jamilet said softly.

"How do you know if you don't give me a chance?"

"Because nobody except Tía Carmen understands. She's the only one who isn't afraid."

"Afraid of what?"

It was as though another voice responded, and she heard its echo from far away; the words resonated like a chant. *The reason,* it said. "The reason I always wear long sleeves. The reason I'm not like other girls."

Eddie stuffed his hands in his pockets. "Okay . . . what's the reason?"

She was close to the edge, one foot hovering over the void between who she was and who she might be. She stood there poised for several seconds. All at once, she felt her body losing its form, and every part of her being melting into nothingness as she considered stepping across, but hope for a better life was unable to reconstruct her, and she wavered. Her legs grew heavy and the heaviness traveled up to her lungs, making it difficult to breathe. Eddie was saying something, asking her questions filled with concern, but he was still on the other side, and she was no longer listening intently. No longer was she trying to fit her brain and her soul into his so that he might wallow in her adoration. No doubt he was missing this feeling, and wondering what was wrong.

Without another word, she spun on her heel and started running straight toward the trees, her feet pounding the ground with unbelievable speed, her sweater trailing behind her like a cape in the wind, and her hair flapping in front of her face so that, at one point, she was nearly blinded. She didn't think about Eddie, she could only run as far away from the edge as she could, running as she should have before the rocks hit her so many years ago. But before she could make it to the street, Eddie was on top of her, and they were rolling over each other in the grass, and he was speaking angrily to her, telling her not to run away like a crazy dog. He

pinned her down by the wrists, and straddled her. He was panting and flushed, and his perfectly white shirt had become marred
across the front with dirt.

"You can run fast, girl," he said, and his face moved in closer,
as though he might kiss her. "What could be so bad to make you
run like that?"

He wasn't expecting an answer, so perplexed was he by her
sudden transformation. She looked eerily beautiful to him, like a
fragile bird, easy to scare into submission, but if he let go for just a
second, she'd disappear again.

Jamilet moved her head from side to side, looking past him,
toward the sky, as she tried again to find the words. She'd never
spoken about the mark to anyone who didn't already know about
it. Revealing it to the uninitiated was like trying to describe love in
three or four words. It was beyond her, and yet it was the essence
of who she was, and why she was.

But when she refocused on his face, his eyes were intent on
the curve of her neck beyond the strap of her shirt. During their
tussle, her clothes had shifted, and he could see the fine edges
of the mark for himself, like delicate fingers curling around her
throat. He sat up, still straddling her, his eyes unwavering and
steady on the mark.

"What's that on your neck?" he asked, concerned that he might
have hurt her. He loosened his grip on her wrists, and she flung
her arms free. In one smooth movement she pushed him off and
onto his back. She scrambled to her feet in a flash, but before she
could take another step, Eddie grabbed her foot, knocking her off
balance, and she fell hard, on her stomach. He was on top of her
again, and she felt her sweater coming off and her new shirt pulled
up so that most of the mark was visible. Her hands grabbed fists
full of dirt as she waited. The smell of the earth and the fresh air
on her skin created such a peaceful sensation that she wondered
if she might be dying. She closed her eyes, as though to let death
know that she accepted its arrival.

She imagined his face, round startled eyes, mouth slightly

open in shock. He had momentarily lost the ability to speak, but she felt much better nonetheless. This she had lived before. She knew what would come next, and how the scene would unfold, as it had so many times before.

"It's a birthmark," she said, spitting out dirt as she spoke. "And it doesn't hurt."

He was breathing hard, as he hadn't had the sense to look away. She thought of warning him that the more he looked at the mark, the worse it would get, but she remained quiet. It was almost over.

"Why didn't you tell me?" he finally asked, but he sounded different, as though humbled by something he couldn't understand.

"I never tell anyone," Jamilet answered. She felt Eddie's weight lift off her, and he stood up. She stood as well, brushing the dirt from her pants, her stomach, her arms, and her hair, and then giving herself a good shake.

Eddie watched her, surprised by her ability to move normally after what he'd just seen. "Is it there like . . . I mean, can you get rid of it?"

Jamilet felt strangely powerful when she saw the wonder and the fear in his eyes. She could have told him of her plans to see a doctor, and the stash of money she had in her room, but she would sound like a silly child, as though announcing that one day she planned to be a famous movie star. "There's nothing I can do," she said, and as she heard herself say these words, for the first time in her life she accepted their truth. Her grandmother had known it. Her aunt in her own way had tried to tell her, and even Dr. Martinez knew, but it was only then, while staring into Eddie's shrinking face, that she knew she'd live with the mark until the day she died.

Neither of them made any attempt to leave, although it was almost dark. Eddie started to look around and stomp his feet like a restless horse. He grew still and asked, "Do you want me to walk you home?"

The tenderness in his eyes fought with his desire to break out in a full run, and get as far away from her as he could. She knew it, as well as the fact that she could hold him for only a moment or two longer in this unsettled trance born of disgust and pity. "I know the way," she said, and then she released him.

Later that night, while she lay in bed exhausted, Jamilet decided that it felt good to hate. The feelings packed up inside her made her feel dense and strong, and no longer like the flimsy creature she'd known herself to be who could be carried off by the wind, or shaken by a good cough. And while she was thinking about it, she hated her weak-minded foolishness too, and the wimpy way she agreed with everybody all the time—this cowardice masquerading as kindness made her sick to her stomach. And she hated where she came from and who she was, and the fact that her life was small enough to fit into a shoe box. She was lulled to sleep by her steely resolve to hate. Perhaps hate would put a little meat on her bones.

26

WITH BREAKFAST TRAY held high, Jamilet knocked once, then entered before hearing Señor Peregrino give his permission. He was still in bed, which wasn't surprising because she had arrived earlier than usual. He preferred his breakfast after his shower, but Jamilet decided that it was unreasonable for him to expect her to go up to the fifth floor first thing in the morning, back down, and then up again, just because he liked his coffee hot enough to scald the feathers off a chicken. He'd have to settle for coffee hot enough to dissolve a teaspoon or two of sugar.

She set the tray on his desk with a thud, and turned to see if the sound had disturbed him, but he hadn't stirred. She lifted the tray, set it down again, and then dropped the coffee spoon into the cup, but still, no sign that he'd heard her. She proceeded to the bathroom next. Señor Peregrino had always directed her to tidy the bath *after* he'd showered, as the lingering steam resulted in mold, and this disgusted him. But Jamilet decided that she'd clean the bathroom while he slept. Why wait until later when the heat of the day would be at its worst?

She'd already started to wipe down the shower door when she heard him calling for her, his voice confused and still gruff with sleep. Jamilet quickly went to his bedside, her expression set, with chin up and eyes clear. "Yes, Señor?" she said, practically standing at attention.

"What are you doing here so early?" he asked as he propped himself up on his pillows, his hair standing on end like an enormous white flame.

"I'm doing my job, Señor. That should be obvious." She glanced at him to see if her curt reply had produced sufficient shock, and quickly looked away before she could appreciate it in full bloom.

"Do excuse my feeble mind," he retorted.

Jamilet pushed her shoulders back. "And I've decided that it's much more convenient that I bring your breakfast up first thing in the morning instead of waiting until after you shower. It would save me going up and down the stairs so often, which I *hate.*"

Señor Peregrino flinched at the word "hate," not only because she'd never used it before but because of the way she'd said it, as if she wasn't talking, but was spitting. He sat up more fully to get a better look at her. "You don't even look like yourself this morning," he said, squinting. "Did you cut your hair?"

"I like it short. It's easier for me."

"Turn around," he commanded. She hesitated, but then did as she was told. "It looks like you chopped it off without looking, as if you did it in the dark."

Jamilet hung her head and said nothing. Señor Peregrino got out of bed to get the breakfast tray himself and brought it back to his bed. Out of the corner of her eye, she saw his bare feet shuffling across the floor and back to his bed again. She heard him preparing his coffee and the coarse sound of a buttered knife move across the toast. "I know what you're doing," he said. "You're punishing yourself, hoping that self-cruelty will inspire you somehow, and discourage the world."

"I don't know what you're talking about, Señor."

"Oh, yes you do, my dear." He took a bite of his toast, and spoke before he had completely swallowed, causing him to cough a little. "And only matters of the heart can provoke such drama. I would venture to guess that the young man for whom you suffered a swollen jaw not long ago is at the heart of this."

She sighed and felt unexpectedly relieved. "I decided that I hate him, Señor."

"Have you? Well, you should know by now that you can't choose to hate any more than you can choose to love."

Jamilet spun around in a flash, her fists tight at her sides. "Oh, yes you can, Señor. Just like I can choose to get up before dawn, even though my body and mind are telling me to keep sleeping. Before long I'm not tired anymore, and I don't even think about going back to bed. I can choose to love and to hate in the same way."

"Perhaps." Señor Peregrino sipped his coffee. "But you have to fool yourself into believing that will alone defines reality, beyond experience, and even beyond the wildest hopes of your heart. You must deny your heart, your mind, and your body all at once."

Jamilet reached around to feel the stubble on the back of her neck. She'd cut her hair so short that it was necessary to wear her collar up or else risk revealing the mark.

"Sit down and have some coffee with me," Señor Peregrino said.

She sat and accepted the cup, allowing the warmth of it to reach through her fingers and palms, up to her arms, until her shoulders were as round and sluggish as she felt. After a shared breakfast of coffee and toast with jam, the story resumed.

***

The morning we stood on Monte de Gozo, and saw the cathedral spires as though floating in the distance, the sun was already making its ascent into the pale sky. It was difficult for me to accept that our journey was nearly over. Santiago had grown into much more than a destiny in my mind; it was the culmination of all that it meant to be human, and I feared that my spirit, no more than a wisp on this earth, would evaporate when the clouds decided to part.

The four of us hiked down the mountain toward the city below, and for the first time, I heard Rosa sing, her soft voice dispersing like the mist. I joined her, and together our song spilled out
over the hills, as my heart surged with the joyous realization that
I was living my destiny—to love this remarkable woman until the
day I died, to raise our children with her, and to become lost in
our union forever.

Then I felt Rosa's hand slip into mine. No longer concerned
that Tomas and Jenny were watching, we walked together toward
the cathedral as if it were our wedding day. I turned to see Rosa's
face, radiant in the fragile light of morning. She'd flung her hood
back and the dew in her hair appeared like a thousand glistening
diamonds. Neither of us dared to look back at our companions,
but I felt their bitterness, darker than the clouds overhead, a disappointment equal to our joy.

We momentarily lost sight of the cathedral as we made our
way through the labyrinth of narrow streets that circled the old
city, but then all at once we found ourselves in the main square.
The cathedral of Santiago soared up toward the heavens in all
its glory. It was grander than I had imagined, and the dark gray
stone of the facade seemed to breathe with the life of the countless faithful who'd worshipped at her feet over the ages. And at the
very crest of the tallest spire stood the statue of the apostle Santiago, with his pilgrim's staff and wide-brimmed hat, welcoming
all who were as he had been—a pilgrim of faith, a courageous and
wandering soul, a child of God.

Rosa and I entered the main doors of the sanctuary, feeling as
two drops in a vast river of life. Once inside we took our place in
line, along with hundreds of other pilgrims, so that we might see
Santiago's crypt, touch his cape and embrace him, thus officially
completing our pilgrimage. Immediately thereafter, we planned
to find a priest who'd marry us, right then and there if necessary.
We weren't concerned with shaking the dust of the road from our
shoes, we were desperate only to fulfill the destiny we knew belonged to us. Listening to the whispered prayers and the weeping

of the pilgrims around us, I realized that with Rosa beside me, I was as close to God as I would ever be. Overcome with emotion I cupped her face in my hands and kissed her with the sacred tenderness reserved for a saint. I kissed her again to let her know I was a man who loved her with all of my soul. And I kissed her a third time because the taste of her lips was exquisite.

And together we mounted the steps that led to the crypt of our saint. If moments in life could be strung like pearls along the chain of our existence, this would have been the most precious jewel of all.

"We must thank Santiago," Rosa said. "We must thank him as pilgrims, and as two people who will soon be man and wife."

"Yes," I agreed enthusiastically. "We must ask him to bless our marriage and the many children we'll have, and the grandchildren and great-grandchildren." Holding her as I was, I had every intention of getting started with the matter of procreation as quickly as possible.

When we entered the crypt, our eyes squinted at the remarkable sight—the intricacy of gold carvings surrounding us at every turn, from floor to ceiling, inspired awe. And the golden statue of Santiago was the most magnificent of all. He faced out toward the congregation, with his back turned to us. We embraced him together, and our prayers swept across the interior of the cathedral, out through the tinted glass and moss-covered stone, beyond the thickening clouds, escaping into the heavens and reaching the ear of God.

It was difficult to find a priest who'd see us, as they were busy with the duties of their *oficio*, all the more pressing on Sundays. While a pilgrim mass was celebrated daily, on Sundays the ceremony called for the use of the *botafumeiro*, an enormous incense pot that swung from the rafters during the service. And it was not entirely for religious purposes, as it was also known that over the centuries, it had effectively masked the malodorous fumes emanating from those who hadn't seen soap and water in months.

But eventually we encountered a young priest leaving the confessional. Fatigued and diminished by the constant barrage of sins he'd been subjected to absolve, he tried his best to avoid us, but it was Rosa who captivated him with her sweet entreaty. He gazed reverently at her face while she spoke, and when she was finished, agreed to marry us the next morning at eleven for a small fee. I remember how he quickly glanced at her midsection as we left to see if she were with child.

We remained for the mass and watched as the *botafumeiro* swung from the eaves, filling the nave with clouds of sweet smoke. Try as I might to keep my eyes on the altar, I couldn't help but turn and gaze at the woman standing next to me who was so soon to become my wife. All said and told, we'd probably spoken fewer than a hundred words to each other, yet I felt that she was part of my spirit. While the other pilgrims asked God to absolve them of their sins so they could return home with their place in heaven assured, I thanked God for the heaven I'd already found and for the wondrous blessing of Rosa's love. "I'll be good to her, dear Lord," I vowed. "I'll protect her from all harm, and faithfully provide for our children."

The mass was concluded with the singing of hymns from all over the world. Voices could be heard singing in French and Italian and Greek and English as all faces turned toward the altar in praise of the apostle Santiago. Then we filed out into the square, which was bathed with a brilliant golden light. The sun had decided to make an appearance, as if persuaded by the ecstatic song that broke out among the pilgrims. We were swept up in the joyfulness of the crowd, laughing and singing along with them, and even sharing in a swallow or two of wine from another pilgrim's wine bag. It was then that I saw Tomas standing at the doorway of the *refugio*, watching us as if we were the only people in the square. Rosa saw him too, but Jenny was nowhere in sight.

I asked Rosa to go inside so that I might speak with Tomas alone. I had decided while in the midst of my prayers during the mass that I would tell Tomas of our plans to marry, before and not after the ceremony as we had planned, and ask him to be our witness. This I hoped would be a decisive step toward the healing of our relationship.

It was the first time Rosa passed by Tomas without drawing his gaze, or prompting a smile. His eyes, somber and grave, stayed affixed to mine.

I drew in my breath, straightened my shoulders, and mustered up the courage for my task. "I haven't been honest with you, my friend—" But he did not allow me to finish.

"I once considered you to be the most noble man I knew. Now I wonder if you might not be the devil himself," he said.

"Because of Rosa?" I placed my hand on his shoulder.

He immediately shrugged it off. "You promised to leave her to me, and I trusted you."

"It's true that I broke my promise, but you must forgive me and understand that it was impossible to keep myself from falling in love with Rosa. We're getting married—tomorrow morning, and I'd like you to be at my side when we do."

"And what about Jenny?" he asked.

"What about her?"

"She's so overcome with grief that she was barely able to make it here even with my help."

"Jenny will get over her obsession with me, I have no doubt of that."

He came in closer to me and whispered, "But I will never get over Rosa, and I intend to tell her now how I feel—today. And then we'll see what she decides."

"Do as you wish, but she won't betray me, Tomas. You're wasting your time."

"Give me the afternoon to speak with her," he replied. "At least give me that."

Reluctantly, I conceded, and entered the building in search of a room and much-needed rest. Later that evening, when I heard the sound of the dinner bell echoing throughout the stone corridors of the *refugio*, I figured that they'd had enough time to talk and set about looking for Rosa. It was only right that we should enjoy this meal together on the eve of our wedding, and it was well known that the meals provided for pilgrims at this hostel were the best on the *camino*. There would be plenty of fresh meat and vegetables, and good-quality wine, all lovingly prepared for those who'd found the strength and inspiration to finish their journey. I looked forward to sharing this experience with Rosa, but as I made my way to the dining room I was unable to rid myself of an anxiety that had settled on my brain like an annoying fly. Could it be that Rosa was actually taking time to seriously consider Tomas's proposal? Jenny's words kept repeating themselves over and over again in my mind: "He is able to give her a life that you never could. They are meant to be together, Antonio, just as we are." It seemed absurd to think that Rosa would be persuaded by such an argument. And yet, I was unable to put the thought out of my mind.

I entered the dining room to find a large and elegant space overflowing with countless jovial pilgrims. Hanging on the stone walls were colorful tapestries that reached from floor to ceiling and there were many long tables laid end to end, upon which were placed massive bowls filled with fragrant stews and mountains of bread still steaming from the oven. Although in one corner two men played the guitar and flute, it was impossible to hear their music over the sound of clinking glasses and hundreds of voices eager to divulge the miracles that had taken place while on the *camino*.

I spotted Tomas sitting alone at one of the tables and went to sit with him. Without a word, he served me a plate of food, and I began to eat, but was only able to get down a mouthful or two. His plate was also untouched, and his expression glum.

I pushed my food away. "Have you spoken with Rosa?"

He nodded. "I have emptied my heart and my soul. I've done everything within my power to persuade her to make a life with me."

"And what did she say?" I asked, sounding like an impertinent child.

"Don't you know, Antonio? Hasn't she come looking for you

to tell you herself? Just a few hours ago, you were so sure of her love." He folded his arms across his chest and sneered. "Well, if she hasn't told you, then neither will I."

My fists clenched with fury and for the first time in my life I thought I might strike him. Instead, I stormed out of the room, my long strides resulting in several collisions with baffled pilgrims who knew better than to start a quarrel when they saw the loathing on my face. I looked for Rosa in the women's dormitory, but was told that she wasn't there. I walked the grounds of the hostel, and searched in every public room I could find, and even made my way to the well where some of the women were washing. Back in my room, I collapsed on the mat on the floor. My mind was an old rag used one too many times, yet I persisted in wringing out the anxieties contained within its fibers. My God, I'd waited long enough, and it was cruel to keep me waiting much longer. Didn't my love realize that I desperately needed to see her again, and hold her in my arms?

The room was dark, and I was preparing to resume my search for Rosa when the door opened and I saw her standing on the threshold, appearing as a column of light. She glanced over her shoulder to make sure the corridor was empty, then entered, closing and locking the door behind her. "Antonio," she whispered, breathless with fear. "I need to see you alone. Tomas doesn't know that I'm here."

"What does it matter if he knows? We're together, as we're meant to be, and we're free to tell the world."

Appearing like an angel who'd lost her way, she knelt beside me and placed her fingers on my lips. Her gaze intensified, but she did not speak right away. Finally, she whispered, "I saved you once before and I'm going to save you again."

"The only way you can save me is by leaving with me this instant," I said. "We'll steal away into the night and never look back."

She spoke as though in a trance. "Sometimes it is impossible to run away, Antonio, as much as we may want to."

"Don't torture me with such words, Rosa. The only thing that matters is the love we have for each other. Don't be tempted by Tomas and his wealth and empty promises. Come away with me now, before it's too late." Kneeling before her, I pressed her hands against my forehead and began to weep, fearing that I'd already lost her.

"May God forgive me," she whispered and then stood up, and without another word she removed her skirt and let it fall in a heap to the floor. Moments later, her blouse fluttered down, only to be followed by a series of undergarments each smaller than those that preceded it, until she stood before me wearing nothing at all.

Overcome, I reached up for her and pulled her down to me. Our union was ecstasy, every movement a submission to the truth in our hearts, a consummation of our perfect love. Words were no longer necessary to assure me of her devotion. I had no doubt that she would be mine forever.

I can't be certain of how much time we lay together, only that we were still breathless with passion when she hastily took up her clothing and dressed. Pressing into my hands the small Bible she'd carried with her on the *camino,* she said, "Always remember that everything I do, I do because I love you."

"What are you saying, Rosa?"

"I'm saying that even though I love you with all my heart, I have decided to go away with Tomas. We must face the harsh realities of this life, Antonio. We are both poor, and we will always be poor if we stay together, but now we have a chance for a better life—I with Tomas and you with Jenny. We must accept these miracles we've found on our journey."

"No, I won't accept it, Rosa. I'll never accept it. I can't believe what you're saying."

"Believe it, Antonio, because I have never spoken a truer word in all my life. After this day, you will never see me again."

The words struck me like a lethal blow to the chest. I couldn't believe what came from her mouth, yet there was no mistaking the conviction in her eyes. And I could only watch, paralyzed and miserable, as she walked out of the room, taking everything that was hopeful and beautiful in my life away with her into the Galician mist.

※

Señor Peregrino's eyes were half open, fluttering between waking and sleeping. He hadn't spoken for several minutes, but Jamilet remained mesmerized as she watched the steady rise and fall of his chest. He'd succumb to sleep at any moment if she didn't say something.

"So then what did you do?" she asked abruptly.

His eyes widened slightly as he continued, "The next morning, once I had sufficiently recovered from my stupor, I set out with a vengeance to find Tomas and Rosa. The more I thought about it, the more I realized that something other than money must have influenced Rosa's decision, and even if I had to beat the truth out of Tomas, I intended to discover what it was. But it was Jenny who I found waiting for me in the square, her hand coiled around a scroll of some sort. It seems that the priest we'd arranged for earlier had been put to good use, and Jenny wasted no time in showing me the place on the marriage certificate that revealed Rosa and Tomas's signatures. After seeing this, I staggered back to my room as though I were delirious with drink, but I would neither eat nor drink anything for several days.

"To think that Rosa had actually married Tomas, and that they were husband and wife nearly destroyed me. I couldn't comprehend it. The pieces just didn't fit together in any way that made sense. But Jenny stayed by my side during those difficult days, all the while speaking gently and persuasively as I wept and raged like a madman. She told me that all women are practical creatures at their core, and that poor women are even more so. She said that I should forgive Rosa for her feminine weakness in these matters and get on with my life, and many more things besides. I didn't know what to believe, or even if I was dead or alive. All I knew was that in order to survive, I had to hold on to something and the only lifeline within reach was Jenny. She convinced me that in time she'd cure my broken heart, and before the week's end she'd bought passage on a ship that took us far away from Santiago, from Spain, and from everything else I knew."

Señor Peregrino pressed both palms to his eyes, and shook his head as though reacting to a severe and sudden headache. "Over the years, I managed to delude myself into believing that my deep love for Rosa had been a mere obsession fueled by nothing other than youthful lust. As I resigned myself to a life with Jenny, I learned how to appreciate her many talents. She was undoubtedly a clever woman, and if nothing else, we proved to be good business partners. I grew to love not the woman at my side so much as the life that we'd made together—a life dedicated to the acquisition of wealth and the power that goes along with it. Although still young, Jenny and I decided not to have children, but to vigorously pursue our chosen professions, and we acquired numerous businesses over the years, including a chain of hospitals and asylums, Braewood among them."

"You own *this* hospital?" Jamilet asked, incredulous.

Señor Peregrino nodded, as though guilty of the fact, and lowered his hands from his face. "I was able to put everything behind me. I suppose you could even say that I made peace with the fact that Rosa had chosen a life of wealth with Tomas over a humble shepherd's life with me. And whenever I thought of her, which was less and less as time passed, I hoped that she was as comfortable with him as I was with Jenny." He opened his desk drawer and took out the letters he incessantly studied, spreading them over the top of his desk. "But when I found these letters, everything changed."

"Why, Señor?"

He chuckled bitterly. "Betrayal reveals itself in the most insidious ways, my dear. It's a snake that slithers through the years undetected, then quite suddenly you find that it's been hiding in your bed all along, ready to devour you in your sleep." He snatched the letter closest to him and dangled it in front of Jamilet's eyes. "These were written when I was still a young man, but I first laid eyes on them only three years ago. I found them while searching for an old set of golf clubs in the attic. They had been stashed away in a shoe box that quite literally fell on my head while I was moving things around. I can't imagine why Jenny kept them, perhaps because she thought she might need them if legal complications arose, and Jenny has always worried so about legalities. Sometimes I wish that she'd thrown them out, and that I'd never found them." Señor Peregrino's eyes began to fade once again.

"Why? Who wrote them?" Jamilet asked.

Señor Peregrino answered, "Tomas, of course, and it was shocking to see how many he'd written and the mysterious invoices that accompanied his letters. But even more so to put this puzzle together piece by piece until the dreadful scene was complete." He tossed the letter he held back onto his desk with the others. "What I learned was that when Andres challenged Tomas and me to the duel, Rosa secretly begged Jenny to help her put an end to it. While we agonized on that night we thought might be our last, they schemed and then bargained with Andres, who finally agreed to give up the duel and Rosa as well if Jenny made the payments for a prime piece of grazing land he'd had his eye on in the northwest of Spain. So long as Jenny made the payments, he'd leave Tomas and me alone. But that wasn't the worst of it. Before the deal was struck, Jenny told Rosa that she would go along with it only if Rosa also agreed to leave me to her, and Rosa consented.

With head held high, Señor Peregrino declared, "I was right. Rosa did not turn away from my love for money and other worldly comforts. She did so to save my life. That's why she was so desperate to keep our love a secret. Had Jenny found out that Rosa had violated their agreement, she would have ceased the payments, and Andres would have come after me as he'd promised—he was not the sort of man who'd ever forgive and forget." Señor Peregrino sighed wearily. "I suppose that as the journey neared its end

Rosa hoped that we might find a way to escape, but both Jenny and Tomas, who was by then involved in the scheme as well, were successful in convincing her that there was no escape, and that Andres would hunt me down and kill me whether I was married to her or not. But if she had told me the truth, I know we would have found our miracle." His eyes glittered for an instant. "My only comfort was in learning that the marriage certificate Jenny had produced was a fake and that Rosa never truly married Tomas. She left Santiago soon after and didn't contact him again until some years later."

Señor Peregrino began searching frantically for a specific letter among the collection before him. And when he found it, he tenderly kissed the corner of the yellowed page and pressed it to his heart. "When I read this letter, it was no longer possible to put things out of my mind, as I had been able to do for so many years." He turned to Jamilet, his eyes gleaming. "You see, my dear, on the last night that Rosa and I were together, she became pregnant with our child. She never planned to let me know of it and was prepared to raise the child alone. But when she grew deathly ill a few years later, she contacted Tomas for fear that our child, still so young and vulnerable, would be orphaned. Tomas then wrote to Jenny, and . . ." He sighed bitterly, placed the letter down, and retrieved a small leather Bible from his desk, staring longingly at it. "I don't know what happened after that. The letters revealed nothing more, and when I confronted Jenny, she denied knowing anything about it, and said that I had misinterpreted everything. She even accused me of writing the letters myself in order to torture her with painful memories of the past. Such a cold hatred grew between us that I could barely look at her without wishing to destroy her.

"The only feeling within me stronger than my hate for Jenny was my desire to find my child. I made endless inquiries with authorities here and abroad. In my business dealings, I'd acquired friends in high places, and I asked them for favors that might help me in my quest. I even enlisted the assistance of a private detective, the most expensive one I could find, but you have no idea how difficult it is to find the nameless child of a woman who died so long ago. I didn't even know if our child was a boy or a girl.

"When I had no choice but to accept that I'd failed, I began to falter. For weeks, I didn't speak to anyone. I refused to eat, hardly slept, and was unable even to work. Eventually, I refused to set foot out of my front door. Everyone believed that I'd gone mad, and if I should try to explain what was fueling my madness, Jenny was always nearby to explain how years of hard work and stress had finally caught up with me. There was no way of convincing anyone of the truth. Even good friends, who were once in a position to help, began to doubt me. I was stripped of all hope and dignity, and before long, I stopped caring about anything at all."

"And what about Jenny? What happened to her?" Jamilet asked, all at once remembering the janitor's story about how the fifth-floor patient had cut up his wife into a thousand little pieces. After hearing all of this, it seemed a likely outcome. "Did you kill her, Señor? Is . . . is that how you ended up here?"

Señor Peregrino placed the Bible back in the drawer, and clasped his hands together. "I cannot deny that the thought crossed my mind once or twice, but no, I didn't kill Jenny. She continues to pursue me, and finds it impossible to leave me in peace even now as I live my hermit's life."

"But I'm the only one who comes here, Señor."

"Yes, that's true, but Jenny is never far away. You see, my dear," Señor Peregrino said, gathering his letters together and putting them back in the drawer, "Jenny and Nurse B. are one and the same."

27

IT WAS THE FIRST MORNING since the incident at the park that Jamilet awoke without thinking about Eddie. She did not remember to renew her vow to hate him, nor did she painfully relive their tender moments together at the fence when she passed by it on her way to work. When she walked through the gate and up the path to the main entrance of the hospital, she heard the singing again, sweetly rising and lingering about the treetops. She stopped to listen more intently, and admire the mystical tones. It was an ancient song, yet as familiar to her as a lullaby. She resumed her walk, stepping softly, as she imagined the pilgrims had done when reaching the crest of a steep hill, contemplating the journey that lay ahead, and the miles they'd already traveled. She didn't understand the words of the chant, but they twisted melodically and found their place in her soul, deciphering their own meaning, and gnawing at the edges of her hopes and fears.

Jamilet entered the hospital as always, punched in her time card, and proceeded up the five stories to her post. Now that the story was finished, she felt as though she were on the threshold of something extraordinary, and hesitated outside Señor Peregrino's door, feeling almost as she had on her first day. She knocked, and entered after he acknowledged her. She found him still in bed, his eyes shimmering and a faint smile hovering about his lips. It was then that she saw the open suitcase on his desk, and the neat piles of clothing on the chair. His shoes were lined up against the wall, and the drawers of his wardrobe were open and nearly empty. Noting her confusion, he said, "As interminable as my stay here has been, it now seems to have passed so quickly. Time can be as moody and petulant as a spoiled child, I'm afraid."

Jamilet's face was blank. "Where are you going, Señor?"

He blinked once. "The appointed hour has arrived. I'm going to Spain, to Santiago de Compostela, as I've been planning to do all along."

Upon hearing his words, Jamilet felt an unexpected sadness descend upon her. It was so strong that she immediately found an excuse to interrupt their discussion, and in a semi-bewildered state went about her usual duties in the bathroom. She didn't want Señor Peregrino to see the tears that kept welling up in her eyes, and she needed time to compose herself. She reported to the kitchen at the normal hour for his breakfast, and when she returned she felt better. But she noticed that Señor Peregrino was behaving a bit oddly as well. She'd never seen him smile in such a secretive manner. He asked her to sit and share a cup of coffee with him, as these moments would soon end. But he said this strangely too, as though stifling giggles.

"It looks like you're almost packed," Jamilet observed between sips of coffee. "When do you leave?"

"Tomorrow evening."

"And what is the weather like in Santiago?" she asked, trying to sound casual, hoping that this would keep her strong emotions at bay.

"You wouldn't be asking me that if you'd listened carefully to my story, Jamilet."

She became flustered, and her cup rattled on its saucer. "Well, I know there's plenty of rain and mist, but it's summertime. Does it rain in the summer too?"

"Perhaps," he said, watching her closely. "But enough talk about weather. I'm ready for my breakfast now." He raised his arms and Jamilet took the tray to him, positioning it carefully on his lap. She lifted the dome off the plate, and sat in her chair as he ate. He appeared to have a fine appetite, with little concern about the adventure that awaited him.

"Why are you leaving now, Señor?"

He nodded, and swallowed. "This coming Sunday is the twenty-fifth of July, the holiest day of the year in Santiago, and if I leave tomorrow night I'll make it just in time." When he was finished with his breakfast, he raised his arms again so that Jamilet could remove the tray. Then he pushed back the covers and swung his legs out of the bed. His feet were searching for his slippers, but then he became still, and locked his eyes on Jamilet's face. "Some months ago you asked me if my story were true or pretend. Do you remember what I said to you then?"

Jamilet nodded. "You said that everything in life is an illusion and that truth is only what we choose to believe."

"That's correct. And now I must ask you, do you believe that my story is true, or a delusion?"

Jamilet was stunned by his question, and wondered why Señor Peregrino, as certain as he was of his own truth, would care what she thought. Even so, she had to admit that from the beginning she was drawn to his story, and to the power of his convictions, but she didn't know enough about the art of deception to be sure of much else. Did truth, even in its crudest form, draw you in, like the warmth of the sun? Could it claim itself to be by its mere presence? She felt incapable of answering such questions; nevertheless, she knew that she believed in him. She couldn't find the words to describe this feeling so essential to her being. She simply knew that she believed, like she did in the sky above, although she'd never touched it and couldn't prove to herself or anyone that the expanse of nothingness was indeed the sky and not an illusion.

"I believe that your story is true, Señor," she said.

He smiled in response and, still looking at her intently, said, "I've been waiting for the right time to tell you that some weeks ago, I experienced a revelation. It came to me at the point when sleep had begun to creep into my brain, but it was so powerful that I was unable to close my eyes for some time afterward." He shuddered, as though a remnant of this experience were still afflicting him. "I heard a voice, as strong as thunder, yet tender enough to suspend all of my fears. The voice told me that while I would never find the child I was searching for, I should no longer despair, because my grandchild had found me." He clasped his hands together. "And you, my dear, are that grandchild."

Jamilet stood up abruptly. "Señor!"

He stood as well, and shuffled along to the bathroom, unperturbed. "It's only right that you should accompany me to Spain so that we may honor your grandmother Rosa and express our gratitude to Santiago together. And you needn't worry about the expense or any details. I've already made the necessary arrangements."

"This isn't a revelation, Señor. You . . . you made it all up!"

He was almost to the bathroom door when Jamilet ran in front of him, blocking the entrance. "Señor, I am not your granddaughter," she said, with rigid arms down at her sides and fists clenched. "I don't believe that part of your story—not at all!"

"That may be, but I'm certain that I believe you are my granddaughter more than you believe you're not. Now, if you'll kindly step away . . ."

He had started to move past her when Jamilet blurted out, "My mother was born in a brothel. Her mother was a prostitute. It's well-known by everyone in the village. She sold her body for money, and probably died from some horrible disease that comes from doing too much of whatever it was she did. Was Rosa a prostitute, Señor? Is that what we should believe?" The startled expression on Señor Peregrino's face encouraged her to continue. "And my mother wasn't her first child. Tía Carmen came first, and looking at her anyone would know that neither you nor Rosa could have been her parent."

Señor Peregrino hung his head and appeared distressed. Then he raised it slowly, his eyes sparkling with fresh resolve. "I can't concern myself with such details now. How my daughter ended up in a Mexican brothel, I'll never know. Perhaps that is where Jenny put her, God only knows what treachery she's capable of. Or, perhaps it isn't your mother we should consider, but your father . . ."

"He was a rapist and a drunk, Señor! I swear it!"

Señor Peregrino closed the door without another word, and promptly opened the faucets, which squealed and moaned before releasing a rush of water that effectively drowned out all other sounds.

Jamilet squeezed her face into the doorjamb and yelled, "I'll get proof, Señor, and you'll see that what you're saying is crazy."

She listened for a moment or two with her ear pressed against the door, but there was no response from him, only the gushing sound of the shower. A few moments later she heard chanting, soft and reverent, yet bright enough to lift the heaviest fog.

Dressed in a white linen shirt and dark slacks, Señor Peregrino was waiting at his desk when Jamilet returned later that day with his lunch tray. He slid a sealed envelope toward the edge of the desk, and said nothing, but it was clear that he meant for her to take it.

Jamilet approached cautiously. After she'd left him to his shower that morning, she'd retreated to the adjacent office, praying that his earlier insanity would lift so that when she returned, all would be back to normal. But whenever she thought about the fact that Señor Peregrino actually wanted her to be his grand-daughter, her good sense was interrupted by an unexpected warm fluttering in the pit of her stomach. It made her feel as though she might float out of the window, to frolic in the treetops and enjoy this balmy weather born of hope.

It was in the afterglow of this state of mind that she opened the envelope. There she found her original documents, just as she remembered them, her birth certificate and the identification card

Carmen had bought for her downtown. But there was something else, and she studied it more closely. It was another card with nine digits stamped across the front, like the one Carmen had given her, but this one had her true name.

Señor Peregrino leaned back in his chair with arms folded across his chest, apparently quite pleased with himself. "I have friends in immigration, and enough money to be bold with the favors I ask," he said slyly.

"I don't understand, Señor."

He uncrossed his arms and leaned forward in his chair. "You can throw that false Social Security card your aunt gave you away. This one is legal—it's the real thing."

Overwhelmed, Jamilet asked, "Why did you do this, Señor?"

His eyes wandered the ceiling and he scratched his chin as he thought about it. "I asked myself that very question months ago when I began this whole process. I didn't know the answer then, but if nothing else, I've learned that it's a wise man who obeys the dictates of his heart. Anyway," he said, with practical cheer, "it's quite difficult to travel abroad without proper identification and a passport, at least not by plane."

Jamilet stared at the new document and allowed herself to entertain the vision she'd been resisting all morning. She's onboard a plane bound for Spain, with Señor Peregrino sitting beside her. As the plane flies across the Atlantic, they happily peer out of the small windows and watch the clouds drift by while sipping coffee and sharing stories. Then, all at once, Jamilet shook the fog from her head and returned the documents to their envelope. "Señor, I don't want to disappoint you, but I can't force myself to believe something I know isn't true. We both know that I'm not your *real* granddaughter. Maybe you just decided that you needed a miracle, and that this was it."

His expression stiffened. "This is a miracle, Jamilet. Make no mistake about that."

"How can it be, Señor? A miracle is like when the doctor tells you that you're going to die and nothing will save you, and then suddenly you're cured. Or . . . or like when you don't have enough money to pay the rent, and you find an envelope stuffed with just what you need on the sidewalk. Miracles happen like magic."

"And who says that miracles happen like magic? Who invented that rule? Was it you?"

"No. Everybody just knows that's how it is."

"And what I know is that we make our own miracles." He held out his hands to her. "Come here, child." She stepped in closer to give him her hands and he pressed them into his own. "Magic is for weak-hearted fools, whereas miracles are born of faith, and nothing else. You are my granddaughter because I will it with all of who I am."

Inspired by the strength of his words and the warmth of his touch, Jamilet understood for the first time exactly what he meant. "Just because we say it's true, it becomes true."

"That's right, and you must choose your stories, and believe in them with all your heart, and all your soul—your entire being. Do you understand what I'm saying, Jamilet?"

"I think so."

He released her hands, and cleared his throat. "I'm aware of the fact that I'm not the most patient man. I can be moody at times, even difficult by some accounts, but I'm basically a simple and good-hearted soul, and relatively well educated. Under my tutelage you'll apply your capabilities in an honorable fashion." He addressed her as sincerely as he ever had. "Will you have me for your grandfather, Jamilet?"

"Señor, anyone would be lucky to have you as their grandfather."

"Then you accept my proposal?"

"I . . . I guess . . ."

"Guessing isn't good enough, my dear."

Jamilet gathered her conviction and poured it into every word. "I accept you as my grandfather, Señor, with all of my heart."

Satisfied by the sincerity of her declaration, he opened the first drawer of his desk to retrieve Rosa's small leather Bible, cracked and worn with the years. He asked Jamilet to place her hand upon it, and he did the same. His voice took on a singsong quality, and he strung out the words all on the same note as they echoed softly in the room. "By the power of this holy book, and by the love and will of our eternal souls, I hereby declare that you, Jamilet, and I, Antonio, are from this moment and forevermore to be known as granddaughter and grandfather. And may the truth of our relationship be known to any and all who care to hear of it."

He placed the Bible back in the drawer and cleared a space on his desk. He looked up, bright-eyed and resolved. "Now then, we have many things to plan for our trip, but first I believe we should have some lunch."

28

⌐

T HE BEER CAN slipped out of Carmen's hand and hit the floor. "You what?" she asked, her eyes round with disbelief.
Jamilet swallowed hard. "I'm going to Spain tomorrow night with Señor Peregrino," she said.

"You're kidding, right?" Carmen tried to force a smile, but she knew her niece wasn't the type to joke around.

"No, Tía. We became grandfather and granddaughter," Jamilet said, dreading the revelation, but knowing there'd be no better test for her conviction than this. "We vowed with our hands on the Bible and everything. He said—"

"He's a goddamned pervert! I knew it the first day you told me about him. Didn't I warn you?" Carmen bounded over to the phone, nearly slipping on the beer that had spilled on the floor. "I'm calling the cops."

"He hasn't done anything wrong, Tía. He's just a nice old man who wants to believe in miracles. It would all make sense to you if you heard his story. He walked for hundreds of miles to Santiago—"

"Let me tell you a story," Carmen said with one hand on the phone. "Once upon a time there was this dirty old man who thought to himself, gee wouldn't it be nice if I had myself a young piece of ass? I think I'll make up a crazy story only a stupid girl would believe, and get myself some. If she's really stupid, I'll convince her she's my granddaughter and take her away somewhere. And if she's a total retard, I'll tell her she has to blow on my thingy or the plane will fall out of the sky."

"He'd never say that. You don't understand—"

"No, *you* don't understand what comes next, but he won't tell you that part of the story until you're all alone . . ."

"We've been alone."

"No," Carmen said, her face contorting, "I mean *alone* . . . away from the hospital, away from everything, you stupid girl."

Jamilet had never risked any kind of confrontation with her aunt before, yet she was prepared to do whatever was necessary to protect Señor Peregrino and their relational oath. The blood raced through her veins, and she felt short of breath when she said, "Put down the phone, Tía."

"Yeah, right." Carmen started dialing. "I'll ask for the pervert department," she said, punching the numbers with enough force to splinter the fingers of an ordinary hand. "Do you expect me to allow my dead sister's daughter to go off with a fucking pervert?"

"Put down the phone, Tía."

Watching Jamilet approach, she said, "You take another step and I'll kick your ass all the way to Spain and save the old man the airfare."

Jamilet stood still. What she said next was the worst thing she could think of saying, yet she felt she had no choice. She had to say it for the sake of believing beyond all doubt and making the miracle happen, just like Señor Peregrino said it would. She took a deep breath and expelled the content of her lungs along with the words, "You don't care about me. All you care about is not having someone around to do your cooking, and cleaning, and laundry, and to . . . to keep the rats out."

Carmen held the phone away from her ear and stared at her niece. "What did you say?"

"Admit it, Tía. All you're worried about is losing your slave."

It took a moment or two for Carmen to recover from the

shock, and when she did she began to seethe as her fingers curled into fists. "After all I've done for you, you have the fucking balls to tell me that?" She fumed and trembled and scrunched her toes. She threw the phone off the table as Jamilet sprang back against the couch, almost toppling over the side, but she regained her balance soon enough to get away from Carmen, who was shoving furniture, lunging about like a bull, and ranting at the top of her lungs. "And you think everyone's supposed to feel sorry for you 'cause of that thing on your back!" she screamed. "Well I don't, okay? I don't feel one fuckin' bit sorry for you!" Just then, Louis walked in through the front door, and everyone froze. The couch was diagonal across the living room, the pillows were on the floor, and the table blocked the kitchen entrance. With fists raised, Carmen's eyes were still intent on Jamilet, who stood cornered at the other end of the room.

"What's going on?" Louis asked, his eyes flitting nervously between them. "Carmen, talk to me."

She shook her head, too angry to speak, tears blurring her vision.

"Jamilet?"

Jamilet explained, wincing internally at her shorthand explanation. It sounded even more preposterous than the version she'd given her aunt, but she had little energy to spare on credibility.

Louis raised his hands, dedicating one to each of them. "Okay now, Jamilet, you believe this old guy at the hospital is your grandfather, or you want to believe it. He says he wants you to go to Spain with him for something . . . I didn't get that part too good." He turned to Carmen. "And you think the old man's a pervert, and you're mad at Jamilet for saying you treat her like a slave." He turned bug eyes on both of them. "Is that right?"

Carmen's voice eased out of her throat like black tar. "Close enough. And she can find somewhere else to call home if she's going to be such a bitch."

Louis turned both hands toward Carmen, palms massaging the air between them as if he were some kind of snake charmer, but Carmen didn't back down. "I told you the first day you came here, little girl—I don't like people lying to me."

Jamilet tried to concentrate on her aunt's words and the sight of her familiar face, but she felt as though she were standing on a flat, desolate plain with nothing but the path of the *camino* ahead of her. And it was only Señor Peregrino whom she recognized, and only his chanting that she heard. She was walking beside him now, and realized that she had been for some time. Nothing but their journey was real to her anymore.

Louis was still rattling off one rationalization after another, assuming a false calm. He hoped to inspire something of the like in Carmen, but she shoved him aside with an undignified sweep of her arm, causing him to teeter on one foot. "All right already, I didn't say she had to leave right this minute and spend the night under the bridge or anything." She stuck out her chin at Jamilet. "Maybe your grandpapa will take you in. I'm sure he can find room for you at the looney bin—that's where you belong, if you ask me."

"We leave tomorrow," Jamilet said. "Can I stay until then?"

"Whatever," Carmen said, and then she flashed her niece a sarcastic grin. "And while you're in Spain pick me up some castanets, 'cause I've decided that I'm gonna quit my job and become a flamenco dancer. That's my secret dream, you know." She pushed her belly out and raised her arms over her head. "Don't you think I'd make a good dancer?" she said, sticking out one foot, and bending at the knees like a sumo wrestler. "Open the window, Louis," she commanded while striking another pose that made her look even more ridiculous. "When the talent agent from the Folkloric Ballet de Mexico walks by, I want to make sure he gets a good look at me. I'm sure he'll want to sign me up right away."

In spite of his effort to remain serious, Louis coughed to cover up his laughter, but Carmen didn't miss it. "What? You don't think he's gonna come?" She shoved his arm and then resumed her dramatic pose. "Don't you know there's magic in the air? You should rub my belly and make a wish."

Unable to resist, Louis gingerly patted her belly and closed his eyes tight, so that the creases around his eyes became dimples. "I wish I was rich enough to make things right for my Carmencita." He opened one eye to see how this had gone over. "I'll build her a castle and every room will have a TV and—"

Carmen slapped his hand away. "I don't want none of that crap," she said. "I just want to live an honest life." She released her pose, and pointed a thick finger at Jamilet. "That should be enough for anybody."

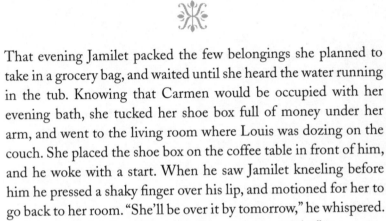

That evening Jamilet packed the few belongings she planned to take in a grocery bag, and waited until she heard the water running in the tub. Knowing that Carmen would be occupied with her evening bath, she tucked her shoe box full of money under her arm, and went to the living room where Louis was dozing on the couch. She placed the shoe box on the coffee table in front of him, and he woke with a start. When he saw Jamilet kneeling before him he pressed a shaky finger over his lip, and motioned for her to go back to her room. "She'll be over it by tomorrow," he whispered. "But I think it's better if you stay out of sight tonight."

"I want to give you something, Louis—"

"Tomorrow, tomorrow," he repeated. "She'll be pissed as hell if she knows we're talking right now."

"I won't be here tomorrow."

Louis sucked in his mustache. "You know she'd never kick you out. It's just her anger talking."

"I know it is, and I know it sounds crazy, but I really am going to Spain with Señor Peregrino tomorrow." She pushed the shoe box to the edge of the table, toward Louis. "I've been saving this money, and the only reason I could save so much was because Tía never let me pay for rent or food. I think it's enough to get your wife and kids over the border. And then you can live an honest life." Jamilet put the box on his knees. "Tía will like that."

"I can't take your money," he said, glancing at the bathroom door for fear he'd spoken too loudly.

"You're not taking it—I'm giving it to you. It's no good having money without a purpose for it. So, it's better for me if you take it."

She stopped talking when they heard the water start to drain from the tub. Louis hastily shoved the shoe box under the couch. "Get back in your room. We'll talk about this tomorrow."

"All I ask is that you make things right, Louis," Jamilet said, and then she tiptoed down the hall to her room.

Jamilet left for work the next morning at the usual hour, walking slowly in honor of the fact that this would be the last time. Already feeling a bit nostalgic, she realized that she'd miss the routine of her days—making the morning coffee, walking to work, attending to Señor Peregrino, returning home for her evening duties, and then spending time with Carmen and Louis. She wondered if she'd be putting in a full day before they left for the airport. Señor Peregrino said they'd be leaving in the evening, but hadn't mentioned the exact time.

She'd had difficulty sleeping the night before, her mind alive with the adventure that awaited her. Every time she closed her eyes she saw herself standing before the grandeur of the cathedral at Santiago and feeling like one drop in the river of life, as Señor Peregrino had described. Undoubtedly it would change her life forever, and maybe there was even the chance for a miracle . . . the only miracle she had ever hoped for.

Jamilet quickened her pace, and made it to the hospital a few minutes early. She proceeded to punch in as she did every morning, but was unable to locate her time card. She tried to calm her nerves while searching down the column of names again, and for a moment feared that she'd forgotten everything Señor Peregrino had taught her. Before long she became aware of Ms. Clark's glare boring through the back of her head.

"Nurse B. has your time card," she mumbled. "You'd better go see her." She returned to her desk, where an untidy pile of papers awaited her.

When Jamilet entered Nurse B.'s office, she saw that her employer was not alone. Across from her in the chair that Jamilet usually occupied sat a man Jamilet had never seen before, wearing a crumpled shirt and tie, and horn-rimmed glasses perched on his greasy nose. Normally she would have remained silent while waiting for her superior to set the tone, but she was flustered with not having found her time card, and eager to get upstairs. Jamilet also realized, while staring into those strange yellow-gray eyes, that this was the first time she'd faced Nurse B. while knowing her true identity. Although Nurse B. was decidedly unpleasant, Jamilet had no doubt that Jenny would be even more so.

"My time card is missing," Jamilet blurted out. "And . . . and I'll be late with Señor Peregrino's breakfast if I don't hurry."

"Don't concern yourself with that now, Monica. We have more pressing things to discuss," she said, flexing her fingers.

"Is this about Señor Peregrino?" Jamilet asked.

An impatient huff escaped from Nurse B.'s throat. "I told you not to refer to him that way. But yes, this has to do with your patient, and the fact that his condition has obviously worsened. I was hoping that your longevity, if nothing else, would encourage a better response, but it's clear that his delusions have only become more involved and—"

The man coughed and leaned forward in his chair. "This situation doesn't warrant an unnecessary review of Mr. Calderon's pathology. I think it best that you proceed with essential information only."

Nurse B. considered the man's advice, and her fingers curled back up into her palms. "You're right Mr. Simpson," she said before turning to Jamilet. "I received a call from your aunt early this morning, and she informed me of your ridiculous plan to leave today with your patient. To Spain. I . . . I believe that's what she said."

Jamilet's bag of belongings dropped to the floor. "Tía Carmen called you?"

"She did the right thing," Nurse B. said. Then she glanced at Mr. Simpson, who was engrossed in organizing his documents on her desk, and continued. "If you recall, when you started your employment here, I informed you that your patient was free to come and go as he wished. You have become quite *intimate*, I know," she said in a belittling tone. "So perhaps he informed you that if he didn't cooperate with his treatment, and demonstrate some sort of improvement by leaving his room on occasion for meals or by taking a stroll in the garden, he would be placed on an involuntary conservatorship. What that means is that at approximately three o clock this afternoon, he will lose the legal right to make decisions for himself. Mr. Simpson," she said, nodding at the man seated in front of her, "is the attorney who will see to it."

Nurse B. went on with eyes half closed, as though reciting the words from a professional journal she had long ago memorized. "Delusional patients like Mr. Calderon can be persuasive, and quite believable. They're capable of inventing elaborate stories in order to support their delusions. Sometimes," she said, slowing her speech, as though speaking with an idiot who was also deaf, "they incorporate others into their delusional stories. And sometimes," she said, slower still, "these others believe the delusion just as much as they do. Among professionals, this is called a 'folie à deux,' or a shared delusion. It's most likely to occur when a close bond has been established between the delusional patient and someone else who may have the need to believe similarly." A sad and somewhat patronizing smile crept over Nurse B.'s haggard face. "He says the same thing every year—that he's waiting for the '*appointed hour*,' and that at the '*appointed hour*' he'll leave his room with a suitcase packed, and head off to Spain. Isn't that right, Mr. Simpson?"

He nodded, irritated that Nurse B. hadn't followed his recommendation to stick to the essential information, and kept his eyes focused on his various documents. "I'll need you to sign where it's highlighted," he said to Nurse B.

But Nurse B.'s discourse seemed to have renewed her agitation, and she didn't appear to have heard the attorney's request. "That is the reason I instructed you to refrain from unnecessary conversation with him in the first place. Do you know that in all the time he's been here he's never so much as set foot out of his room? How can he possibly board a plane and go to Spain? That's the most preposterous thing I've ever heard. Your patient knows very well that if he were able to leave his room and . . . and tell Mr. Simpson to stop the legal proceedings himself, then that would be something else entirely. But as it stands there's no doubt in my mind that what your patient needs is to be placed on conservatorship so that he can receive the treatment he sorely needs. And as for you," she continued while pounding her plump fingers on the desk, "your services are no longer required. In fact, I don't want to see you on the grounds of this hospital ever again. I'll have your final check mailed to your home."

Jamilet stood motionless in the center of the room. "You can't do that to him," she said.

"I've given him a fair chance," Nurse B. continued, her face reddening. "But he hasn't been willing to speak with me, or to see his psychiatrist, and he has certainly never left his room."

Jamilet felt her lungs constricting in her chest, and she began breathing much as Nurse B., in short little spasms and gasps, but what she had to say next was intended not for her employer, but for Jenny. "He won't speak with you because he hates you. You should have let him marry the woman he loved. If he'd married Rosa, none of this would have happened."

"Nurse B., your signature please," the attorney repeated, but this time she definitely hadn't heard a word he said. Slowly, she stood up from her chair and leaned over her desk, toward Jamilet, her face contorting and her eyes bulging with pent-up emotion. "I gave everything I had to that man," she seethed. "And he chose a life with me. Now because of a few dusty letters, he wants to pretend that the past forty years were a lie." The rage she'd been saving for so long began to sputter and boil to the surface. She raised a clenched fist in the air. "I won't have it!" she yelled as she slammed her fist on the desk. Mr. Simpson jumped nearly a foot in the air, and looked up from his work with a shocked and horrified expression.

Jamilet, however, remained calm. "Perhaps," she said, "he'd come out of his room if you told him what happened to his child. Perhaps the truth will cure him."

Nurse B. clasped her hands together, weaving her fingers into a fierce knot. "You have gone too far, and I have indulged you for far too long. If you don't leave this instant, I'll call security and have you removed by force!"

Jamilet picked up her bag of belongings, and headed for the door. But before leaving she turned around and said, "It's never too late to do the right thing, Jenny."

"Get out!" she yelled while pointing to the door.

Jamilet left the building confused and frantic enough to be on the verge of tears, but she couldn't allow herself to lose her bearings now. She needed time and space to think. She made her way back down toward the gate, stumbling on the path as she went, and nearing the very spot where she and Eddie had come through the trees that first night. She ducked into the darkness of their cover and waited for her heart to stop pounding, and for an idea to come to her.

From where she was hiding she could still see most of the building, and the fifth-floor window of Señor Peregrino's room. It was slightly open, as she'd left it the night before, but Señor Peregrino wasn't there waving at her and urging her to come up, as she'd hoped he would be. Her eyes scanned the rest of the building, and she noticed that one of the windows on the first floor had been left open. Without hesitating she ran back up the path toward the open window. While crouching behind an overgrowth of bushes, she peeked inside and saw two patients still asleep. Soon they would be summoned for their breakfasts and baths. She didn't have much time.

After hastily stuffing her possessions under the bushes, she proceeded to open the window a bit wider, but the stiff wooden frame moaned, and one of the patients opened his eyes to find Jamilet with one leg slung over the windowsill. She froze and then breathed a sigh of relief when she saw that it was Charlie. He started to clap his hands with glee at the sight of his friend. Jamilet put her finger to her lips, and immediately he quieted down. She'd finally managed to squeeze herself through when she heard the unmistakable footsteps of authority approaching. She jumped away from the window and made it to Charlie's bedside only seconds before the charge nurse appeared in the doorway. She was obviously irritated, and in no mood for nonsense. "The two of you should have been showering a half hour ago. I told you—" She stopped when she saw Jamilet. "What are you doing here?"

Jamilet flashed her ID badge, thankfully still in her possession. "I work here. On . . . on the fifth floor."

The nurse propped her hands on her hips. "Yes, I've seen you around, but what are you doing here? And why didn't I see you come in? No one gets onto my floor without my authorization." Her eyes darted toward the open window.

Jamilet took a deep breath. "I . . . I wanted to wake Charlie because I know he's always late for breakfast."

The nurse turned toward the patient. "How'd she get in here, Charlie?"

Charlie's eyes flew open, and he shrugged.

She pointed a finger at him. "You tell me the truth or I'll see to it that you don't get your cigarettes today, and I'll know if you're lying."

"She came in," he said nervously, while twisting his blankets in between his tar-stained fingers. "That's all."

"Yes, but *how* did she come in?" the nurse asked, narrowing her eyes. "Did she come in through the door?"

Charlie shook his head. "No, she didn't come in through the door."

"How about the window, Charlie? Did she come in through the open window?"

He began to tremble, and Jamilet knew that for Charlie, as with most of patients, the prospect of losing their cigarettes for an entire day was intolerable—a fate worse than death.

"It's okay, Charlie," Jamilet said, her face red with shame. "You can tell her the truth."

Charlie gazed at Jamilet for some time and then his trembling ceased. All at once he smiled a glorious smile, and pointed up toward the ceiling. "She came through the clouds, just like an angel," he said. "And every time she comes down from heaven she brings me Jell-O and butterscotch pudding." He turned to the nurse with all sincerity when adding, "And sometimes a muffin too. I like blueberry the best."

The nurse rolled her eyes. "Get out of bed and into the shower, Charlie. And you," she said, pointing at Jamilet this time, "get off my floor before I report you."

Jamilet hurried to the kitchen and collected Señor Peregrino's breakfast, which had been prepared for delivery as usual. She proceeded to the elevator that took her up four floors, and then to the narrow staircase up to the fifth, expertly balancing the tray, as she'd learned to do over the months. She was strong enough now to carry a tray twice as heavy if necessary.

She knocked twice, and entered, although she'd heard no reply from Señor Peregrino. He was still in bed with his blankets pulled up over his head. Stepping over his suitcase, she placed the tray on the night table, and went directly to the bathroom to begin her morning chores.

She returned with his laundry in her arms, and found him sitting up in bed watching her, looking as though he might melt with despair. She greeted him as usual, dropped the armload in the center of the room, and opened the window more widely so the morning breeze could sweep in with a fresh hand.

"They've spoken to you?" he asked gravely.

"Yes," she said. "And Jenny fired me too. She said that she never wanted to see me on the hospital grounds again."

Jamilet left the window and began preparing his coffee while shaking her head. With all the delays, it was barely hot enough to dissolve a teaspoon of sugar. She took it to him anyway, but he waved it away with a shaky hand. "Then why are you here?" he asked.

Jamilet prepared a cup for herself, and pulled up a chair to sit near him. She took a sip, and considered him with clear and curious eyes. "Where else would you expect me to be on a beautiful morning like this, if not with my grandfather?"

Señor Peregrino's chin eased down to his chest. Jamilet had nearly finished her coffee before he spoke again. "Your company has proved to be entertaining these past few months, I can't deny that, but the truth is . . . I've . . . I've grown tired of you, and . . . and I no longer think our previous arrangement a sensible one. In fact, it's preposterous to go through with such a charade. You'll have your choice of jobs with your papers now, so leave me be. I'm not anybody's grandfather, least of all yours."

Jamilet set her cup down and leaned forward. "I know what you're doing," she said softly. "You're trying to punish yourself and discourage the world. But it won't work, Grandfather. You can't run from the truth."

Señor Peregrino raised his head, and wiped his eyes with his sleeve. "The truth is that our little game is finished. My foolish agony prevents me from setting foot outside my room, and so we won't be going anywhere. What's more, what little freedom I have will soon be taken from me. I can't be wasting my time with this nonsense!" He clenched his fists, and a slight tremor of rage overtook him.

Jamilet leaned in closer, her eyes shining. "The truth is that we took a vow, you and I. We put our hands on the Bible and every-thing, and you can't change that now no matter what Jenny and that attorney downstairs say about it." Gazing at him, she said, "Tell me again how it is with miracles, Grandfather."

His lips quivered slightly when he said, "I don't recall."

"Yes you do. You said that we conceive our own miracles, and that we must decide what is real by choosing our own stories, and believing in them with all of who we are."

His eyes flickered and he glanced in her direction, although he dared not look at her fully. "I so wanted to make a miracle happen for us, my dear. But I'm afraid that the only thing that seems real for me today is the trembling I feel whenever I step out that door. After all that's happened, I don't know if I'll ever be able to face the world again."

Jamilet took his clenched hand into her own, and immediately his fingers loosened as she tugged gently on his arm. "It's a beauti-ful morning. Come to the window with me and see for yourself. The way the light is shimmering through everything, it reminds me of the mornings you told me about in Spain."

Begrudgingly, Señor Peregrino allowed himself to be pulled out of bed, and guided to the open window. He and Jamilet stood there together looking down at the garden for some time. Then she said, "You know, if I could choose from all the people in the whole world who I'd want for my grandfather, I'd choose you. I'd say that's quite a miracle, wouldn't you?"

Señor Peregrino sighed weakly. "I suppose it is," he said.

Jamilet tilted her head so that it lightly touched his shoul-der. "I love you, Grandfather," she said. "And I'm so glad I found you."

He pressed her hand. "And I you, my dear."

Jamilet left him at the window, and went to the open suitcase where she pulled out trousers, a shirt, and a pair of shoes. She placed them on the bed, and turned to face him, her eyes glitter-ing with determination. "I'm going to leave for a moment so that you can get dressed. And when I get back, we're going to walk the *camino* together so that we can thank Santiago for granting us our miracles."

Chanting echoes reverberated from above and below, seeping through the walls of the building in mournful wails that all at once softened the hospital's harsh reality. The notes of the song fell as tenderly as a child's tears, growing more intense as they descended, filling the corridors with such resonance that everyone was forced to stop and listen. Patients and staff alike exchanged baffled glances, as if to confirm that what they heard was real and not imagined.

Señor Peregrino and Jamilet emerged from the elevator on the first floor hand in hand. His song spread out before them like a verdant path, twisting and winding its way out toward the front door of the hospital. He didn't stop singing until they stood in the doorway of Nurse B.'s office.

When she saw them standing there together, like a portrait in a frame, her mouth dropped open and she floated up from her chair, her eyes focusing and refocusing on the scene before her. "Antonio, you . . . you're here, you left your room."

Mr. Simpson looked up from his work, clearly disappointed.

Señor Peregrino cleared his throat, and patted Jamilet's hand. "My granddaughter and I will be taking our breakfast in the garden this morning. It's such a lovely day, and I'm sure the fresh air will do us good." Before they turned to go outside he added, "And you can tear up those papers, Jenny. You won't have any need for them, as I'll be going home soon. Or wherever it is that I choose to go."

They strolled out toward the garden and selected the bench beneath the largest tree. Señor Peregrino looked about, and when his eyes met Jamilet's their triumphant smiles grew into laughter as light as the breeze. Moments later, an orderly appeared with a fresh pot of coffee while Nurse B. watched them from her office window, her expression filled with wonder.

As custom dictated, Señor Peregrino prepared the coffee and they sipped away, enjoying it in this new venue, and marveling at how wonderful the taste was. A peaceful silence passed between them, and it seemed that Señor Peregrino was on the verge of dozing off when something caught his eye. He pointed down toward the main road and said, "There seems to be a young man watching us. Do you know him?"

Jamilet looked to where he pointed and saw Eddie standing at the gate. Her heart began to beat furiously at the sight of him. When Eddie saw that she'd spotted him, he waved her over and pointed at his watch to let her know that he didn't have much time.

"Yes, I know him," she muttered.

"It appears that he has an urgent need to speak with you. Perhaps you should go see what he wants."

Jamilet was flustered and unsure of what to do. She knew that Eddie had to get to work and didn't have much time to spare. For a moment, she was tempted to drop everything and run to him as fast as her feet could carry her, but she didn't. Instead, she turned back to Señor Peregrino, and inhaled deeply. Her voice was clear and confident when she said, "I'm sure that we'll have a chance to talk later, and I'm enjoying this time with you, Grandfather. The coffee is especially delicious this morning, don't you think?"

"Yes it is," he replied, smiling with pleasure.

When Jamilet turned to look again, Eddie was gone. She relaxed and allowed her gaze to wander up to the branches of the tree, and she watched the leaves flutter gently in the breeze. "May I ask you for a favor, Grandfather?"

"Anything, my dear."

"Since I listened to your story, will you listen to mine? It will explain the reason I left Mexico to come here."

He turned to her, clearly intrigued. "Of course I will. When will you begin this story?"

Jamilet placed her coffee cup down, then stood up, holding both of her hands out to him. "Soon, very soon. But first I'd like you to teach me how to sing one of your songs—how about the one that you and Rosa sang together?"

Chuckling, he set his coffee cup down and eased himself up from the bench. "Very well, I'll teach you the song that Rosa and I sang as we made our way down the Monte de Gozo and into Santiago, but I warn you, it's not an easy one to learn. Some of the notes are quite high, and you'll have to practice to get it right."

It took several attempts before Jamilet was able to sing along without stumbling or depending on Señor Peregrino to lead, but her voice proved to be a sweet and delightful complement to his. And although she would learn many of his songs, her favorite would always be the one they sang together that first summer morning they strolled the perimeter of the hospital grounds arm in arm, as if wandering the highlands of Galicia.

Santiago de Compostela, this path we pilgrims trod
We receive the rain as blessing
The sun as praise from God
No longer do we count the miles
To reach this field of stars
The journey is its own reward
And worship fills the hours

Santiago, Santiago, Santiago
Please pray for me
As I walk upon your *camino*
Searching for my Destiny

Santiago de Compostela, the pilgrim saint endows
A staff to guide my wandering
A hat to shade my brow
I ask that when you see me fall down on bended knee
If miracles grow like flowers
Save one small bloom for me

Acknowledgments

I owe a debt of gratitude to those who continue to support my literary efforts with such sincere hearts and insightful minds. My agent, Moses Cardona, upon whose wise counsel and inspiration I can always rely; my editors, Amy Tannenbaum and Johanna Castillo, who have steered this novel toward a shore more lovely than I had imagined; and my husband, Steven, who never stops believing in me.